DETECTIVES 2

DETECTIVES 2

HAGAR OF THE PAWN-SHOP

FERGUS HUME

THE ADVENTURES OF A LADY PEARL-BROKER

BEATRICE HERON-MAXWELL

COACHWHIP PUBLICATIONS

Greenville, Ohio

2 Detectives: Hagar of the Pawn-Shop / The Adventures of a Lady Pearl-Broker
© 2013 Coachwhip Publications
No claim made on public domain material.
Cover image: Key (cc) Sarah Brooks

Hagar of the Pawn-Shop, by Fergus Hume (1897)
The Adventures of a Lady Pearl-Broker, by Beatrice Heron-Maxwell (1899)

ISBN 1-61646-184-5
ISBN-13 978-1-61646-184-3

CoachwhipBooks.com

CONTENTS

HAGAR OF THE PAWN-SHOP

FERGUS HUME

I

The Coming of Hagar

JACOB DIX was a pawnbroker, but not a Jew, notwithstanding his occupation and the Hebraic sound of his baptismal name. He was so old that no one knew his real age; so grotesque in looks that children jeered at him in the streets; so avaricious that throughout the neighborhood he was called "Skinflint." If he possessed any hidden good qualities to counterbalance his known bad ones, no person had ever discovered them, or even had taken the trouble to look for them. Certainly Jacob, surly and uncommunicative, was not an individual inclined to encourage uninvited curiosity. In his pawn-shop he lived like an ogre in a fairy-tale castle, and no one ever came near him save to transact business, to wrangle during the transaction thereof, and to curse him at its conclusion. Thus it may be guessed that Jacob drove hard bargains.

The pawn-shop—situated in Carby's Crescent, Lambeth—furthermore resembled an ogre's castle inasmuch as, though not filled with dead men's bones, it contained the relics and wreckage, the flotsam and jetsam, of many lives, of many households. Placed in the center of the dingy crescent, it faced a small open space, and the entrance of the narrow lane which led therefrom to the adjacent thoroughfare. In its windows—begrimed with the dust of years—a heterogeneous mixture of articles was displayed, ranging from silver teapots to well-worn saucepans; from gold watches to rusty flatirons; from the chisel of a carpenter to the ivory framed mirror of a fashionable beauty. The contents of Dix's window

9

typified in little the luxury, the meanness, the triviality and the
decadence of latter-day civilization.

There was some irony, too, in the disposition of incongruous
articles; for the useful and useless were placed significantly in prox-
imity, and the trifles of frivolity were mingled with the necessaries
of life. Here a Dresden china figure, bright-hued and dainty, sim-
pered everlastingly at a copper warming-pan; there a silver-
handled dagger of the Renaissance lay with a score of those cheap
dinner-knives whose bluntness one execrates in third-rate restau-
rants. The bandaged hand of a Pharaohonic mummy touched an
agate saucer holding defaced coins of all ages, of all nations.
Watches, in alternate rows of gold and silver, dangled over fantastic temples and ships of ivory carved by laborious Chinese artifi-
cers. On a square of rich brocade, woven of silks, multi-colored as
a parrot's plumage, were piled in careless profusion medals,
charms, old-fashioned rings set with dim gems, and the frail glass
bangles of Indian nautch-girls. A small cabinet of Japanese lacquer, black, with grotesque gilded figures thereon; talismans of
coral from Southern Italy, designed to avert the evil eye; jeweled
pipes of Turkey, set roughly with blue turquoise stones; Georgian
caps with embroideries of tarnished gold; amulets, earrings, brace-
lets, snuff-boxes and mosaic brooches from Florence—all these fri-
volities were thrown the one on top of the other, and all were over-
laid with fine gray dust. Wreckage of many centuries; dry bones of
a hundred social systems, dead or dying! What a commentary on
the durability of empire—on the inherent pride of pigmy man!

Within doors the shop was small and dark. A narrow counter,
running lengthways, divided the whole into two parts. On the side
nearest the entrance three wooden screens by their disposition
formed four sentry-boxes, into which customers stepped when bent
on business. Jacob, wizen, cunning, and racked by an eternal
cough, hovered up and down the space within the counter, wran-
gling incessantly with his customers, and cheating them on every
occasion. He never gave the value of a pawned article: he fought
over every farthing; and even when he obtained the goods at his

own price he grudged payment; for every coin he put down was a drop of blood wrung from his withered heart. He rarely went outside the shop; he never mingled with his fellow-creatures; and, the day's chicanery ended, he retired invariably into a gloomy back parlor, the principal adornment of which was a gigantic safe built into the wall. Here he counted his gains, and saw doubtful customers not receivable in the shop, who came by stealth to dispose of stolen goods. Here, also, in his lighter moments, he conversed with the only friend he possessed in Carby's Crescent—or, indeed, in London. Jacob was in no danger of becoming a popular idol.

This particular friend was a solicitor named Vark, who carried on a shady business, in a shady manner, for shady clients. His name—as he declared himself—proved him to be of Polish descent; but it was commonly reported in the neighborhood that Vark was made to rhyme with shark, as emblematic of the estimation in which he was held. He was hated only one degree less than Jacob, and the two,—connected primarily as lawyer and client,—later on, had struck up a mistrustful friendship by reason of their mutual reputation and isolation. Neither one believed in the other; each tried to swindle on his own account, and never succeeded; yet the two met nightly and talked over their divers rascalities in the dingy parlor, with a confidence begotten by an intimate knowledge of each other's character. The reputations of both were so bad that the one did not dare to betray the other. Only on this basis is honor possible among thieves.

Late one foggy November night Jacob was seated with his crony over a pinched little fire which burnt feebly in a rusty iron grate. The old pawnbroker was boiling some gruel, and Vark, with his own private bottle of gin beside him, was drinking a wineglass of it, mixed sparingly with water. Mr. Dix supplied this latter beverage, as it cost nothing, but Vark—on an understanding which dated from the commencement of their acquaintance—always brought his own liquor. A guttering candle in a silver candlestick—a pawned article—was placed on the deal table, and gave forth a miserable light. The fog from without had percolated into the room,

so that the pair sat in a kind of misty atmosphere, hardly illumi-
nated by the farthing dip. Such discomfort, such squalor, was only
possible in a penurious establishment like that of Jacob.

Vark was a little, lean, wriggling creature, more like a worm
than a man made in the image of his Creator. He had a sharp nose,
a pimply face, and two shifty, fishy eyes, green in hue like those of
a cat. His dress was of rusty black, with a small—very small—display of linen; and he rubbed his hands together with a cringing
bow every time Jacob croaked out a remark between his coughs.
Mr. Dix coughed in a rich but faded dressing-gown, the relic of
some dandy of the Regency; and every paroxysm threatened to
shake his frail form to pieces. But the ancient was wonderfully
tough, and clung to life with a kind of desperate courage—though
Heaven only knows what attraction the old villain found in his
squalid existence. This tenacity was not approved of by Vark, who
had made Jacob's will, and now wished his client to die, so that
he, as executor, might have the fingering of the wealth which Dix
was reported to possess. The heir to these moneys was missing,
and Vark was determined that he should never be found. Meanwhile, with many schemes in his head, he cringed to Jacob, and
watched him cough over his gruel.

"Oh, dear, dear!" sighed Mr. Vark, speaking of his client in the
third person, as he invariably did, "how bad Mr. Dix's cough is to-
night! Why doesn't he try a taste of gin to moisten his throat?"

"Can't afford it!" croaked Jacob, pouring the gruel into a bowl.
"Gin's worth money, and money I ain't got. Make me a little present
of a glass, Mr. Vark, just to show that you're glad of my company."

Vark complied very unwillingly with this request, and poured
as little as he well could into the proffered bowl. "What an engag-
ing man he is!" said the lawyer, smirking—"so convivial, so full of
spirits!"

"Your spirits!" retorted Jacob, drinking his gruel.

"What wit!" cried Vark, slapping his thin knees. "It's better than
Punch!"

"Gin-punch! gruel-punch!" said Dix, encouraged by this praise.

"He, he! I shall die with laughing! I've paid for worse than that at the theater!"

"More fool you!" growled Jacob, taking up the tongs. "You shouldn't pay for anything. Here, get out! I'm going to put out the fire. I ain't going to burn this expensive coal to warm you. And the candle's half-burnt too!" concluded Jacob, resentfully.

"I'm going—I'm going," said dark, slipping his bottle into his pocket. "But to leave this pleasant company—what a wrench!"

"Here, stop that stuff, you inkpot! Has my son answered that advertisement yet?"

"Mr. Dix's son hasn't sent a line to his sorrowing parent," returned the lawyer. "Oh, what a hard-hearted offspring!"

"You're right there, man," muttered Jacob, gloomily. "Jimmy's left me to die all alone, curse him!"

"Then why leave him your money?" said Vark, changing into the first person, as he always did when business was being discussed.

"Why, you fool?—'cause he's Hagar's son—the bad son of a good mother."

"Hagar Stanley—your wife—your gipsy wife! Hey, Mr. Dix?"

Jacob nodded. "A pure-blooded Romany. I met her when I was a Crocus."

"Crocus for Cheap Jack!" whined Vark; "the wit this man has!"

"She came along o' me to London when I set up here," continued Jacob, without heeding the interruption, "and town killed her; she couldn't breathe in bricks and mortar after the free air of the road. Dead—poor soul!—dead; and she left me Jimmy—Jimmy, who's left me."

"What a play of fancy—" began Vark; when, seeing from the fierce look of Jacob that compliments on the score of the dead wife were not likely to be well received, he changed his tone. "He'll spend your money, Mr. Dix."

"Let him! Hagar's dead, and when I die—let him."

"But, my generous friend, if you gave me more power as executor—"

"You'd take my money to yourself," interrupted Dix with irony. "Not if I know it, you shark! Your duty is to administer the estate by law for Jimmy. I pay you!"

"But so little!" whined Vark, rising; "if you—"

At this moment there came a sharp knock at the door of the shop, and the two villains, always expectant of the police, stared at one another, motionless with terror for the moment. Vark, who always took care of his skin, snatched up his hat and made for the back-door, whence, in the fog, he could gain his own house un-questioned and unseen. Like a ghost he vanished, leaving Jacob motionless until aroused by a repetition of the knock.

"Can't be peelers," he muttered, taking a pistol out of a cup-board, "but it might be thieves. Well, if it is—" He smiled grimly, and without finishing his sentence he shuffled along to the door, candle in hand. A third knock came, as the clock in the shop struck eleven.

"Who is there, so late?" demanded Jacob, sharply.

"I am—Hagar Stanley!"

With a cry of terror, Mr. Dix let the candle fall, and in the dark-ness dropped also. For the moment,—so much had his thoughts been running on the dead wife,—the unexpected mention of her name made him believe that she was standing rigid in her wind-ing-sheet on the other side of the door. One frail partition between the living and the dead! It was terrible!

"The ghost of Hagar!" muttered Dix, white and shaking. "Why has she come out of her grave?—and so expensive it was; bricked; with a marble tombstone."

"Let me in! let me in, Mr. Dix!" cried the visitor, again rapping.

"She never called me by that name," said Jacob, reassured, and scrambling for the candle; then, having lighted it, he added aloud: "I don't know any one called Hagar Stanley."

"Open the door, and you will. I'm your wife's niece."

"Flesh and blood!" said the old man, fumbling at the lock—"I don't mind that."

He flung wide the door, and out of the fog and darkness a young girl of twenty years stepped into the shop. She was dressed in a dark red garment made of some coarse stuff, and over this she wore a short black cloak. Her hands were bare, and also her head, save for a scarlet handkerchief, which was carelessly twisted round her magnificent black hair. The face was of the true Romany type: Oriental in its contour and hue, with arched eyebrows over large dark eyes, and a thin-lipped mouth beautifully shaped, under a delicately-curved nose. Face and figure were those of a woman who needed palms and desert sands and golden sunshine, hot and sultry, for an appropriate background; yet this Eastern beauty appeared out of the fog like some dead Syrian princess, and presented herself in all her rich loveliness to the astonished eyes of the old pawnbroker.

"So you are the niece of my dead Hagar?" he said, staring earnestly at her in the thin yellow light of the candle. "Yes, it's true. She looked like you when I met her in the New Forest. What d'ye want?"

"Food and shelter," replied the girl, curtly. "But you'd better shut the door; it might be bad for your reputation if any passer-by saw you speaking to a woman at this time of night."

"My reputation!" chuckled Jacob, closing end bolting the door. "Lord! that's past spoiling. If you knew how bad it is, you wouldn't come here."

"Oh, I can look after myself, Mr. Dix, especially as you're old enough to be my great-grandfather twice over."

"Come, come! Civil words, young woman!"

"I'm civil to those who are civil to me," retorted Hagar, taking the candle out of her host's hands. "Go on, Mr. Dix, show me in; I'm tired, and want to sleep. I'm hungry, and wish food. You must give me bed and board."

"Infernal insolence, young woman! Why?"

"Because I'm kin to your dead Hagar."

"Aye, aye, there's something in that," muttered Dix, and dominated, in spite of his inherent obstinacy, by the imperious spirit of the girl, he led her into the dingy parlor. Here she removed her cloak and sat down, while Jacob, in an unusual spirit of hospitality, induced by the mention of his late wife, produced some coarse victuals.

Without a word he placed the food before his guest; without a word she ate, and was refreshed. Jacob marveled at the self-possession of the gipsy, and was rather pleased than otherwise with her bold coolness. Only when she had finished the last scrap of bread and cheese did he speak. His first remark was curt and rude—designedly so.

"You can't stay here!" said the amiable old man

The girl retorted in kind: "I can, and I shall, Mr. Dix."

"For what reason, you jade?"

"For several—and all good ones," said Hagar leaning her chin on her hands and looking steadily at his wrinkled face. "I know all about you from a Romany chal who was up here six months ago. Your wife is dead; your son has left you; and here you live alone, disliked and hated by all. You are old and feeble and solitary; but you are by marriage akin to the gentle Romany. For that reason, and because I am of your dead rani's blood, I have come to look after you."

"Jezebel! That is, if I'll let you!"

"Oh, you'll let me fast enough," replied the woman, carelessly. "You are a miser, I have heard; so you won t lose the chance of getting a servant for nothing."

"A servant! You?" said Dix, admiring her imperial air.

"Even so, Mr. Dix. I'll look after you and your house. I'll scrub and cook and mend. If you'll teach me your trade, I'll drive a bargain with any one—and as hard and fast a one as you could drive yourself. And all these things I'll do for nothing."

"There's food and lodging, you hussy."

"Give me dry bread and cold water, your roof to cover me, and a bundle of straw to sleep on. These won't cost you much, and I ask for nothing more—Skinflint."

"How dare you call me that, you wild cat!"

"It's what they call you hereabouts," said Hagar with a shrug. "I think it suits you. Well, Mr. Dix, I have made my offer."

"I haven't accepted it yet," snapped Jacob, puzzled by the girl. "Why do you come to me? Why don't you stay with your tribe?"

"I can explain that in five minutes, Mr. Dix. We Stanleys are just now in the New Forest. You know it?"

"Truly lass," said Dix, sadly. "'Twas there I met my Hagar."

"And it is from there that I, the second Hagar, come," replied the girl. "I was with my tribe, and I was happy till Goliath came."

"Goliath?" inquired Jacob, doubtfully.

"He is half a Gorgio and half Romany—a red-haired villain, who chose to fall in love with me. I hated him. I hate him still!"—the woman's bosom rose and fell in short, hurried pantings—"and he would have forced me to be his wife. Pharaoh—our king, you know—would have forced me also to be this man's rani, so I had no one to protect me, and I was miserable. Then I recalled what the chal had told me about you who wed with one of us; so I fled hither for your protection, and to be your servant."

"But Goliath—this red-haired brute?"

"He does not know where I have gone, he will never find me here. Let me stay, Mr. Dix, and be your servant. I have nowhere to go to, no one to seek, save you, the husband of the dead Hagar, after whom I am named. Am I to stay or go, now that I have told you the truth?"

Jacob looked thoughtfully at the girl, and saw tears glistening in her heavy eyelashes, although her pride kept them from falling. Moved by her helplessness, mindful of the wife whom he had loved so well, and alive to the advantage of possessing a white slave whom he could trust, the astute ancient made up his mind.

"Stay," said he, quietly. "I shall see if you will be useful to me—useful and faithful, my girl. If so, bread and bed shall be yours."

"It's a bargain," said Hagar, with a sigh of relief. "And now, old man, let me rest in peace, for I am weary, and have walked many a long mile this day."

So in this fashion came Hagar to the pawnshop; and it was for this reason that Vark, to his great astonishment, found a woman—and what is more, a young and beautiful woman—established in the house of Jacob Dix. The news affected the neighborhood like a miracle, and new tales were repeated about Dix and his house-keeper, who, report said, was no better than she should be. But

Hagar did not mind evil tongues; nor did the old man. Without a spark of love or affection between them, they worked together on a basis of mutual interest; and all the days that Jacob lived Hagar served him faithfully. Whereat Vark wondered.

It was not an easy life for the girl. Jacob was a hard master, and made her pay dearly for bed and board. Hagar scrubbed walls and floors; she mended such pawned dresses as required attention; and cooked the frugal meals of herself and master. The old pawnbroker taught her how to depreciate articles brought to be pawned, how to haggle with their owners, and how to wring the last sixpence out of miserable wretches who came to redeem their pledges. In a short time Hagar became as clever as Jacob himself, and he was never afraid to trust her with the task of making bargains, or with the care of the shop. She acquired a knowledge of pictures, gems, silverware, china—in fact, all the information about such things necessary to an expert. Without knowing it, the untaught gipsy girl became a connoisseur.

It required all Hagar's patience to bear cheerfully the lot which she had chosen voluntarily. Her bed was hard, her food meager; and the old man's sharp tongue was perpetually goading her by its bitterness. Jacob, indeed,—sure of his slave, since she had no other roof save his to cover her,—exercised all the petty arts of a tyrant. He vented on her all the rage he felt against the son who had deserted him. Once he went so far as to attempt a blow; but a single glance from the fierce eyes of Hagar made him change his intention; and, cowed for once in his tyranny, Jacob never lifted his hand again against her. He saw plainly enough that if he once raised the devil in this child of the free gipsy race, there would be no laying it again. But, actual violence apart, Hagar's life was as miserable as a human being's well could be.

Stifled in the narrow shop in the crowded neighborhood, she longed at times for the free life of the road. Her thoughts recalled the green woods, so cool and shady in summer; they dwelt on the brown heath lonely in the starlight, with the red flare of the gipsy fire casting fantastic shadows on caravan and tent. In the darkness of night she would murmur the strange words of the "calo jib," like

some incantation to compel memory. To herself, while arranging
the curiosities in the shop window, she would sing fragments of
Romany songs set in minor keys. The nostalgia of the wilds, of the
encampment and the open road, tortured her in the heats of summer; and when winter descended she longed or the chill breath of
country winds sweeping across moors laden with snow, over pools
rigid in the cold embrace of smooth and glassy ice. In the pawn-
shop she was an exile from her dream paradise of roaming liberty.

To make bad worse, Vark fell in love with her. For the first time
in his narrow, selfish life, a divine passion touched the gross soul
of the thieves' lawyer. Ravished by the dark loveliness of the girl,
dominated by her untamed spirit, astonished by her clear mind
and unerring judgment, Vark wished to possess this treasure. There
was also another reason for the offer of marriage which he made,
and this reason he put into words when he asked Hagar to become
his wife. It took Vark twelve months to make up his mind to this
course; and his wrath may be guessed when Hagar refused him
promptly. The miserable wretch could not believe that she was in
earnest.

"Oh, dear, sweet Hagar!" he whined, trying to clasp her hand,
"you cannot have heard what your slave said!"

Hagar, who was mending some lace and minding the shop in
the absence of Jacob, looked up with a scornful smile. "What you
call yourself in jest," said she quietly, "I am in reality; I sold myself into bondage for bare existence a year ago. Do you want to
marry a slave, Mr. Vark?"

"Yes, yes! Then you will no longer need to work like a servant."

"I would rather be a servant than your wife, Mr. Vark."

"The girl's mad! Why?"

"Because you are a scoundrel."

Vark grinned amiably, in no wise disturbed by this plain-speaking.
"My Cleopatra, we are all scoundrels in these parts. Jacob Dix is—"

"Is my master!" interrupted Hagar, sharply. "So leave him
alone. But this offer of yours, my friend. What benefit do you pro-
pose to gain if I accept it? You're not asking me to be your wife
without some motive."

"Why, that's true enough, my beauty!" chuckled Vark. "Lord, how cunning you are to guess! The motive is double: one part love—"

"We'll say nothing about that, man! You don't know what love is! The other motive?"

"Money!" said Vark, curtly, and without wasting words.

"H'm!" replied Hagar, with irony. "Mr. Dix's money?"

"What penetration!" said the lawyer, slapping his knee. "My word, here's intelligence!"

"We'll pass over the usual compliments, Mr. Vark. Well, how is Mr. Dix's money to benefit you through me?"

"Why," said Vark, blinking his green eyes, "the old man's got a fancy for you, my dear; and all the liking he had for me he's given to you. Before you came, he made a will in favor of his lost son, and appointed me executor. Now that he sees what a sharp one you are, he has made a new will—"

"Leaving all the money to me, I suppose? That's a lie!"

"It is a lie," retorted Vark, "but one I wasn't going to tell you. No; the money is still left to the son; but you are the executor under the new will. Now d'ye see?"

"No," said Hagar, folding up her work, "I don't."

"Well, if I marry you, I'll administer the estate in your name—"

"For the benefit of the lost heir? Well?"

"That's just it," said Vark, laying a lean finger on her knee—"the lost heir. Don't you understand? We needn't look for him, so we can keep the moneys in our own hands, and have some fine pickings out of the estate."

Hagar rose, and smiled darkly. "A nice little scheme, and worthy of you," said she, contemptuously; "but there are two obstacles. I'm not your wife, and I am an honest girl. Try some of your lady clients, Mr. Vark. I'm not for sale!"

When she walked away Vark scowled. A scoundrel himself, he could not understand this honesty which stood in the way of its own advancement. Biting his fingers, he stared after Hagar, and wondered how he could catch her in his net.

"If that old miser would only leave her his heiress!" he thought; "she'd have no scruples about taking the money then; and if she had the money, I'd force her to be my wife. But Jacob is set on giving all his wealth to that infernal son of his, who so often wished his father to die. Aha!" sighed Vark, rubbing his hands, "I wish I could prove that he tried to kill the old man. Jacob wouldn't leave him a penny then, and Hagar should have the money, and I would have her. What a lovely dream! Why can't it come true?"

It was such a lovely dream, and offered such opportunities for scoundrelly dealings, that Vark set to work at once to translate it into actual facts. He had many of the letters and bills of the absent Jimmy, who had been accustomed to come to him for the money refused by the paternal Dix. Counting on the old man's death, Vark had lent the son money for his profligacy at a heavy percentage, and intended to repay himself out of the estate. Now that Hagar was to handle the money instead of himself, he thought that there might be some difficulty over his usury, owing to the girl's absurd honesty. He therefore determined to give proofs to Jacob that the absent son had designed to rid himself of a troublesome father by secret murder. Once Dix got such an idea into his head, he might leave his wealth to Hagar. The heiress would then be wooed and won by skilful, scheming Mr. Vark. It was a beautiful idea, and quite simple.

Among his many shady clients Vark possessed one who was a clever forger, and who occasionally retired to one of Her Majesty's prisons for too frequently exercising his talents in that direction. At the present moment he was at large. Vark gave him a bundle of Jimmy's letters, and the draft of a memorandum which he wished to be imitated in the handwriting of the absent heir. When this was ready, Vark watched his opportunity and slipped it into a Chinese jar in the back parlor, in which he knew Jimmy had been accustomed to keep tobacco. This receptacle stood on a high shelf, and had not been touched by Jacob since his son's departure. Vark, like the clever scoundrel he was, ascertained this fact by the thick and undisturbed dust which coated jar and shelf. The trap being thus prepared, it only remained to lead Jacob into it; and this Mr. Vark arranged to do in the most skilful manner. He quite counted on success, but one necessary element thereto he overlooked, and that was the aid of Hagar. But as he had designed the whole scheme primarily for her benefit, he never thought she would refuse to forward its aim. Which blindness showed that he was incapable of appreciating or even understanding the honesty of the girl's character.

According to his custom, he came one evening to converse with Jacob. The room with its solitary candle, the starved fire, and the foggy atmosphere, were the same as on the night when Hagar had arrived, save that now Hagar herself sat sewing by the table. She frowned when Vark came cringing into the room, but beyond greeting him with a slight nod she took no notice of the smiling scoundrel. Vark produced his bottle of gin, and set down near the fire, opposite to Jacob, who on this night looked very old and feeble. The old man was breaking up fast, and was more querulous and crabbed than ever. As usual, he asked Vark if Jimmy had answered the advertisement, and as usual he received a negative reply. Jacob groaned.

"I'll die this winter," said he, with moody face, "and no one will be by to close my eyes."

"What is this I hear Mr. Dix say!" cried Vark, smilingly. "He forgets our beautiful Hagar."

"Hagar is all very well, but she is not Jimmy."

"Perhaps, if our dear friend knew all, he would be pleased that she isn't."

Hagar looked up in surprise at the significant tones of Vark, and Jacob scowled. "What d'ye mean, you shark?" he demanded, a light coming into his faded eyes.

"Why," replied the lawyer, luring on the old pawnbroker, "Jimmy was a scoundrel."

"I know that, man!" snapped Jacob.

"He wanted your money."

"I know that also."

"He wished for your death."

"It's probable he did," retorted Jacob, nodding; "but he was content to let me take my own time to die."

"H'm! I'm not so sure of that!"

Guessing that Vark had some scheme in his head which he was striving to bring to fulfilment, Hagar dropped her sewing, and looked sharply at him. As Vark spoke she saw him glance at the Chinese jar, and mentally wondered what possible connection that could have with the subject of conversation. On this point she was soon enlightened.

"Vark," said Dix, seriously, "are you going to tell me that Jimmy wished to kill me?"

The lawyer held up his hands in horror. "Oh, dear, that I should be so misunderstood!" he said in a piteous tone. "Jimmy was not so bad as that, my venerable friend. But if some one else had put you out of the way, he would not have been sorry."

"Do you mean Hagar?"

"Let him dare to say so!" cried the girl, leaping to her feet with flaming eyes. "I do not know your son, Mr. Dix."

"What!" said Vark, softly; "not red-haired Jimmy!"

Hagar sat down with a pale face. "Red-haired!" she muttered. "Goliath! No, it is impossible!"

Vark looked at Hagar, and she stared back at him again. With the approaching senility of old age, Jacob had ceased to take part in the conversation, and was moodily staring at the miserable fire, a trembling and palsied creature. The idea hinted at by Vark—that Hagar had been employed by Jimmy to destroy him—so stupefied his brain that he was incapable of even expressing an opinion. Seeing this, the lawyer glided away from the dangerous topic, to carry out the second part of his scheme.

"Oh, dear, dear!" he said, hunting in his pockets. "My pipe is empty, and I have no tobacco with me."

"Then go without it, Mr. Vark!" said Hagar, sharply. "There's no tobacco here."

"Oh, yes; I think in that jar," said the lawyer, pointing one lean finger at the high shelf—"Jimmy's jar."

"Leave Jimmy's jar alone!" mumbled Jacob, savagely.

"What! will not Mr. Dix spare one tiny pipe of tobacco for his old friend?" whined Vark, going towards the shelf. "Oh, I think so; I am certain," and with this one of his long arms shot upwards to seize the jar. Jacob rose unsteadily as Vark took down the article, and he scowled fiercely at the daring of his visitor. Indifferent to what was going on, Hagar continued her sewing.

"Leave that jar of Jimmy's alone, I tell you!" snarled Dix, seizing the poker. "I'll break your fox's head if you don't!"

"Violence—and from gentle Mr. Dix!" cried Vark, still gripping the jar. "Oh, no, no, not at all! If he—"

At this moment Jacob lost patience, and delivered a swinging blow at the lawyer's head.

Ever watchful, Vark threw himself to one side, and the poker crashed down on the jar, which he held in his hands. In a moment it lay in fragments on the floor. A pile of broken china, a loose bit of dried tobacco, and a carelessly folded paper.

"See what your angry passion has done!" said Vark, pointing reproachfully to the débris. "You have broken poor Jimmy's jar!"

Jacob threw the poker inside the fender, and bent to pick up the folded paper, which he opened in a mechanical manner. Always methodical, Hagar went out of the room to fetch a dust-pan and broom. Before she could return with them she was recalled by a cry from Vark; and on rushing back she saw Jacob prone on the floor among the broken china. He had fainted, and the paper was still clutched in his hand.

"Bring water—salts!" cried Vark, his eyes filled with a triumphant light at the success of his plot. "My venerable friend is ill!"

"What have you been doing to him?" demanded Hagar, as she loosened the scarf round the old man's neck.

"I? Nothing! He read that paper which fell out of the jar—Jimmy's jar," added Vark, pointedly—"and went down like a ninepin!"

There was a jug of water on the table, used by Vark for diluting his gin, so Hagar sprinkled the wrinkled face of her master with this fluid, and slapped his hands. Vark looked on rather anxiously. He did not wish the old man to die yet; and Jacob was a long time coming out of his swoon.

"This paper made him faint," said Vark, removing it from Jacob's feeble grasp. "Let us see what it says." He knew the contents quite well, but nevertheless he read it aloud in a distinct voice for the benefit of Hagar. Thus ran the words: "Memo.: To extract the juice of foxglove—a poison difficult to trace—nothing can be proved after death. Small doses daily in old man's tea or gruel. He would die in a few weeks without suspicion. Will trust nobody, but will prepare drug myself."

Hagar looked steadily at Vark. "Who wrote that," she said in a low voice—"the old man's son or—you?"

"I?" cried Vark, with well-simulated indignation, "why should I write it?—or how could I write it? The penmanship is that of James Dix; it was concealed in his tobacco-jar; the jar was broken by accident; you saw it yourself. Do you dare to—"

"Be silent!" interrupted Hagar, raising Jacob's head; "he is reviving."

The old pawnbroker opened his eyes and looked wildly around. Little by little his senses returned to him, and he sat up. Then, with the aid of Hagar, he climbed into his chair, and began to talk and sigh.

"Little Jimmy wants me to die," he moaned, feebly. "Hagar's son wants to kill me. Foxglove poison—I know it! Not a trace does it leave after death. Hagar's son! Hagar's boy! Parricide! Parricide!" he cried, shaking his two fists in the air.

"He wanted the money, you know," hinted Vark, softly.

"He shall not have the money!" said Jacob with unnatural energy. "I'll make a new will—I'll disinherit him! Parricide! Hagar shall have all!"

"I, Mr. Dix? No, no!"

"I say yes, you jade! Don't cross a dying man. I am dying; this is my death-blow. O Jimmy, Jimmy! Wolf's cub! My will! my will!"

Pushing back Hagar, who strove to keep him in his chair, he snatched up the candle and staggered towards the safe to get his will. While he was looking within, Vark hastily fumbled in his capacious pockets. When Jacob replaced the candle on the table, Hagar saw thereon a sheet of paper covered with writing; also pen and ink. Jacob, clutching the will, beheld these things also, and anticipated the question on Hagar's lips.

"What's all this?"

"Your new will, Mr. Dix," explained Vark, smoothly. "I never did trust your son, and I knew some day that you would find him out. I therefore prepared a will by which you left everything to Hagar. Or," added the lawyer, taking another document from his pocket, "if you chose to make me your heir—"

"You? You? Never!" shrieked Jacob, shaking his fist. "All shall go to Hagar, the namesake of my dead wife. I'm glad you had the sense to see, that failing Jimmy, I'd leave her my money."

"Mr. Dix," interrupted Hagar, firmly, "I do not want your money; and you have no right to rob your son of—"

"No right! No right, you jade! The money is mine! mine! It shall be yours. I could have forgiven anything to Jimmy save his wish to poison me."

"I don't believe he did wish it," said Hagar, bluntly.

"But the paper—his own handwriting!" cried Vark.

"Yes, yes; I know Jimmy's handwriting," said Jacob, the veins in his forehead swelling with rage. "He is a devil—a par—par—!" The violence of his temper was such that Hagar stepped forward to soothe him. Even Vark felt alarmed.

"Keep quiet, you old fool!" said he, roughly; "you'll break a blood-vessel! Here, sign this will. I'll witness it; and—" He stopped, and whistled shrilly. A man appeared. "Here is another witness," said Vark. "Sign!"

"It's a plot! a plot!" cried Hagar. "Don't sign, Mr. Dix. I don't want the money."

"I'll make you take it, hussy!" snarled Jacob, crushing the will up in his hand. "I shall leave it to you—not to Jimmy, the parricide. First I'll destroy this." With the old will he approached the fire, and threw it in. With the swiftness of a swallow Hagar darted past him and snatched the document away from the flames before it was even scorched. Jacob staggered back, mad with rage. Vark ground his teeth at her opposition. The stranger witness looked stolidly on.

"No!" cried Hagar, slipping the will into her pocket. "You shall not disinherit your son for me!"

"Give—give—will!" panted Jacob, and, almost inarticulate with rage, he stretched out his hand. Before he could draw it back he reeled and fell; a torrent of blood poured from his mouth. He was dead.

"You fool!" shrieked Vark, stamping. "You've lost a fortune!"

"I've saved my honesty!" retorted Hagar, aghast at the sudden death. "Jimmy shall have the money."

"Jimmy! Jimmy!" sneered Vark, wrathfully. "Do you know who Jimmy is?"

"Yes—the rightful heir!"

"Quite so, you jade—and the red-haired Goliath who drove you to this pawn-shop!"

"It is a lie!"

"It is the truth! You have robbed yourself to enrich your enemy!"

Hagar looked at the sneering face of Vark; at the dead man lying at her feet; at the frightened countenance of the witness. She felt inclined to faint, but, afraid lest Vark should steal the will which she had in her pocket, she controlled herself with a violent effort. Before Vark could stop her, she rushed out of the room, and into her bedroom. The lawyer heard the key turn in the lock.

"I've lost the game," he said, moodily. "Go and get assistance, you fool!" this to the witness; then, when the man had fled away, he continued: "To give up all that money to the red-haired man whom she hated! The girl's mad!"

But she was only honest; therefore her conduct was unintelligible to Vark. So this was how Hagar Stanley came to take charge of the pawn-shop in Carby's Crescent, Lambeth. Her adventures therein may be read hereafter.

2

The First Customer and the Florentine Dante

IT HAS BEEN explained otherwhere how Hagar Stanley, against her
own interests, took charge of the pawn-shop and property of Jacob
Dix during the absence of the rightful heir. She had full control of
everything by the terms of the will. Jacob had made many good
bargains in his life, but none better than that which had brought
him Hagar for a slave—Hagar, with her strict sense of duty, her
upright nature, and her determination to act honestly, even when
her own interests were at stake. Such a character was almost unknown amongst the denizens of Carby's Crescent.

Vark, the lawyer, thought her a fool. Firstly, because she refused to make a nest-egg for herself out of the estate; secondly,
because she had surrendered a fine fortune to benefit a man she
hated; thirdly, because she declined to become Mrs. Vark. Otherwise she was sharp enough—too sharp, the lawyer thought; for with
her keen business instinct, and her faculty for organizing and ad-
ministering and understanding, he found it impossible to trick her
in any way. Out of the Dix estate Vark received his due fees and no
more, which position was humiliating to a man of his intelligence.

Hagar, however, minded neither Vark nor any one else. She
advertised for the absent heir, she administered the estate, and
carried on the business of the pawn-shop; living in the back-
parlor meanwhile, after the penurious fashion of her late master.
It had been a shock to her to learn that the heir of the old pawnbroker was none other than Goliath, the red-haired suitor who had
forced her to leave the gipsy camp. Still, her honesty would not

permit her to rob him of his heritage; and she attended to his interests as though they were those of the man she loved best in the world. When Jimmy Dix, alias Goliath, appeared to claim the property, Hagar intended to deliver up all to him, and to leave the shop as poor as when she entered it. In the mean time, as the months went by and brought not the claimant, Hagar minded the shop, transacted business, and drove bargains. Also, she became the heroine of several adventures, such as the following:

During a June twilight she was summoned to the shop by a sharp rapping, and on entering she found a young man waiting to pawn a book which he held in his hand. He was tall, slim fair-haired and blue-eyed, with a clever and intellectual face, lighted by rasher dreamy eyes. Quick at reading physiognomies, Hagar liked his appearance at the first glance, and, moreover, admired his good looks.

"I—I wish to get some money on this book," said the stranger in a hesitating manner, a flush invading his fair complexion; "could you—that is, will you—" He paused in confusion, and held out the book, which Hagar took in silence.

It was an old and costly book, over which a bibliomaniac would have gloated.

The date was that of the fourteenth century the printer a famous Florentine publisher of that epoch; and the author was none other than one Dante Alighieri, a poet not unknown to fame. In short, the volume was a second edition of "La Divina Commedia," extremely rare, and worth much money. Hagar, who had learnt many things under the able tuition of Jacob, at once recognized the value of the book; but with keen business instinct—notwithstanding her prepossession concerning the young man—she began promptly to disparage it.

"I don't care for old books," she said, offering it back to him. "Why not take it to a secondhand bookseller?"

"Because I don't want to part with it. At the present moment I need money, as you can see from my appearance. Let me have five pounds on the book until I can redeem it."

Hagar, who already had noted the haggard looks of this customer, and the threadbare quality of his apparel, laid down the

Dante with a bang. "I can't give five pounds," she said bluntly. "The book isn't worth it!"

"Shows how much you know of such things, my girl! It is a rare edition of a celebrated Italian poet, and it is worth over a hundred pounds."

"Really?" said Hagar, dryly. "In that case, why not sell?"

"Because I don't want to. Give me five pounds."

"No; four is all that I can advance."

"Four ten," pleaded the customer.

"Four," retorted the inexorable Hagar. "Or else—"

She pushed the book towards him with one finger. Seeing that he could get nothing more out of her, the young man sighed and relented. "Give me the four pounds," he said, gloomily. "I might have guessed that a Jewess would grind me down to the lowest."

"I am not a Jew, but a gipsy," replied Hagar, making out the ticket.

"A gipsy!" said the other, peering into her face. "And what is a Romany lass doing in this Levitical tabernacle?"

"That's my business!" retorted Hagar, curtly. "Name and address?"

"Eustace Lorn, 4: Castle Road," said the young man, giving an address near at hand. "But I say—if you are true Romany, you can talk the calo jib."

"I talk it with my kind, young man; not with the Gentiles."

"But I am a Romany Rye."

"I'm not a fool, young man! Romany Ryes don't live in cities for choice."

"Nor do gipsy girls dwell in pawn-shops, my lass!"

"Four pounds," said Hagar, taking no notice of this remark; "there it is, in gold; your ticket also—number eight hundred and twenty. You can redeem the book whenever you like, on paying six per cent. interest. Good night."

"But I say," cried Lorn, as he slipped money and ticket into his pocket, "I want to speak to you, and—"

"Good night, sir," said Hagar, sharply, and vanished into the darkness of the shop. Lorn was annoyed by her curt manner and his sudden dismissal; but as there was no help for it, he walked out into the street.

"What a handsome girl!" was his first thought; and "What a spitfire!" was his second.

After his departure, Hagar put away the Dante, and, as it was late, shut up the shop. Then she retired to the back-parlor to eat her supper—dry bread-and-cheese with cold water—and to think over the young man. As a rule, Hagar was far too self-possessed to be impressionable; but there was something about Eustace Lorn—she had the name pat—which attracted her not a little. From the short interview she had not learnt much of his personality. He was poor, proud, rather absent-minded; and—from the fact of his yielding to her on the question of price—rather weak in character. Yet she liked his face, the kindly expression of his eyes, and the sweetness of his mouth. But after all he was only a chance customer; and—unless he returned to redeem the Dante—she might not see him again. On this thought occurring to her, Hagar called common-sense to her aid, and strove to banish the young man's image from her mind. The task was more difficult than she thought.

A week later, Lorn and his pawning of the book were recalled to her mind by a stranger who entered the shop shortly after midday. This man was short, stout, elderly and vulgar. He was much excited, and spoke badly, as Hagar noted when he laid a pawnticket number eight hundred and twenty on the counter.

"'Ere, girl," said he in rough tones, "gimme the book this ticket's for."

"You come from Mr. Lorn?" asked Hagar, remembering the Dante.

"Yes; he wants that book. There's the brass. Sharp, now, young woman!"

Hagar made no move to get the volume, or even to take the money. Instead of doing either, she asked a question. "Is Mr. Lorn ill, that he could not come himself?" she demanded, looking keenly at the man's coarse face.

"No; but I've bought the pawn-ticket off him. 'Ere, gimme the book!"

"I cannot at present," replied Hagar, who did not trust the looks of this man, and who wished, moreover, to see Eustace again.

"Dash yer imperance! Why not?"

"Because you did not pawn the Dante; and as it is a valuable book, I might get into trouble if I gave it into other hands than Mr. Lorn's."

"Well, I'm blest! There's the ticket!"

"So I see; but how do I know the way you became possessed of it?"

"Lorn gave it me," said the man, sulkily, "and I want the Dante!"

"I'm sorry for that," retorted Hagar, certain that all was not right, "for no one but Mr. Lorn shall get it. If he isn't ill, let him come and receive it from me."

The man swore and completely lost his temper—a fact which did not disturb Hagar in the least. "You may as well clear out," she said, coldly. "I have said that you shan't have the book, so that closes the question."

"I'll call in the police!"

"Do so; there's a station five minutes' walk from here."

Confounded by her coolness, the man snatched up the pawn-ticket, and stamped out of the shop in a rage. Hagar took down the Dante, looked at it carefully, and considered the position. Clearly there was something wrong, and Eustace was in trouble, else why should he send a stranger to redeem the book upon which he set such store? In an ordinary case, Hagar might have received the ticket and money without a qualm, so long as she was acting rightly in a legal sense; but Eustace Lorn interested her strangely—why, she could not guess—and she was anxious to guard his interests. Moreover, the emissary possessed an untrustworthy face, and looked a man capable, if not of crime, at least of treachery. How he had obtained the ticket could only be explained by its owner; so, after some cogitation, Hagar sent a message to Lorn. The gist of this was, that he should come to the pawn-shop after closing time.

All the evening Hagar anxiously waited for her visitor, and—such is the inconsequence of maids—she was angered with herself

for this very anxiety. She tried to think that it was sheer curiosity
to know the truth of the matter that made her impatient for the
arrival of Lorn; but deep in her heart there lurked a perception of
the actual state of things. It was not curiosity so much as a wish to
see the young man's face again, to hear him speak, and feel that he
was beside her. Though without a chaperon, though not brought
up under parental government, Hagar had her own social code,
and that a strict one. In this instance, she thought that her mental
attitude was unmaidenly and unworthy of an unmarried girl.
Hence, when Eustace made his appearance at nine o'clock, she was
brusque to the verge of rudeness.

"Who was that man you sent for your book?" she demanded,
abruptly, when Lorn was seated in the back-parlor.

"Jabez Treadle. I could not come myself, so I sent him with the
ticket. Why did you not give him the Dante?"

"Because I did not like his face, and I thought he might have
stolen the ticket from you. Besides, I"—here Hagar hesitated, for
she was not anxious to admit that her real reason had been a desire to see him again—"besides, I don't think he is your friend,"
she finished, lamely.

"Very probably he is not," replied Lorn, shrugging his shoulders. "I have no friends."

"That is a pity," said Hagar, casting a searching glance at his
irresolute face. "I think you need friends—or, at all events, one
staunch one."

"May that staunch one be of your own sex," said Lorn, rather
surprised at the interest this strange girl displayed in his welfare—
"yourself, for instance?"

"If that could be so, I might give you unpalatable advice, Mr.
Lorn."

"Such as—what?"

"Don't trust the man you sent here—Mr. Treadle. See, here is
your Dante, young man. Pay me the money, and take it away."

"I can't pay you the money, as I have none. I am as poor as Job,
but hardly so patient."

"But you offered the money through that Treadle creature."

"Indeed no!" explained Eustace, frankly. "I gave him the ticket, and he wished to redeem the book with his own money."

"Did he really?" said Hagar, thoughtfully. "He does not look like a student—as you do. Why did he want this book?"

"To find out a secret."

"A secret, young man—contained in the Dante?"

"Yes. There is a secret in the book which means money."

"To you or Mr. Treadle?" demanded Hagar.

Eustace shrugged his shoulders. "To either one of us who finds out the secret," he said, carelessly. "But indeed I don't think it will ever be discovered—at all events by me. Treadle may be more fortunate."

"If crafty ways can bring fortune, your man will succeed," said Hagar, calmly. "He is a dangerous friend for you, that Treadle. There is evidently some story about this Dante of yours which he knows, and which he desires to turn to his own advantage. If the story means money, tell it to me, and I may be able to help you to the wealth. I am only a young girl, it is true, Mr. Lorn; still, I am old in experience, and I may succeed where you fail."

"I doubt it," replied Lorn, gloomily; "still, it is kind of you to take this interest in a stranger. I am much obliged to you, Miss—"

"Call me Hagar," she interrupted, hastily. "I am not used to fine titles."

"Well, then, Hagar," said he, with a kindly glance, "I'll tell you the story of my Uncle Ben and his strange will."

Hagar smiled to herself. It seemed to be her fate to have dealings with wills—first that of Jacob; now this of Lorn's uncle. However, she knew when to hold her tongue, and saying nothing, she waited for Eustace to explain. This he did at once.

"My uncle, Benjamin Gurth, died six months ago at the age of fifty-eight," said he, slowly. "In his early days he had lived a roving life, and ten years ago he came home with a fortune from the West Indies."

"How much fortune?" demanded Hagar, always interested in financial matters.

"That is the odd part about it," continued Eustace; "nobody ever knew the amount of his wealth, for he was a grumpy old curmudgeon, who confided in no one. He bought a little house and garden at Woking, and there lived for the ten years he was in England. His great luxury was books, and as he knew many languages—Italian among others—he collected quite a polyglot library."

"Where is it now?"

"It was sold after his death along with the house and land. A man in the city claimed the money and obtained it."

"A creditor. What about the fortune?"

"I'm telling you, Hagar, if you'll only listen," said Eustace, impatiently. "Well, Uncle Ben, as I have said, was a miser. He hoarded up all his moneys and kept them in the house, trusting neither to banks nor investments. My mother was his sister, and very poor; but he never gave her a penny, and to me nothing but the Dante, which he presented in an unusual fit of generosity."

"But from what you said before," remarked Hagar, shrewdly, "it seemed to me that he had some motive in giving you the Dante."

"No doubt," assented Eustace, admiring her sharpness. "The secret of where his money is hidden is contained in that Dante."

"Then you may be sure, Mr. Lorn, that he intended to make you his heir. But what has your friend Treadle to do with the matter?"

"Oh, Treadle is a grocer in Woking," responded Lorn. "He is greedy for money, and knowing that Uncle Ben was rich, he tried to get the cash left to him. He wheedled and flattered the old man; he made him presents, and always tried to set him against me as his only relative."

"Didn't I say the man was your enemy? Well, go on."

"There is little more to tell, Hagar. Uncle Ben hid his money away, and left a will which gave it all to the person who should find out where it was concealed. The testament said the secret was contained in the Dante. You may be sure that Treadle visited me at once and asked to see the book. I showed it to him, but neither of us could find any sign in its pages likely to lead us to discover the hidden treasure. The other day Treadle came to see the Dante

again. I told him that I had pawned it, so he volunteered to redeem it if I gave him the ticket. I did so, and he called on you. The
result you know."

"Yes; I refused to give it to him," said Hagar, "and I see now
that I was quite right to do so, as the man is your enemy. Well, Mr.
Lorn, it seems from your story that a fortune is waiting for you, if
you can find it."

"Very true; but I can't find it. There isn't a single sign in the
Dante by which I can trace the hiding-place."

"Do you know Italian?"

"Very well. Uncle Ben taught it to me."

"That's one point gained," said Hagar, placing the Dante on the
table and lighting another candle. "The secret may be contained in
the poem itself. However, we shall see. Is there any mark in the
book—a marginal mark, I mean?"

"Not one. Look for yourself."

The two comely young heads, one so fair, the other so dark,
were bent over the book in that dismal and tenebrous atmosphere.
Eustace, the weaker character of the twain, yielded in all things to
Hagar. She turned over page after page of the old Florentine edition, but not one pencil or pen-mark marred its pure white surface
from beginning to end. From "L'Inferno" to "Il Paradiso" no hint
betrayed the secret of the hidden money. At the last page, Eustace,
with a sigh, threw himself back in his chair.

"You see, Hagar, there is nothing. What are you frowning at?"

"I am not frowning, but thinking, young man," was her reply.
"If the secret is in this book, there must be some trace of it. Now,
nothing appears at present, but later on—"

"Well," said Eustace, impatiently, "later on?

"Invisible ink."

"Invisible ink!" he repeated, vaguely. "I don't quite understand."

"My late master," said Hagar, without emotion, "was accustomed to deal with thieves, rogues, end vagabonds. Naturally, he
had many secrets, and sometimes by force of circumstances, he
had to trust these secrets to the post. Naturally, also, he did not

wish to risk discovery, so when he sent a letter, about stolen goods for instance, he always wrote it in lemon-juice."

"In lemon-juice! And what good was that?"

"It was good for invisible writing. When the letter was written, it looked like a blank page. No one, you understand, could read what was set out, for to the ordinary eye there was no writing at all."

"And to the cultured eye?" asked Eustace, in ironical tones.

"It appeared the same—a blank sheet," retorted Hagar. "But then the cultured mind came in, young man. The person to whom the letter was sent warmed the seeming blank page over the fire, when at once the writing appeared, black and legible."

"The deuce!" Eustace jumped up in his excitement. "And you think—"

"I think that your late uncle may have adopted the same plan," interrupted Hagar, coolly, "but I am not sure. However, we shall soon see." She turned over a page or two of the Dante. "It is impossible to heat these over the fire," she added, "as the book is valuable, and we must not spoil it; but I know of a plan."

With a confident smile she left the room and returned with a flat iron, which she placed on the fire. While it was heating Eustace looked at this quick-witted woman with admiration. Not only had she brains, but beauty also; and, man-like, he was attracted by this last in no small degree. Shortly he began to think that this strange and unexpected friendship between himself and the pawnbroking gipsy beauty might develop into something stronger and warmer. But here he sighed; both of them were poor, so it would be impossible to—

"We will not begin at the beginning of the book," said Hagar, taking the iron off the fire, and thereby interrupting his thoughts, "but at the end."

"Why?" asked Eustace, who could see no good reason for this decision.

"Well," said Hagar, poising the heated iron over the book, "when I search for an article I find it always at the bottom of a heap of things I don't want. As we began with the first page of this book and found nothing, let us start this time from the end, and perhaps we shall learn your uncle's secret the sooner. It is only a whim of mine, but I should like to satisfy it by way of experiment."

Eustace nodded and laughed, while Hagar placed a sheet of brown paper over the last page of the Dante to preserve the book from being scorched. In a minute she lifted the iron and paper, but the page still showed no mark. With a cheerful air the girl shook her head, and repeated the operation on the second page from the end. This time, when she took away the brown paper, Eustace, who had been watching her actions with much interest, bent forward with an ejaculation of surprise. Hagar echoed it with one of delight; for there was a mark and date on the page, half-way down, as thus:

> Oh, abbondante grazia ond'io presumi
> Ficcar lo viso per la luce eterna $\quad$ 27.12.38.
> Tanto, che la veduta vi consumi!

"There, Mr. Lorn!" cried Hagar, joyously—"there is the secret! My fancy for beginning at the end was right. I was right also about the invisible ink."

"You are a wonder!" said Eustace, with sincere admiration; "but I am as much in the dark as ever. I see a marked line, and a date, the twenty-seventh of December, in the year, I presume, one thousand eight hundred and thirty-eight. We can't make any sense out of that simplicity."

"Don't be in a hurry," said Hagar, soothingly; "we have found out so much, we may learn more. First of all, please to translate those three lines."

"Roughly," said Eustace, reading them, "they run thus: 'O abundant grace, with whom I tried to look through the eternal light so much that I lost my sight.'" He shrugged his shoulders. "I don't see how that transcendentalism can help us."

"What about the date?"

"One thousand eight hundred and thirty-eight," said Lorn, thoughtfully; "and this is ninety-six. Take one from the other, it leaves fifty-eight, the age at which, as I told you before, my uncle died. Evidently this is the date of his birth."

"A date of birth—a line of Dante!" muttered Hagar. "I must say that it is difficult to make sense out of it. Yet, in figures and letters, I am sure the place where the money is concealed is told."

"Well," remarked Eustace, giving up the solution of this problem in despair, "if you can make out the riddle it is more than I can."

"Patience, patience!" replied Hagar, with a nod. "Sooner or later we shall find out the meaning. Could you take me to see your uncle's house at Woking?"

"Oh, yes; it is not yet let, so we can easily go over it. But will you trouble about coming all that way with me?"

"Certainly! I am anxious to know the meaning of this line and date. There may be something about your uncle's house likely to give a clue to its reading. I shall keep the Dante, and puzzle over the riddle; you can call for me on Sunday, when the shop is closed, and we shall go to Woking together."

"O Hagar! how can I ever thank—"

"Thank me when you get the money, and rid yourself of Mr. Treadle!" said Hagar, cutting him short. "Besides, I am only doing this to satisfy my own curiosity."

"You are an angel!"

"And you a fool, who talks nonsense!" said Hagar, sharply. "Here is your hat and cane. Come out this way by the back. I have an ill enough name already, without desiring a fresh scandal. Good night."

"But may I say—"

"Nothing, nothing!" retorted Hagar, pushing him out of the door. "Good night."

The door snapped to sharply, and Lorn went out into the hot July night with his heart beating and his blood aflame. He had seen this girl only twice, yet, with the inconsiderate rashness of youth, he was already in love with her. The beauty and kindness and brilliant mind of Hagar attracted him strongly; and she had shown him such favor that he felt certain she loved him in return. But a girl out of a pawn-shop! He had neither birth nor money, yet he drew back from mating himself with such a one. True, his mother was dead, and he was quite alone in the world—alone and poor. Still, if he found his uncle's fortune, he would be rich enough to marry. Hagar, did she aid him to get the money, might expect reward in the shape of marriage. And she was so beautiful, so clever! By the time he reached his poor lodging Eustace had put all scruples out of his head, and had settled to marry the gipsy as soon as the lost treasure came into his possession. In no other way could he thank her for the interest she was taking in him. This may seem a hasty decision; but young blood is soon heated; young hearts are soon filled with love. Youth and beauty drawn together are as flint and tinder to light the torch of Hymen.

Punctual to the appointed hour, Eustace, as smart as he could make himself with the poor means at his command, appeared at the door of the pawn-shop. Hagar was already waiting for him, with the Dante in her hand. She wore a black dress, a black cloak, and a hat of the same somber hue—such clothes being the mourning she had worn, and was wearing, for Jacob. Averse as she was to using Goliath's money, she thought he would hardly grudge her these garments of woe for his father. Besides, as manageress of the shop, she deserved some salary.

"Why are you taking the Dante?" asked Eustace, when they set out for Waterloo Station.

"It may be useful to read the riddle," said Hagar.

"Have you solved it?"

"I don't know; I am not sure," she said, meditatively. "I tried by counting the lines on that page up and down. You understand—twenty-seven, twelve, thirty-eight; but the lines I lighted on gave me no clue."

"You didn't understand them?"

"Yes I did," replied Hagar, coolly. "I got a second-hand copy of a translation from the old bookseller in Carby's Crescent, and by counting the lines to correspond with those in the Florentine edition I arrived at the sense."

"And none of them point to the solution of the problem?"

"Not one. Then I tried by pages. I counted twenty-seven pages, but could find no clue; I reckoned twelve pages; also thirty-eight; still the same result. Then I took the twelfth, the twenty-seventh, and the thirty-eighth page by numbers, but found nothing. The riddle is hard to read."

"Impossible, I should say," said Eustace, in despair.

"No; I think I have found out the meaning."

"How? how? Tell me quick!"

"Not now. I found a word, but it seems nonsense, as I could not find it in the Italian dictionary which I borrowed."

"What is the word?"

"I'll tell you when I have seen the house."

In vain Eustace tried to move her from this determination. Hagar was stubborn when she took an idea into her strong brain; so she simply declined to explain until she arrived at Woking—at the house of Uncle Ben. Weak himself, Eustace could not understand how she could hold out so long against his persuasions. Finally he decided in his own mind that she did not care about him. In this he was wrong. Hagar liked him—loved him; but she deemed it her duty to teach him patience—a quality he lacked sadly. Hence her closed mouth.

When they arrived at Woking, Eustace led the way towards his late uncle's house, which was some distance out of the town. He addressed Hagar, after a long silence, when they were crossing a piece of waste land and saw the cottage in the distance.

"If you find this money for me," he said, abruptly, "what service am I to do for you in return?"

"I have thought of that," replied Hagar, promptly. "Find Goliath—otherwise James Dix."

"Who is he?" asked Lorn, flushing. "Some one you are fond of?"

"Some one I hate with all my soul!" she flashed out; "but he is the son of my late master, and heir to the pawn-shop. I look after it only because he is absent; and on the day he returns I shall walk out of it, and never set eyes on it, or him again."

"Why don't you advertise?"

"I have done so for months; so has Vark, the lawyer; but Jimmy Dix never replies. He was with my tribe in the New Forest, and it was because I hated him that I left the Romany. Since then he has gone away, and I don't know where he is. Find him if you wish to thank me, and let me get away from the pawn-shop."

"Very good," replied Eustace, quietly. "I shall find him. In the mean time, here is the hermitage of my late uncle."

It was a bare little cottage, small and shabby, set at the end of a square of ground fenced in from the barren moor. Within the quadrangle there were fruit trees—cherry, apple, plum, and pear; also a large fig-tree in the center of the unshaven lawn facing the house. All was desolate and neglected; the fruit trees were unpruned, the grass was growing in the paths, and the flowers were straggling here and there, rich masses of ragged color. Desolate certainly, this deserted hermitage, but not lonely, for as Hagar and her companion turned in at the little gate a figure rose from a stooping position under an apple-tree. It was that of a man with a spade in his hand, who had been digging for some time, as was testified by the heap of freshly-turned earth at his feet.

"Mr. Treadle!" cried Lorn, indignantly. "What are you doing here?"

"Lookin' fur the old un's cash!" retorted Mr. Treadle, with a scowl directed equally at the young man and Hagar. "An' if I gets it I keeps it. Lord! to think as 'ow I pampered that old sinner with figs and such like—to say nothing of French brandy, which he drank by the quart!"

"You have no business here!"

"No more 'ave you!" snapped the irate grocer. "If I ain't, you ain't, fur till the 'ouse is let it's public property. I s'pose you've come 'ere with that Jezebel to look fur the money?"

Hagar, hearing herself called names, stepped promptly up to Mr. Treadle, and boxed his red ears. "Now then," she said, when the grocer fell back in dismay at this onslaught, "perhaps you'll be civil! Mr. Lorn, sit down on this seat, and I'll explain the riddle."

"The Dante!" cried Mr. Treadle, recognizing the book which lay on Hagar's lap—"an' she'll explain the riddle—swindling me out of my rightful cash!"

"The cash belongs to Mr. Lorn, as his uncle's heir!" said Hagar, wrathfully. "Be quiet, sir, or you'll get another box on the ears!"

"Never mind him," said Eustace, impatiently; "tell me the riddle."

"I don't know if I have guessed it correctly," answered Hagar, opening the book; "but I've tried by line and page and number, all of which revealed nothing. Now I try by letters, and you will see if the word they make is a proper Italian one."

She read out the marked line and the date. "'Ficcar lo viso per la luce eterna, 27th December, '38.' Now," said Hagar, slowly, "if you run all the figures together they stand as 271238."

"Yes, yes!" said Eustace, impatiently; "I see. Go on, please."

Hagar continued: "Take the second letter of the word 'Ficcar.'"

"'I.'"

"Also the seventh letter from the beginning of the line."

Eustace counted. "'L.' I see," he went on, eagerly. "Also the first letter, 'F,' the second again, 'i,' the third and the eighth, 'c' and 'o.'"

"Good!" said Hagar, writing these down. "Now, the whole make up the word 'Ilfico.' Is that an Italian word?"

"I'm not sure," said Eustace, thoughtfully. "'Ilfico.' No."

"Shows what eddication 'e's got!" growled Mr. Treadle, who was leaning on his spade.

Eustace raised his eyes to dart a withering glance at the grocer, and in doing so his vision passed on to the tree looming up behind the man. At once the meaning of the word flashed on his brain.

"'Il fico!'" he cried, rising. "Two words instead of one! You have found it, Hagar! It means the fig-tree—the one yonder. I believe the money is buried under it."

Before he could advance a step Treadle had leaped forward, and was slashing away at the tangled grass round the fig-tree like a madman.

"If 'tis there, 'tis mine!" he shouted. "Don't you come nigh me, young Lorn, or I'll brain you with my spade! I fed up that old uncle of yours like a fighting cock, and now I'm going to have his cash to pay me!"

Eustace leaped forward in the like manner as Treadle had done, and would have wrenched the spade out of his grip, but that Hagar laid a detaining hand on his arm.

"Let him dig," she said, coolly. "The money is yours; I can prove it. He'll have the work and you the fortune."

"Hagar! Hagar! how can I thank you!"

The girl stepped back, and a blush rose in her cheeks. "Find Goliath," she said, "and let me get rid of the pawn-shop."

At this moment Treadle gave a shout of glee, and with both arms wrenched a goodly-sized tin box out of the hole he had dug.

"Mine! mine!" he cried, plumping this down on the grass. "This will pay for the dinners I gave him, the presents I made him. I've bin castin' my bread on the waters, and here it's back again."

He fell to forcing the lid of the box with the edge of the spade, all the time laughing and crying like one demented. Lorn and Hagar drew near, in the expectation of seeing a shower of gold pieces rain on the ground when the lid was opened. As Treadle gave a final wrench it flew wide, and they saw—an empty box.

"Why—what," stammered Treadle, thunderstruck—"what does it mean?"

Eustace, equally taken aback, bent down and looked in. There was absolutely nothing in the box but a piece of folded paper. Unable to make a remark, he held it out to the amazed Hagar.

"What the devil does it mean?" said Treadle again.

"This explains," said Hagar, running her eye over the writing. "It seems that this wealthy Uncle Ben was a pauper."

"A pauper!" cried Eustace and Treadle together.

"Listen!" said Hagar, and read out from the page: "When I returned to England I was thought wealthy, so that all my friends and relations fawned on me for the crumbs which fell from the rich man's table. But I had just enough money to rent the cottage for a term of years, and to purchase an annuity barely sufficient for the necessities of life. But, owing to the report of my wealth, the luxuries have been supplied by those who hoped for legacies. This is my legacy to one and all—these golden words, which I have proved true: 'It is better to be thought rich than to be rich.'"

The paper fell from the hand of Eustace, and Treadle, with a howl of rage, threw himself on the grass, loading the memory of the deceased with opprobrious names. Seeing that all was over, that the expected fortune had vanished into thin air, Hagar left the disappointed grocer weeping with rage over the deceptive tin box, and led Eustace away. He followed her as in a dream, and all the time during their sad journey back to town he spoke hardly a word. What they did say—how Eustace bewailed his fate and Hagar comforted him—is not to the point. But on arriving at the door of the pawn-shop Hagar gave the copy of Dante to the young man. "I give this back to you," she said, pressing his hand. "Sell it, and with the proceeds build up your own fortune."

"But shall I not see you again?" he asked, piteously.

"Yes, Mr. Lorn; you shall see me when you bring back Goliath."

Then she entered the pawn-shop and shut the door. Left alone in the deserted crescent, Eustace sighed and walked slowly away. Hugging to his breast the Florentine Dante, he went away to make his fortune, to find Goliath, and—although he did not know it at the time—to marry Hagar.

3

The Second Customer and the Amber Beads

AFTER THE EPISODE of the Florentine Dante, Hagar lost her high spirits. She had sent Eustace away to make his fortune, and to discover, if possible, the lost heir of Jacob Dix. By this act of self-
denial, as it really was, she had deprived herself of all pleasure;
she had robbed herself of what might have been a bright future;
consequently she was less cheerful than of yore. Nevertheless, she
felt convinced that Lorn loved her, and that he would earn her gratitude—possibly her hand—by returning with Goliath at his heels.
When that event took place she would recover at once her spirits
and her lover; but at present the business of the pawn-shop took
up her undivided attention, and forced her to put away sad thoughts
and melancholy considerations. Also, Providence provided distrac-
tion for her dismal humors by sending her a negress to pawn a
necklace of amber beads. Although Hagar did not know it at the
time, this was the beginning of a second and rather more serious
adventure.

It was drawing to night one August evening when the woman
made her appearance, and the atmosphere of the pawnshop was
darker than usual. Still, it was sufficiently light for Hagar to see
that her customer was a tall and bulky negress, arrayed in a gaudy
yellow dress, neutralized by trimmings of black jet beading. As
the evening was hot and close, she wore neither cloak nor jacket,
but displayed her somewhat shapeless figure to the full in this
decidedly startling costume. Her hat was a garden of roses—red,
white and yellow; she wore a large silver brooch like a shield, an

extensive necklace of silver coins, and many bangles of the same metal on her black wrists. As a contrast to these splendors she wore no gloves, nor did she hide her coal-black face with a veil. Altogether, this odd customer was the blackest and most fantastically-dressed negress that Hagar had ever seen, and in the dim light she looked a striking but rather alarming figure.

On Hagar coming to the counter this black woman produced out of a silver-clasped sealskin satchel a necklace, which she handed silently to Hagar for inspection. As the light was too imperfect to admit of a close examination, Hagar lighted the gas, but when it flamed up the negress, as though unwilling to be seen too clearly in the searching glare, stepped back hastily into the darkness. Hagar put this retrograde movement down to the natural timidity of a person unaccustomed to pawning, and took but little notice of it at the time. Afterwards she had cause to remember it.

The necklace was a string of magnificent amber beads threaded on a slender chain of gold. Each bead was as large as the egg of a sparrow, and round the middle of every single one there was a narrow belt of tiny diamonds. The clasp at the back was of fine gold, square in shape, and curiously wrought to the representation of a hideous Ethiopian face, with diamonds for eyes. This queer piece of jewelry was unique of its kind, and, as Hagar rapidly calculated, of considerable value. Nevertheless, she offered, according to custom, as low a sum as she well could.

"I'll give five pounds on it," said she, returning to the counter.

Rather to her surprise, the negress accepted with a sharp nod, and then took out of her bag a scrap of paper. On this was written laboriously: "Rosa, Marylebone Road." The name and address were so imperfect that Hagar hesitated before making out the pawn-ticket.

"Have you no other name but Rosa?" she asked, sharply.

The negress shook her head, and kept well in the shadow.

"And no more particular address than Marylebone Road?"

Again the black woman made a negative sign, whereat, annoyed by these gestures, Hagar grew angered.

"Can't you speak?" she demanded, tartly. "Are you dumb?"

At once the negress nodded, and laid a finger on her lips. Hagar drew back. This woman was black, she was dumb, she gave half a name, half an address, and she wished to pawn a valuable and unique piece of jewelry. The whole affair was queer, and, as Hagar considered, might be rather dangerous. Perhaps this silent negress was disposing of stolen goods, as the necklace seemed too fine for her to possess. For the moment Hagar was inclined to refuse to do business; but a glance at the amber beads decided her to make the bargain. She could get it cheap; she was acting well within the legal limits of business; and if the police did appear in the matter, no blame could be attached to her for the transaction. Biased by these considerations, Hagar made out the ticket in the name Rosa, and took a clean new five-pound note out of the cash-box. As she was about to give ticket and money across the counter she paused. "I'll take the number of this note," she thought, going to the desk; "if this negress can't be traced by name or address, the bank-note number will find her if it is necessary."

Deeming this precaution judicious, Hagar hastily scribbled down the number of the five-pound note, and returning to the counter, gave it and the ticket to her queer customer. The negress stretched out her right hand for them; and then Hagar made a discovery which she noted mentally as a mark of identification if necessary. However, she said nothing, but tried to get a good look at the woman's face. The customer, however, kept well in the shadow, and swept note and ticket into her bag hurriedly. Then she bowed and left the shop.

Six days later Hagar received a printed notice from New Scotland Yard, notifying to all pawn-brokers that the police were in search of a necklace of amber beads set with diamonds, and clasped with a negro's face wrought in gold. Notice of its whereabouts was to be sent to the Detective Department without delay. Remembering her suspicions, and recalling the persistent way in which the negress had averted her face, Hagar was not much surprised by this communication. Curious to know the truth, and to learn what crime might be attached to the necklace, she wrote at once about the matter. Within four hours a stranger presented himself to see the amber beads, and to question her concerning the woman who had pawned the same. He was a fat little man, with a healthy red face and shrewd twinkling eyes. Introducing himself as Luke Horval, of the detective service, he asked Hagar to relate the circumstances of the pawning. This the girl did frankly enough, but without communicating her own suspicions. At the conclusion of her narrative she displayed the amber beads, which were carefully examined by Mr. Horval. Then he slapped his knee, and whistled in a thoughtful sort of way.

"I guessed as much," said he, staring hard at Hagar. "The negress did it."

"Did what?" asked the girl, curiously.

"Why," said Horval, "murdered the old woman."

Murder! The word had a gruesome and cruel sound, which caused Hagar's cheek to pale when it rang in her ears. She had connected the amber beads with robbery, but scarcely with the taking of life. The idea that she had been in the company of a murderess gave Hagar a qualm; but, suppressing this as a weakness, she asked Horval to tell her the details of the crime and how it bore on the pawning of the amber beads.

"It's just this way, miss," explained the detective, easily. "This Rosa is the nigger girl of Mrs. Arryford—"

"Is Rosa her real name?"

"Oh, yes; I s'pose she thought she might lose the beads if she gave a wrong one; but the address ain't right. It's the other end of London as Mrs. Arryford lives—or rather lived," added Horval, correcting himself, "seeing she now occupies a Kensal Green grave—Campden Hill, miss; a sweet little house in Bedford Gardens, where she lived with Rosa and Miss Lyle."

"And who is Miss Lyle?"

"The companion of Mrs. Arryford. A dry stick of a spinster, miss; not to be compared with a fine girl like you."

Hagar did not deign to notice the compliment, but sharply requested Mr. Horval to continue his story, which he did, in no wise abashed by her cold demeanor.

"It's just this way, miss," said he again; "the old lady, the old maid and the nigger wench lived together in Bedford Gardens, a kind of happy family, as one might say. Mrs. Arryford was the widder of a West Indian gent, and as rich as Solomon. She brought those amber beads from Jamaica, and Rosa was always wanting them."

"Why? The necklace was very unsuitable to one of her condition."

"'Twasn't exactly the cost of it as she thought about," said Horval, nursing his chin, "but it seems that the necklace is a fetish, or charm, or lucky-penny, as you might say, to bring good fortune to the wearer. Mrs. Arryford was past wanting good luck, so hadn't no need for the beads. Rosa asked her for them, just for the good luck of them, as you might say. The old girl wouldn't part, as she was as superstitious as Rosa herself over that necklace; so in the end Rosa murdered her to get it."

"How do you know she did?" asked Hagar, doubtfully.

"How do I know?" echoed the detective in surprise. "'Cause I ain't a fool, miss. Last week Mrs. Arryford was found in her bed with a carving knife in her heart, as dead as a door-nail, and the beads were missing. Miss Lyle, she didn't know anything about it, and Rosa swore she hadn't left her room, so, you see, we couldn't quite hit on who finished off Mrs. Arryford. But now as I know Rosa pawned these beads, I'm sure she did the job."

"What made you think that the beads might have been pawned?"

"Oh, that was Miss Lyle's idea; a sharp old girl she is, miss. She was very fond of Mrs. Arryford, as she well might be, seeing as the old lady was rich and kept her like a princess. Often she heard Rosa ask for those beads, so when Mrs. Arryford was killed and the beads missing she told me as she was sure Rosa had done the trick."

"But the pawning?"

"Well, miss," said Horval, scratching his chin, "it was just this way. Miss Lyle said as how Rosa, to get rid of the necklace until the affair of the murder was blown over, might pawn it. I thought so too, so I sent a printed slip to all the pop-shops in London. You wrote that the beads were here, so it seems as Miss Lyle was right."

"Evidently. By the way, who gets the money of Mrs. Arryford?"

"A Mr. Frederick Jevons; he's a nephew of Miss Lyle's."

"A nephew of Miss Lyle's!" echoed Hagar, in surprise. "And why did Mrs. Arryford leave her money to him instead of to her relatives?"

"Well, it's just this way, miss," said Horval, rising. "She hadn't got no relatives; and as Mr. Jevons was a good-looking young chap, always at the house to see his aunt, she took a fancy to him and left the money his way."

"You are sure that Miss Lyle is no relation to Mrs. Arryford?"

"Quite sure. She was only the old girl's companion."

"Was Mrs. Arryford weak in the head?"

"Not as I ever heard of," said Mr. Horval, with a stare, "but you can find out, if you like, from Miss Lyle."

"Miss Lyle! How am I to see her?"

"Why," said the detective, clapping on his hat, "when you come to see if Rosa is the same nigger as pawned the amber beads. Just leave someone to look after the shop, miss, and come with me right away."

With true feminine curiosity, Hagar agreed at once to accompany the detective to Campden Hill. The shop was delivered into the charge of Bolker, a misshapen imp of sixteen, who for some months had been the plague of Hagar's life. He had a long body and long arms, short legs and a short temper, and also a most malignant eye, which indicated only too truly his spiteful nature. Having given a few instructions to this charming lad, Hagar departed with Horval in the omnibus, and arrived at Bedford Gardens early in the afternoon.

The house was a quaint, pretty cottage, which stood in a delightful garden—once the solace of poor dead Mrs. Arryford's soul—and was divided from the road by a tall fence of iron railings closed in with wooden planks painted a dark green. The room into which the detective and gipsy were shown was a prim and rather cosy apartment, which bore the impress of Miss Lyle's old-maidism in the disposition of the furniture. When they were seated here, and were waiting for Miss Lyle, who had been advised of their arrival, Hagar suddenly asked Horval a leading question.

"Is Rosa dumb?" she demanded.

"Bless you, no!" answered Horval. "It's true as she don't talk much, but she can use her tongue in nigger fashion. Why do you ask?"

"She said she was dumb when she pawned the beads."

"Oh, that was 'cause she was too 'cute to let her voice betray her," replied Horval, smiling. He had humor enough to note Hagar's unconscious bull; but as she was likely to be useful to him in the conduct of the case, he did not wish to anger her by remarking on it.

When Miss Lyle made her appearance, Hagar, after the manner of women, took immediate note of her looks and manner. The old maid was tall and lean and yellow, with cold gray eyes, and a thin-lipped, hard-tempered mouth, turned down at the curves. Her iron-gray hair was drawn tightly off her narrow forehead and screwed into a hard-looking knob behind. She wore a black stuff gown, somber and lusterless; collar and cuffs of white linen, and cloth slippers, in which she glided noiselessly. Altogether an unpromising, hard woman, acidulated and narrow-minded, who looked disapprovingly on the rich beauty of Hagar, and remarked her graces with a jaundiced eye and a vinegary look. The cough with which she ended her inspection showed that she condemned the girl at first sight.

"Is this young person necessary to your conduct of the case?" said Miss Lyle, addressing herself to Horval, and ignoring Hagar altogether.

"Why, yes, miss," replied Horval, on whom the antagonistic attitude of the two women was not lost. "She keeps the pawn-shop at which Rosa pawned the beads!"

Miss Lyle gave a start of virtuous horror, and her thin lips wreathed in a viperous smile. "The wretch did kill my poor friend, then," she said in a soft and fluty voice. "I knew it!"

"She pawned the amber beads, Miss Lyle, but—"

"Now, don't say the wretch didn't kill my martyred friend," snapped Miss Lyle, going to the bell-rope; "but we'll have her in, and perhaps this young person will recognize her as the viper who pawned the beads."

"It is to be hoped so," said Hagar, very dryly, not approving of being spoken at in the third person; "but the negress kept her face turned away, and I might not—"

"It is your duty to recognize her," exclaimed Miss Lyle, addressing herself to the girl for once. "I am convinced that Rosa is a dangerous criminal. Here she is—the black Jezebel!"

As the last word fell from her mouth the door opened, and Rosa entered the room, whereat Hagar uttered an exclamation of surprise. This negress was rather short, and more than a trifle stout. It is true that she wore a yellow dress trimmed with black jet beading; that silver ornaments were on her neck and wrists; also that she was without the wonderful hat. Still, Hagar was surprised, and explained her ejaculation forthwith.

"That is not the woman who pawned the beads!" she declared, rising.

"Not the woman?" echoed Miss Lyle, virulently. "She must be! This is Rosa!"

"Yis, yis! I Rosa," said the negress, beginning to weep, "but I no kill my poo' dear missy. Dat one big lie."

"Are you sure, miss, that this is not the woman?" asked Horval, rather dismayed.

Hagar stepped forward, and looked sharply at the sobbing negress up and down. Then she glanced at the woman's hands and shook her head.

"I am prepared to swear in a court of law that this is not the woman," she said, quietly.

"Rubbish, rubbish!" cried Miss Lyle, flushing. "Rosa coveted the necklace, as it was connected with some debased African superstition, and—"

"It one ole fetish!" interrupted Rosa, her eyes sparkling fire at the old maid, "and ole missy she did wish to gib it me, but you no let her."

"Certainly not!" said Miss Lyle, with dignity. "The necklace was not fit for you to wear. And because I persuaded Mrs. Arryford not to give it to you, you murdered her, you wretch! Down on your knees, woman, and confess!"

"I no 'fess!" exclaimed the terrified negress. "I no kill my missy! I no gib dose amber beads for money. If dose beads mine, I keep dem; dey a mighty big fetish, for sure!"

"One moment," said Horval, as Miss Lyle was about to speak again, "let us conduct this inquiry calmly, and give the accused every chance. Miss," he said, turning to Hagar, "on what day, at what time, was it that the beads were pawned?"

Hagar calculated rapidly, and answered promptly: "On the evening of the 23d of August, between six and seven o'clock."

"Ah!" exclaimed Miss Lyle, joyfully—"and on that very evening Rosa was out, and did not return till nine!"

"Me went to see Massa Jevons for you," said Rosa vehemently; "you send me."

"I send you! Just listen to the creature's lies! Besides, Mr. Jevons's rooms are in Duke Street, St James's, whereas it was at Lambeth you were."

"I no go to dat gem'man's house. You send me to de train Waterloo!"

"Waterloo!" said Horval, looking sharply at Rosa. "You were there?"

"Yis, masse; me dere at seven and eight."

"In the neighbourhood of Lambeth," murmured Horval. "She might have gone to the pawn-shop after all."

"Of course she did!" cried Miss Lyle, vindictively—"and pawned the amber beads of my poor dead friend!"

"She did nothing of the sort!" interposed Hagar, with spirit. "Whosoever pawned the beads, it was not this woman. Besides, how do you know that Rosa killed Mrs. Arryford?"

"She wanted the beads, young woman, and she killed my friend to obtain them."

"No, no! dat one big lie!"

"I am sure it is!" said Hagar, her face aflame. "I believe in your innocence, Rosa. Mr. Horval," she added, turning to the detective, "you can't arrest this woman, as you have no grounds to do so."

"Well, if she didn't pawn those beads—"

"She did not, I tell you."

"She did!" cried Miss Lyle angrily. "I believe you are an accomplice of the creature's!"

What reply Hagar would have made to this accusation it is impossible to say, for at this moment a young man walked into the room. He was good-looking in appearance, and smart in dress, but there was a haggard look about his face which betokened dissipation.

"This," said Miss Lyle, introducing him, "is my nephew, the heir to the property of my late dear friend. He is resolved, as such heir, to find out and punish the assassin of his benefactress. For my part, I believe Rosa to be guilty."

"And I," cried Hagar, with energy, "believe her to be innocent!"

"Let us hope she is," said Jevons, in a weary voice, as he removed his gloves. "I am tired of the whole affair."

"You are bound to punish the guilty!" said Miss Lyle, in hard tones.

"But not the innocent," retorted Hagar, rising.

"Young woman, you are insolent!"

Hagar looked Miss Lyle up and down in the coolest manner; then her eyes wandered to the well-dressed figure of Jevons, the heir. What she saw in him to startle her it is difficult to say; but after a moment's inspection she turned pale with suppressed emotion. Stepping forward, she was about to speak, when, checking herself suddenly, she beckoned to Horval, and advanced towards the door.

"My errand here is fulfilled," she said, quietly. "Mr. Horval, perhaps you will come with me."

"Yes, and you can go also, Rosa," cried Miss Lyle, angered by the insulting gaze of the girl. "I am mistress here in my nephew's house, and I refuse to let a murderess remain under its roof!"

"Be content," said Hagar, pausing at the door. "Rosa shall come with me; and when you see us again with Mr. Horval, you will then learn who killed Mrs. Arryford, and why."

"Insolent hussy!" muttered Miss Lyle, and closed the door on Hagar, Horval and the black woman.

The trio walked away, and shortly afterwards picked up an omnibus, in which they returned to the Lambeth pawnshop. Hagar talked earnestly to Horval the whole way; and from the close attention which the detective paid to her it would seem that the conversation was of the deepest interest. Rosa, a dejected heap of misery, sat with downcast eyes, and at intervals wiped away the tears which ran down her black cheeks. The poor negress, under suspicion as a thief and a murderess, turned out of house and home, desolate and forsaken, was crushed to the earth under the burden of her woes. On her the fetish necklace of amber beads had brought a curse.

On arriving at the shop Hagar conducted Rosa into the back parlor; and after a further conference she dismissed the detective.

"You can stay with me for a week," she said to Rosa.

"And den what you do?"

"Oh," said Hagar, with an agreeable smile, "I shall take you with me to denounce the assassin of your late mistress."

All that week Rosa stayed in the domestic portion of the pawn-shop, and made herself useful in cooking and cleaning. Hagar questioned her closely concerning the events which had taken place on the night of the murder in the house at Bedford Gardens, and elicited certain information which gave her great satisfaction. This she communicated to Horval when he one day paid her a hurried visit. When in possession of the facts, Horval looked at her with admiration, and on taking his leave he paid her a compliment.

"You ought to be a man, with that head of yours," he said; "you're too good to be a woman!"

"And not bad enough to be a man," retorted Hagar, laughing. "Be off with you, Mr. Horval, and let me know when you want me up West."

In four more days Horval again made his appearance, this time in a state of the greatest excitement. He was closeted with Hagar for over an hour, and at its conclusion he departed in a great hurry. Shortly after noon Hagar resigned the shop into Bolker's charge, put on hat and cloak, and ordered Rosa to come with her. What the reason of this unexpected departure might be she did not inform the negress immediately; but before they reached their destination Rosa knew all, and was much rejoiced thereat.

Hagar took Rosa as far as Duke Street, St James's, and here, at the door of a certain house, they found the detective impatiently waiting for them.

"Well, Mr. Horval," said Hagar, coming to a stop, "is he indoors?"

"Safe and sound!" replied Horval, tapping his breastcoat pocket—"and I have got you know what here. Shall we come up?"

"Not immediately. I wish to see him by myself first. You remain outside his door, and enter with Rosa when I call you."

Mr. Horval nodded, with a full comprehension of what was required of him, and the trio ascended the dark staircase. They paused at a door on the second landing. Then Hagar, motioning to her companions that they should withdraw themselves into the gloom, rapped lightly on the portal. Shortly afterwards it was opened by Mr. Frederick Jevons, who looked inquiringly at Hagar. She turned her face towards the light which fell through the murky staircase window, whereat, recognizing her, he stepped back in dismay.

"The pawn-shop girl!" said he in astonishment. "What do you want?"

"I wish to see you," replied Hagar, composedly, "but it is just as well that our conversation should be in private."

"Why, you can have nothing to say to me but what the whole world might hear!"

"After I have mentioned the object of my visit you may think differently," said Hagar, with some dryness. "However, we'll talk here if you wish."

"No, no; come in," said Jevons, standing on one side. "Since you insist upon privacy, you shall have it. This way."

He showed her into a large and rather badly furnished room. Evidently Mr. Fred Jevons had not been rich until he inherited the fortune of Mrs. Arryford.

"I suppose you will be moving to the Bedford Gardens house soon?" said Hagar, sitting composedly in a large armchair.

"Is that what you came to speak to me about?" retorted Jevons, rudely.

"Not exactly. Perhaps, as you are impatient, we had better get to business."

"Business! What business can I have to do with you?"

"Why," said Hagar, quietly, and looking directly at him, "the business of those amber beads which you—pawned."

"I," stammered Jevons, drawing back with a pale face.

"Also," added Hagar, solemnly, "the business which concerns the commission of a crime."

"A—a—a crime!" gasped the wretched creature.

"Yes—the most terrible of all crimes—murder!"

"What—what—what do you—you mean?"

Hagar rose from her chair, and, drawn to her full height, stretched out an accusing arm towards the young man. "What I mean you know well enough!" she said, sternly. "I mean that you murdered Mrs. Arryford!"

"It's a lie!" cried Jevons, sinking into a chair, for his legs refused to support him longer.

"It is not a lie—it is the truth! I have evidence!"

"Evidence!" He started up with dry and trembling lips.

"Yes. Through her influence over Mrs. Arryford, your aunt induced her to make you her heir. You are fond of money; you are in debt, and you could not wait until the old lady died in the course of nature. On the night of the murder you were in the house."

"No, no! I swear—"

"You need not; you were seen leaving the house. To throw suspicion on Rosa you disguised yourself as a negress, and came to pawn the amber bead necklace at my shop. I recognized that the supposed black woman was minus the little finger of the right hand. You, Mr. Jevons, are mutilated in the same way. Again, I paid you with a five-pound note. Of that note I took the number. It has been traced by the number, and you are the man who paid it away. I saw—"

Jevons jumped up, still white and shaking. "It's a lie! a lie!" he said, hoarsely. "I did not kill Mrs. Arryford; I did not pawn the beads. I did—"

"You did both those things!" said Hagar, brushing past him. "I have two witnesses who can prove what I say is true. Rosa! Mr. Horval!"

She flung the outside door wide open, while Jevons again sank into the arm-chair, with an expression of horror on his white face. "Rosa! Horval!" he muttered. "I am lost!"

Rosa and the detective entered quickly in response to Hagar's call, and with her looked down on the shrinking figure of the accused man.

"These are my witnesses," said Hagar, slowly. "Rosa!"

"I saw dat man in de house when my missy died," said the negress. "I hear noise in de night; I come down, and I see Massa Jevons run away from de room of my missy, and Missus Lyle let him out by de side door. He kill my poo' missy—yes, I tink dat."

"You hear," said Hagar to the terrified man. "Now, Mr. Horval."

"I traced the five-pound note you gave him by its number," said the detective. "Yes, he paid it away at his club; I can bring a waiter to prove it."

"You hear," said Hagar again; "and I know by the evidence of your lost finger that you are the man, disguised as a negress, who pawned the necklace which was stolen from the person of Mrs. Arryford, after you murdered her. The dead woman, as Rosa tells us, wore that necklace night and day. Only with her death could it have been removed. You murdered her; you stole the necklace of amber beads."

Jevons leaped up: "No, no, no!" he cried, loudly, striking his hands together in despair. "I am innocent!"

"That," said Horval, slipping the handcuffs on his wrists, "you shall prove before a judge and jury."

When Jevons, still protesting his innocence, was removed to prison, Hagar and the negress returned to Carby's Crescent. It can easily be guessed how she had traced the crime home to Jevons. She had noticed that the negress who pawned the beads had no little finger. On being brought face to face with Rosa, she had seen that the woman had not lost the finger; and when Jevons had removed his gloves she had seen in his right hand the evidence that he was one with the mysterious black woman of the pawn-shop.

Still, she was not certain; and it was only when Rosa had deposed
to the presence of the man at midnight in the Bedford Gardens
house, and when Horval had traced the five-pound note of which
she had taken the number, that she was certain that Jevons was
the murderer. Hence the accusation; hence the arrest. But now the
fact of his guilt was clearly established. To obtain the wealth of
Mrs. Arryford the wretched man had committed a crime; to hide
that crime and throw the blame on Rosa he had pawned the amber
beads; and now the amber beads were about to hang him. In the
moment of his triumph, when preparing to enjoy the fruits of his
crime, Nemesis had struck him down.

The news of the arrest, the story of the amber beads, was in all
the papers next day; and next day, also, Miss Lyle came to see
Hagar. Pale and stern, she swept into the shop, and looked at Hagar
with a bitter smile.

"Girl!" she said, harshly, "you have been our evil genius!"

"I have been the means of denouncing your accomplice, you
mean," returned Hagar, composedly.

"My accomplice; no, my son!"

"Your son!" Hagar recoiled, with a startled expression. "Your
son, Miss Lyle?"

"Not Miss, but Mrs. Lyle," returned the gaunt, pale woman;
"and Frederick Jevons is my son by my first husband. You think
he is guilty; you are wrong, for he is innocent. You believe that you
will hang him; but I tell you, girl, he will go free. Read this paper,"
she said, thrusting an envelope into the hand of Hagar, "and you
will see how you have been mistaken. I shall never see you again
in this life; but I leave my curse on you!"

Before Hagar could collect her wits, Miss—or rather Mrs.—Lyle,
as she called herself, went hurriedly out of the shop. Her manner
was so wild, her words so ominous of evil, that Hagar had it on her
mind to follow her, and, if possible, prevent the consequences of
her despair. She hurried to the door, but Mrs. Lyle had disappeared,
and as there was no one to mind the shop, Hagar could not go
after her. Luckily, at this moment Horval turned the corner, and
at once the girl beckoned to him.

"Miss Lyle—did you see her?"

"Yes," said Horval, with a nod, "she's on her way across West-minster Bridge."

"Oh, follow her—follow her quickly!" cried Hagar, wildly, "she is not herself; she is bent on some rash deed!"

Horval paused a moment in bewilderment; then, grasping the situation, he turned, without a word, and raced down the street in the trail of Miss Lyle. Hagar watched his hurrying figure until it turned the corner; then she retreated to the back parlor, and hurriedly opened the envelope. On the sheet of paper she found within the following confession was written:

"I am not a spinster, but a widow," began the document abruptly—"a twice-married woman. By my first husband I had Frederick Jevons, who passes as my nephew, and whom I love better than my own soul. When my second husband, Mr. Lyle, died, I cast about for some means of employment, as I was poor. Mrs. Arryford advertised for an unmarried woman as a companion; she absolutely refused to have any companion but a spinster. To get the situation, which was a good one, as Mrs. Arryford was rich, I called myself Miss Lyle, and obtained the place. Mrs. Arryford had no relatives and much money, so I schemed to obtain her wealth for my son, whom I introduced as my nephew. Rosa, the black maid, had a great deal of influence over her weak-minded mistress, and in some way—I don't know how—she fathomed my purpose. It was a battle between us, as Rosa was determined that I should not get the money of Mrs. Arryford for my son. Finally I triumphed, and Frederick was left sole heir of all the old lady's wealth. Then Rosa learnt, by eavesdropping, the true relationship between myself and Frederick. She told her mistress, and with Mrs. Arryford I had a stormy scene, in which she declared her intention of revoking her will and turning me and my son out on the world as paupers. I begged, I implored, I threatened; but Mrs. Arryford, backed up by that wicked Rosa, was firm. I sent for my son to try and soften the old lady, but he was not in town, and did not come to see me till late at night. When he arrived I told him that I had killed Mrs. Arryford. I did so to prevent her altering her will, and out of love for my dear son, lest he should lose the money. Frederick was horrified, and rushed from the house. I believe Rosa saw me let him out by the side door. I was determined to throw the blame on Rosa, as I hated her so. Knowing that she coveted the necklace of amber beads, I stole it from the neck of the dead woman and gave it to my son next day. I suggested that he should dress up as Rosa, and pawn the necklace, so that she might be suspected. To save me, he did so. I obtained a dress that Rosa was fond of wearing—yellow silk trimmed with black beads; also the jewelry of the creature. Frederick blackened his face, and pawned the beads in a pawn-shop at Lambeth. I sent Rosa on a pretended errand to Waterloo Station, at the time Frederick was pawning the beads, so as to get evidence against her that she was in the neighborhood. Then I suggested to Horval, the detective, that the beads might have been pawned. He found the shop, and I thought my plot had succeeded; that Rosa would be condemned and hanged. Unfortunately, the woman who kept the pawn-shop was clever, and traced Frederick by means of his mutilated right hand. I hate her! Frederick is now in prison on a charge of murder, which he did not commit. I am guilty. I killed Mrs. Arryford. Frederick knows nothing. He helped me to save myself by trying to throw the blame on Rosa. All useless. I am guilty, and I am determined that he shall not suffer for my sin.

Officers of the law, I command you to release my son and arrest me. I am the murderess of Mrs. Arryford. I swear it."

"Julia Lyle.

"Witnesses:
"Amelia Tyke (housemaid). "Mark Drew (butler)."

Hagar let the document fall from her hands with a sensation of pity for the wretched woman.

"How she must love her son," thought the girl, "to have murdered a kind and good woman for his sake! It is terrible! Well, I suppose he will now be released and will enter into possession of the wealth his mother schemed to obtain for him. But he must do justice to Rosa for all the trouble he has caused her. He must give her an annuity, and also the necklace of amber beads, which has been the cause of tracing the crime home to its door. As for Mrs. Lyle—"

At this moment, white and breathless, Horval rushed into the parlor. Hagar sprang to her feet, and looked anxiously at him, expectant of bad news. She was right.

"My girl," cried Horval, hoarsely, "Miss Lyle is dead!"

"Dead? Ah!" said Hagar to herself. "I thought as much."

"She threw herself over Westminster Bridge, and has just been picked out of the water—dead!"

"Dead!" said Hagar again. "Dead!"

"As a door-nail!" replied the detective in a perplexed tone. "But why—why did she commit suicide?"

Hagar sighed, and in silence handed to the detective the confession of the dead woman.

4

The Third Customer and the Jade Idol

HAGAR WAS A SHREWD, clear-headed girl, who, having been educated in the hard school of Jacob Dix, knew the value of money and the art of driving good bargains. Otherwise she was uncultured and uneducated, although, to speak truly, she had a considerable knowledge of pictures and china, of gems and silverware. But a schoolboy knew more than she did as regards bookish information. She was ignorant of geography, as that science had been taught neither in the gipsy camp nor in the Lambeth pawn-shop. China was to her—ware, and not a vast empire of the East. But when the third customer came to pawn an idol of sea-green jade Hagar learnt something concerning the Celestial Kingdom.

The man was a sailor, with a coarse face reddened by wind and salt water, and two twinkling blue eyes, which peered at her shrewdly from under shaggy eyebrows. He had strong white teeth, which glistened through a heavy mustache, a head of fair curly hair, and a heavily-built figure well supported on stalwart legs. His rough trousers of blue serge, his black pilot jacket with brass buttons, and his gaudy loose cravat were all redolent of the ocean wave. Rings of gold in his large red ears added to his queer aspect; and he rolled into the shop like one to whom the firm earth is strange after the swinging and pitching of a ship.

This mariner cast uneasy glances over his shoulder as he entered the shop, and finally swung into one of the sentry boxes like a vessel coming to anchor. Here he took off his gold-banded cap and wiped his rough brow with a red handkerchief of Chinese silk.

Hagar, with her hands resting lightly on the counter, waited for him to speak, and was rather surprised when he still kept silent, and still continued to glance over his shoulder in the direction of the door. Finally she lost patience.

"Well, what can I do for you?" she asked sharply.

The mariner leant across the counter, and spoke in a hoarse voice like the roaring of waves. "Nathaniel Prime is my name, miss," he said; almost in a whisper—"Nat fur short; and I'm third mate on board a tea ship as trades from Hong Kong to London's port and back agin."

"Well, Mr. Prime," said Hagar, as he paused, "what do you want?"

Nat pulled a small parcel wrapped in a blue check handkerchief out of his pocket, and plumped it on the counter. "I've a small article here, miss, as I wants to lodge with you fur safe keeping."

"Oh," said Hagar, adapting this speech to her own ideas, "you want to pawn something. What is it?"

"It's Kwan-tai—that's what it is, miss."

Hagar drew back. "What gibberish are you talking?" she asked, frowning.

"Chinese," replied the mariner promptly. "Kwan-tai is the god of war in China, miss. This"—he unrolled the handkerchief and displayed a particularly ugly idol—"is his image. I got it from his temple in the Street of the Water Dragon in Canton. Jest look at it, miss—but wait a bit." He rolled back to the door, stepped out on to the pavement, and looked to right and left. Apparently he was satisfied with this survey, for with a complacent whistle he returned to continue the conversation. "I thought that blamed Chinaman might be arter me," said he, slipping a plug of tobacco into his capacious mouth; "he'd knife me like pie to get that d—d thing there."

"Knife you, man! What do you mean?"

"Why," said Mr. Prime, "this China devil—Yu-ying is his name—wants to git that there god; so, as I don't want a bowie exploring my inside, I think it's good biz to leave it with you fur safe keeping."

Hagar put down the idol and stepped back. "So you want to transfer the danger to me?" she said, dryly. "No, thank you; take that ugly thing away!"

"Now, don't you make any mistake, miss," said Nat, pushing back the idol in his turn. "Yu-ying don't know as I'm on this lay. All I wants is to leave Kwan-tai in this here strop for a week. There ain't no danger in that."

Hagar picked up the god again and considered. It was a revoltingly ugly figure carved out of green jade, and had diamonds for eyes, crossed legs, and two large, fan-like hands resting on a protuberant stomach. Not a desirable article to possess, save as a curiosity; but no doubt it had some sacred significance in the almond eyes of Yu-ying; hence his desire to obtain it, even at the cost of a man's life. For a moment or two Hagar hesitated as to taking Kwan-tai in pawn; but as there seemed to be no immediate danger and might not be any, she resolved to trade. Hagar was so far Hebraic that she never lost the chance of making a bargain; but then, according to some folk, the Romany are one of the ten lost tribes.

"I'll give you thirty shillings on it," she said, abruptly.

"Thirty bob it is," assented Nat, promptly, "as all I want is to leave this 'ere idol in your diggings fur safety. If 'twas pawning, I guess thirty quid 'ud be nearer my price. I reckon that there piece of jade is worth two hundred pound!"

"I don't know the market value of jade," retorted Hagar, impatiently. "All my business with you is to lend money on the thing. It's thirty shillings or nothing."

"Don't I tell you it's a deal?" said Mr. Prime, shifting the quid of tobacco to the other side of his mouth. "Give us a scratch of the pen to say as you've got Kwan-tai in charge."

"Name and address?" demanded Hagar, making out the ticket.

"Nathaniel Prime, mariner, 20, Old Cloe Street, Docks," said the sailor. "It's a pub, y' know, miss—the Nelson. I'll stand you a drink if you looks me up, and proud to do it fur a slap-up gal like yourself!"

"Here's the ticket and the money, Mr. Prime. If that's all your business, get out sharp!"

"Sharp's the word," said the obedient mariner, slipping the thirty shillings into his pocket; "and if Yu-ying comes smelling round here, jest you up anchor and steer fur me at the Nelson. I'm the bad man from the back of beyond when that heathen's about!"

Mr. Prime nodded in a friendly way to Hagar, and rolled out of the shop door. She heard him singing a chanty as he left Carby's Crescent, and it was only when the roar of his lusty voice died away that she bethought herself of the diamond-eyed idol. Kwan-tai was a very ugly deity, but curious and attractive in his way; so, for the furtherance of business, and to see if there was any truth in Nat's story about Yu-ying, the girl placed the Chinese god in the shop window. He smiled as complacently there, out of his almond eyes, amongst the dusty wrecks as formerly he had beamed on his worshipers in the Street of the Water Dragon in far Canton.

Now, if there be one vice above another which ruins the female sex, it is that of curiosity. Here was Hagar told a surprising fact concerning the idol Kwan-tai, and at once she resolved to test if Nat's story was true. By putting the jade god in the window, she afforded Yu-ying a chance of seeing it; and then, if he wanted to possess the talisman—as it apparently was—she expected that he would enter the shop and offer to purchase it. Not for a moment did she think that he would kill her, or even attempt her life. That statement she believed to be an embellishment of Prime's to adorn his queer story.

"And I don't believe a word of it!" said the doubting Hagar. "However, the jade idol is exposed in the shop window, and we will see what will come of it."

Greatly to her surprise, trouble came of her folly, and that speedily. At noon next day she was eating her simple dinner in the back parlor with the door leading into the shop open, so that she might hear the approach of possible customers. Most of the inhabitants of the Crescent were within doors at the midday meal and the little square was quite deserted. Suddenly Hagar heard the crash of glass, and sat paralyzed for the moment in sheer astonishment at the unusual sound. When she recovered her wits and the use of her limbs, she ran rapidly into the shop, and beheld the warning of Nat Prime verified to the letter. The middle pane of the shop window was broken, and the jade idol was gone. With an ejaculation of surprise and Hagar sprang to the door, and saw a blue-bloused figure racing down the narrow street which led to the thoroughfare.

"The Chinaman! the Chinaman!" cried Hagar, giving chase. "Thief! stop—stop—thief! Yu-ying! Yu-ying!"

Followed by a crowd, which had collected like magic in answer to her cries, Hagar sped as lightly as a deer down the alley. But she was no match for the nimble Chinaman. When she reached the crowded street, Yu-ying—as it doubtless was—could not be seen. She appealed to the bystanders, to a stolid policeman, to the cab-drivers; but all to no purpose. Certainly they had seen the Chinese thief flying out of the Carby Crescent *cul-de-sac*, but no one had taken particular notice of him. Hagar ran this way, that way; looked, questioned, considered; all in vain. Yu-ying had vanished as though the earth had swallowed him up, and with him the jade idol of Nat Prime. Blaming herself for her credulity and headstrong folly in putting Kwan-tai into the window, Hagar returned crest-fallen to the pawn-shop. Having placed a temporary barricade before the broken pane, and having sent for the glazier to mend it, Hagar sat down to consider what was to be done relative to the theft.

Assuredly Prime would return at the end of the week to redeem the jade god, and Hagar did not know what excuse to make for its loss. Without doubt, Yu-ying had followed Nat to the shop on the previous day, and had ascertained the fact of the pawning. He had watched his opportunity to steal the god, as he evidently preferred this illegitimate way, to buying it in a proper manner. Probably Yu-ying, with the astuteness of the Chinese character, guessed that Hagar could not and would not sell it; hence his raid on the shop window. However, the idol was gone, and Hagar judged it wise to advise Nat Prime immediately of the loss. It might be that he knew the whereabouts of Yu-ying, and could tax him with the theft. Thinking this the best course to adopt under the circumstances, Hagar wrote to Prime at the address he had given her. Then she prepared to receive him, and to make the best of a bad business. In her letter she made no mention of the theft.

It was two days before Prime appeared in person to answer her note; and he explained his negligence by stating that he had been down at Brighton to interview a friend. Then he asked to see the jade idol, to assure himself that it was safe. When Hagar told him of its loss, and of Yu-ying's exploit, his rage was frightful. He swore volubly for ten minutes; and such was his command of bad language that he scarcely repeated himself in delivering a string of oaths. In his subsequent conversation it may be as well to omit these flowers of speech.

"I knew that blamed Chinaman had followed me!" he said, when somewhat calmer, "if y' mind, miss, I went to look if the coast wor clear. He must ha' sneaked round the corner, I guess. Cuss all Celestials, say I!"

"I am sorry the idol is gone, Mr. Prime—"

"Now, miss, don's 'ee say another word. How was a young gal like you to best a Chinky? Why, Yu-ying 'ud have the teeth out of yer 'ead afore ye cud say knife!"

"Still, I am to blame," persisted Hagar. "I should not have put the jade god in the window."

"Winder or no winder, it 'ud have been jest the same," returned Nat, gloomily; "if Yu-ying hadn't got the god so easily, he'd have burgled the shop to get it. Aye, miss, and have cut your throat into the bargain!"

"Why does he want this idol so particularly?"

"Fur the same reason as I do. Fifty thousand pounds is the reason!"

"Fifty thousand pounds!" echoed Hagar, drawing back: "the idol isn't worth that!"

"Not in itself, miss; but it kin git that cash. I reckoned to have it myself, and chuck deep-sea sailing; but now I opines that blamed John Chinaman's scooped the pool."

"Why don't you look up Yu-ying and tax him with the theft?"

"He'd only lie, miss; and as fur looking him up, I guess he's made himself mighty scarce by this time. But I'll go on the trail, anyhow. Good-day t' ye, miss, and don't you put trust in them Chinese devils."

After which speech Nat rolled away with a philosophical air, leaving Hagar very regretful for having contributed to the loss of the idol by her negligence and perverse folly. All the same, she did not believe the statement about the fifty thousand pounds. Yet, as she might have argued, but did not, Nat had told the truth concerning the desire of Yu-ying to possess the idol, so why should he not have spoken truly concerning the money? And, after all, Hagar knew no details likely to confirm the tale. On consideration she dismissed Nat and Yu-ying and the jade Kwan-tai from her thoughts, and considered that she had purchased a new experience at the cost of thirty shillings.

In the meantime, Nat was seated in the taproom of the Nelson, down the docks way, with a pipe in his mouth and a tankard of beer before him. For several days he had sat thus alone waiting— as would appear from his expectant attitude—for some visitor. Four days after the loss of the idol, he was no longer by himself, for in a chair near him sat a dried-up, alert man clothed in black, with bright eyes and a keen expression. This individual was a gentleman—a doctor—and the visitor expected by Nat Prime.

"If y'd on'y come a week ago, I'd not have pawned the idol," said Nat, in a gloomy tone, "an' the blamed thing wouldn't have been lost."

"Yes, yes; I see, I see. But why did you pawn it?" asked the doctor, fretfully.

"Why," said Prime, drily, "'cause I didn't want my throat cut by Yu-ying; as long as I carried that idol on me, my life wasn't worth a red cent!"

"How did Yu-ying learn the value of the idol?"

"He was a priest in the war-god's temple, I reckon. I've seed him do joss-pigeon a dozen times; and when he kim on board the Havelock as stewart I guessed as he wos arter the idol. But I slept with one eye open," added Nat, triumphantly, "an' I guess he didn't best me till I put Kwan-tai into that blamed pop-shop!"

"But I don't see how he gained a knowledge of the iron box in London," persisted the doctor, irritably, "or learnt about Poa's treasure."

Prime drank some beer, and leant forward to speak, emphasizing his remarks by means of his pipe stem. "Now, look'ee here, Dr. Dick," said he, slowly, "what wos it y' told me a year ago, afore I went this trip to Chiner?"

"Why," said Dr. Dick, thoughtfully, "I told you that my uncle had been at the sack of the Summer Palace in Pekin. Chinese helped to loot the place as well as the French and English. Among these a priest called Poa collected a number of small gold images of Kwan-tai to the value of fifty thousand pounds, and fled with them to England. He placed these in an iron box, and left it with a countryman of his own in London. After selling a few of the images he returned to China, and to his service as a priest in the Temple of Kwan-tai in Canton. He intended to send for the iron box, and restore the images of the god to his temple; but, struck down by sickness, he was unable to carry out his intention. Fearful of being tortured for sacrilege if he told the truth, Poa wrote in Chinese characters a description of the whereabouts of the treasure in London, and placed the paper in the interior of a small jade idol, with diamond eyes, which stood in the Kwan-tai Temple in the Street of the Water Dragon. My uncle did some service for Poa, who, out of gratitude, told him the secret. Shortly afterwards he died, and my uncle, unable to gain access to the temple and steal the idol, was forced to return to England. He took up his residence at Christchurch, Hants, and died there, leaving a paper telling the story of Poa's treasure. I found the paper two years ago, and knowing you were trading to Canton, I came up to see you."

"Yes," said Prime, taking up the thread of the story, "and you asked me to get the jade idol out of that there temple. Well, I stole it, and I believe that pig of a Yu-ying saw me stealing. Any rate, he turned up aboard of the Havelock, and somehow—I can't guess in what way—he learnt the whole yarn, and tried to git back the idol. I bested him on the voyage; and when I kim ashore I expected to find you and get the iron box right away. I—"

"I was ill," interrupted Dick, impatiently. "I couldn't come up. You might have got the treasure yourself and then shared it with me."

"Now, that's blamed silly, doctor! I couldn't read the Chinese writing which I found inside the idol; and as you're a Chinese scholard—taught by your uncle, y' said—I waited fur you to kim up and read it. Fur safety, I put the idol in the pop-shop, and Yu-ying—cuss him—followed me and stole it. So I guess by this time he's got the whole lot of the golden gods."

"Probably; but how did he learn that they were in existence, and that the production of the jade idol was necessary to obtain the treasure of Poa?"

"Can't say, sir, onless that Poa told some of his brother priests."

"Poa died fifteen years ago," replied Dick, sharply; "if he had told them on his death-bed, they would not have waited all this time to get the treasure."

"Well, I calc'late as they've annexed the same this trip," said Nat, coolly.

While thus conversing, the landlord of the Nelson entered the tap-room, and informed Prime that a lady wished to see him. Rather surprised—for he had few female friends—Nat instructed that the visitor should be admitted. In a moment or so she appeared on the threshold, and, to his still greater surprise, Nat beheld Hagar.

"'Tis the pop-shop gal!" he said, rising. "And what might you want, miss?"

"To restore to you the jade idol," replied Hagar, taking the god Kwan-tai out of her pocket.

"Glory alleluia!" shouted Nat, snatching it from her grasp. "How the creation did you git it?"

"When I opened the shop door this morning, it was hanging to the knob by a string."

"Yu-ying couldn't make anything out of it, I guess. Here, doctor, see if the paper's inside."

Dick, in a state of considerable excitement, having been previously instructed by his uncle's paper how to discover the secret, unscrewed the head of the idol. When removed, a cavity was revealed; inside the cavity a strip of rice paper, scrawled with Chinese characters in vermilion.

While he was deciphering these, Nat turned to Hagar.

"Thankee, miss," he said, graciously. "If we git the money, I'll give 'ee a pound or so."

"I don't want it," replied Hagar, abruptly. "Give me the pawn-ticket and thirty-one shillings—that is what I gave you, and the percentage. Then I'll go."

Nat produced money and ticket from his pocket, and gave them into her hand. "But I'd like to do summat fur you gitting that idol back," said he, wistfully.

"Well, Mr. Prime," said Hagar, pausing at the door, with a smile, "when you get the fifty thousand pounds you talk about, reward me by coming to the shop, and telling me the story. I should like to know why Yu-ying stole the god; also why he restored it."

"I'll tell 'ee, never fear, miss; and a rum yarn it is. Y' won't take a drain, miss? No? Well, good day! good day, and thankee."

When Hagar retired Nat came back to the table, and found that Dr. Dick had ascertained the meaning of the Chinese characters. They gave the address of one Yeh, who kept an opium shop—or rather den—in Vesey Street, Whitechapel.

"We must go there," said Dick, rising, "and interview this Yeh. I dare say he has the iron box in charge."

"I guess some Chinky of sorts has the box," assented Nat, "but 'twon't be Yeh. If Poa lef' the box along o' him, I surmise he's dead and buried by this time. Even Chinamen ain't immortal."

"Yeh or another—what does it matter, Prime? All we have to do is to show Kwan-tai's jade image to the custodian of the box, and it will be handed over to us."

"That's so," replied Nat, glancing at his watch. "Seems as we've got the whole arternoon to engineer the job. Let's grub a bit, and start right away for Whitechapel."

While at the meal, Prime seemed thoughtful, and did not respond very enthusiastically to Dr. Dick's delight at discovering the whereabouts of the treasure. Dick commented on this.

"You don't seem over-pleased, Nat," he said; in a piqued tone, "yet your share will be twenty-five thousand pounds; and you ought to be both contented and delighted. What's your trouble?"

"Yu-ying, doctor. I don't trust that heathen a cent. What did he give back the jade god for?"

"Because he couldn't find the secret of opening it," replied Dick; "and seeing that the image was no good, he restored it to its proper owner."

Nat shook his head. "As a priest of the temple, Yu-ying is the proper owner of that there god," said he, doubtfully. "I stole it, y' know, so 'twasn't mine; not much. No, doctor; there's something queer about the biz. Guess this Chinky's rubbin' it in with salt."

"What do you mean, Nat?"

"Why," said Mr. Prime, coolly, "'twouldn't surprise me to find as how Yu-ying has lifted the lot of them gods of gold, and he's sent back Kwan-tai so as we kin take a squint at the empty box. It 'ud be like a Chiner devil to play low in that style."

"I hope not, I trust not!" cried Dick, turning pale. "But we had better make certain of what has been done. Come, Nat; let us start for Whitechapel at once."

Still shaking his head, for a long acquaintance with Chinamen had inspired him with a wholesome mistrust of the race, Nat paid his bill, and set out for Whitechapel in the company of Dr. Dick.

"You take my word for it, doctor," said he, when they were in the train, "there's a big sell waiting for us at the end of this trip. I guess 'twasn't honesty has made that Celestial give back the jade idol."

On arriving at Whitechapel, the two adventurers had some difficulty in discovering Vesey Street; and it was quite an hour before they ascertained its whereabout. It proved to be a narrow and dirty alley of no great length, midway in which was placed the dwelling of Yeh. A red-painted sign, sprinkled with golden Chinese characters, announced that the house was "the Abode of a Hundred Blessings," and that Yeh was a dealer in goods from the Flowery Land. Dick translated this for the benefit of Nat, who could speak but not read Chinese, and commented thereon.

"Either the original Yeh is in existence, or this is a son of his," he said, and on Nat grunting assent they both stopped at the door of the house which they fondly hoped contained the treasure of Poa, the golden idols of the Imperial dynasty of T'sin.

In answer to their knock, a sleek, soft-footed China-boy, dressed in a blue indigo-hued blouse and with his pigtail down, appeared to admit them. Nat, as more experienced in Chinese speech, explained that they wanted to see Yeh. After some hesitation, the boy conducted them through a long dark passage into a rather large room piled up with goods, amongst which moved three or four Chinamen. These packages were the ostensible reason of Yeh's business; but at the back of the shop, through another dark passage, there was an opium den. The boy spoke to a spectacled Chinese merchant about the two Englishmen, whereupon he came forward and addressed them in his own tongue.

"What can your vile slave do for the lords who honor his despicable house?" asked the suave Celestial, with all the flowery humbug of Chinese speech. Nat, conversant with such rhodomontade, replied in a similar fashion. "Your humble guests would see the learned and respectable Yeh."

"He is my worshipful father," said the Chinaman, with a bow. "And what would the gracious lords with the reverend Yeh?"

For answer, Nat pulled the jade idol out of his pocket; at the sight of which the son of Yeh went as green as the god's image. Down he fell on his knees and knocked his forehead three times on the floor; after which, without wasting time in explanation, he conducted the two Europeans into the opium den. Here, on a kind of elevated platform, and under the smiling face of a particularly ugly Joss, sat Yeh, the merchant, a very old and wrinkled man. He wore heavy spectacles with tortoiseshell rims; also a thickly-wadded blouse of red silk embroidered elaborately in gold thread. Like his son, he was likewise greatly struck by the sight of jade Kwan-tai, and, like him, made genuflections.

"The learned Poa was my much-esteemed friend," he said, bowing to the Europeans; "with me he left an iron box, to be delivered to him who showed me the image of the mighty war-god. But Poa did not say that the sacred jade god would be shown twice!"

"Oho!" cried Dick, in disgust. "Yu-ying!"

"You know the name, I see," said Yeh, a trifle grimly; "this priest of the temple in the Street of the Water Dragon is your much-admired friend?"

"Yes, yes!" said Nat, eagerly; "we gave him the jade god so that he should come and look at the iron box of Poa; but we did not tell him to take it away."

"He obeyed your commands, my lord," replied Yeh, rising stiffly; "he looked at the box, but he did not take it away."

Dr. Dick jumped up with a cry of relief and delight. "Then the box is here!" he said, in excited tones. "Take us to see it at once!"

"It waits your noble presence in another room."

So speaking, Yeh, followed by the anxious adventurers, passed through a little door into a kind of strong room, dimly lighted by a small grated window. In a corner, towards which the old Chinaman pointed, there was a large iron box painted black, upon the lid of which were inscribed some Chinese characters in white paint. From a nail above this Yeh took a small copper key, and presented it to Dick with a bow. Then he turned to go, "My lords can look at Poa's secret alone," said he, backing with many bows to the door. "Who am I that I should meddle with the business of those favored by Kwan-tai?"

On being left alone, the two men looked at one another in some surprise and a little doubt. "The job's been easier than I thought," said Nat, after a pause. "All the same, I guess as Yu-ying's got some trick to play us."

"Impossible!" replied Dick, going on his knees before the box. "Here is the key, and within, no doubt, we shall find the golden gods of T'sin."

"Well," said Nat, with a nod, "if everything's square, I'll never cuss a heathen Chinee again. Open the box, doctor."

The key turned easily in the lock, and Dick flung back the lid. In an instant a flare of fire spouted out with a great roar. The two men, the room, and the greater part of Yell's dwelling were blown to shreds. They had expected to find a fortune, instead of which they discovered dynamite and a terrible death.

Two months after this, when London had almost forgotten the mysterious explosion in Vesey Street, Whitechapel, a Chinaman was reporting himself to the priests of Kwan-tai's temple, Canton, in this fashion:

"Most holy men," said he, pointing to a number of golden images which lay on a lacquer table before him, "here are the images of Kwan-tai, the gods of the Imperial House of T'sin, brought back from the dark land of the Outer Barbarians by your servant Yu-ying. When your greatnesses found the confession of the evil priest Poa that he had stolen the gods, and had confided the secret of their whereabouts to the jade image of Kwan-tai, you ordered your unworthy slave to search and find the treasure, so that it should be restored to the temple in the Street of the Water Dragon. But before your servant could depart to the Land of Darkness, a foreign devil, also possessed of Poa's secret, stole the jade image which contained the name of the hiding-place. I, foolish Yu-ying, followed the barbarian in a tea-junk to his own land; but it was many days before I could get the jade image. Then the foreign devil pawned for gold the sacred idol of war, and it was placed in the window of the shop. I broke the window, most reverend priests; I stole the image, and going to the house of Yeh, I recovered the golden idols which are now before you. But I wished to punish Yeh for his sacrilege in conspiring with Poa against Kwan-tai; and also to kill the foreign devil who had thieved the jade god. To this end I removed the golden idols from the box, and in their place I left a dangerous powder of the barbarians, which they call dynamite. This I arranged with care so that when the lid of the box was flung open it would rush out like the breath of the Fire Dragon, and slay those who came to steal the gods. As I intended, holy ones, so it happened, as I have learnt since. The foreign devil and a friend were shattered, and also the house of Yeh was destroyed. It was for this end that I restored the idol Kwan-tai to the pawn-shop; and thus did I lure the foreign devils to their deaths. Now, no one knows the truth, mighty servants of Kwan-tai, save yourselves. Say, have I done well?"

And all the sleek priests answered with one voice: "Yu-ying, you have done well. Your tablet shall be placed in the temple of Kwan-tai."

And while this explanation was being made, Hagar, in far-off London, was waiting for the return of Nat Prime to hear the story of the jade idol. But he never appeared.

5

The Fourth Customer and the Crucifix

MENTION HAS BEEN made of Bolker, the misshapen imp, who was Hagar's factotum and the plague of her life. With her clear brain and strong will, she could manage most people, but not this deformed street arab, whose nature seemed to be compounded of all that was worst in human beings. He lied freely, he absented himself from the shop when he had no business to do so, he even stole little things, when he thought it was safe to run the risk with so vigilant a mistress; but, notwithstanding all these vices, Hagar kept him as servant. Her reason was that he possessed three redeeming virtues: he was an excellent watch-dog, he was admirable at clinching bargains, and he was cunning enough not to lose his situation. Clever servants have been retained by mistrustful mistresses for less reasonable qualities.

When Hagar went out on business—which she frequently did— Bolker stayed to look after the shop, and to receive such customers as might present themselves. To these he gave as little as he possibly could on the articles they wished to pawn; and when Hagar returned he had usually some tales to tell of excellent business having been transacted for the good of the shop. Then Hagar would reward him with a little money and Bolker would take unauthorized leave to misconduct himself generally on the proceeds. This program never varied.

One day Hagar returned late in the evening, having been in the country on an excursion connected with a copper key. This adventure will be related another time, for the present story deals with the strange episode of the silver crucifix. It was this article which Bolker had ready to show Hagar when she entered the pawn-shop at eight o'clock.

"See here, missus!" said Bolker, pointing to the wall at the back of the shop; "there's a fine thing I got for you—cheap!"

It may be here remarked that Bolker had been to school, and having a remarkably clever brain as a set-off against his deformed body, he had succeeded in gaining a certain amount of learning, and also a mode of speaking, as regards both diction and accent, much above the ordinary conversation of his class. Proud of this superiority, the clever imp spoke always slowly and to the point, so that he might preserve his refined speech.

"Dirt cheap, missus!" added Bolker, who used vulgar words when excited, and he was so now. "Ten pound I lent on it; the silver itself is worth more than that!"

"Oh, I can always trust your judgment in these matters," laughed Hagar, and took down the crucifix to examine it more particularly.

It was over a foot long, made of refined silver now somewhat tarnished from neglect and exposure to the air; and the workmanship was peculiarly fine and delicate. The figure of the Christ crowned with a thorn-wreath was exquisite; and the arms of the cross itself, enchased with arabesque patterns, were beyond all praise from an artistic point of view. Altogether, this silver crucifix, obtained by the crafty Bolker for ten pounds—a sum greatly below its real value—was a remarkably fine sample of Renaissance workmanship in the style of Cellini. Learned in such things, Hagar, even in the yellow glow of the badly lighted lamp, saw its magnificence and worth at a glance. She patted Bolker's red head of hair with approval.

"Good little man!" said she, in a pleased tone. "You always do well when I am out of the shop. There is half-a-crown. Go and enjoy yourself, but don't make yourself sick with smoking a pipe as you did last time, my boy. But one moment," she added; "who pawned this?"

"Gemma Bardi, 167, Saffron Hill."

"An Italian woman. Like enough, as the crucifix is of the Renaissance," said Hagar, musingly. "What was she like, Bolker?"

"Oh, a fine, handsome girl," replied Bolker, leering in a man-about-town style; "black hair and eyes the same just like yours, missus, only I guess you're the finer woman of the two. Here—don't you box my ears," shouted the imp, wriggling out of Hagar's grip, "or I shan't tell you what I found out!"

"About this crucifix?" asked Hagar, dropping her hands.

"Yes. 'Tain't a crucifix; it's a dagger."

"A dagger, you young fool! What are you talking?"

"Sense, missus—as I always do. Look here, if you don't believe me."

Bolker took the presumed crucifix in his lean, small hands, and with deft fingers he touched a concealed spring set where the four arms of the cross joined. At once the lower and longer arm, with the silver Christ attached thereto, slid down, and lo! the cross was changed into a slender and, sharp-pointed poniard, the handle of which was formed by the upper arms and the, so to speak, haft of the cross. The symbol of Christ, of peace, of faith, had become a deadly and dangerous weapon of bloodshed. Hagar was so startled that Bolker, the discoverer, grinned.

"It's fine, ain't it?" he said, gloating over the shining blade. "It would stick a man like fun! I dare say it's been through lots. My eye, what larks!"

The joy of the boy was so grim and unnatural that Hagar snatched the crucifix—or rather the poniard, as it was now—from his grasp, and pushed him out of the shop with the sharp command that he was to put up the shutters. When he had done so, and all was safe for the night, he went away to enjoy himself with his half-crown; while Hagar carried the newly-pawned article into the back parlor to examine it anew, as she ate her frugal supper. The crucifix, which was at once a symbol of peace and war attracted her strangely.

Why did it possess these dual characteristics? To what end had its maker placed in the hands of priests this deadly and concealed weapon? The hands of the Christ were not attached to the cross bars; and the sheath—as it might be—of the poniard slipped easily

off the blade, figure and all. Hagar wondered in her imaginative
fashion if it had glimmered, a symbol of Christianity over the dying, or had flashed cruelty into the heart of some helpless human
being. From the old bookseller in Carby's Crescent she had heard
some strange stories of the Italian Renaissance—that wild and con-
tradictory time. Religion had then gone hand in hand with paganism; Savonarola had grown up beside the Medici; Popes had de-
creed peace, and had plunged whole nations in war; and the laugh
of a friend had oftentimes been but a prelude to the death-blow.
Of this many-sided, sinful epoch the crucifix dagger was a symbol;
it represented at once its art, its religion, and its lust of blood.
Hagar evoked strange visions in her dingy parlor from that strange
piece of silver.

Afterwards, in the imperative demands of business, Hagar forgot her dreams about the crucifix, and looked upon it as an article
of value merely pawned by its owner, and which would be redeemed
in due time. A month later the ticket made out in the name of
Gemma Bardi was brought to her by a man of the same nationality. This tall, slender, supple Italian, with oval olive face and fierce
eyes had come to take the crucifix out of pawn. Although he produced the ticket and offered the money, Hagar hesitated at giving
the article to him.

"It was pawned by Gemma Bardi," said she, taking down the
crucifix from where it hung in the obscurity.

"My wife," replied the man, briefly.

"She sent you to redeem it?"

"*Gran Dio!* Why not?" he broke out, impetuously. "I am Carlino
Bardi, her husband. She pawned the crucifix against my will, while
I was absent in the country with my organ. Now that I have returned, I come with ticket and money to redeem it. I do not wish
to lose the Crucifix of Fiesole."

"The Crucifix of Fiesole," repeated Hagar—"is that what it is
called?"

"Of a surety, signorina; and it is worth much money."

"More than ten pounds, I am sure," said Hagar, smiling, as she
picked up the note silently placed on the counter by Carlino. "Well,

I have no right to refuse you the crucifix. You give me the ticket, principal, and interest, so all is legal and shipshape. Take up your cross."

"My cross!" echoed Carlino, with a flash from his big eyes. "Gemma is my cross."

"Your wife! That is a strange way to speak of one dear to you."

"Dear to me, signorina! That may be; but she is dear also to Pietro Neri. May the pains of hell seize him!"

"Why? What has he done?"

"Run away with Gemma," said Bardi, fiercely. "Oh, she went cheerfully enough. To get the money for my dishonor she pawned the crucifix."

"Oh. So she did not send you to redeem it?"

"No," replied Carlino, with tranquil insolence. "That was a lie I told to get back my property without trouble. But now it is mine"— he clasped the silver Christ convulsively to his breast. "I shall make Gemma and Pietro pay for their evil deed!"

"You speak English well for a foreigner."

"I ought to," answered the man, indifferently. "I have been ten years in England, and I have almost forgotten my Tuscan tongue. But I remember still what Tuscan husbands do to faithless women and their paramours. We kill them!"—his voice leaped an octave to a shrill scream of wrath—"we kill the man and the woman!"

Thrilled by the terrible hatred of this passionate Latin nature, Hagar started back. The man was leaning across the counter, and showed no disposition to depart; nor did she want him to leave her, for there had come upon her a desire to learn the history of the Fiesole crucifix. Bending forward, she touched it lightly with the tips of her fingers.

"How did this come into your possession?" she asked.

"I stole it from a painter in Florence."

"You stole it!" echoed Hagar, confounded by the frankness of this admission.

"Yes. I was the model of an artist—one Signor Ancillotti, who had a studio in Piazza San Spirito, hard by the Ponte Santa Trinita of the Arno. This crucifix hung in his rooms, and once, when I was posing as his model, he told me the legend which gave it the name of the Crucifix of Fiesole. It was the story which made me steal it."

"But why? What is the story?"

"A common one," said Bardi, bitterly—"man's love and a woman's faithlessness to her husband There was a silversmith in Florence, what time the Magnificent ruled, who was called Guido. He had one fair wife whom he loved very dearly. She did not care for his love, however, and fled with a young Count of good family, one Luigi da Francia. From France, you understand, for from that country the race had come to Florence in the days of the Republic. Luigi was handsome and rich; Guido, ugly and rather poor, although a clever craftsman; so you cannot wonder that the wife— Bianca was her name—fled from the one's arms to the other's palace. Guido determined upon revenge, and manufactured this crucifix."

"But I don't understand how—"

"No more did any one else," said Bardi, cutting her short. "When Guido finished the crucifix he disguised himself as a priest, and went up to see Count Luigi in his palace at Fiesole. Afterwards the nobleman and Bianca were found dead with dagger thrusts in their hearts, and Guido was missing. Between the corpses lay this silver crucifix; but no one ever knew how they died."

"Why not? Guido killed them with his dagger."

"No," said Bardi, shaking his head. "Guido had no dagger with him at the time. Count Luigi was always afraid of assassination, for he had many enemies; and every visitor was searched by his retainers to see that they carried no concealed weapons. Guido, the supposed priest, was searched also, and had nothing on him but the silver crucifix. So the legend grew that whosoever had a faithless wife, the possession of the Crucifix of Fiesole would give him power to slay her and her lover, as Guido had slain his two deceivers. Therefore," added Bardi, grimly, "as I had then married Gemma, and thought that some day she might be faithless, I stole the crucifix from Signor Ancillotti. It seems I was right to do so."

"A strange story," said Hagar, meditatively "and stranger still that the means by which Guido slew were not discovered long ago."

"Do you know how he killed them?"

"Certainly. By means of that crucifix."

Bardi looked at the cross eagerly, and a lurid light came into his eyes as he gazed. "How?" he questioned, loudly. "Tell me, signorina."

But Hagar refused to impart that knowledge.

The story of the man deserted by his wife was so similar to that of the faithless Bianca and the forsaken Guido that Hagar dreaded lest Bardi should learn the secret of the concealed dagger and repeat the Cinque de Cento tragedy of Fiesole. With this idea in her mind she wished the Italian to depart, ignorant of the devilish ingenuity of the cross. But Fate willed that in her despite Bardi should gain the evil knowledge. He learnt it forthwith from the lips of Bolker.

"Hullo!" cried that imp, as he entered the shop, to see Carlino holding the crucifix. "You have got that dagger?"

"Dagger!" said Bardi, with a start.

"Bolker, you wretched child, hold your tongue!" said Hagar, vehemently.

"Why should I? My tongue's my own, and if that cove wants to know how this crucifix can be changed into a dagger, it's only fair. See here!" and before Hagar could interfere Bolker had the cross in his hands, and a finger on the spring. "You touch this, and the lower part of—"

"Ah!" cried Bardi, snatching back the cross, and examining the deadly mechanism. "I see now how Guido killed his enemies. Gemma does not know of this; Pietro is ignorant; but they shall learn—both. I—I, the betrayed husband, shall teach it to them."

"Bardi!" said Hagar, catching him by the arm, "do not take—"

"It is mine—mine!" he interrupted, furiously. "I go to search for the evil ones! I go to put the Crucifix of Fiesole to the use for which it was created by Guido! Look in the papers, signorina, and sooner or later you will see again the tale of Luigi, of Bianca, of the deceived Guido!"

He tore his sleeve from her grip, and rushed furiously from the shop, racing out of the crescent into the crowded streets, wherein he was soon lost. Hagar ran to the door, but could not stop his mad career; so all she could do was to rage at Bolker, the mischief-maker, who, comprehending nothing of the Italian's excitement, was standing open-mouthed in the shop.

"You imp! You goblin!" raged Hagar, boxing his large ears. "You have put murder into that man's head!"

"Murder!" repeated Bolker, dodging her slaps, "what do you mean?"

"The man's wife has deceived him. He'll kill her with that dagger!"

"Jiminy!" said the imp, a light breaking in on his brain. "Kill her with a crucifix! What a rum murder it will be! I'll keep my eye on the papers, you bet!"

After which speech he ran out of the shop to escape further punishment, while Hagar was left to bewail the perverse fate which had sent the talkative lad to Bardi at so critical a moment. However, it was not her fault that he had gained the fatal knowledge; nor could it be laid to her charge if he did use the crucifix-dagger to kill Gemma and Pietro. Salving her conscience thus, Hagar waited for the consummation of the tragedy, and daily, as advised by the Italian, she read the papers to see if it occurred. But for many weeks nothing came of her reading, and Hagar concluded that either the man had not found his wife, or, having found her, had condoned her offense against his honor. Which conclusion showed how little Hagar knew of the fierce and passionate Tuscan nature.

In the meanwhile Bardi, his heart filled with vengeful hatred, was tracking his runaway wife and her lover with dogged persistence. The cost of his travels was little, as his profession was that of an organ-grinder, and with his box of music he could earn his livelihood on the road. Whither they had gone he did not learn for a long time; but at length he ascertained definitely that the pair were in the southern counties of England. Pietro was an organ-man also; and with Gemma was now no doubt tramping from village to village, earning a pittance. The ten pounds obtained for the crucifix would not last forever, and then the pair would be reduced to gain a livelihood by the organ. Bardi cursed both, as he thought of them living together; and felt that the silver cross was safe in his breast when he started on their trail. With that infernal weapon of Guido's he intended to kill those who had deceived him, and repeat in the nineteenth century the wild tragedy of Fiesole.

For some weeks he saw nothing of the couple, but from sundry sources he discovered their whereabouts. Yet as soon as he arrived in some town or village where he had been advised of their presence he would learn that they had departed in some unknown direction. Whether they knew, or did not know, that he was tracking them, Bardi could not say; but certainly at many times when just within his reach they would elude him in the most exasperating fashion. Any one less bent upon revenge would have given up the task; but, sustained by undying hatred, Carlino followed the weary trail with the persistence of a bloodhound. As soon might the twain expect to escape death as to elude the betrayed husband, the deceived friend.

It was at Daleminster that he found them, and revenged himself on the infidelity of the one, the treason of the other. Daleminster is a quiet, desolate cathedral town, very quaint, very beautiful, set in the very heart of Midland cornfields, and made up of ancient red-roofed houses which cluster round the great minster of Saint Wulf's. There it rises, a poem in stone, with its great central tower soaring into the misty blue of English skies; and its magnificent facade carved with saints, and angels, and grotesque faces of peering devils—a strange medley of Heaven and hell. Before it, extends a little square, in the center of which rises an ancient cross sculptured with religious imagery. It was near this relic of medieval piety that Carlino saw his wife.

The day was dull and rainy—April weather, of storm, with occasional bursts of sunshine. In that desolate and forsaken square, where the grass sprang greenly betwixt worn stones, Gemma, in the gay colors of her Neapolitan garb, stood grinding Italian melodies out of the organ. Pietro was not with her, and Carlino wondered for a moment if he had deserted her, now that the moneys obtained for the silver crucifix were expended. The woman appeared sad and lamentable enough as she looked to right and left in the hope of gaining stray coppers. The melancholy music of "Ah, che la morte" was sighing forth in the damp air, when her wandering gaze alighted suddenly on the man she had betrayed. With folded arms Bardi looked at her as the music faltered and stopped; but for the time being he said nothing. Nor did the woman; she was as petrified as any of the grim and saintly statues which looked down upon them both.

"Where is he?" demanded Bardi, in the Italian tongue.

Gemma put her hand to the necklace of blue beads dangling from her brown throat, and strove to speak. Her face was set and white, her lips were dry with fear, and she could only stare at Carlino with terrified eyes. The man came a step nearer and laid a persuasive hand on her white linen sleeve. She shuddered and drew away.

"Where is your lover?" demanded Bardi, in silky tones. "Has he left you?"

"No," she replied, hoarsely, finding her voice at last. "He is ill."

"Here—in this town?"

"Yes. He caught cold; it settled on his lungs; he is very ill."

Gemma uttered these staccato sentences in a mechanical manner, as though compelled to do so against her will, under the mesmeric gaze of the man. The unexpected appearance of Bardi stunned and appalled her; she could not think what to do; her brain refused to act. At length a request made by Carlino released her from the mesmeric spell which enchanted and froze her.

"Lead me to him," said he, in a quiet way. "I wish to see him."

Gemma felt the blood rush from her heart to her face, and sprang back with a loud cry, which echoed through the lonely square and down the desolate streets.

"No, no, no!" she cried, vehemently. "You will kill him!"

"Why? I have not killed you, and you are the guiltier of the two. Pietro was my very good friend until you tempted him with your beauty. Kill Pietro!"—the man laughed in a jeering manner—"woman, I have let you live."

"Oh, I hate you! I hate you!" said Gemma, drawing her black brows together, and sending a flash at him from her somber eyes. "I love Pietro!"

"I know you do. So much that you left me for him, and pawned the silver Christ of Fiesole to pay for the journey."

"I left the pawn-ticket behind," she muttered, sullenly.

"I know it. Here is the crucifix!" and with that Bardi drew it from his bosom to hold it before her eyes. She shrank back before the symbol of faith, and uttered a low cry, at which her husband jeered.

"*Dio!*" said he, scoffingly. "You have religion still, I see; yet I thought you would have finished with such things when you were base enough to leave me. Why did you sell the crucifix and fly, Gemma? Did I beat you, or starve you?"

"You would not let me have money!" cried Gemma, dashing the tears from her eyes; "whenever I wanted a ribbon or a silver brooch you refused to give me a single *soldo*."

"And why?" was the swift answer. "Because I was saving all, that we could go back to Italy and buy a little vineyard near my own village—near Lastra-a-Signa. There is one I know of at Mosciano, which my father wrote and told me was for sale at a small price. I have the money now, and I intended to tell you of it; but I came back to find that you had fled with that infamous Pietro."

Gemma sobbed. Like most women, she had a practical side to her character, and the vineyard would have been a little heaven to her, setting aside the joy of returning to Signa. She would not have fled had she known of these plans, as she had not loved Pietro over-much. Besides, he beat her, now that the money was gone; and they earned very little by the organ. It was horrible to think that she had lost all, for a few months of illicit love.

"O Carlino, forgive me!" she moaned, stretching out her arms.

"Lead me to Pietro and I shall see," he replied, and took her organ—or rather Pietro's—on his strong shoulders.

Without a word, Gemma led the way out of the square, down tortuous streets into a poor part of the town. She was afraid of Carlino, and could not quite understand what he intended to do to Pietro. Probably he would kill him; and then he would be arrested and hanged. But then the money would come to her, and she would have all the vineyard to herself. Again, Carlino might forgive Pietro, and take her back. Gemma was a clever woman, and trusted to extricate herself out of all difficulties by her wiles. Still, she knew Carlino's violent temper, and she dreaded the worst. At the door of the poor house where she lived with her lover she stopped, and faced Bardi with a resolute air.

"Pietro is within," she said, hurriedly, "ill in bed; but I shan't take you to him unless you swear that you intend him no harm."

"I swear by this crucifix!" said Bardi, thinking of it as a dagger and not as a cross.

"Have you a knife on you?" demanded Gemma, still doubtful.

"No," smiled Bardi, thinking how the old Fiesole tragedy was repeating itself. "I have nothing with me but this crucifix." Then, as she still seemed dubious, he added: "You can see for yourself if you like."

Not knowing what to make of this smiling complacency, so different to his usual stern demeanor, Gemma passed her hands through his clothes to feel if he had any weapon concealed therein. Her fears were groundless. Bardi wore little clothing, and she assured herself beyond all doubt that he was unarmed; he had nothing wherewith to kill Pietro. Certainly he might strangle him with his bare hands; but that was not the Tuscan fashion of disposing of a rival. Perhaps, after all, he meant to forgive Pietro.

"You see," said Carlino, when her arms dropped, "I am unarmed; I have nothing with me save this silver crucifix. As Pietro is so ill he may like to look at it."

His look as he said this was hardly pleasant, and a glimpse of it might have put the woman on her guard; but it was lost on her, as already she had turned her back, and was climbing the crazy stairs. Bardi followed her, carrying the organ on his broad back, and holding in his two hands the silver crucifix, like some priest bearing the Host to the dying. Gemma conducted him into a bare garret on the topmost story. Here Carlino put down the organ and looked around.

In a corner near the window Pietro, wild-looking, with his unshaven beard of a week's growth, lay on a pile of straw roughly covered with some pieces of coarse sacking. He was emaciated and haggard about the face, and his skin was flushed red with the burning of the fever which consumed him. At times a dry hacking cough would echo through the bleak room, and the man would fall back on the poor bed in a paroxysm of pain. Clearly he was very ill, as Gemma had said, and not long for this world; knowledge that he was dying did not move Carlino's determination. He had come hither to slay Pietro with the crucifix, and he was bent upon executing his purpose.

"Carlino!" cried the sick man, raising himself on one elbow with a look of mingled terror and surprise. "You here?"

"Yes," said Gemma, moving towards her lover; "he has come to forgive you and to take me back."

"That is so," answered Bardi, raising the crucifix aloft. "I swear by this cross. Dear Pietro," he added, moving towards the bed, "I know you were tempted and—"

"Keep off! Keep off!" screamed Neri, shrinking back. "Liar! you have come to kill me. I see it in your eyes!"

"No, no," said Gemma, soothingly; "he has no weapon."

"None, my wife!" echoed Bardi, touching the spring of the cross—"only this dagger!" and Gemma saw the silver Christ fall on the floor, while the cross which had borne Him remained, a poniard, in the right hand of her deceived husband. With a cry of horror, she flung herself on the sick man.

"Me first! Me first!"

"No! You later!" cried Bardi, dragging her off. "This for—"

"Carlino!" shrieked Neri, as the dagger flashed downward—"for the love of—"

The rest of the cry ended in a gurgle, as a stream of blood burst from his breast and stained the bedclothes.

"Murderer! Assassin!" gasped Gemma, scrambling on her hands and knees towards the door. "I shall—"

"Die!" snarled Bardi. "Die!"

When it was all over, he stood looking at the two dead bodies, and began to think of his own safety. His plan was soon made.

"I shall wound myself, and say that there was a struggle," he muttered; "that they tried to kill me, and I struck in self-defense. One little wound will be evidence enough to save my life."

He placed the dagger at his throat, and setting his teeth with stern determination, he inflicted upon himself a slight gash. Then he rent his clothes as evidence of the clutching of hands, and thrust the stained dagger into the grip of the dead woman.

"She tried to kill me because I slew Pietro in self-defense," he said, rehearsing the story to himself; "so now I—ah! *Dio!* What is this?"

A cold feeling, as of iced water, was creeping through his veins, a film of gray mist swam before his eyes, and in his throat, where he had inflicted that lying wound, there rose a ball which choked him. He staggered and fell on his knees and hands, striking the silver image of the Christ across the room. The walls spun round and round, his eyes grew dark, and with a sob of agony he pitched forward on to the bodies of his victims—dead.

One week later Hagar was rewarded for her searching by reading the conclusion of the tragedy of the Fiesole Crucifix. The journal explained the finding of the three dead bodies, and commented upon the deadly ingenuity of the weapon used, which was at once a dagger and a crucifix. It added that one of the men and the woman had been struck to the heart, and so had died; but mentioned that the third corpse had a slight wound only, inflicted on the neck. "Quite insufficient to cause death," said the sapient reporter; "therefore, how the other man died—his name has been ascertained to be Carlino Bardi—is a mystery."

It might have been to the Press; but Hagar was better informed. A short time previously, Bolker had confessed that when he discovered the secret of the crucifix a thin piece of paper had been wrapped round the blade of the poniard. This he had kept, not that it was of value, or that he had any reason to withhold it from his mistress, but simply out of a thievish magpie propensity which was inherent in his nature. Finding it one day in his pocket—for he had forgotten all about it—he gave it to Hagar. As it was written in Italian, and she was ignorant of the language, Hagar took it to the old bookseller, of whom mention has been made, to have it translated.

This was done by a customer of his, and the following translation was handed to Hagar the next day:

> "I, Guido, of Florence, have manufactured this dagger, hidden in this silver crucifix, to slay Count Louis from France and my faithless wife, Bianca, who with him has deceived me. As I may not be able to strike them to the heart, I have anointed this blade with a deadly poison, so that the slightest scratch of the poniard causes death. I write this warning and place it within the crucifix, so that he who finds it may beware of touching the point; and that he may use it upon a faithless wife, as it is my intention to do.— Signed at Florence in Tuscany.
>
> > "Guido."

Hagar looked at this paper, after reading the report of the tragedy, and mused. "So," said she to herself, "Carlino killed his wife and her lover; but how did it come about that he wounded himself, and died of the poison?"

There was no answer to this question, for Hagar never learnt that Bardi had inflicted the wound on himself to save his life, hereby slaying himself as surely as the law would have done.

6

The Fifth Customer and the Copper Key

THE SEVERAL ADVENTURES in which she had been engaged begot in
Hagar a thirst for the romantic. To find that strange stories were
attached to many pawned articles; to ascertain such histories of
the past; to follow up their conclusions in the future—these things
greatly pleased the girl, and gave her an interest in a somewhat
dull life. She began to perceive that there was more romance in
modern times than latter-day sceptics are willing to admit. Tropi-
cal scenery, ancient inns, ruined castles, are not necessary to en-
gender romance. It is of the human heart, of human life; and even
in the dingy Lambeth pawn-shop it blossomed and bloomed like
some rare flower thrusting itself upward betwixt the arid city
stones. Romance came daily to the gipsy girl, even in her prosaic
business existence.

Out of a giant tooth, an unburied bone, a mighty footprint,
Cuvier could construct a marvelous and prehistoric world. In like
manner, from some trifle upon which she lent money, Hagar would
deduce tales as fantastic as the Arabian Nights, as adventurous as
the story of Gil Blas. Of such sort was the romance brought about
by the pawning of the copper key.

The man who pawned it was in appearance like some Eastern
mage; and the key itself, with its curious workmanship, green with
verdigris, might have served to unlock the tower of Don Roderick.
Its owner entered the shop one morning shortly before noon, and
at the sight of his wrinkled face, and the venerable white beard

which swept his breast, Hagar felt that he was a customer out of the common. With a gruff salutation, he threw down a paper parcel, which clanged on the counter.

"Look at that," said he, sharply. "I wish to pawn it."

In no wise disturbed by his discourtesy, Hagar opened the package, and found therein a roll of linen; this, when unwound, revealed a slender copper key of no great size. The wards at the lower end were nearly level with the stem of the key itself, as they consisted merely of five or six prickles of copper encircling at irregular intervals the round stem. The handle, however, was ornate and curious, being shaped like a bishop's crozier, while within the crook of the pastoral staff design the letters "C.R." were interwoven in an elaborate monogram. Altogether, this key—apparently very ancient—was a beautiful piece of workmanship, but of no value save to a dealer in rarities. Hagar examined it carefully, shook her head, and tossed it on the counter.

"I wouldn't give you five shillings on it," said she, contemptuously; "it is worth nothing."

"Bah, girl! You do not know what you are talking about. Look at the workmanship."

"Very fine, no doubt; but—"

"And the monogram, you blind bat!" interrupted the old man. "'C.R.'—that stands for Carolus Rex."

"Oh," said Hagar, picking up the key again, and taking it to the light of the window; "it is an historic key, then?"

"Yes. It is said to be the key of the box in which the First Charles kept the treasonous papers which ultimately cost him his head. Oh, you may look! The key is authentic enough. It has been in the Danetree family for close on two hundred and fifty years."

"And are you a Danetree?"

"No; I am Luke Parsons, the steward of the family."

"Indeed!" said Hagar, with a piercing glance. "Then how comes the key into your possession?"

"I don't recognize your right to ask such questions," said Parsons, in an angry tone. "The key came into my possession honestly."

"Very probably; but I should like to know how. Do not get in a rage, Mr. Parsons," added Hagar, hastily; "we pawnbrokers have to be very particular, you know."

"I don't know," snapped the customer; "but if your curiosity must be satisfied, the key came to me from my father Mark, a former steward of the Danetrees. It was given to him by the then head of the family some sixty years ago."

"What are all these figures graven on the stem?" asked Hagar, noting a number of hieroglyphic marks.

"Ordinary Arabic numerals," retorted Parsons. "What they mean I know no more than you do. If I did I should be rich," he added, to himself.

"Ah! there is some secret connected with these figures?" said Hagar, overhearing.

"If there is, you won't find it out," replied the old man, ungraciously; "and it is none of your business, anyhow! What you have to do is to lend money on the key."

Hagar hesitated. The article, notwithstanding its workmanship, its age, and its historical associations, was worth very little. Had its interest consisted of these merely, she would not have taken the key in pawn. But the row of mysterious figures decided her. Here was a secret, connected—as was probable from the remark of the old man—with a hidden treasure. Remembering her experience with the cryptogram of the Florentine Dante, Hagar determined to retain the key, and, if possible, to discover the secret.

"If you are really in want of money, I will let you have a pound on it," she said, casting a glance at the threadbare clothes of her customer.

"If I did not need money, I should not have blundered into your spider's web," he retorted. "A pound will do; make out the ticket in the name of Luke Parsons, The Lodge, Danetree Hall, Buckton, Kent."

In silence Hagar did as she was bid; in silence she gave him ticket and money; and in silence he walked out of the shop. When alone she took up the key, and began to examine the figures without loss of time. The learning of many secrets had created in her a burning desire to learn more. If ingenuity and perseverance could do it, Hagar was bent upon discovering the secret of the copper key.

This mysterious object was so covered with verdigris that she was unable to decipher the marks. With her usual promptness, Hagar got the necessary materials, and cleaned the key thoroughly. The figures—those, as Parsons had said, of Arabic numerals—then appeared clearer, and Hagar noted that they extended the whole length of the copper stem. Taking paper and pencil, she copied them out carefully, with the following result:

"20211814115251256205255—H—38518212."

"An odd jumble of figures!" said Hagar, staring at the result of her labors. "I wonder what they mean."

Unversed in the science of unraveling cryptograms, she was unable to answer her own question; and after an hour of profitless investigation, which made her head ache, she numbered the key according to the numeral of the ticket, and put it away. But the oddity of the affair, the strange circumstance of the figures with the letter "H" stranded among them, often made her reflective, and she was devoured by curiosity—that parent of all great discoveries—to know what key and figures meant. Nevertheless, for all her thought no explanation of the problem presented itself. To her the secret of the key was the secret of the Sphinx—as mysterious, as unguessable.

Then it occurred to her that there might be some story, or legend, or tradition attached to this queer key, which might throw some light on the mystery of the figures. If she learnt the story, it was not improbable that she might gain a hint therefrom. At all events, Parsons had spoken of concealed riches connected with the reading of the cypher. To attempt to unravel the problem without knowing the reason for which the figures were engraved was, vulgarly speaking, putting the cart before the horse. Hagar determined that the cart should be in its proper place, viz., at the tail of the animal. In other words, she resolved first to learn the legend of the key, and afterwards attempt a reading of the riddle. To get at the truth, it was necessary to see Parsons.

No sooner had Hagar made up her mind to this course than she resolved to carry out her plan. Leaving Bolker to mind the shop, she went off down to Kent—to the Lodge, Buckton, that address which Parsons had given to be written on the ticket. With her she took the key, in case it might be wanted, and shortly after midday she alighted at a little rural station.

Oh, it was sweet to be once more in the country, to wander through green lanes o'er-arched with bending hazels, to smell the perfume of Kentish orchards, to run across the springy turf of wide moors golden with gorse! Such a fair expanse was stretched out at the back of the station, and across it—as Hagar was informed by an obliging porter—Danetree Hall was to be found. At the gates thereof, in a pretty and quaint lodge, dwelt surly Mr. Parsons, and thither went Hagar; but in truth she almost forgot her errand in the delights of the country.

Her gipsy blood sang in her veins as she ran across the green sward, and her heart leaped in her bosom for very lightness. She forgot the weary Lambeth pawn-shop; she thought not of Eustace Lorn; she did not let her mind dwell upon the return of Goliath and her subsequent disinheritance; all she knew was that she was a Romany lass, a child of the road, and had entered again into her kingdom. In such a happy vein she saw the red roofs of Danetree Hall rising above the trees of a great park; and almost immediately she arrived at the great iron gates, behind which, on one side of a stately avenue, she espied the lodge wherein dwelt Parsons.

He was sitting outside smoking a pipe, morose even in the golden sunlight, with the scent of flowers in his nostrils, the music of the birds in his ears. On seeing Hagar peering between the bars of the gate he started up, and literally rushed towards her.

"Pawn-shop girl!" he growled, like an angry bear. "What do you want?"

"Civility in the first place; rest in the second!" retorted Hagar, coolly. "Let me in, Mr. Parsons. I have come to see you about that copper key."

"You've lost it?" shouted the gruff creature.

"Not I; it's in my pocket. But I wish to know its story."

"Why?" asked Parsons, opening the gates with manifest reluctance.

Without replying Hagar marched past him, into his garden, and the porch of his house. Finally she took her seat in the chair Parsons had vacated. The old man seemed rather pleased with her ungracious behavior, which matched so well with his own; and after closing the gates he came to stare at her brilliant face.

"You're a handsome woman, and a bold one," said he, slowly. "Come inside, and tell me why you wish to know the story of the key."

Accepting the invitation with civility, Hagar followed her eccentric host into a prim little parlor furnished in the ugly fashion of the early Victorian era. Chairs and sofa were of mahogany and horsehair; a round table, with gilt-edged books lying thereon at regular intervals, occupied the center of the apartment, and the gilt-framed mirror over the fireplace was swathed in green gauze. Copperplate prints of the Queen and the Prince Consort decorated the crudely-papered walls, and the well-worn carpet was of a dark-green hue sprinkled with bouquets of red flowers. Altogether a painfully ugly room, which made any one gifted with artistic aspirations shudder, Hagar, whose eye was trained to beauty, shuddered duly, and then took her seat on the most comfortable of the ugly chairs.

"Why do you want to know the story of the key?" asked Parsons, throwing his bulky figure on the slippery sofa.

"Because I wish to read the riddle of the key."

Parsons started up, and his face grew red with anger. "No, no! You shall not—you must not! Never will I make her rich!"

"Make who rich?" asked Hagar, astonished at this outburst.

"Marion Danetree—the proud hussey! My son loves her, but she disdains him. He is breaking his heart, while she laughs. If that picture were found she would be rich, and despise my poor Frank the more."

"The picture? What picture?"

"Why, the one that is hidden," said Parsons in surprise. "The clue to the hiding-place is said to be concealed in the figures on

the key. If you find the picture, it will sell for thirty thousand
pounds, which would go to that cruel Miss Danetree."

"I don't quite understand," said Hagar, rather bewildered.
"Would you mind telling me the story from the beginning?"

"As you please," replied the old man, moodily. "I'll make it as
short as I can. Squire Danetree, the grandfather of the present lady,
who is the only representative of the family, was very rich, and a
friend of George the Fourth. Like all the Danetrees, he was a scamp,
and squandered the property of the family in entertainments
during the Regency. He sold all the pictures of the Hall save one,
'The Nativity,' by Andrea del Castagno, a famous Florentine painter
of the Renaissance. The King offered thirty thousand pounds for
this gem, as he wished to buy it for the nation. Danetree refused,
as he had some compunction at robbing his only son, and wished
to leave him the picture as the only thing saved out of the wreck.
But as time went on, and money became scarce, he determined to
sell this last valuable. Then the picture disappeared."

"How did it disappear?"

"My father hid it," replied Parsons, coolly. "It was not known
at the time, but the old man confessed on his death-bed that, determined to save the family from ruin, he had concealed the picture while Squire Danetree was indulging in his mad orgies in London. When my father confessed, the spendthrift squire was dead,
and he wished the son—the present Miss Danetree's father—to
possess the picture and to sell it, in order to restore the fortunes
of the family."

"Well, did he not tell where the picture was hidden?"

"No; he died on the point of revealing the secret," said Parsons. "All he could say was 'The key! the key!' Then I knew that the
hiding-place was indicated by the row of figures graven on the stem
of the copper key. I tried to make out the meaning; so did my son;
so did Squire Danetree and his daughter. But all to no purpose.
None can read the riddle."

"But why did you pawn the key?"

"It wasn't for money, you may be sure of that!" snapped the old
man—"or I should not have taken a paltry pound for it. No, I

pawned it to put it beyond my son's reach. He was always poring over it, so I thought he might guess the meaning and find the picture."

"And why not? Don't you want it found?"

Parsons's face assumed a malignant expression. "No!" said he, sharply—"for then Frank would be foolish enough to give the picture to Miss Danetree—to the woman who despises him. If you guess the riddle, don't tell him, as I don't want to make the proud jade rich."

"I can't guess the riddle," replied Hagar hopelessly. "Your story does not aid me in the least."

While thus speaking, her eyes wandered to the wall at the back of the glum old steward. Thereon she saw in a frame of black wood one of those hideous samplers which our grandmothers were so fond of working. It was a yellow square, embroidered—or rather stitched—with the alphabet in divers colors, and also an array of numerals up to twenty-six. Hagar idly wondered why the worker had stopped at that particular number; and then she noticed that the row of figures was placed directly under the row of letters. At once the means of reading the key riddle flashed on her brain. The cypher was exceedingly simple. All that had to be done was to substitute letters for the figures. Hagar uttered an ejaculation which roused old Parsons from his musings.

"What's the matter?" said he, turning his head: "what are you looking at, girl? Oh," he added, following her gaze, "that sampler; 'twas done by my mother; a rare hand at needlework she was! But never mind her just now. I want to know about that riddle."

"I can't guess it," said Hagar, keeping her own counsel, for reasons to be revealed hereafter. "Do you wish your key back? I have it here."

"No; I don't want my son to get it, and make that proud wench rich by guessing the riddle. Keep the key till I call for it. What! are you going? Have a drink of milk?"

The offer was hospitably made, but Hagar declined it, as she had no desire to break bread with this malignant old man. Making a curt excuse, she took her leave, and within the hour she was on her way back to London, with a clue to the cypher in her brain. The sampler had revealed the secret; for without doubt it was from his wife's needlework that the Parsons of sixty years before had got the idea of constructing his cryptogram. In the sampler the figures were placed thus:

A	B	C	D	E	F	G	H	I	J	K	L	M	N	O
1	2	3	4	5	6	7	8	9	10	11	12	13	14	15

P	Q	R	S	T	U	V	W	X	Y	Z
16	17	18	19	20	21	22	23	24	25	26

and Parsons had simply substituted figures for letters. The thing was so plain that Hagar wondered why, with the key-sampler staring him in the face, the steward had not succeeded in reading the riddle.

When back in the shop, she applied her test to the figures on the key, and found out the meaning thereof. Then she considered what was the best course to pursue. Clearly it was not wise to tell Parsons, as he hated Miss Danetree, and if he found the picture through Hagar's aid he might either hide it again or destroy it. Should she tell Miss Danetree herself, or Frank Parsons, the despised lover? After some consideration the girl wrote to the latter, asking him to call on her at the shop. She felt rather a sympathy with his plight after hearing his father's story, and wished to judge for herself if he was an eligible suitor for Miss Danetree's hand. If she liked him, and found him worthy, Hagar was resolved to tell him how to find the picture, and by doing so thus aid him to gain the hand of the disdainful beauty. If, on the other hand, she did not care for him, Hagar concluded to reveal her discovery to Miss Danetree herself. Her resolution thus being taken, she waited quietly for the arrival of the steward's son.

When he presented himself, Hagar liked him very much indeed, for three reasons. In the first place, he was handsome—a sure passport to a woman's favor; in the second, he had a fine frank nature, and a tolerably intelligent brain; in the third, he was deeply in love with Marion Danetree. This last reason influenced Hagar as much as anything, for she was at a romantic age, and took a deep interest in love and lovers.

"It is most extraordinary that my father should have pawned the key," said Frank, when Hagar had told her story, less the explanation of the riddle.

"It may be extraordinary, Mr. Parsons, but it is very lucky—for you."

"I don't see it," said Frank, raising his eyebrows. "Why."

"Why," replied Hagar, drawing the key out of her pocket, "because I have discovered the secret."

"What! Do you know what that line of figures means?"

"Yes. When I paid my visit to your father, I saw an article in his room which gave me a clue. I worked out the cypher, and now I know where the picture is hidden."

Young Parsons sprang to his feet with glowing eyes. "Where—oh, where?" he almost shouted. "Tell me, quick!"

"For you to tell Miss Danetree, no doubt," said Hagar, coolly.

At once his enthusiasm died away, and he sat down, with a frown on his face. "What do you know about Miss Danetree?" he asked, sharply.

"All that your father told me, Mr. Parsons. You love her, but she does not love you; and for that your father hates her."

"I know he does," said the young man, sighing, "and very unjustly. I will be frank with you, Miss Stanley."

"I think it is best for you to be so, as I hold your fate in my hands."

"You hold—fate! What do you mean?"

Hagar shrugged her shoulders in pity at his obtuseness. "Why," she said, quietly, "this picture is worth thirty thousand pounds, and Miss Danetree is worth nothing except that ruined Hall. If I tell you where to find that picture, you will be able to restore her fortunes, and make her a comparatively rich woman. Now you cannot read the cypher; I can; and so—you see!"

Young Parsons laughed outright at her comprehensive view of the situation, although he blushed a little at the same time, and gave an indignant denial to the hinted motive which prompted Hagar's speech. "I am not a fortune-hunter," he said, bluntly; "if I learn the whereabouts of Castagno's 'Nativity,' I shall certainly tell Mar—I mean Miss Danetree. But as for trading on that knowledge to make her marry me against her will, I'd rather die than act so basely!"

"Ah, my dear young man, I am afraid you have no business instincts," said Hagar, dryly. "I thought you loved the lady."

"You are determined to get at the truth, I see. Yes; I do love her."

"And she loves you?"

Parsons hesitated, and blushed again at this downright questioning. "Yes; I think she does—a little," he said, at length.

"H'm! That means she loves you a great deal."

"Well," said the young man, slyly, "you are a woman, and should be able to read a woman's character. Don't you think so?"

"Perhaps. But you forget that I have not seen this particular woman—or rather angel, as I suppose you call her."

"You are a queer girl!"

"And you—a love-sick young man!" rejoined Hagar, mimicking his tone. "But time passes; tell me about your wooing."

"There is little to tell," rejoined Frank, dolefully. "My father is, as you know, the steward of the Danetree family; but as they were ruined by the Regency squire, his duties are now light enough. Miss Danetree is the last of the race, and all that remains to her is the Hall, the few acres which surround it, and a small income from the rents of two outlying farms. I was brought up from childhood with Marion—I must call her so, as it is the name which comes easiest to my lips—and I loved her always. She loves me also."

"Then why will she not marry you?"

"Because she is poor and I am poor. Oh, my position as son of her steward would not stand in the way could I support her as my wife. But my father always refused to let me learn a profession or a trade, or even to earn my own livelihood, as he desired me to succeed him as the steward of the Danetree property. In the old days the post was a good one; but now it is worth nothing."

"And your father dislikes Miss Danetree."

"Yes, because he thinks she scorns me—which she does not. But she will not let me tell him the truth until there is a chance of our marriage."

"Well," said Hagar, producing the paper on which was written the line of figures, "I am about to give you that chance. This cypher is quite easy; figures have been substituted for letters—that is all. A is set down as one, B as two, and so on."

"I don't quite understand."

"I will show you. These figures must be divided into numbers, and a letter set over each. Now, the first number is twenty, and the twentieth letter of the alphabet is 'T.' The twenty-first letter is 'U.' Then come the eighteenth and the fourteenth letters. What are they?"

Frank counted. "'R' and 'N,'" he said, after a pause. "Ah! I see the first word is T, U, R, N,—that is turn!"

"Exactly; represented by numbers, 20, 21, 18, 14. Now you understand, so I need not explain further. Here is the cypher written out."

Young Parsons took up the paper and read as follows:

T	u	r	n	k	e	y	l	e	f	t	e	y	e
20	21	18	14	11	5	25	12	5	6	20	5	25	5

8	c	h	e	r	u	b
H	3	8	5	18	21	2

"Turn key left eye eighth cherub!" repeated Parsons, in puzzled tones. "I have no doubt that you have solved the problem correctly; but, I do not know what the sentence means."

"Well," said Hagar, rather sharply, "it means, I should think, that the left eye of some cherub's head is a keyhole, into which is to be thrust the copper key upon which the figures are engraved. Doubtless, by turning the key the wall will open, and the picture will be discovered."

"What a clever girl you are!" cried Parsons, in admiration.

"I use my brains, that is all," said Hagar, coolly. "I'm afraid you don't. However, are there a number of sculptured cherubs in Danetree Hall?"

"Yes; there is a room called 'The Cherubs' Room,' from a number of carved heads. How did you guess that there was more than one?"

"Because the letter 'H' corresponds with the figure eight; so no doubt there are more than eight heads. All you have to do is to take this copper key, put it into the left eye of the eighth cherub, and find the picture. Then you can marry Miss Danetree, and the pair of you can live on the thirty thousand pounds. If she is as clever as you, you'll need it all."

Quite impervious to Hagar's irony, Frank Parsons took his leave with many admiring words and protestations of gratitude. When he found the picture he promised to let Hagar know, and to invite her to Danetree Hall to see it. Then he departed, and it was only when she was left alone that Hagar reflected she had not got back the pound lent on the key. But she consoled herself with the reflection that she could demand it when the hidden picture was discovered. Principal and interest was what she required; for Hagar was nothing if not businesslike.

That same evening Frank was seated in the prim little parlor with his dour father. He had been up to the Hall, and had proved the truth of Hagar's reading by discovering the picture; also he had seen Marion Danetree, and told her of the good fortune which was coming. She would be able to buy back the lost acres of the family, to restore and refurnish the old house, to take up her position again in the county, and reign once more as the lady of Danetree Hall. All this Frank told his father, and the old man's brow grew black as night.

"You have made her rich!" he muttered—"that proud girl who looks upon you as dirt beneath her feet."

Frank smiled. He had not told his father the termination of the interview with Marion; nor did he intend to do so at present.

"We'll talk of Marion and her pride to-morrow," he said, rising; "I am going to bed just now; but you know how I discovered

the picture, and how it has been restored to the Danetrees as grandfather wished."

When his son left the room, Luke Parsons sat with folded hands
and a dull pain in his heart. It was gall and wormwood to him that
the woman who rejected Frank should acquire wealth and regain
her position through the aid of the man she despised. Oh, if he
could only hide the picture, or even destroy it!—anything rather
than that proud Marion Danetree should be placed on an eminence
to look down on his bright boy. To rob her of this newly-found
wealth—to take away the picture—Parsons felt that he would commit even a crime.

And why should he not? Frank had left the key on the table—
the copper key which was to be placed in the left eye of the cherub.
Parsons knew well enough—from the explanation of his son—how
the key was to be used; how his father had designed the hiding-
place of the Castagno picture. The lock and key which had belonged
to the First Charles had been given to the old man by his master.
He had placed the first behind the cherub, with the keyhole in the
left eye, so as to keep the panel or portion of the wall in its place;
and on the second he had graven the numbers indicating the local-
ity. Parsons rose to his feet and stretched out his hand for the copper key. When he touched it, all his scruples vanished. He made
up his mind then and there to go up that night to the Hall and
destroy the picture. Then Marion Danetree would no longer be rich,
or benefit by the secret which Frank had discovered. It will be seen
that Mr. Parsons never thought of Hagar's share in the reading of
the cypher.

As steward he had keys of all the doors in the Hall, and was
able easily to gain admission at whatever hour he chose. He chose
to enter now, and with a lantern in his hand, and a clasp-knife hidden in his pocket, he went on his errand of destruction. Unlocking
a small side door under the greater terrace, he passed along the
dark underground passages, ascending to the upper floor, and in a
short space of time he found himself in "The Cherubs' Room."

It was a large and lofty apartment, paneled with oak darkened
by time and carved with fruit and flowers and foliage after the mode

of Grinling Gibbons. Between each panel there was a beautifully-carven cherub's head, with curly hair, and wings placed crosswise under the chin. The moonlight streaming in through the wide and uncurtained windows showed all these things clearly to the wild eyes of the old man; and he made haste to fulfil his task before the moon should set and leave him in darkness. Swinging the lantern so that its yellow light should illuminate the walls, Parsons counted the cherubs' heads between the panels, starting from the door, and was rewarded by finding the one he sought. The left eye of this face was pierced, and into it he inserted the slender copper stem of the key. There was a cracking sound as he turned it, and then the whole of the panel swung outward to the left. On the back of this he beheld the picture of Andrea del Castagno. The sight of it was so unexpected that he started back with a cry, and let fall the lantern, which was immediately extinguished. However, this mattered little, as he had ample light in the rays of the summer moon. In the white radiance he relighted his candle, and then, betwixt the yellow glare of the one and the chill glimmer of the other, he examined the gem of art which, in the interests of mistaken pride, he proposed to destroy. It was beautiful beyond description.

Under a lowly roof of thatched straw lay the Divine Child, stretching up His little Hands to the Holy Mother. With arms crossed upon her breast in ecstatic adoration, Mary bent over Him worshiping; and in the dim obscurity of the humble dwelling could be seen the tall form and reverend head of Joseph. Above spread the dark blue of the night sky, broken by golden dashes of color, in which were seen the majestic forms of wide-winged angels looking earthward. At the top of the picture there was a blaze of light radiating from the Godhead, and in the arrowy beam streaming downward floated the white specter of the Holy Dove. The marvelous beauty of the picture lay in the dispersion and disposition of the various lights: that mild luster which emanated from the Form of the Child, the aureole hovering round the bowed head of Mary; the glory of the golden atmosphere surrounding the angels; and, highest and most wonderful of all, the fierce white light which showered down, blinding the terrible, from the unseen Deity. The picture was majestic, sublime: a dream of lovely piety, a master-piece of art.

For the moment Parsons was spellbound before this wonderful creation which he intended to destroy. Almost he was tempted to forego his evil purpose, and to spare the beautiful vision which spread itself so gloriously before trial. But the thought of Marion and her scorn, of Frank and his hopeless love, decided him With a look of hatred he opened the knife, and raised the blade to slash the picture.

"Stop!"

With a cry, Parsons dropped the knife and wheeled round at that imperious command. At the further end of the room, candle in hand, stood the tall form of a woman. She wore a dressing-gown hastily thrown over her shoulders; her hair was loose, her feet were bare; and she approached the steward noiselessly and swiftly. It was Marion Danetree, and her eyes were full of anger.

"What are you doing here at this time of night?" she demanded haughtily of the sullen old man. "I heard a cry and the noise of a fall, and I came down."

"I want to spoil that picture," said Parsons between his teeth.

"Destroy Castagno's 'Nativity'? Take away my only chance of restoring the family fortunes? You are mad."

"No; I am Frank's father. You despise him; you hate him. Through him you have found the picture; but now—" He picked up the knife again.

"Wait a moment!" said Marion, comprehending Parsons's mo-tive; "if you destroy that picture, you prevent my marriage with Frank."

"What?"—the knife crashed on the floor—"are you going to marry my boy?"

"Yes. Did not Frank tell you? When we discovered the picture together this afternoon, he asked me to be his wife. I consented only too gladly."

"But—but I thought you despised him!"

"Despise him? I love him better than all the world! Go away, Mr. Parsons, and thank God that He sent me to prevent you committing a crime. I shall bring that picture to Frank as my dowry. He shall take my name, and there will once more be a Squire Danetree at the Hall."

"O Miss Danetree—Marion—forgive me!" cried Parsons, quite broken down.

"I forgive you; it was love for Frank made you think of this folly. But go—go! it is not seemly that you should be here at this hour of the night."

Parsons closed up the panel in silence, locked it, and turned to go. But as he passed her he held out his hand.

"What is this?" asked Marion, smiling.

"My gift to you—my marriage gift—the copper key which has brought you a husband and a fortune."

7

The Sixth Customer and the Silver Teapot

OF ALL THE PEOPLE with whom Hagar had to do while managing the
Lambeth pawn-shop, she liked always to remember Margaret Snow.
The memory of that pale, blind old maid, with her sorrowful story
and her patient endurance, never died out of the girl's heart. The
pitiful little episode of the silver teapot, which she pawned so unwillingly, and only out of sheer necessity; the sad tale recounted
by the crushed creature, and the unexpected part which she took
herself in the conclusion of such tale: all these things served to
keep green the memory of the sad woman whom Hagar called her
sixth customer. There was even something ludicrous in parts of
the affair; something naive and childlike in the absolute simplicity of the romance; but Hagar never saw its humor. All she knew
was that Margaret was a martyr and a saint, and that the world
was the loser for not knowing her story. Such as it is, the tale runs
thus:

It was dusk one November evening when Margaret entered the
shop, with a parcel tied up in an old towel. Hagar knew her well by
sight as a blind woman who lived in an attic at the top of the end
house in Carby's Crescent, and as one who earned a hard and penurious living by weaving hand-baskets of straw for a great empo-
rium at the corner of the outside street. These baskets—a special-
ity of the great shop—were given to customers in which to carry
away small parcels; and as the demand was constant, the supply
was the same. Margaret could always sell as many of these baskets
as she could weave; but, although skilful and nimble with her long

fingers, she could rarely earn more than ten shillings a week. On this she had to live, and dress, and buy food, so her existence was really a kind of miracle. Still, she had never asked charity of a single soul, being proud and reserved: and in all the years she had dwelt in Carby's Crescent she had never entered the pawn-shop. Knowing this, Hagar was astonished to see her standing in one of the sentry-boxes, with the bundle placed on the counter before her.

"Miss Snow!" cried Hagar, in sheer surprise. "What is the matter? Is there anything that I can do for you?"

The thin pale face of the woman flushed as she heard herself called by her name; and her voice was hesitating and low as she laid one slender finger on the bundle, before making reply.

"I have been ill, Miss Stanley," she explained, softly, "so I have not done much work lately. Very little money has come in. I—I am obliged to—to pay my rent and—and—" She broke down altogether, and added desperately: "Please lend me something on this."

Hagar became a business woman at once "What is it?" she said, undoing the bundle deftly.

"It is—it is—a silver teapot," faltered Miss Snow; "the only valuable I possess. I wish to pawn it for three months, until I can redeem it. I—I—hope to repay the money by then. Three—three pounds will be—" Her voice died away in her throat: and Hagar saw her poor thin hand steal up to her averted face to brush away a tear.

The teapot was a square one of Georgian design, with fluted sides, an elegantly-curved spout, and a smooth handle of ivory. Hagar was quite willing to lend on it the required three pounds, as the silver was worth more, until she made a curious discovery. The lid of the pot was closed tightly, and soldered all round, in a manner which made it quite impossible to be opened. This odd circumstance rendered the teapot for all practical purposes entirely useless; no one could use an hermetically sealed vessel.

"Why is this teapot closed?" asked Hagar in surprise.

"It was done thirty years ago by my order," replied the blind woman, in a calm voice; then, after a pause, she added in faint and hesitating tones: "There are letters in it."

"Letters? Whose letters?"

"Mine and—a person's with whom you have no concern. Please do not ask any more questions, Miss Stanley. Give me the money and let me go. I hope to redeem the teapot in three months."

Hagar hesitated and looked doubtful. "As it is sealed up, the teapot is hardly of much use," she said, after a pause. "Take it back, my dear Miss Snow, and I'll lend you the three pounds."

"Thank you, no," replied the old maid, coldly. "I take charity from no one. If you can't lend the money on the teapot, give me back my property."

"Oh, well, I'll take it in pawn if you like," rejoined Hagar, with a shrug. "Here are three sovereigns, and I'll make out the ticket at once."

The hand of the blind woman closed on the money with a sigh of mingled regret and relief. When Hagar returned with the ticket she saw that Margaret was fondling the piece of silver as though unwilling to part with it. She drew back, flushing, on hearing the approaching foot-steps of Hagar, and taking the ticket in silence, moved away with tears running down her withered cheeks. Hagar was touched by this mute misery.

"Can you find your way back home in the darkness?" she called out.

"My dear," said the elder woman with dignity, "day and night are the same to me. You forget that I am blind. Also," she added, with an attempt at lightness, "I know every inch of this neighborhood."

When she departed Hagar put away the teapot, and wondered a little over the odd circumstance of it being closed, and containing love-letters. She was certain that the letters were full of love from the faltering way in which Margaret had mentioned them; also because they were her own and "a person's with whom you have no concern."

That last sentence, as spoken by the blind woman, showed Hagar only too truly her indomitable reserve and pride. She must have been reduced to her last crust before she could have brought herself to pawn the queer casket—and a teapot as a receptacle for love-letters was very queer indeed—which contained the evidence of her youth's dead romance. Thirty years ago the teapot had been sealed; Hagar knew also that thirty years ago the heart of this blind and unattractive old maid had been broken. Here indeed was material for a true romance—and that of the strangest, the most pitiful.

"What a strange place is a pawn-shop!" said Hagar, philosophizing to herself. "All the flotsam and jetsam of human lives drift into it. Broken hearts, wrecked careers, worn-out and dead romances—this is the place for them all. I should like to know the story of that sealed-up teapot."

Indeed, so curious she was to know it that she felt half-inclined to call on the old maid, and ask for information. But Hagar, although a poor girl, and a wandering gipsy, and the manageress of a low London pawn-shop, had a natural instinct of delicacy which withheld her from forcing the confidence of one disinclined to give it.

Miss Snow was a lady born, as all Carby's Crescent knew, and her unbending pride was proverbial. The few words with which she had checked Hagar's inquiries about the letters enshrined in the teapot showed plainly enough that the subject of the hinted romance was not one to be touched upon. Hagar therefore kept the teapot in the shop, and forbore to call upon its owner.

For some weeks Margaret continued to weave her baskets and take them to the shop which employed her. She went to church every Sunday morning, according to her usual custom; and other than these outings she remained secluded in her freezing garret. In that year the winter was particularly severe in London, and snow fell thickly before Christmas. In her desire to save money for the redemption of the teapot, Margaret denied herself a fire, and reduced the amount of food she took, to as little as would sustain life. In her thin clothing and well-worn shoes she went to shop and church amid falling snow, and in the teeth of cutting winds. Naturally, with lack of clothing, food and fire, with her weight of years, and emaciated frame, she fell ill. One morning she did not appear, and the woman of the house went up to find her in bed.

Still, her bold spirit, her inborn pride, kept her resolute to refuse charity; and she wove her baskets sitting up in her buckle-bed, between bouts of pain and anguish. In these straits she must have died, but that God in His pity for this helpless and tortured woman sent an angel to aid her. The angel was Hagar; and a very practical angel she proved to be.

Learning from the gossip of the neighborhood that Miss Snow was ill, and remembering the episode of the silver teapot, Hagar marched up to the freezing garret and took charge of the old maid. Margaret objected with all her feeble force; but the kind-hearted gipsy girl was not to be deterred from what she conceived to be her duty.

"You are ill and alone, so I must look after you," she said, throwing a rug, which she had brought, over the poor woman.

"But I cannot pay you. All I have of value is the silver teapot."

"Well," said Hagar, proceeding to kindle a good fire, "that is safe in my shop, so don't trouble about it. As to payment, we'll talk about that when you get better."

"I shall never get better," groaned Margaret, and turned her face to the wall. And indeed, Hagar thought, that was true enough. Worn by years of cold and privation, Margaret's body was too feeble to resist much longer the inroads of disease. When she left her garret again it would be feet foremost; and another London pauper would be added to the great army of the unknown dead. With Margaret the sands of time were running out very rapidly.

Hagar was like a sister to her. She kept her supplied with fire and food and blankets; she gave her wine to drink; and, when she could get away from the shop, she came oftentimes to sit by that poor bedside. It was on such an occasion that she heard the one romance of Margaret's life, and learnt why the love-letters—they truly were love-letters—had been placed in the silver teapot.

It was late in December, and the ground was white with snow. The shops, even in Carby's Crescent, were being decked with holly and mistletoe for the season of Yule; and, after closing the premises, Hagar had come to pass an hour with Margaret. There was a good fire—one which would have made wrathful the miserly heart of the late Jacob Dix—and a fair amount of light from two candles placed on the mantelpiece. Margaret was cheerful, even gay, on this evening; and with her hand in Hagar's she thanked the girl for her kindness.

"But indeed thanks are weak," said the blind woman; "you have fed the hungry and clothed the naked. After thirty years of doubt, my dear, you have restored my faith in human nature."

"How did you lose it?"

"Through a man, my dear; one who said that he loved me, yet who broke off our engagement without any reason."

"That was strange. Why did you not ask him for his reason?"

"I could not," said Margaret, with a sigh; "he was in India. But it is a long story, my dear. If you care to listen—"

"I shall be delighted," said Hagar, quickly—"especially if it explains why you sealed up the letters in the teapot."

"Yes; it explains that. In that teapot—which was the only present I ever received from John Mask—I placed his cruel letters thirty years ago; also mine to him, which he sent back."

"Why did he send back your letters?" asked Hagar.

"I don't know; I cannot say; but he returned them. Oh!" she cried with a burst of anguish, "how cruel, how cruel! and I loved him so—I loved him! But he forgot me and married Jane Lorrimer. Now they are rich and prosperous and happy, while I—I am dying a pauper in a garret. And the silver teapot is pawned," she finished pathetically.

Hagar patted the thin hand which gripped the bedclothes. "Tell me the story," said she, soothingly—"that is, if it will not cause you too much pain."

"Pain," echoed Margaret, bitterly. "When the heart is broken it feels no pain, and mine was broken thirty years ago by John Mask." She remained silent for a moment, and then continued: "I lived at Christchurch, in Hants, my dear, in a little cottage just outside the town. This I inherited from my parents, together with a trifle of money—not much, indeed, but sufficient to live upon. Both my father and mother had died, leaving me alone in the world at the age of twenty; so I lived in my cottage with Lucy Dyke and a little maid as my servants. Lucy was near my own age, and looked after the house well. I was blind, you see, my dear," said Margaret, softly "and could do nothing for myself. Dear Lord! but I have had to earn my own living since then."

Overcome by bitter memories, she paused for a moment. Hagar did not dare to break the silence; and in a short time Margaret resumed her tale.

"Also, I had a dear friend called Jane Lorrimer, who lived near with her parents, and who visited me constantly. We were like sisters, and I loved her better than any one in the world till John Mask came to Christchurch. He was visiting the rector of the parish, and I met him. Although I never saw his face, I was told that he was very handsome; and he had a sweet low voice, which charmed me greatly. You know, my dear, how we poor blind folk love a sympathetic voice. Well, I loved John, but I had no idea that there would be any return of that love; for how could a blind girl hope that a handsome young man would look on her—especially," added Margaret in a melancholy tone, "when Jane was so handsome?"

"But he did not love Jane," observed Hagar, significantly.

"No," said the blind woman, proudly; "he loved me, and this he told me after we had known each other a year. We became engaged, and life was then at its brightest for me. However, he was going out to India to be a tea-planter; and he said when he was settled there and had made a fair amount of money that he would send for me. Alas! alas! that promise was never kept."

"Why wasn't it?" asked Hagar, bluntly.

"Who can tell?" said Margaret, sadly. "Not I; not Jane. She was as surprised as I was when the end came. Although blind, my dear, I can write fairly well, and John made me promise to correspond with him. I did so for more than a year, and he answered faithfully."

"Who read his letters to you?"

"Sometimes Jane, sometimes Lucy Dyke. Ah! they were both good friends to me in my trouble. At first John's letters were very affectionate, but as the months went by they grew colder and colder. Oftentimes Jane said that she would not read them to me. I wrote to John asking the meaning of this change; but his replies were not satisfactory. At last, eighteen months after his departure, I received back my letters."

"Really! Did Jane or Lucy bring them to you?"

"No; Jane was absent in London seeing friends; and Lucy at the moment was out of the house. The little maid brought me the packet. I opened it, thinking it might be a present from John, as he had given me nothing but the silver teapot, which he presented to me before he departed. I made the little maid wait till I opened the packet; and I asked her to read the letter from John enclosed."

"Did she?"

"Yes; oh, the pain of it!" cried Margaret. "He said that it was best that our engagement should end, and that he returned to me my letters, thirteen in all. Not an excuse, or a sigh, or a regret. Only two curt, cruel lines, breaking off our engagement, and the packet of my letters. I was distracted with grief; and I placed the letters in my bosom while I wept."

"What did Lucy say when she returned?"

"She was very angry with the little maid for having read the letter to me and causing me such pain. She wanted me to destroy my own letters, but I refused. I kept them by me day and night; John had touched them, and they were all that remained to me of him. Then I saw that my romance was dead and done with. I took my own letters and those he had written me, and tying them up in a bundle, I placed them with my own hands in the silver teapot. Then I went to a jeweler, and had the lid closed. It has not been opened since."

"Did you tell Lucy or Jane that you had done this?"

"I told no one. I kept my own secret, and none guessed what the teapot contained of my one hour of happiness. Then shortly afterwards misfortunes fell on me. I lost my money through the wickedness of my trustee, and had to give up my house and dismiss Lucy and my little maid. Jane went out to India to an uncle, and she took with her Lucy as maid. In six months from her departure I heard that she had married John Mask."

"Did she write and tell you so?"

"No; she never wrote to me, nor did he. As for myself, after receiving back my letters with those cruel two lines, after enshrining them in the teapot, I strove to forget him. I never wrote a line to him; I never mentioned him. He had treated me cruelly, and he was dead to me. That was the end of my romance, my dear."

"And how did you come to London?"

"I lost my all, as I told you," said Margaret, simply; "and, as I could not bear to live poor where I had been well off, I left Christchurch and came to London. Oh, my dear, why should I tell you of the miseries I endured! Blind and poor and friendless, I suffered greatly; but it was all nothing compared to the suffering of that hour when John broke my heart. Finally, I drifted here, to earn my bread by weaving baskets; and here I die. Alas! poor Margaret Snow!"

"And John Mask and his wife?"

"They live in the West End, in Berkeley Square, rich and prosperous, with sons and daughters by their side. Lucy is the housekeeper. Oh, I learnt it all from a friend of mine in Christchurch. Ah! how happy—how happy they are!"

"Did you reveal yourself to them?"

"No. Why should I? They would not care for me to haunt them like a ghost of the past. They are rich and honored and happy."

"And you lie here, poor and dying!" said Hagar, bitterly.

"Yes; it is hard—hard. But I must not complain. God has sent you to me to make my last moments happy. You are good—good, my dear. You have done much for me; but one thing more you must do. Open the teapot."

"What!" cried Hagar, in surprise—"open what has been closed for thirty years!"

"Yes; I wish you to read me John's letters before I die. Let me go to my rest knowing that he loved me once. To-morrow, my dear, you must do this for me. Promise."

"I promise," said Hagar, folding the blankets over her. "To-morrow I shall have the teapot opened, and bring you the letters—your own and John Mask's."

With this promise she took her leave for the night, after first seeing that Margaret was warm and comfortable. In her own bed, Hagar meditated on the sadness of the story which had been told to her, on the passionate love of the man for the blind woman, which had died away so strangely. That he should have ceased to love Margaret was not uncommon, as men, particularly when absent, are only too often prone to forget those they leave at home; but it was curious that he should have married Jane Lorrimer. A doubt stole into Hagar's mind as to whether Margaret had been treated fairly; whether there might not have been other reasons for the sudden ending of her romance than she knew of. For such suspicion Hagar had no grounds to go upon; but all the same she could not rid her mind of the doubt. Perhaps the letters might set it at rest; perhaps all had happened as Margaret had told. Nevertheless, Hagar was anxious that the morrow should come—that the teapot should be opened and the letters read. Then she would learn if treachery and woman's wiles had parted the lovers, or if the story was merely one—as Margaret believed—of a faithless man and a broken-hearted woman.

The next day Hagar left the shop in charge of Bolker, and took the silver teapot to a jeweler in the adjacent thoroughfare. He soon melted the solder, and opened the lid. Within, beneath a pile of dried rose-leaves, she found the packet of letters, tied up with a blue ribbon. There was something sacrilegious to her imaginative mind, in thus disturbing the relics of this dead-and-done-with romance; and it was with reverent care that Hagar carried the teapot and its contents to the house in Carby's Crescent. After thirty years of moldering under the rose-leaves, these letters, yellow and faded, were restored to the light of day; and the woman who had written them when young and fair was now lying withered and dying in the winter of her age. Hagar was profoundly moved as she sat by that humble bedside with the ancient love-letters on her lap.

"Read them all," said Margaret, with the tears running down her face; "read the letters of John in which he told me of his love thirty years ago. Thirty years! Ah, dear God! when I was young and fresh! Oh, oh, oh! Youth and love!" she wept, beating the bedclothes with trembling hands—"love and youth! Gone! gone!—and I lie dying!"

Steadying her voice with an effort in the presence of this sacred grief, Hagar read the letters written from India by the absent lover. There were ten or twelve of them—charming letters, full of pure and undying love. From first to last there was no sentiment but what breathed devotion and trust. The writer spoke tenderly of his poor blind love; he promised to make her life happy, to strew her path with roses, and in every way to show himself worthy of honor and affection. Up to the twelfth letter there was not a hint of parting or of a desire to break off the engagement; only in the thirteenth letter—two curt lines, as Margaret had said—came the announcement, with the swiftness and unexpectedness of a thunderbolt. "It is better that our engagement should end," wrote John, coldly; "therefore I return you the thirteen letters you wrote me." And that was all. This unexpected communication, coming so suddenly after the fervor of the dozen letters, took away Hagar's breath.

"Excepting in the last I do not see anything cruel or cold in these letters, Miss Snow," said Hagar, when she had ended her reading.

Margaret put up one thin hand to her head. "No, no," she stammered, confusedly; "and yet I am sure John wrote cruelly. It is so long ago that perhaps I forget; but his last letters were cold, and hinted at a desire that we should part. I remember Jane and Lucy reading them to me."

"I don't see any hint of that," replied Hagar, doubtfully; "in fact, in the last two or three he asks, as you have heard, why you wish the marriage postponed."

"I never wished that!" murmured Margaret, perplexed. "I wanted to marry John and be with him always. Certainly I never said such a thing when I wrote to him. Of that I am sure."

"We can soon prove it," said Hagar, taking up the other packet. "Here are your letters to John—all of them. Shall I read them?"

Receiving an eager assent, the girl arranged the epistles in order of dates, and read them slowly. They were scrawled rather than written, in the large, childish handwriting of the blind; and most of them were short, but the first six were full of love and a desire to be near John. The seventh letter, which was better written than the previous ones, breathed colder sentiments; it hinted that the absent lover could do better than marry a blind girl, who might be a drag on him, it said.

"Stop! Stop!" cried Margaret, breathlessly. "I never wrote that letter!"

She was sitting up in the bed, with her gray hair pushed off her thin, eager face; and turning her sightless eyes towards Hagar, she seemed almost to see the astonished face of the girl in the intensity of her desire.

"I never wrote that letter!" repeated Margaret, in a shrill voice of excitement; "you are making some mistake."

"Indeed I read only what is written," said Hagar; "let me continue. When I finish the other five letters we shall discuss them. But I fear—I fear—"

"You fear what?"

"That you have been deceived. Wait—wait! say nothing until I finish reading."

Margaret sank back on her pillow with a gray face and quick in-drawn breathing. She dreaded what was coming, as Hagar well knew; so the girl continued hurriedly to read the letters, lest she should be interrupted. They were all—that is, the last five or six—written in better style of handwriting than the former ones; and each letter was colder than the last. The writer did not want to leave her quiet English home for distant India. She was afraid that the engagement was a mistake; when she consented to the marriage she did not know her own mind. Moreover, Jane Lorrimer loved him; she was—

"Jane!" interrupted Margaret, with a cry—"what had Jane to do with my love for John? I never wrote those last letters; they are forgeries!"

"Indeed they look like it," said Hagar, examining the letters; "the handwriting is that of a person who can see—much better than the writing of the early letters."

"I always wrote badly," declared Margaret, feverishly. "I was blind; it was hard for me to pen a letter. John did not expect—expect—oh, dear Lord, what does it all mean?"

"It means that Jane deceived you."

"Deceived me!" wailed Margaret, feebly—"deceived her poor blind friend! No, no!"

"I am certain of it!" said Hagar, firmly. "When you told me your story, I was doubtful of Jane; now that I have read those forged letters—for forged they are—I am certain of it. Jane deceived you, with the aid of Lucy!"

"But why, dear Lord, why?"

"Because she loved John and wished to marry him. You stood in the way, and she removed you. Well, she gained her wish; she parted you from John, and became Mrs. Mask."

"I can't believe it; Jane was my friend."

"Naturally; and for that reason deceived you," said Hagar, bitterly. "Oh, I know well what friendship is! But we must find out the truth. Tell me the exact address of Mrs. Mask."

"For what reason?"

"Because I shall call and see her. I shall learn the truth, and right you in the eyes of John."

"What use?" wept Margaret, bitterly. "My life is over, and I am dying. What use?"

Feeble and hopeless, she would have made no effort herself; but Hagar was determined that the secret, buried in the silver teapot for thirty years, should be known, if not to the world, at least to John Mask. These many days he had deemed Margaret faithless, and had married a woman who, he believed, gave him that love which the blind girl had refused. Now he should learn that the wife was the traitress, that the rejected woman had been true and faithful even unto death. Hagar made up her mind to this course, and forcing the address from the unwilling lips of Margaret, she went the very next day to the stately mansion in Berkeley Square. So came Nemesis to the faithless friend after the lapse of thirty years. The justice of the gods is slow, but it is certain.

Margaret lay weeping in her bed. As yet her feeble brain could not grasp the truth. John, whom she had believed faithless, had been true; and in his eyes all these years it was she who had been cruel. To her all was confusion and doubt. Not until the afternoon of the next day did she learn the truth for certain. It was Hagar who told it to her.

"I went to the house in Berkeley Square," said Hagar, "and I asked for Mrs. Mask. She was out, and I saw the housekeeper—none other than your former servant, Lucy Dyke; Mrs. Jael now," added the girl, contemptuously—"well off, trusted, and comfortable. That is the reward of her treachery."

"No, no! Lucy—surely she did not deceive me?"

"I made her confess it," said Hagar, sternly. "I told her of the letters in the teapot; of your hard life, and of your dying bed. At first she denied everything; but when I threatened to tell Mr. Mask the wretch confessed the truth. Yes, my poor Miss Snow, you were deceived—bitterly deceived—by your friend and your servant. They made a sport of your blindness and love."

"Cruel! cruel!" moaned Margaret, trembling violently.

"Yes, it was cruel; but it is the way of the world," said Hagar, with bitterness. "It seems that Jane was in love with your John; but as he was true to you, she could not hope to marry him. Determined, however, to do so, she bribed Lucy with money, and the pair resolved to part you from John by means of lying letters. Those you wrote to India never reached him. Instead of your epistles, Jane wrote those which I read to you, urging a breaking-off of the engagement, and hinting at her own love. John thought they came from you, and wrote back—as you have heard now—asking why you wished the marriage broken off. When Lucy or Jane read the letters to you thirty years ago, they altered the sense so that you should think John cruel. But why explain further?" cried Hagar, with a burst of deep anger. "You saw—you know how they succeeded. John broke off the engagement and sent you back your letters. For that your treacherous enemies were not prepared. If Lucy had been in the house, you would never have received the packet. No wonder she wanted you to burn the letters, seeing that the forged ones were amongst them. Had you not hidden them away in the silver teapot, Lucy would have found means to destroy them. However, you know how they have been preserved these thirty years, to prove the truth at last. Revenge yourself, Miss Snow! Jane is the honored wife of John; Lucy is the confidential housekeeper, comfortable and happy. Tell John the truth, and punish these vixens!"

"Oh, what shall I do? What can I do?" cried Margaret. "I do not want to be cruel, but they ruined my life. Jane—"

"She is coming to see you; and John also," said Hagar, rapidly. "The two will be here in an hour. Then you can denounce the treachery of Jane, and show John those letters to prove it. Ruin her! She ruined you."

Margaret said nothing. She was a religious woman, and nightly recited the Lord's Prayer; "Forgive us our trespasses, as we forgive them that trespass against us." Now—and in no idle fashion— she was called upon to prove the depth of her belief—the extent of her charity. She was asked to forgive her bitterest enemies those two women who had ruined her life, and who had built up prosperous existences on such ruins. It was hard to say "Go in peace" to these. Hagar was implacable, and urged revenge; but Margaret—weak, sweet soul—leant to the side of charity. Waiting the arrival of her false friend, her lost lover, she prayed for guidance and for strength to sustain her in the coming ordeal. It was the last and most painful phase of her long, long martyrdom.

Mrs. Mask arrived an hour later, as Hagar had announced, but alone. Her husband had been detained by business, she explained to the girl, and would come on later. Like herself, he was anxious to see their dying friend.

"Does he know the truth?" asked Hagar before admitting the visitor.

Jane was now a large and prosperous woman, with an imperious temper, and in an ordinary case would have replied sharply. But the discovery of her treachery, the knowledge that her victim was dying, had broken her down entirely. With a pale face and quivering lips, she shook her head, and signed that she could not bring herself to speak. Hagar stood aside and permitted her to pass

in silence. She would have lashed the perfidious woman with her
tongue, but deemed it more just that the traitress should be punished by the friend she had wronged so bitterly. Mrs. Mask entered the room, and slowly walked over to the bedside. The blind
woman recognized her footstep: yes! recognized it, even after these
many years.

"Jane," said Margaret, reproachfully, "have you come to look
at your work?"

The prosperous lady recoiled as she saw the wreck of the merry,
happy girl she had known thirty years before. Tongue-tied by the
knowledge that Margaret spoke truly, she could only stand like a
culprit beside the bed, and like a culprit await her sentence. Hagar
remained at the door to listen.

"Have you nothing to say?" gasped Margaret, faintly—"you who
lied about me with your accomplice—who made my John believe
me faithless? My John! alas, he has been yours—won by dishonor—
these thirty years!"

"I—I loved him!" stammered the other woman at last, goaded
into defending herself.

"Yes, you loved him and betrayed me. For years I have suffered
hunger and cold; for years I have lived with a broken heart, alone
and miserably!"

"I—I—oh, I am sorry!"

"Sorry! Can your sorrow give me back thirty years of wasted
life—of long-enduring agony? Can sorrow make me what I should
have been—what you are—a happy wife and mother?"

"Margaret," implored Jane, sinking on her knees, "forgive me!
In spite of all my prosperity, I have suffered in secret. My sin has
come home to me many a time, and made me weep. I searched for
you when I returned to England; I could not find you. Now I am
willing to make what expiation you wish."

"Then tell your husband how you tricked him and ruined me."

"No—no! Anything but that, Margaret! For God's sake! I should
die of shame if he knew. He loves me now; we are old; we have
children. Two of my boys are in the army; my daughter is a wife

and mother. What you will, but not that; it would destroy all; it would kill me!"

She bowed her head on the bed-clothes and wept. Margaret reflected. Her revenge was within her grasp. John was coming, and a word from her would make him loathe the woman he had loved and honored these many years—would make him despise the mother of his children. No, she could not be so cruel as to ruin the innocent to punish the guilty. Besides, Jane had loved him, and it was that love which had made her sin. Margaret raised herself feebly, and laid her thin hand on the head of the woman who had martyrized her.

"I forgive you, Jane. Go in peace. John shall never know."

Jane lifted up her face in amazement at this God-like forgiveness. "You will not tell him?" she muttered.

"No. No one shall tell him. Hagar, swear to me that you will keep silent."

"I swear," said Hagar, a little sullenly. "But you are wrong."

"No; I am right. To gain forgiveness we must forgive others. My poor Jane, you were tempted, and you fell. Of Lucy I shall say nothing; God will bring home her sin to her in—Ah! dear Lord! Hagar! I—I—I die!"

Hagar ran to the bedside, and placed her arms round the lean frame of poor Margaret. Her face was gray, her eyes glazed, and her body fell back in the arms of Hagar like a dead thing. She was dying; the end of her martyrdom was at hand.

"Give! give—" she whispered, striving to raise one feeble hand.

"The teapot!" said Hagar. "Quick—give it to her!"

Jane seized the teapot—ignorant that it contained the letters which proved her guilt—and placed it in the hands of the poor soul. She clasped it feebly to her breast, and a smile of delight crept slowly over her gray face.

"John's gift!" she faltered, and—died.

A moment later the door was pushed open, and a portly man with gray hair entered the room. He saw Jane sobbing by the bedside, Hagar kneeling with tears in her eyes, and on the bed the dead body of the woman he had loved.

"I am too late," said he, approaching. "Poor Margaret!"

"She has just died," whispered Hagar. "Take your wife away."

"Come, my dear," said John, raising the repentant woman; "we can do no good. Poor Margaret! to think that she would not marry me! Well, it is best so; God has given me a good and true wife in her place."

"A good and true wife!" muttered Hagar, with irony.

With Jane on his arm, the former lover of Margaret moved towards the door. "I shall of course see to the funeral," he said in a pompous tone. "She shall be buried like a princess."

"Indeed, Mr. Mask!—and she lived like a beggar!"

A faint flush of color crept into the man's cheeks, withered with age. "That was not my fault," he said, haughtily; "had I known of her wants, I would have helped her; though, indeed," he added, bitterly, "she deserves little at the hands of one whom she wronged so deeply. I loved her, and she was faithless."

"Ah!" cried Hagar, and for the moment she felt inclined to tell the truth, but the memory of her promise restrained her; also a glance at the white face of Jane, who thought that her secret was about to be revealed.

"What do you say?" asked John, looking back.

"Nothing. But—the silver teapot?"

"My gift. Let it be buried with her."

He passed through the door without another word, leaving Hagar alone with the dead. Had he known of the contents of the teapot which the dead woman held clasped in her arms, he might not have departed with his wife by his side. But he went out ignorant and happy.

Hagar looked at the retiring forms of the married pair; at the white face of the dead woman at the bare, bleak room and the silver teapot. Then she laughed!

8

The Seventh Customer and the Mandarin

THERE WAS SOMETHING very queer about that lacquer mandarin; and something still queerer about the man who pawned it. The toy itself was simply two balls placed together; the top ball, a small one, was the head, masked with a quaintly-painted face of porcelain, and surmounted by a pagoda-shaped hat jingling with tiny golden bells. The large ball below was the body, gaily tinted to imitate the official dress of a great Chinese lord; and therefrom two little arms terminating in porcelain hands, exquisitely finished even to the long nails, protruded in a most comical fashion. Weighted dexterously within, the mandarin would keel over this side and that, to a perilous angle, but he never went over altogether. When set in motion the big ball would roll, the arms would wag, and the head nod gravely, a little red tongue thrusting itself out at every bow. Then the golden bells would chime melodiously, and rolling, wagging, nodding, the mandarin made all who beheld him laugh, with his innocent antics. He was worthy, in all his painted beauty, to be immortalized by Hans Andersen.

"A very pretty toy?" said Hagar, as the quaint thing tipped itself right and left, front and back. "It comes from China, I suppose?"

She asked this question of the customer, who demanded two pounds on the figure; but in place of answering her, he burst out into a hoarse laugh, and leered unpleasantly at the girl.

"Comes from other side of Nowhere, I reckon, missus!" he said, in a coarse voice; "and a bloomin' rum piece of goods 'tis, anyhow!"

Hagar did not like the man's looks at all, although she was by no means exacting on the score of personal beauty—especially with regard to the male sex. Still, there was something brutal about this fellow which revolted her every sense. He had a bullet-head, with a crop of closely-cut hair; a clean-shaven face of a blue-black dirty hue, where the beard had been removed; a low forehead, a snub nose, a large ugly mouth, and two cunning gray eyes which never looked any one straight in the face. This attractive gentleman wore a corduroy suit, a red linen handkerchief round his throat, and a fur cap with earflaps on his head. Also he carried a small black pipe between his teeth, and breathed therefrom an atmosphere of the vilest tobacco. Certainly the toy was queer; but the man queerer. Not at all the sort of person likely to be in possession of so delicate a work of Chinese art and fancy.

"Where did you get this?" demanded Hagar, drawing her black brows together and touching with one finger the swaying mandarin.

"It's all on the square, missus!" growled the man in an injured tone. "I didn't prig the blessed thing, if that's yer lay. A pal o' mine as is a sailor brought it from Lord-knows-where an' guv it me. I wants rhino, I do; so if you kin spring two quid—"

"I'll give you twenty shillings," said Hagar, cutting him short.

"Oh, my bloomin' eyes! if this ain't robbery an' blue murder!" whined the man; "twenty bob! why, the fun you gits out of it's worth more!"

"That's my offer—take it or leave it. I don't believe you came honestly by it, and I'm running a risk in taking it."

"Sling us the blunt, then!" said the customer, sullenly; "it's the likes of you as grinds down the likes of me! Yah! you an' yer preachin'."

"In whose name am I to make out the ticket?" asked Hagar, coldly.

"In the name of Mister William Smith—Larky Bill they calls me; but 'tain't hetiikit to put h'endearin' family names on pawn-tickets. I lives in Sawder Alley, Whitechapel."

"Why didn't you go to a nearer pawn-shop, then?" said Hagar, taking down Mr. Smith's address, without smiling at his would-be wit.

"That's my biz!" retorted Bill, scowling. "'Ere, gimme the tin; an' don't you arsk no questions an' you won't be tol' no lies! D'ye see?"

Hagar stamped her foot. "Here's the money and the ticket. Take yourself and your insolence out of my shop. Quick!"

"I'm gitting!" growled the man, shuffling towards the door. "See 'ere, missus; I comes fur that doll in three months, or it may be four. If it ain't all right an' 'anded up to me proper, I'll break your neck!"

"What's that you say?"

Hagar was over the counter, and close at hand by this time. Larky Bill stared open-mouthed at her spirit. "You say another word, my jail-bird," said Hagar, seizing his ear, "and I'll put you into the gutter!"

"Lordy! what a donah!" muttered Bill, rubbing his ear when he found himself outside. "She'll look arter the toy proper. Three months. Tck!" he rapped his thumbnail against his teeth. "I can't get less from the beak; but I've bested Monkey anyhow!"

And with these enigmatic words, Mr. Smith turned on his heel and went to Whitechapel. There his forebodings were realized, for at the very door of his own house in Sawder Alley, he was taken in charge by a grim policeman, and sent to prison for four months. He had stolen some fruit off a coster's barrow on the day previous to his arrest, and quite expected to be—as he phrased it—nabbed for the theft. Therefore he employed the small remnant of freedom still remaining to him in pawning the mandarin in the most distant pawn-shop he could think of, which happened to be Hagar's. As Mr. Smith left the court to do his four months, a wizen-faced man slouched close to him.

"Bill," he growled, edging against the policeman, "where's that doll?"

"That's all right, Monkey! I've put it where you won't git it!" grunted Smith.

When Black Maria rolled away with Bill inside, the man he had called Monkey stood on the edge of the pavement and cursed freely till a policeman moved him on. He had a particular desire to gain

possession of that doll, as he called it; and it was on this account
that Larky Bill had taken the trouble to hide it. Monkey never
thought of a pawn-shop. It was a case of diamond cut diamond;
and one rogue had outwitted the other.

In the meantime, Hagar, quite unaware of the value attached
to the Chinese toy, placed it away among other pawned articles
upon a high shelf. But it did not always remain there, for Bolker, a
child in many ways, notwithstanding his precocious intelligence,
found it out, and frequently took it down to play with. Hagar would
not have permitted this had she known, as the toy was given into
her charge to keep safe, and she would have been afraid of Bolker
spoiling the painting or rubbing off the gilding. Bolker knew this,
and was clever enough to play with the mandarin only when Hagar
was absent. He placed it on the counter, and made it sway in its
quaint fashion. The waving arms, the nodding head, and the rose-
leaf of a tongue slipping in and out, enchanted the lad, and he would
amuse himself for hours with it. It was strange that a gilded toy,
no doubt made for the amusement of grave Chinese Emperors,
should descend to afford pleasure to an arab of London City. But
the mandarin was an exile from the Flowery Land, and rocked as
merrily in the dingy pawn-shop as ever he had done in the porcelain palaces of Pekin.

A month or two after the mandarin had been pawned, Bolker
announced in the most unexpected manner that he intended to
better himself. He had been given, he said, the post of shop-boy in
a West-end bookseller's establishment; and as he was fond of lit-
erature, he intended to accept it. Hagar rather wondered that any
one should have placed sufficient confidence in this arab to give
him a situation; but she kept her wonderment to herself, and permitted him to go. She was sorry to lose the benefit of his acute
intelligence, but personally she had no great love for this scamp-
ish hunchback; so she saw him depart without displaying much
sorrow. Thus Bolker vanished from the pawn-shop and from
Carby's Crescent, and ascended into higher spheres.

Nothing new happened after his departure. The mandarin remained untouched on the shelf, and the dust collected over his

motionless figure. Hagar quite forgot about the toy and its pawner; and it was only when Larky Bill was released from prison and came to claim his property that she recalled the incident. She took down the figure, dusted it carefully, and set it swaying on the counter before Mr. Smith. Neither Bill nor Hagar noticed that it did not roll as easily and gracefully as usual.

"Here's the quid and interest and ticket," said Bill, tendering all three. "I'm glad to get this 'ere back again. No one's touched it, 'ave they?"

"No. It has been on that shelf ever since you pawned it. Where have you been?"

Larky Bill grinned. "I've been stayin' at a country 'ouse of mine fur my 'ealth's sake," he said, tucking the mandarin under his arm. "Say, missus, a cove called Monkey didn't come smellin' round 'ere fur this h'image?"

"Not that I know of. Nobody asked for the toy."

"Guess it's all right," chuckled Bill, gleefully. "Lord, to think as how I've done that bloke! Won't he cuss when he knows as I've got 'em!"

What "them" were Mr. Smith did not condescend to explain at that particular moment. He nodded familiarly to Hagar, and went off, still chuckling with the mandarin in charge. Hagar put away the money, and thought that she had seen the last of Bill; but she reckoned wrongly. Two hours afterwards he was back in the shop, mandarin and all, with a pale face, a wild eye, and a mouth full of abuse. At first he swore at large without giving any explanation; so Hagar waited till the bad language was ended, and then asked him quietly what was the matter. For answer Bill plumped down the Chinese toy on the counter, and clutched his fur cap with both hands.

"Matter, cuss you!" he shrieked, furiously—"as if ye didn't know! I've been robbed!"

"Robbed! What nonsense are you talking? And what have I to do with your being robbed?"

Bill gasped, and pointed to the mandarin, who was rolling complacently, with a fat smile on his porcelain visage. "That—that doll!" he spluttered. "I've been robbed!"

"Of the doll?" asked Hagar, impatiently.

"Y' young Jezebel! Of the dimins—dimins!"

"Diamonds!" echoed the girl, starting back in astonishment.

"Yes! Y' know, hang you, y' know! Twenty thousan' pount of dimins! They was in that doll—inside 'im. They ain't there now! Why not? 'Cause you've robbed me! Thief! Yah!"

"I did not know that there were any jewels concealed in the mandarin," said Hagar, calmly. "Had I known I should have informed the police."

"Blown the gaff, would ye? An' why?"

"Because a man in your position does not possess diamonds, unless he steals them. And now I think of it," added Hagar, quickly, "about the time you pawned this toy Lady Deacey's jewels were stolen. You stole them!"

"P'raps I did, p'raps I didn't!" growled Bill, mentally cursing Hagar for the acuteness of her understanding. "'Tany rate, 'twarn't your biz to prig 'em!"

"I tell you I never touched them! I did not know they were in there!"

"Then who did, cuss you? When I guv you the doll, the dimins were inside; now they ain't. Who took 'em?"

Hagar pondered. It was certainly odd that the diamonds should have been stolen. She had placed the mandarin on the shelf on the day of its pawning, and had not removed it again until she had returned it to its owner. Seeing her silent, Bill turned the toy upside down, and removed a square morsel of the lacquer, which fitted in so perfectly as to seem like one whole piece. Within was the dark hollow of the ball—empty.

"I put them dimins into 'ere with my own 'and," persisted Bill, pointing one grimy finger at the gap; "they were 'ere when I popped it; they ain't 'ere now. Where are they? Who's bin playing with my property?"

"Bolker!" cried Hagar, without thinking. It had just flashed across her mind that one day she had found Bolker amusing himself with the mandarin. At the time she had thought nothing of it, but had replaced the toy on its shelf, and forbidden the lad to meddle with it. But now, recalling the episode, and connecting it with Bolker's sudden departure, she felt convinced that the imp had stolen the concealed jewels. But—as she wondered—how had he become cognizant that twenty thousands pounds' worth of diamonds was hidden in the hollow body of the doll? The thing puzzled her.

"Bolker?" echoed Larky Bill, wrathfully. "And who may that cuss be?"

"He was my shop-boy; but he left three months ago to better himself."

"I dessay! With my dimins, I'll bet. Where is he, that I may cut his bloomin' throat!"

"I shan't tell you," said Hagar, alarmed by the brutal threat of the man, and already regretting that she had been so candid.

"I'll make you! I'll twist your neck!" raged Bill, mad with anger.

He placed his great hands on the counter to vault over; but the next moment he dropped back before the shining tube of a neat little revolver, which leveled itself in Hagar's hands. She had lately purchased it for defense.

"I keep this always by me," said she, calmly, "to protect myself against such rogues as you!"

Bill stared at her blankly, then turned on his heel and left the shop. At the door he paused and shook his fist.

"I'll find that Bolker, and smash the life out of him!" he said, hoarsely; "then, my fine madam, I'll come back to lay you out!" after which he vanished, leaving the mandarin, with its eternal smile, still rocking on the counter.

Hagar put away the pistol, and took up the figure. Now that she knew about the diamonds, and had forced Bill to admit, as he had done indirectly, that they had been stolen from Lady Deacey, she thought it possible that the Chinese toy might belong to the same owner. In spite of her fearlessness, Hagar was not altogether happy in her mind as regards the burglar. If he did not find the diamonds, he was quite capable of returning to murder her. On the whole, Hagar concluded that it would be just as well for society at large, and herself in particular, if Mr. Smith were restored to the prison whence he had lately emerged. After some consideration she resolved to see Vark, the lawyer, and tell him the episode of the mandarin, taking the image with her as evidence. Vark, if anyone, would be able to deal with the intricacies of the affair.

In the meantime, Bill Smith had repaired to the public-house which guarded the narrow entrance to Carby's Crescent, and there was drowning his regrets in strong drink. As he drained his tankard of ale, he fell into conversation with the fat landlord—a brutal-looking prize-fighter, who looked as though he had been in jail—quite a bird of Mr. Smith's feather. These two congenial spirits recognized each other, and became friendly—so friendly, indeed, that Bill thought it a good opportunity to extract information regarding the whereabouts of Bolker. He was too wise to explain his reason for making these inquiries.

"That's a fine gal in the pawn-shop, hay!" said he, with a leer.

"Wot—'Agar? She's a plum, ain't she?—but not for every man's pickin'; oh, no; not she! 'Agar kin look arter herself proper!" said the landlord.

"Does she mind that shorp all alone?"

"Jus' now she does," replied mine host. "She 'ad a boy, a wicked little 'unchback devil; Bolker's 'is name. But he's hoff; gitting a wage in West-end, as I do 'ear."

"Wes'-end?" said Bill, reflectively. "An' where might 'e 'ang out there?"

"Ho, in a swell, slap-up book-shop. Juppins, Son an' Juppins, Les'er Square way. 'Is parients live down 'ere, but Bolker's that set up with 'is good luck as 'e looks down on 'em."

"Do he now!" said Bill, amiably. "I'd twist 'is neck if he wos my kid. No more booze, thankee. I'm orf t' see a pal o' mine."

The result of this conversation was that Mr. Smith repaired to Leicester Square and loafed up and down the pavement before the book-shop. He saw Bolker several times during the day; for, having been told by the landlord that the lad was a hunchback, he had no difficulty recognizing him. Up till the evening he kept a close watch, and when Bolker had put up the shutters and was walking home towards Lambeth, Bill followed him stealthily. All unknowing that he was followed by a black shadow of crime and danger,

Bolker paused on Westminster Bridge to admire the red glories of the sunset; then plunged into the network of alleys which make up Lambeth. In a quiet lane by the river he was gripped from behind; a large hand was clapped over his mouth to prevent his crying out, and he was dragged down on to a ruined wharf which ran out through green slime into the turbid waters of the stream.

"Now, then, I've got ye!" said his captor in a savage tone—"an' I've got a knife too, y' bloomin' thief! Jes' y' answer me strife, or I'll cut yer 'ead orf!"

Bolker gasped with alarm; but, not recognizing the threatening face of the man before him, he recovered a little of his native impudence, and began to bluster.

"Here, now, what do you mean by this? What have I done?"

"Done, y' whelp! Opened that doll an' prigged them dimins!"

"Larky Bill!" cried Bolker, at once recognizing his peril. "Here, let me go!"

"Not till y' give up my property—my dimins."

"What property? What diamonds?"

"Oh, y' know what 'm drivin' at, cuss you! Y're the 'unchback as wos in the shorp kep' by that foine gal 'Agar. I popped that doll, with dimins in 'is innards, an' you stole 'm."

"I did nothing of the sort. I—"

"'Ere! drop yer lies, y' imp! Y' know moy naime, y' did, so y' knows more! Jes' look et this knoif! S'elp me but I'll slip it int' ye, ef y' don't tell!"

He threw the terrified boy across his knee, and placed the cold steel at his throat. The rose-red sky spun overhead in the eyes of Bolker, and he thought that his last hour had come. To save himself there was nothing for it but confession.

"What! wait! I'll tell you!" he gasped. "I did take the diamonds."

"Y' young cuss!" growled Bill, setting the lad on his feet again with a jerk. "An' 'ow did y' know they was inside that himage?"

"Monkey told me."

Bill started to his feet with an oath, but still kept his grip on Bolker's shoulder to prevent him getting away. "Monkey," he said, fiercely. "Wot did 'e tell y'?"

"Why, that Lady Deacey's diamonds were inside the mandarin."

"How did Monkey come to find that doll?"

"He got the office from a girl called Eliza, who saw you pawning the toy."

"Liz sold me," muttered Bill. "I thought as I sawr'er on that doy. She' mus' ha' twigged that doll under m' arm, and guessed as I popped it. Gord! I'll deal with 'er laiter, I will! Garn, y' doryg and tell me th' rest!" he added, shaking the boy.

"There is no more to tell," whimpered Bolker, his teeth chattering. "Monkey couldn't get the mandarin, 'cause he had not the ticket. He made friends with me, and asked me to steal it. I wouldn't, until he told me why he wanted it. Then he said that you had stolen twenty thousand pounds' worth of diamonds from Lady Deacey's house in Curzon Street, and had hidden them in the mandarin. He said we'd go whacks if I'd steal them for him. I couldn't get the mandarin, as Hagar's so sharp she would have missed it, and put me in jail for stealing it; so I opened the doll, and took out the diamonds which were in a leather bag."

"Moy bag, moy dimins!" said Bill, savagely. "What did y' do with 'em?"

"I gave them to Monkey, and he cleared out with them. He never gave me a single one; and I don't know where to find him."

"I does," growled Mr. Smith, releasing Bolker, "an' I'll fin' 'im and slit his bloomin' throat. 'Ere! I say, y' come back!" for, taking advantage of his release, Bolker was racing up the wharf.

Bill gave chase, as he wanted to obtain further information from the lad; but Bolker knew the neighborhood better than the burglar, and soon eluded him in the winding alleys.

"It don't matter!" said Bill, giving up the chase and wiping his brow. "Monkey's got the swag. Might ha' guessed as he'd round on me. I'll jest see 'im and Liz, and if I don't make 'm paiy fur this, maiy I—!" Then he clinched his resolve with an oath, which it is unnecessary to repeat here. After relieving his feelings thus, he went in search of his perfidious friend, with murderous thoughts in his heart.

At first he thought that it would be difficult to find Monkey. No doubt the man on obtaining the diamonds had gone off to America, North or South, so as to escape the vengeance of his pal—Bill had always been Monkey's pal—and to live comfortably on the fruits of his villainy. Later on the burglar learnt, rather to his surprise, that Monkey was still in London, and still was haunting the thieves' quarter in Whitechapel. Bill wondered at this choice of a residence when the man had so much money in his possession; but he ascribed this longing to Monkey's love for his old haunts and associates. Nevertheless, knowing that Bill was out of prison, it was strange that the man did not look after his skin.

"'E knows wot I am when I'm riz!" said Bill to himself, as he continued his search, "so he ought to get orf while 'is throat ain't cut! Blimme; but I'll 'ave a drop of 'is 'eart's blood fur every one of them bloomin' dimins!"

One evening he found Monkey in the parlor of a low public-house called the Three Kings, and kept by a Jew of ill-fame, who was rather a fence than a landlord.

His traitorous friend, more wizened and shriveled up than ever, was seated in a dark corner, with an unlighted pipe in his mouth, a half-drained tankard of bitter before him, and his hands thrust moodily into his pockets. If Monkey had the diamonds, his appearance belied their possession, for he looked anything but prosperous. There was no appearance of wealth in his looks or manner or choice of abode.

"Wot, Bill, ole pal!" he said, looking up when Mr. Smith hurled himself into the room. "Y've got h'out of quod!"

"Yus! I've got trout to slit yer throat!"

"Lor!" whined Monkey, uncomfortably. "Wot's you accusin' me fur? I ain't done nuffin', s'elp me!"

Bill drew a chair before that of Monkey, and taking out his knife played with it in a significant manner. Monkey shrank back before the glitter of the blade and the ugly look in his pal's eyes, but he did not dare to cry out for assistance, lest the burglar should pounce on him.

"Now, look 'ee 'ere, Monkey," said Bill, with grim deliberation, "I don't want none of yer bloomin' lip, ner his eiather! D' y' see? I've seen that beast of a kid as you put up to steal my dimins, and—"

"Yah! that kid!" cried Monkey, with sudden ferocity. "Wish I'd 'im 'ere; I'd squeeze the 'eart out o' him!"

"Wot fur? Didn't 'e git y' the swag—moy swag—cuss y'?"

"No, 'e didn't; an' ef 'e ses 'e did, 'e's a liar—a bloomin' busted liar, s'elp me! I tell you, Bill, 'e kep' them shiners to 'imself, cuss 'im!"

"Thet's a d—d lie, y' sneakin' dorg!" said Bill, politely.

"M' I die if 'tain't gorspel truth!" yelped Monkey. "Look 'ee 'ere, ole pal—"

"Don't y' call me pal!" interrupted Bill, savagely. "I ain't no pal of yourn, y' terbaccer-faiced son of a bloomin' 'angman! Liz blew the gaff on me poppin' that himage, and y' tried to git m' swag when I was doin' time. An' y' did get it, y'—!"

"I didn't!" snapped Monkey, interrupting in his turn. "The kid stuck to the swag, I tell y'. 'Course I knowed of them dimins!"

"'Course y' did!" growled William, ironically. "Didn't I tell y' 'ow I cracked that crib in Curzon Street, an' prigged th' dimins an' th' himage? Yah! y' cuss!"

"I knows y' did, Bill. An' you tole me 'ow y' stowed the swag inside the doll. My heye! that was sharp of y'; but y' moight 'ev trusted a pal! I didn't know y' popped the doll till Liz told me. She sawr y' goin' in t' that popshorp with the Chiner thing under yer arm; an'—"

"And you'd set 'er arter me!" cried Bill! savagely. "She didn't git int' Lambeth on the chance!"

"Yus," said Monkey, doggedly, "I did put 'er on yer trail. Y' hid the dimins in that image, and cleared out with it. I couldn't foller meself, so I set Liz ont' ye. She tole me as 'ow y'd popped th' thing; so when y' wos doin' time I tried to git it again, tho' that young cuss 'es sold me."

"Blimme! but I've a moind to slit yer throat!" said Bill, furiously. "Wot d' y' mean tryin' to coller my swag?"

"Why, fur yer own sake, Bill, s'elp me. I thort the gal might fin' out. But y' needn't git up, Bill; I didn't git them dimins. The boy hes them."

"That's a lie. I tell y'!"

"'Tain't! When I tole the kid about the dimins he stole 'em sure, an' lef' th' doll so es the pawn-shop gal wouldn't fin' out. But I never saw 'im agin, though I watched the shorp like a bloomin' tyke. The boy cleared out with them dimins. I wish I'd 'im 'ere! I'd choke the little devil!"

Bill reflected, and slipped the knife into his pocket. Without doubt Monkey was speaking the truth; he was too savagely in earnest to be telling a falsehood. Moreover, if he really possessed the diamonds, he would not remain hard up and miserable in the thieves' quarter of dingy Whitechapel. No; Bolker had kept the jewels, and had deceived Monkey; more than that, in the interview on the ruined wharf he had deceived Bill himself. Priding himself on his astuteness, Mr. Smith felt savage at having been sold by a mere boy.

"If I kin on'y git 'im agin!" he thought, when leaving the Three Kings, "I'll take the 'ead orf 'm, and chuck 'is crooked karkuss int' the river mud!"

But he found it difficult to lay hands on Bolker, although for more than a week he haunted the shop in Leicester Square. Warned by his one experience that Bill was a dangerous person to meddle with, Bolker had given notice to his employers, and at present was in hiding. Also, he was arranging a little scheme whereby to rid himself of Larky Bill's inopportunities. Vark was the man who undertook to carry out the details of the scheme; and Hagar was consulted also with regard to its completion. These three people, Vark, Hagar, and Bolker, laid an ingenious trap for unsuspecting Bill, into which he walked without a thought of danger. He had been betrayed by Monkey, by Bolker, by Liz; now he was going to be sold by Vark, the lawyer. Truly, the fates were against Bill at this juncture.

Vark was a thieves' lawyer, and had something in him of a latter-day Fagin; for he not only made use of criminals when he could do so with safety, but also he sold them to justice when they became dangerous. As he saw a chance of making money out of Bill Smith, he resolved to do so, and sent for the man to visit him at once. As Vark had often done business with the burglar, Bill had no idea that it was in the lawyer's mind to betray him, and duly presented himself at the spider's office in Lambeth, like a silly fly. The first thing he saw on entering the room was the mandarin swaying on the table.

"You are astonished to see that," said Vark, noticing his surprise. "I daresay; but you see, Bill, I know all about your theft of the Deacey diamonds."

"Who tole you?" growled Bill, throwing himself into a chair.

"Hagar of the Pawn-shop," replied Vark, slowly and with significance.

Bill's eyes lighted up fiercely, in precisely the way Vark wished. The lawyer had not forgiven Hagar for refusing to marry him, and for curtailing his pickings in the Dix estate. For these reasons he wished her evil; and if he could inoculate the burglar's heart with a spite towards her he was bent on doing so. It appeared from Bill's next speech that he had succeeded.

"Oh, 'twas that gal, wos it?" said Mr. Smith, quietly. "I might ha' guessed it, by seein' that himage. Well, I owe 'er one, I do, and I guess I'll owe 'er another. But that's my biz; 'tain't yourn. Wot d'ye want, y' measly dorg?" he added, looking at the lean form of Vark in a surly manner.

"I want to see you about the Deacey diamonds. Why did you not bring them to me when you stole them?"

"Whoy? 'Cause I didn't b'lieve in ye!" retorted Bill. "I know'd I wos in fur toime when I prigged them apples, an' I wasn't going to trust my swag to y' or Monkey. Y'd ha' sold me."

"Well, Monkey did sell you."

"Yah! 'e didn't get much on th' deal!"

"No; but Bolker did."

"Bolker!" echoed Bill, grinding his teeth: "d' y' know that crooked cuss? Y' do! Well, see 'ere!"—Bill drew his clasp-knife out of his pocket and opened it—"I'm goin' to slip that int' 'im fust toime as I claps eyes on 'is ugly mug!"

"You'd better not, unless you want to be hanged."

"Wot d' I care?" growled Bill, sulkily; "scragged, or time with skilly an' hoakum. It's all th' saime t' me."

"I suppose you wonder where the diamonds are?"

"Yus. I want 'em!"

"That's a pity," said Vark, with irony—"because I am afraid you won't get them."

"Where is them dimins?" asked Bill, laying his open knife on the table.

Vark passed over the question. "I suppose you know that the police are after you for the Deacey robbery?" he said, slipping his hand idly across the table till it was within reach of the knife. "Oh, yes; Lord Deacey offered a reward for the recovery of the jewels. That has been paid, but as you are still at large, the police want you, my friend!"

"Oh, I ain't afraid of y' givin' me up; I'm too useful t'y', I am, and I knows too much about y'. The pealers shawn't put me in quod this toime. Who got the reward?" he asked suddenly.

"Bolker got it."

"D—n him! Bolker!"

"Yes. Monkey made a mistake when he trusted the lad. Bolker thought that he would make more out of honesty than by going shares with Monkey. When he found the jewels, he went off with them to Scotland Yard. Lady Deacey has them now, and Bolkers," added Vark, smiling, "has money in the bank."

"Cuss 'im; whoy didn't I cut 'is bloomin' throat down by the river?"

"That is best known to yourself," replied Vark, who was now playing with the knife. "You are in a tight place, my friend, and may get some years for this robbery."

"Yah! No one knows I did it!"

"There is the evidence against you," said Vark, pointing to the mandarin. "You stole that out of Lord Deacey's drawing-room along with the diamonds. You pawned it, and Hagar can swear that you did so. Bolker can swear that the stolen diamonds were inside. With these two witnesses, my poor Bill, I'm afraid you'd get six years or more!"

"Not me!" said Bill, rising. "Y' won't give me up; and I ain't feared of any one else."

"Why not? There is a reward offered for your apprehension."

"What d' I care? Who'll git it?"

"I will!" replied Vark, coolly, rising.

"You?" Bill recoiled for a moment, and sprang forward. "Cuss you! Y'd sell me, y' shark! Gimme my knife!"

"Not such a fool, Mr. Smith!"

Vark threw the knife into a distant corner of the room, and leveled a revolver at the bullet head of the advancing burglar. Bill fell back for the moment—fell into the arms of two policemen.

He gave a roar like a wild beast.

"Trapped, by—!" he yelled, and struggled to get free.

The next moment Hagar and Bolker were in the room, and Bill glared at one and the other.

"Y' trapped me, d—n y'!" said he; "wait till I git out!"

"You'll kill me, I suppose?" said Hagar, scornfully.

"No; shawn't kill you, nor yet that little devil with th' 'unch. There's on'y one cove as I'd swing for—that beastly thief of a lawyer!"

Vark recoiled before the glare in the man's eyes; and as Bill, foaming and cursing, was hurried out of the room, he looked at Hagar with a nervous smile.

"That's bluff," he said, feebly.

"I don't think so," replied Hagar, quietly. "Good-by, Mr. Vark. I'm afraid you won't live more than seven years; there will be a funeral about the time of Larkey Bill's release."

When she went out, Bolker grinned at the lawyer and, with frightful pantomime, he drew a stroke across his neck. Vark looked at the clasp knife in the corner and shivered. The mandarin on the table rolled and smiled always.

9

The Eighth Customer and the Pair of Boots

HE WAS A VERY little lad, reaching scarcely to the top of the counter; but he had a sharp, keen face, intelligent beyond his years with the precocity taught by poverty. Hagar, looking at his shock of red hair, and the shrewd blue eyes which peered up at her face, guessed that he was Irish; and when he spoke, his brogue proved her guess to be a correct one. She stared at the ragged, bare-footed urchin with some amusement, for this was the smallest customer she had yet had. But Micky—so he gave his name—was quite as sharp as customers of more mature years—in fact, sharper. He bargained astutely with Hagar, and evidently had made up his small mind not to leave the shop until he obtained his own price for the article he was pawning. This was a pair of strong laborer's boots, hob-nailed and stout in the soles. The red-haired boy heaved them on to the counter with a mighty clatter, and demanded seven shillings thereon.

"I'll give you five," said Hagar, after examination.

"Ah, now, would ye?" piped the brat, with shrill impudence. "Is it taking the bread out av me mouth ye w'uld be afther? Sure, me mother sid sivin bob, an' 'tis sivin I want."

"Where is your mother, boy? Why did she not come herself?"

"Mother's comforting herself wid the drink round the carner; an' sure I'm aqual to gittin' th' dirthy money meself! Sivin bob, alannah, ant may the hivins be yer bed!"

"Where did you get these boots?" said Hagar, asking another question, and ignoring the persuasive tone of the lad. "I see there are letters marked in nails on the two soles."

"Ah! there moight be," assented Micky, complacently; "there's a 'G' on one foot, an' a 'K' on the other; but me fawther's name is Patrick Dooley, an' he's in Amerikey, worse luck. Mother got thim boots foive days gone in the counthry. They wos a prisint, me darlin'; an' as they wos too big fur me an' me mother, we pop them, dear, fur sivin bob."

"Take six," said Hagar, persuasively; "they aren't worth more."

"Howly saints! listen to the lies av her!" shrieked Micky. "Six, is it? An' how can I go to me mother wid a shillin' wrong? Sure, it's breakin' me hid she'd be afther, wid a quart pot! An' what's money to the loikes av you, me dear?"

"Here—here! take the seven shillings!" said Hagar, anxious to rid herself of this shrieking imp. "I'll make out the ticket in the name of Mrs. Dooley."

"Mrs. Bridget Dooley, av Park Lane," said Micky, grandly. "Sure that will do as well as any other place. It's on the tramp we are— bad luck to it! If 'twasn't for thim boots we got in Marlow, it's without a copper we'd be."

"Here! take the ticket and money. I daresay you stole the boots."

"Is it takin' away me characther y'd be afther? Stalin'? Wasn't thim boots a prisint to me, for pure charity an' love av the saints? Ah, well, I'm goin'—I'm goin'! Sivin bob; it's little enough onyhow; but phwat's the use of lookin' for justice to Oireland in the counthry av the Saxon toyrant?" and Micky went out, singing "The Wearing of the Green" in a very shrill and unpleasant voice.

Hagar put the boots away, never expecting that a story could be attached to so ordinary a pawned article. But two days afterwards she was reading an account of a murder, and, to her surprise, the very boots, now reposing on a high shelf in her shop, were mentioned as a link in the chain of evidence likely to hang the assassin. Coincidences occur in real life oftener than the world cares to admit; and this was a case in point. A pair of boots with initials on the soles had been pawned in her shop; and now— scarcely forty-eight hours afterwards—she was reading about them in a newspaper. It was strange—almost incredible; but, to quote a trite and well-worn saying, "Truth is stranger than fiction." Briefly, the history of the crime was as follows:

Sir Leslie Crane, of Welby Park, Marlow, had been shot by his gamekeeper, George Kerris. It seemed that the man was engaged to marry a farmer's daughter, Laura Brenton by name; and Sir Leslie had been paying the girl more attention than was consistent with their respective positions. Kerris had remonstrated with the baronet, who had forthwith discharged him. A week later, Crane, having gone out after dinner for a stroll in the park, had been found dead by a pond known as the Queen's Pool, which was some little distance from the gates. Footmarks had been discovered in the soft mud near the water, which showed that the assassin had worn boots marked on the soles with the letters "G" and "K." These had been traced, through a Marlow bootmaker, to George Kerris. The man had been arrested, but neither denied his guilt nor affirmed his innocence. Still, as the report said, there could be no doubt that he had killed Sir Leslie in a fit of jealous rage, and also because he had been discharged. The boots could not be found, so undoubtedly the man had got rid of them after wearing them on the night of the murder. The report in the paper concluded by stating that the dead baronet was succeeded by his cousin, now Sir Lewis Crane.

"Strange that the boots should have been pawned in London," thought Hagar, when she finished reading this article, "and stranger still that they should have been pawned by that Irish lad! On the day he came here, he said the boots had been given to him five days previously. It is two days since then, so that in all makes seven days. H'm! To-day is the twenty-first of August, so I suppose Kerris must have given the boots to Micky on the fourteenth. Let me see the date of the crime."

On examination she found that the murder had been committed on the night of the twelfth of August, and that Kerris had been arrested on the thirteenth. Here Hagar came to a full stop and reflected. If Kerris had been in jail on the fourteenth—as from the report in the paper he undoubtedly was—he could not have given the boots to Micky on that day. Yet the Irish lad had confessed to

receiving the boots at Marlow, and had given a time which, as reckoned out by Hagar, corresponded with the fourteenth of the month.
But on that day the man who owned the boots was under lock and key.

"There's something wrong here," said Hagar to herself, on making this discovery. "Perhaps Kerris is innocent in spite of the evidence of the boots. What am I to do?"

It was difficult to say. Certainly the accused man did not assert
his innocence—a fact which was rather astonishing on the face of
it. No one would let themselves be hanged for a murder which they
did not commit. Yet, if Kerris were guilty, he must have had an
accomplice, else how could the boots have been given to the Irish
tramp when their owner was in prison? The man, thought Hagar,
might be innocent after all, in spite of his strange silence. Still,
not knowing all the circumstances of the case—save the garbled
and bare report in the newspaper—the girl did not, and could not,
make up her mind in the matter. At the present moment, her sole
course was to write and state that the boots had been pawned. This
Hagar did at once, and the next day received a visit from the detective who had charge of the case.

He was called Julf, a lean, tall, dark and solemn creature, who went
very cautiously to work—especially in cases of murder. He had a conscience, he said, and would never forgive himself did he hang the
wrong criminal. Julf knew how often circumstantial evidence
helped to condemn the innocent; how likely even the most acute
detective was to be deceived by outward appearances; and how intri-
cate and dark were the paths which led to the discoveries of mysterious crimes. Hence he was slow and circumspect in his dealings.

On arriving at the Lambeth pawn-shop he examined the boots,
asked Hagar a few questions, and then sat down with her to thresh
out the matter. Julf saw that the girl was shrewd and clever from
the remarks she had made anent the pawning of the boots; so he
was quite willing to discuss the affair freely with her. In contrast
to many self-sufficient detectives, Julf always believed that two
heads were better than one, especially when the second head was
that of a woman. He had a great respect for the instinct of the
weaker sex.

"I'm afraid the man's guilty, right enough," he said, in his solemn way. "He had quarreled with Sir Leslie over this girl, and had been dismissed for insolence. Besides, he was seen coming out of the park at ten o'clock—just after the murder!"

"Had he his gun with him?"

"No; but that's no matter. Sir Leslie was shot through the heart with a pistol. Now, Kerris had a pistol, but that can't be found either. You didn't have a pistol pawned here, did you?"

"Nothing was pawned but the boots," said Hagar, "and Kerris could not have given them to Micky; it seems that he was in prison on the day the lad got them."

"That is true enough. We must find this boy, and learn who gave him the boots on that day. But if Kerris is innocent, why doesn't he say so?"

"It is a mystery," sighed Hagar. "You say that Kerris's pistol cannot be found?"

"No, not in his house; so I daresay he flung it away after killing Sir Leslie."

"Oh, ho!" said Hagar, shrewdly, "then the weapon with which the murder was committed can't be found either."

"But the pistol is the same; Kerris used it, and then got rid of it."

"Why don't you search for it?"

"We have searched everywhere, but it cannot be found."

"Have you drained the pond near which the crime was committed?"

"Why, no," said Julf, meditatively; "we haven't done that. It's a good idea!"

Hagar sighed impatiently. "I wish I had this case in my own hands!" she said, sharply; "I believe I'd find the assassin."

"We have found him," replied the detective, stolidly. "Kerris killed Sir Leslie."

"I don't believe it!"

"Then why doesn't he deny it?"

"I can't say. Is Kerris much in love with this Laura Brenton?" asked Hagar, turning her large bright eyes on Julf.

"I should think so! He's madly in love with her."

"And she with him?"

"Oh, I don't say that," replied Julf; "that is quite another thing. I fancy from what I have heard that she gave far too much encouragement to that young baronet. Kerris evidently had cause for jealousy; so I do not wonder he killed Sir Leslie."

"You have yet to prove that he did."

"Bah!" said Julf, rising to take his leave. "He quarreled with the baronet: he was discharged. His own pistol is missing, and the dead man was shot with a pistol. Then there is the evidence of the boots with his initials on the soles. You can't get over that. Don't you talk nonsense, my girl; there is a strong case against Kerris."

"I can see that; but there is one point in his favor. He did not give those boots to Micky."

"Evidently not. But to prove that point we must find the lad."

This was easier said than done, for Micky and his mother had disappeared as completely as though the earth had swallowed them up. All the police and detective forces in London tried to find the boy, but could not. Yet on his evidence turned the whole case. And all this time George Kerris, in the Marlow prison, refused to open his mouth. Most people believed him to be guilty on the evidence of the boots; but Hagar, on the evidence of the pawning, insisted that he was innocent. Still, she could not understand why he held his tongue at such a crisis.

It has been stated several times that Hagar found her life in the pawn-shop extremely dull, and seized every opportunity to gain for herself a little diversion. A chance of amusement in unraveling the mystery of the boots offered itself now; and this she resolved to take. Also, the conduct of the case would necessitate a visit into the country; and, weary of the narrow streets of Lambeth, Hagar eagerly desired a breath of fresh air. She left the shop in charge of an elderly man, who had been her assistant since Bolker's departure, and took the train to Marlow. When she arrived there, Julf, more solemn than ever, met her at the railway station.

"Good-day," said he, quietly. "You see I have agreed to let you assist me in finding out the truth of this case; though to my mind the truth is already plain enough."

"I don't believe it, Mr. Julf. Take my word for it, George Kerris is innocent of the crime."

"Is he?" said Julf, in sceptical tones; "then who is guilty?"

"That is what I have come to find out," retorted Hagar. "I am obliged to you for letting me help you, though, to be sure, I do so only to gratify my own curiosity. But you won't repent of your concession. I am to have a free hand?"

"You can do exactly as you like."

"Can I? Then I shall first call and see the new baronet."

Refusing the offer of Julf to accompany her, on the plea that she could execute her business better alone, Hagar walked to Welby Park, which was on the other side of Marlow, and asked to see Sir Lewis Crane. At first, owing to her gipsy-like appearance, she was refused admittance; but on mentioning that her business had to do with the murder of the late baronet, Sir Lewis consented to see her. When face to face with him, Hagar, for reasons of her own, examined him closely.

He was an ugly, elderly little creature, many years older than his dead cousin, and had a mean yellow face, stamped with an expression of avarice. Hagar had seen just such another pinched, cunning look on the face of Jacob Dix, and she knew without much trouble that the man before her was a miser. However, she wasted no time in analyzing his character—knowing that it would reveal itself in the forthcoming conversation—but at once mentioned her business.

"I am come on the part of Mr. Julf to see about this murder," she said, curtly.

Sir Lewis raised his eyes. "I did not know that the Government employed lady detectives!" was his remark.

"I am not a detective, but the owner of the shop in which the boots of George Kerris were pawned."

"The boots which prove his guilt," said Crane, with an air of relief, which did not escape Hagar.

"I rather think that they prove his innocence!" was her cold reply.

"Oh! you are talking about them having been given to that tramp when Kerris was in prison. I know all about that, as the detective told it to me. But, all the same, Kerris is guilty, else he would deny his guilt."

"Have you any idea why he does not do so?"

Crane shrugged his shoulders. "No; unless it is that he knows himself to be guilty."

"I believe him to be innocent."

"Pshaw! My cousin admired Laura Brenton, who was engaged to Kerris, and was foolishly attentive to her. On that score the man was insolent; so Leslie discharged him. In committing the murder, he took a double revenge."

"Where were you, Sir Lewis, when your cousin was killed?"

"In the park," replied the baronet, frankly, "After dinner my cousin and I went out for a stroll. In a short time he made some excuse to leave me, as I believe he wished to meet Laura by the Queen's Pool. I walked in the opposite direction, and shortly afterwards I came back to the house. Leslie had not returned, so I went to look for him, and found his dead body by the Pool."

"Did you hear the pistol shot?"

"Yes; but I paid no attention to it. My cousin was in the habit of firing at a target, and I thought he might be doing so then."

"What! firing at a target in the twilight! Could your cousin see in the dark like a cat?" said Hagar, with irony.

"I don't know anything about that!" retorted Crane, snappishly. "I have told you the story, as you represent the detective Julf. I say no more!"

"I don't want you to say more. May I go and look at the pond?"

"Certainly. One of the servants shall show it to you."

"Can't you come yourself?" said Hagar, with a keen glance.

Crane drew back, and his yellow face grew pale. "No," said he, in an almost inaudible voice. "I have seen enough of that horrible place!"

"Very good; I'll go with the servant," replied Hagar, and marched towards the door.

"What do you want to see the pool for?" he asked, following.

"I wish to find the lost pistol."

When Hagar had taken her departure, Sir Lewis, pale and nervous, stood near the open window. "Confound this woman!" he thought, clenching his hand. "She is far too clever; but I don't think she'll be quite clever enough to find that pistol," he added, in a satisfied tone.

The Queen's Pool was a circular sheet of water filled with lilies, at the lower end of the park. On the way thereto Hagar asked the servant who was guiding her a few questions.

"Was Sir Lewis poor before he got the estate?" she demanded.

"Very poor, miss; hadn't a sixpence but what he got from Sir Leslie."

"Was he on good terms with his cousin?"

"No, miss; they was quarreling fearful. On the night of the murder they had a row royal!"

"What about?" asked Hagar, turning a keen look on the man.

"About money and that gal Laura. Sir Lewis loved her just as much as Sir Leslie; but she didn't care a straw for either of them, being taken up with Kerris."

"How does she take her lover's arrest?"

"Why, miss, she cries, and cries, and swears that he is innocent, and talks nonsense."

"What kind of nonsense? There may be some sense in it?"

"I dursn't tell you, miss," said the servant casting a hurried look round, "it 'ud be as much as my place is worth."

"Oh, I understand," said Hagar, serenely; "this Laura says that Sir Lewis killed his cousin."

"Yes, she do," replied the man, aghast at her penetration; "but how could you guess, miss, is more—"

"Never mind," said Hagar, cutting him short as they arrived at the pool. "Is this the place where the murder was committed?"

"Yes, miss; we found the body there in the mud; and just beside it the marks of the boots."

Hagar reflected, and asked another question. "Did Sir Lewis ever visit Kerris?"

"He did, miss, just two days afore the murder—went to see him about some game."

"Oh, did he?" murmured Hagar to herself. "I think there was something more than game in that visit."

Of this she said nothing to the man, who stood on the bank, watching her searching about the place. The pool was filled with clear water, and on it the lilies floated placidly. Hagar peered in to see if there was any trace of the pistol used to kill Sir Leslie; but although the water was crystal-clear, and she searched carefully, not a sign of the weapon could she see. The grass round the pool was closely shorn, and some little distance up the slope stretched a terrace with a flight of shallow stone steps. On either side of these, at the lower end, were two pillars, bearing urns of marble sculptured in classic fashion with nymphs and dancing fauns. In these bloomed scarlet geraniums, now in full flower; and as Hagar, idly gazing around, caught sight of the vivid blossoms an idea entered her head. Dismissing the man, for whom she had no further use, she moved swiftly towards the terrace, and lifted one of the pots out of its marble urn.

"No sign of a pistol there," she said, replacing the pot with a sense of disappointment. "I may be wrong. Let me examine the other."

This time she was rewarded for her shrewd guess. At the bottom of the right-hand urn, quite concealed by the pot, she found a small pistol. On its stock there was a silver plate, and on that plate a name was engraved. At the sight of this latter the eyes of Hagar glistened with much satisfaction.

"I thought so!" said she to herself, "and now to tell Julf!"

The detective was waiting for her at the park gates, and looked up expectantly as she moved towards him with a smile on her face. With grim satisfaction she placed the pistol in his hand.

"There is the weapon with which Sir Leslie was killed!" she said, in a tone of triumph. "I found it under the geranium pot in one of those urns. What do you think of that?"

"The pistol of Kerris!" said Julf quite amazed.

"No; not the pistol of Kerris, but of the man who murdered Sir Leslie."

"Kerris," repeated Julf, with dogged obstinacy.

"Look at the name on the silver plate, you idiot!"

"Lewis Crane!" read the detective, stupefied then he looked up with an expression of blank astonishment on his solemn face. "What!" he muttered, "do you think Sir Lewis killed his cousin?"

"I am sure of it!" replied Hagar, firmly. "I have just learnt from a servant that he was in love with the girl Laura also, and that he was poor and dependent upon the dead man for money. The two had a quarrel on the night of the murder, as they were walking in the park. Because of this quarrel they parted, each going different ways. Sir Lewis said that he returned home, that he heard the pistol shot, and thought that his cousin was shooting at a target—as if a man would do so in the twilight!" added the girl, contemptuously. "What he really did—Lewis, I mean—was to follow his cousin, and shoot him by the Queen's Pool; then he hid the pistol in the marble urn, and crept back to the house to play his comedy. I tell you, Mr. Julf, that Kerris is innocent. I said so always. Sir Lewis is the guilty person, and he slew his cousin out of jealousy of Laura Brenton, and because he wanted the dead man's money."

"But the boots—the footmarks in the mud?" stammered Julf, quite confounded by this reasoning. "The marks were made by the boots of Kerris."

"I quite believe that," admitted Hagar; "another portion of Sir Lewis's very clever scheme to ward off suspicion from himself. The servant who led me to the Queen's Pool will tell you, as he told me, that Sir Lewis just a day or two before the murder paid a visit to the cottage of Kerris. Now, it is my opinion that while there he stole the boots, and wore them on the night on which he committed the murder, with the intention of throwing the blame on Kerris, whom Laura Brenton loved. Don't you see what his game was, Mr. Julf? He wanted to gain a title and money, so as to marry Laura: so he slew his cousin to get the first, and laid the blame—by circumstantial evidence—on George Kerris, to get the second. Now what do you say?"

"It looks black against Sir Lewis, certainly," admitted Julf; "still, I cannot think that he would dare—"

"Bah! men dare anything to gratify their passions!" retorted Hagar, shrewdly; "besides, he thought that he made all safe for himself by wearing the boots of Kerris. It was Sir Lewis who gave the boots to Micky. Oh, if that boy could only be found!"

"He is found!" said Julf, quickly. "I got a telegram while you were in the park. The police picked him up in Whitechapel, and will send him down here to-morrow. If he can swear that Sir Lewis gave him the boots, I shall get a warrant out for that man's arrest."

"I believe he is guilty," said Hagar, in a meditative fashion, "and yet I am not altogether sure."

"Why not? There is certainly a strong case against him."

"Yes, yes; but why, if Sir Lewis is guilty, should Kerris keep silent, and not declare his innocence? I must see the man and find out. Can I get into the jail?"

"I'll take you there myself to-morrow morning," replied Julf. "I should like to know the reason of his silence also. It can't be love of Sir Lewis as makes him hold his tongue."

"No; that is what puzzles me. After all, like Kerris, the baronet may be innocent."

Julf shook his head. "I can't think where you will find a third party on which to lay the guilt—unless," he added, with an after-thought, "you blame the Irish boy who pawned the boots."

"It may be even him!" said Hagar, seriously. "But we'll know to-morrow, I fancy. Kerris, Sir Lewis, Micky—h'm! I wonder which of the three killed that poor young man."

Hagar thought over this problem for an hour or so, then, not being able to solve it, she put it out of her head for the night. As for Julf, he was so much impressed by Hagar's cleverness in finding the pistol and constructing a case against Sir Lewis—who he now began to believe was guilty—that the next morning, before taking her to see George Kerris in prison, he conducted her to an outlying farm.

"Laura Brenton lives here," he said; "ask her about Sir Lewis, and see if we can strengthen the case against him."

Laura was a fine, tall, handsome girl, somewhat masculine in her looks; but at the present moment she seemed ill, and appeared haggard—which was no wonder, seeing that one of her lovers was dead, and the other in prison. However, she was quite willing to answer Hagar's questions, and declared most emphatically that Kerris was innocent.

"He wouldn't kill a fly!" said she, weeping, "although he was angry with me for meeting Sir Leslie; but I never saw any harm in doing so."

"Opinions differ," said Hagar, coldly, not approving of this morality. "You met Sir Leslie on the night of the murder?"

"I—I didn't!" stammered the girl, fiercely. "Who says so?"

"Sir Lewis. He told me that his cousin left him in the park—after their quarrel—to see you by the Queen's Pool."

This Laura denied flatly. "I went into Marlow on that evening to buy some ribbon," she explained, "but I never went near Welby Park. Sir Lewis is a liar and a murderer!"

"A murderer? Why should he murder his cousin?" asked Hagar, sharply.

"Because he loved me, and I would have nothing to say to him."

"You loved Sir Leslie?"

"I did not!" blazed out the girl, wrathfully. "I loved neither of them, but only George Kerris. He is innocent, and Sir Lewis is guilty. I believe he killed his cousin with the pistol Sir Leslie gave him."

"What do you know about that pistol?"

"Why," explained Laura, quietly, "I went to Welby Park with father to pay the rent, and in the library, on the table, there was a pistol with a silver plate on it. Sir Lewis—he was not the baronet then—told me that Sir Leslie had given it to him, and showed me his own name on the plate. As Sir Leslie was shot with a pistol, I believe Sir Lewis did it."

"But had not George Kerris a pistol also?"

"Yes; an old thing that wouldn't fire straight. I tried it myself at a target which George set up on the farm."

"The pistol isn't in George's house."

"I don't know where it is, then," said the girl, indifferently; "but I am sure of one thing, that George is innocent. Oh, try and get him out of jail!"

"And Sir Lewis hanged?" said Hagar, drily.

"Yes!" cried Laura, fiercely: "he's a murdering beast; I should like to see him dead!"

Rather wondering at the fierceness of the girl, Hagar left her, and went on to the jail in which Kerris was incarcerated. The gamekeeper was a huge blond man, with a fresh, handsome face. Usually his expression was frank and kindly, but now, owing to recent events, he looked sullen. In spite of all Hagar's questioning, he persisted in declining an explanation.

"I'll say neither one thing nor another," he declared; "if I did kill Sir Leslie, or I didn't, is my business. Anyhow, he deserved to be killed."

"Who are you screening?" asked Hagar, changing her tactics.

"No one," replied Kerris, a color rising in his face.

"Yes, you are, else you would not jeopardize your neck. But you shall be saved in spite of yourself. I know who killed Sir Leslie."

"You do?" asked the man, looking up anxiously.

"Yes, his cousin, Sir Lewis. We have found his pistol concealed where the murder took place; he stole your boots to wear them, and throw the blame on you. You came out of Welby Park at ten o'clock, after the murder was committed. Did you not see Sir Lewis?"

"No, I didn't," replied Kerris, hastily. "I saw no one. I heard a shot, and thought poachers might be about, but as Sir Leslie had discharged me I didn't think it was my business to see after them."

"Sir Lewis paid you a visit shortly before the murder?"

"Yes, he did; to see me about some game."

"Did you miss the boots after he left?"

"I never missed them till the night of the murder, when I wanted to put 'em on," said Kerris. "I hadn't worn them for some days, as they were new boots, and rather hurt my feet."

"Then no doubt Sir Lewis stole them for his own purposes," said Hagar triumphantly. "He is guilty, and you—"

"I am innocent!" cried Kerris, proudly. "I don't mind saying it now. I never killed Sir Leslie; I never laid a finger on him."

"And you did not say so before because you are screening some one. Who is it?"

Kerris made no reply, but looked uneasy.

Before Hagar could repeat her question, the answer thereto came from a most unexpected quarter. The door of the cell was opened, and Julf entered, with an expression of profound aston-ishment on his face.

"Here's a go!" he cried to Hagar. "Micky has arrived, and has told me from whom he received the boots!"

"Sir Lewis?"

"No! I have seen Sir Lewis, and he denies his guilt; also, he tells me a story which corroborates Micky's evidence, and explains why Kerris here holds his tongue."

Kerris rose from his seat on the bed with a bound, and strode towards Julf, looking worried and fierce.

"Not a word! not a word!" he said, between his clenched teeth. "Spare her!"

"Her!" cried Hagar, a light breaking in on her. "Laura Brenton?"

"Yes, Laura Brenton," replied Julf, shaking off the gamekeeper. "Micky has seen her; it was she who gave him the boots."

"I told her to; I told her to!" interrupted Kerris, in despair.

"Nonsense! you wish to screen her, as you have tried to do all along. But you are wrong. Laura Benton is not worth your sacrific-ing your life, my man. She is the guilty person who killed Sir Leslie. And why? Because he had cast her off, and was about to marry another woman."

Kerris gave a great cry. "It is false—false! She loved me!"

"She loved herself!" retorted Julf, sharply. "Sir Leslie prom-ised to marry her, and because she could not force him to keep that promise she killed him. It was to throw the blame on you that she stole the boots and wore them on the night she met Sir Leslie by the Queen's Pool. It was to get Sir Lewis into trouble that she stole his pistol to kill his cousin."

"And did she hide it in the urn?" asked Hagar, astonished by these revelations.

"No; Sir Lewis did so. He knew that Laura committed the crime."

"How so?"

"He heard the shot, and went to see who had fired it. By the Queen's Pool he found his cousin's dead body, and picked up his own pistol on the bank. As Laura, to his knowledge, had taken it away from the library on the day she came with her father to pay rent, he knew that she had killed Sir Leslie. To screen her, and not thinking of his own danger should the pistol with his name on it be found, he hid it in the urn where you found it. So, you see, two men have tried to screen this woman, who loved neither of them."

"She loved me—me!" cried Kerris, in agony. "Oh, why did Sir Lewis speak!"

"To save himself from arrest," replied Julf. "He was not so loyal as you, my poor fellow. However, you will soon be released. To-day, I arrest Laura."

And this was done on that very morning. Laura was arrested, and, terrified by the statements of Micky and Sir Lewis, although George Kerris loyally kept silent, she confessed all. Julf's explanation was correct. She had met Sir Leslie on the night of the murder by the Queen's Pool, with the intention of killing him should he persist in his intention of casting her off. He did so, and she killed him. She had stolen the pistol and the boots to throw the blame, should occasion arise, on Sir Lewis and Kerris. Also, she had taken away the pistol of Kerris from his cottage to inculpate him. But for Hagar and the episode of the pawned boots, which Laura had given to Micky to get rid of, she might have succeeded in her vile plans, and have escaped free, to ruin other men. As it was, she confessed her crime, and was condemned to penal servitude for life. She deserved the scaffold, but she escaped that through the leniency of the jury, on the score of her youth and beauty.

Released from the prison into which he had cast himself so madly to save an ungrateful woman, George Kerris came up to Lambeth and redeemed those fatal boots which had been pawned by Micky.

"I am going to Australia," he said to Hagar. "I failed to save her, so I cannot bear to remain at Marlow. I knew she was guilty all along; for she had been in my cottage the day previous to the murder, and had carried off these boots, on the plea that her father wished for a similar pair, and wanted to see them. When the footmarks with my initials were traced in the mud of the pond, I guessed that she had worn the boots, and had killed Sir Leslie. I loved her so dearly that I would have suffered in her place: but you with your clear head found her out, and now she is paying for her wickedness. Life is over for me here; I go to Australia, and I shall take these boots which ruined her with me."

"Why did you do all this for Laura—that worthless woman?"

"Worthless she is, I know," rejoined Kerris; "but—I loved her!" and with a nod he departed, carrying the boots and himself into exile.

10

The Ninth Customer and the Casket

HAGAR HAD ALMOST a genius for reading people's characters in their faces. The curve of the mouth, the glance of the eyes—she could interpret these truly; for to her feminine instinct she added a logical judgment masculine in its discretion. She was rarely wrong when she exercised this faculty; and in the many customers who entered the Lambeth pawn-shop she had ample opportunities to use her talent. To the sleek, white-faced creature who brought for pawning the Renaissance casket of silver she took an instant and violent dislike. Subsequent events proved that she was right in doing so. The ninth customer—as she called him—was an oily scoundrel. In appearance he was a respectable servant—a valet or a butler—and wore an immaculate suit of black broad-cloth. His face was as white as that of a corpse, and almost as expressionless. Two tufts of whisker adorned his lean cheeks, but his thin mouth and receding chin were uncovered with hair. On his badly-shaped head and off his low narrow forehead the scanty hair of iron-gray was brushed smoothly. He dropped his shifty gray eyes when he addressed Hagar, and talked softly in a most deferential manner. Hagar guessed him to be a West-end servant; and by his physiognomy she knew him to be a scoundrel.

This "gentleman's gentleman"—as Hagar guessed him rightly to be—gave the name of Julian Peters, and the address 42, Mount Street, Mayfair. As certainly as though she had been in the creature's confidence, Hagar knew that name and address were false. Also, she was not quite sure whether he had come honestly by the casket which he wished to pawn, although the story he told was a very fair and, apparently, candid one.

"My late master, miss, left me this box as a legacy," he said deferentially, "and I have kept it by me for some time. Unfortunately, I am now out of a situation, and to keep myself going until I obtain a new one I need money. You will understand, miss, that it is only necessity which makes me pawn this box. I want fifteen pounds on it."

"You can have thirteen," said Hagar, pricing the box at a glance.

"Oh, indeed, miss, I am sure it is worth fifteen," said Mr. Peters (so-called): "if you look at the workmanship—"

"I have looked at everything," replied Hagar, promptly—"at the silver, the workmanship, the date, and all the rest of it."

"The date, miss?" asked the man, in a puzzled tone.

"Yes; the casket is Cinque Cento, Florentine work. I dare say if you took it to a West-end jeweler you could get more on it than I am prepared to lend. Thirteen pounds is my limit."

"I'll take it," said Peters, promptly. "I don't care about pawning it in the West-end, where I am known."

"As a scoundrel, no doubt," thought Hagar, cynically. However, it was not her place to spoil a good bargain—and getting the Renaissance casket for thirteen pounds was a very good one—so she made out the ticket in the false name of Julian Peters, and handed it to him, together with a ten-pound note and three sovereigns. The man counted the money, with a greedy look in his eyes, and turned to depart with a cringing bow. At the door of the shop he paused, however, to address a last word to Hagar.

"I can redeem that casket whenever I like, miss?" he asked, anxiously.

"To-morrow, if it pleases you?" replied Hagar, coldly, "so long as you pay me a month's interest for the loan of the money."

"Thank you, miss; I shall take back the box in a month's time. In the meantime I leave it in your charge, miss, and wish you a very good day."

Hagar gave a shudder of disgust as he left the shop; for the man to her was a noxious thing, like a snake or a toad. If instinct were worth anything, she felt that this valet was a thief and a scoundrel, who was abusing the trust his employer placed in him. The casket was far more likely to have been thieved than to have come to Mr. Peters by will. It is not usual for gentlemen to leave their servants legacies of Cinque Cento caskets.

The box, as Peters called it, was very beautiful; an exquisite example of goldsmith's art, worthy of Benvenuto Cellini himself. Probably it was by one of his pupils. Renaissance work certainly, for in its ornamentation there was visible that mingling of Christianity and paganism which is so striking a characteristic of the re-birth of the Arts in the Italy of Dante and the Medici. On the sides of the casket in relief there were figures of dancing nymph and piping satyr; flower-wreathed altar and vine-crowned priest. On the lid a full-length figure of the Virgin with upraised hands; below clouds and the turrets of a castle; overhead the glory of the Holy Ghost in the form of a wide-winged Dove, and fluttering cherubs and grave saints. Within the casket was lined with dead gold, smooth and lusterless; but this receptacle contained nothing.

Without doubt this tiny gem of goldsmith's art had been the jewel-case of some Florentine lady in that dead and gone century. Perhaps for her some lover had ordered it to be made, with its odd mingling of cross and thyrsus; its hints of asceticism and joyous life. But the Florentine beauty was now dust; all her days of love and vanity and sin were over; and the casket in which she had stored her jewels lay in a dingy London pawn-shop. There was something ironic in the fate meted out by Time and Chance to this dainty trifle of luxury.

While examining the box, Hagar noticed that the gold plate of the case within was raised some little distance above the outside portion. There appeared to her shrewd eyes to be a space between the base of the casket and the inner box of gold. Ever on the alert to discover mysteries, Hagar believed that in this toy there was a secret drawer, which no doubt opened by a concealed spring. At once she set to work searching for this spring.

"It is very cleverly hidden," she murmured, having been baffled for a long time; "but a secret recess there is, and I intend to find it.

Who knows but what I may stumble on the evidence of some old Florentine tragedy, like that of the Crucifix of Fiesole?"

Her fingers were slender and nimble, and had a wonderfully delicate sense of feeling in their narrow tips. She ran them lightly over the raised work of beaten silver, pressing the laughing heads of the fauns and nymphs. For some time she was unsuccessful, until by chance she touched a delicately-modeled rose, which was carven on the central altar of one side. At once there was a slight click, and the silver slab with its sculptured figures fell downward on a hinge. As she had surmised, the box was divided within into two unequal portions; the upper one, visible when the ordinary lid was lifted, was empty, as has been said; but in the narrowness of the lower receptacle, between the false and the real bottoms of the box, there was a slim packet. Pleased with her discovery—which certainly did credit to her acute intelligence—Hagar drew out the papers. "Here is my Florentine tragedy!" said she, with glee, and proceeded to examine her treasure-trove.

It did not take her long to discover that the letters—for they were letters, five or six, tied up with rose-hued ribbon—were not fifteenth century, but very late nineteenth; that they were not written in Italian, but in English. Penned in graceful female handwriting upon scented paper—a perfume of violets clung to them still— these letters were full of passionate and undisciplined love. Hagar only read one, but it was sufficient to see that she had stumbled upon an intrigue between a married woman and a man. No address was given, as each letter began unexpectedly with words of fire and adoration, continuing in such style from beginning to end, where the signature appended was "Beatrice." In the first one, which Hagar read—and which was a sample of the rest—the writer lamented her marriage, raged that she was bound to a dull husband, and called upon her dearest Paul—evidently the inamorato's name—to deliver her. The passion, the fierce sensual love which burnt in every line of this married woman's epistles, disgusted Hagar not a little. Her pure and virginal soul shrank back from the abyss revealed by this lustful adoration; trembled at the glimpse it obtained of a hidden life. There was, indeed, no tragedy in these letters as yet, but it might be—with such a woman as she who had penned them—that they would become the prelude to one. In every line there was divorce.

"What a liar that valet is!" thought Hagar, as she tied the letters up again. "This casket was left to him as a legacy, was it? As if a man would entrust such compromising letters to the discretion of a scoundrel like Peters! No, no; I am sure he doesn't know of this secret place, or of the existence of these letters. He stole this casket from his master, and did not know that it was used to hide these epistles from a married woman. I'll keep the casket safely, and see what comes of it when Mr. Peters returns."

But she did not put the letters back in their secret recess. It might be that the valet would return before the conclusion of the month; and if she were out of the shop at the time, her assistant would give back the casket. Hagar felt that it would be wrong to let the letters get into the hands of so unscrupulous a scoundrel as she believed Peters to be. Did he find out the secret of the hiding-place, and the letters were within, he was quite capable of making capital out of them at the expense of the unhappy woman or his own master. He had the face of a blackmailer; so Hagar reclosed the casket, and put away the letters in the big safe in the parlor.

"She is a light woman—a bad woman," she thought, thinking of that Beatrice who had written those glowing letters—"and deserves punishment for having deceived her husband. But I won't give her into the power of that reptile; he would only fatten on her agony. If he comes back for the casket, he shall have it, but without those letters."

Hagar did not think for a moment that Peters knew of the existence of these epistles, else in place of pawning the box he would have levied blackmail on the wretched Beatrice or her lover. But when in two weeks—long before the conclusion of the month—the valet again appeared, he showed Hagar very plainly that he had learnt the secret in the meantime. How and from whom he had learnt it Hagar forced him to explain. She was able to do this, as he wanted back the casket, yet had not the money to redeem it. This circumstance gave her a power over the man which she exercised mercilessly: and for some time—playing with him in cat-and-mouse fashion—she pretended to misunderstand his errand. But at first sight she saw from his greedy eyes and the triumphant look on his face that he was bent on some knavery.

"I wish to look at my box, if you please, miss," said he, on first entering the shop. "I cannot redeem it as yet, but if you would permit me to examine it I—"

"Certainly!" said Hagar, cutting him short; she had no patience with his flowery periods. "Here is the box. Look at it as long as you please."

Peters seized the casket eagerly, opened it, and looked into the empty space within; then he shook it, and turned it upside down, as though he expected the inner box to fall out. In a moment Hagar guessed that he had become aware, since pawning the casket, that it contained a secret receptacle, and was looking for the same. With an ironic smile she watched him fingering the delicate carvings with his clumsy hands, and saw that with such coarse handling the casket would never yield up its secret. She therefore revealed it to him, not for his satisfaction, but because she wanted to know the history of the love-letters. For these, without doubt, the creature was looking, and Hagar congratulated herself that she had obeyed her instinct, and had placed the letters beyond his reach.

"You can't find it, I see," she observed, as Peters put down the casket in disgust.

"Find what?" he asked, with a certain challenge in his regard.

"The secret drawer for which you are looking."

"How do you know that I look for a secret drawer, miss?"

"I can guess as much from the persistent way in which you press the sides of that box. Your late master, who left you the casket as a legacy, evidently did not explain its secrets. But if you wish to know, look here?" Hagar picked up the box deftly, touched the altar rose with a light finger, and revealed to Mr. Peters the secret recess. His face fell, as she knew it would, at the sight of the vacant space.

"Why, it's empty!" he said aloud in a chagrined tone. "I thought—I thought—"

"That you would find some letters within," interrupted Hagar, smartly. "No doubt; but you see, Mr. Peters—if that is your name— I happen to have anticipated you."

"What? You have found the letters?"

"Yes; a neat little bundle of them, which lies in my safe."

"Please give them to me," said the man, with tremulous eagerness.

"Give them to you!" repeated Hagar, contemptuously. "Not I; it is not my business to encourage blackmailing."

"But they are my letters!" cried Peters getting red, but not denying the imputation of blackmailing. "You cannot keep my letters!"

"Yes, I can," retorted Hagar, putting the box on the shelf behind her; "in the same way that I can keep this casket if I so choose."

"How dare you!" said the man, losing all his suavity. "The box is mine!"

"It is your master's, you mean; and the letters also. You stole the casket to get money, and now you would steal the letters, if you could, to extort money from a woman. Do you know what you are, Mr. Peters? You are a scoundrel."

Peters could hardly speak for rage; but when he did find his voice, it was to threaten Hagar with the police. At this she laughed contemptuously.

"The police!" she echoed. "Are you out of your mind? Call a policeman if you dare, and I give you in charge for thieving that box."

"You cannot; you do not know my master's name."

"Do I not?" retorted Hagar, playing a game of bluff. "You forget that the name and address of your master are in those letters."

Seeing that he was baffled in this direction, the man changed his high tone for one of diplomacy. He became cringing and wheedling, and infinitely more obnoxious than before. Hagar could hardly listen to his vile propositions with calmness; but she did so advisedly, as she wished to know the story of the letters, the name of the woman who had written them, and that of the man—Peter's master—to whom they had been sent. But the task was disagreeable, and required a great deal of self-restraint.

"Why not share the money with me?" said Peters, in silky tones; "those letters are worth a great deal. If you let me have them, I can sell them at a high price either to my master or to the lady who wrote them."

"No doubt," replied Hagar, with apparent acquiescence; "but before I agree to your proposal I must know the story."

"Certainly, miss. I shall tell it to you. I—"

"One moment," interrupted Hagar. "Is Peters your real name?"

"Yes, miss; but the address I gave was false; also the Christian name I gave you. I am John Peters, of Duke Street, St. James's, in the employment of Lord Averley."

"You are his valet?"

"Yes; I have been with him for a long time; but I lost some money at cards a week or two ago, so I—I—"

"So you stole this casket," finished Hagar, sharply.

"No miss, I didn't," replied Peters, with great dignity. "I borrowed it from my lord's room for a few weeks to get money on it. I intended to redeem and replace it within the month. I shall certainly do so, if our scheme with these letters turns out successful."

Hagar could scarcely restrain herself from an outbreak when she heard this wretch so coolly discuss the use he intended to make of the profits to be derived from his villainy. However, she kept herself calm, and proceeded to ask further questions with a view to gaining his entire confidence.

"Well, Mr. Peters, we will say you borrowed it," she remarked, ironically; "but don't you think that was rather a dangerous proceeding?"

"I didn't at the time," said Peters, ruefully, "as I didn't know my lord kept letters in it. I did not fancy he would ask after it. However, he did ask two days ago, and found that it was lost."

"Did he think you had taken it?"

"Lor' bless you, no!" grinned the valet. "I ain't quite such a fool as to be caught like that. My lord's rooms have been done up lately, so he thought as perhaps the paper-hangers or some of that low lot stole the box."

"In that case you are safe enough," said Hagar, enraged at the ingenious villainy of the creature. "But how did you come to learn that there were letters hidden in this box? You didn't know of them when you pawned it."

"No, miss, I didn't," confessed Peters, regretfully; "but yesterday I heard my lord say to a friend of his that there were letters to him from a married lady in the secret place of the box, so I thought—"

"That you would find the secret place, and use the letters to get money out of the married lady."

"Yes, I did. That's what we are going to do, ain't it?"

"Is the married lady rich?" asked Hagar, answering the question by asking another.

"Lor', miss, her husband, Mr. Delamere, has no end of money! She'd give anything to get those letters back. Why, if her husband saw them he would divorce her for sure! He's a proud man, is Delamere."

"Has he any suspicion of an intrigue between his wife and Lord Averley?"

"Not he, miss; he'd stop it if he had. Oh, you may be sure she'll give a long price for those letters."

"No doubt," assented Hagar. "Well, Mr. Peters, as I am your partner in this very admirable scheme, you had better let me see Mrs. Delamere. I'll get more out of her than you would."

"I daresay, miss. You're a sharp one, you are! But you'll go shares fair?"

"Oh, yes; if I get a good sum, you shall have half," replied Hagar, ambiguously. "But where does Mrs. Delamere live?"

"In Curzon Street, miss; the house painted a light red. You'll always find her in now about seven. Squeeze her for all she is worth, miss. We've got a good thing on in this business."

"It would seem so," replied Hagar, coolly. "But if I were you, Mr. Peters, I would redeem this casket as soon as I could. You may get into trouble else."

"I'll take the money out of my share of the cash," said the scoundrel. "Don't you take less than five hundred, miss; those letters are worth it."

"Be content; I'll see to all that. To-morrow I shall interview Mrs. Delamere; so if you come and see me the day after, I will tell you the result of my visit."

"Oh, there can only be one result with a sharp one like you," grinned Peters. "You squeeze Mrs. Delamere like an orange, miss. Say you'll tell her husband, and she'll pay anything. Good day, miss. My stars, you're a sharp girl! Good day."

Mr. Peters departed with this compliment, just in time to stop Hagar from an unholy desire to throw the casket at his head. The man was a greater scoundrel even than she had thought; and she trembled to think of how he would have extorted money from Mrs. Delamere had he obtained the letters. Luckily for that lady, her foolish epistles were in the hands of a woman far more honorable than herself.

Although untitled, Mrs. Delamere was a very great lady. Certainly she was a beautiful one, and many years younger than her lord and master. Mr. Delamere was a wealthy commoner, with a long pedigree, and an over-weening pride. Immersed in politics and Blue-books, he permitted his frivolous and youthful wife to do as she pleased, provided she did not drag his name in the mud. He would have forgiven her anything but that. She could be as extravagant as she pleased; gratify all her costly whims; and flirt—if she so chose, and she did choose—with fifty men; but if once the name of Delamere was whispered about in connection with a scandal, she knew well that her husband would seek either a separation or a divorce. Yet, with all this knowledge, pretty, silly Mrs. Delamere was foolish enough to intrigue with Lord Averley, and to write him compromising letters.

She never thought of danger. Averley was a gentleman, a man of honor, and he had told her a dozen times that he always burnt the letters she wrote him. It was therefore a matter of amazement to Mrs. Delamere when a gipsy-like girl called to see her with a sealed envelope, and mentioned that such envelope contained her letters to Averley.

"Letters! letters!" said Mrs. Delamere, brushing her fluffy yellow curls off her forehead. "What do you mean?"

"I mean that your letters to Lord Averley are in this envelope," replied Hagar, looking coldly at the dainty doll before her. "I mean also that did your husband see them he would divorce you!"

Mrs. Delamere turned pale under her rouge. "Who are you?" she gasped, her blue eyes dilating with terror.

"My name is Hagar Stanley. I am a gipsy girl, and I keep a pawn-shop in Lambeth."

"A pawn-shop! How—how did you get my—my letters?"

"The valet of Lord Averley pawned a silver box in which they were concealed," explained Hagar. "He intended to use them as a means to extort money from you. However, I obtained the letters before he did, and I came instead of him."

"To extort money also, I suppose?"

For the life of her, Mrs. Delamere could not help making the remark. She knew that she was speaking falsely; that this girl with the grave, dark, poetic face was not the kind of woman to black-mail an erring sister. Still, the guilty little creature saw that Hagar—this girl from a pawnshop of the slums—was sitting in judgment upon her, and already, in her own mind, condemned her frivolous conduct. Proud and haughty Mrs. Delamere writhed at the look on the face of her visitor, and terrified as she was at the abyss which she saw opening at her feet, she could not help making a slighting remark to gall the woman who came to save her. She said it on the impulse of the moment; and impulse had cost her dearly many a time. But that Hagar was a noble woman it would have cost the frivolous beauty dearly now.

"No, Mrs. Delamere," replied Hagar, keeping her temper—for really this weak little creature was not worth anger—"I do not wish for money. I came to return you these letters, and I should advise you to destroy them."

"I shall certainly do that!" said the fashionable lady, seizing the envelope held out to her; "but you must let me reward you."

"As you would reward any one who returned you a lost jewel!" retorted the gipsy, with curling lip. "No, thank you; what I have done for you, Mrs. Delamere, is above any reward."

"Above any reward!" stammered the other wondering if she heard aright.

"I think so," responded Hagar, gravely. "I have saved your honor."

"Saved my honor!" cried Mrs. Delamere, furiously. "How dare you! How dare you!"

"I dare, because I happen to have read one of those letters; I read only one, but I have no doubt that it is a sample of the others. If Mr. Delamere read what I did, I am afraid you would have to go through the Divorce Court with Lord Averley as co-respondent."

"You—you are mistaken," stammered Mrs. Delamere, drawn into defending herself. "There is nothing wrong between us, I—I swear."

"It is no use to lie to me," said Hagar, curtly. "I have seen what you said to the man; that is enough. However, I have no call to judge you. I came to give you the letters; you hold them in your hand; so I go."

"Wait! wait! You have been very good. Surely a little money—"

"I am no blackmailer!" cried Hagar, wrathfully; "but I have saved you from one. Had Lord Averley's valet become possessed of those letters, you would have had to pay thousands of pounds for them."

"I know, I know," whimpered the foolish little woman. "You have been good and kind; you have saved me. Take this ring as—"

"No, I want no gifts from you," said Hagar, going to the door.

"Why not—why not?"

Hagar looked back with a glance of immeasurable contempt. "I take nothing from a woman who betrays her husband," she said, tranquilly. "Good-night, Mrs. Delamere—and be careful how you write letters to your next lover. He may have a valet also," and Hagar left the magnificent room, with Mrs. Delamere standing in it, white with rage and terror and humiliation. In those few contemptuous words of the poor gipsy girl, her sin had come home to her.

Hagar had come to the West-end to see the woman who had written the letters; now she walked back to her Lambeth pawn-shop to interview the man to whom they had been sent. She was not a girl who did things by halves; and, bent upon thwarting in every way the scoundrelism of John Peters, she had sent a message to his master. In reply Lord Averley had informed her that he would call on her at the time and place mentioned in her letter. The time was nine o'clock; the place, the dingy parlor of the pawnshop; and here Hagar intended to inform Lord Averley of the way in which she had saved Mrs. Delamere from the greed of the valet. Also, she intended to make him take back the casket and repay the money lent on it. In all her dabblings in romance, Hagar never forgot that she was a woman of business, and was bound to get as much money as possible for the heir of the old miser who had fed and sheltered her when she had come a fugitive to London. Hagar's ethics would have been quite incomprehensible to the majority of mankind.

True to the hour, Lord Averley made his appearance in Carby's Crescent, and was admitted by Hagar to the back parlor. He was a tall slender, fair man, no longer in his first youth, with a colorless face, which was marked by a somewhat tired expression. He looked a trifle surprised at the sight of Hagar's rich beauty, having expected to find an old hag in charge of a pawn-shop. However, he made no comment but bowed gravely to the girl, and took the seat she offered to him. In the light of the lamp Hagar looked long and earnestly at his handsome face. There was a look of intellect on it which made her wonder how he could have found satisfaction in the love of a frivolous doll like Mrs. Delamere. But Hagar quite forgot for the moment that the fullest delight of life lies in contrast.

"I have no doubt you wondered at receiving a letter from a pawn-shop," she said, abruptly.

"I confess I did," he replied, quietly: "but because you mentioned that you had my casket I came. It is here, you say?"

Hagar took the silver box off a near shelf, and placed it on the table before him. "It was pawned here two weeks ago," she said, quietly. "I lent thirteen pounds; so, if you give me that sum and the month's interest, you can have it."

Without a word Lord Averley counted out the thirteen pounds, but he had to ask her what the interest was. Hagar told him, and in a few moments the transaction was concluded. Then Averley spoke.

"How did you know it was my casket?"

"The man who pawned it told me so."

"That was strange."

"Not at all, my lord. I made him tell me."

"H'm! you look clever," said Averley, looking at her with interest. "May I ask the name of the man who pawned this?"

"Certainly. He was your valet, John Peters."

"Peters!" echoed her visitor. "Oh, you must be mistaken! Peters is an honest man!"

"He is a scoundrel and a thief, Lord Averley; and but for me he would have been a blackmailer."

"A blackmailer?"

"Yes. There were letters in that casket."

"Were letters!" said Averley, hurriedly, and drew the box towards him. "Do you know the secret?"

"Yes; I found the secret recess and the letters. It was lucky for you that I did so. Your indiscreet speech to a friend informed Peters that compromising letters were hidden in the casket. He came here to find them; but I had already removed them."

"And where are they now?"

"I gave them back to the married woman who wrote them."

"How did you know who wrote them?" asked Lord Averley, raising his eyebrows.

"I read one of the letters, and then Peters told me the name of the lady. He proposed to me to blackmail her. I ostensibly agreed, and went to see the lady, to whom I gave back the letters. I asked you here to-night to return the casket; also to put you on your guard against John Peters. He is coming to see me to-morrow, to get—as he thinks—the money obtained by means of the letters. That is the whole story."

"It's a queer one," replied Averley, smiling. "I shall certainly discharge Peters, but I won't prosecute him for thieving. He knows about the letters, and they are far too dangerous to be brought into court."

"They are not dangerous now, my lord. I have given them back to the woman who wrote them."

"That was very good of you," said Averley, satirically. "May I ask the name of the lady?"

"Surely you know! Mrs. Delamere."

Averley looked aghast for a moment, and then began to laugh quietly. "My dear young lady," he said, as soon as he could bring his mirth within bounds, "would it not have been better to have consulted me before giving back those letters?"

"No," said Hagar, boldly, "for you might not have handed them over."

"Certainly I should not have handed them to Mrs. Delamere!" said Averley, with a fresh burst of laughter.

"Why not?"

"Because she never wrote them. My dear lady, I burnt all the letters I got from Mrs. Delamere, and I told her I had done so. The letters in this casket signed 'Beatrice' were from a different lady altogether. I shall have to see Mrs. Delamere. She'll never forgive me. Oh, what a comedy!" and he began laughing again.

Hagar was annoyed. She had acted for the best, no doubt; but she had given the letters to the wrong woman. Shortly the humor of the mistake struck her also, and she laughed in concert with Lord Averley.

"I'm sorry I made a mistake," she said, at length.

"You couldn't help it," replied Averley rising. "It was that scoundrel Peters who put you wrong. But I'll discharge him to-morrow, and get those letters of Beatrice back from Mrs. Delamere."

"And you'll leave that poor little woman alone," said Hagar, as she escorted him to the door.

"My dear lady, now that Mrs. Delamere has read those letters she'll leave me alone—severely. She'll never forgive me. Goodnight. Oh, me, what a comedy!"

Lord Averley went off, casket and all. Peters never came back to get his share of the blackmail, so Hagar supposed he had learnt from his master what she had done. As to Mrs. Delamere, Hagar often wondered what she said when she read those letters signed "Beatrice." But only Lord Averley could have told her that and

Hagar never saw him again; nor did she ever see Peters the black-mailer. Finally, she never set eyes again on the Cinque Cento Florentine casket which had contained the love-letters of—the wrong woman.

II

The Tenth Customer and the Persian Ring

ONE OF THE LAST customers of any note who came to the Lambeth pawn-shop was a slender, wiry man with an Oriental face, not un-like that of Hagar herself. His countenance was oval, his nose aquiline in shape, and he possessed two dark sparkling eyes; also a long black beard, well trimmed and well kept. In fact, this beard was the neatest thing about him, as his dress—a European garb—was miserably poor, and the purple-hued cloth which he had twisted round his head for a turban was worn and soiled. He was nevertheless a striking figure when he presented himself before Hagar, and she examined him with particular interest. There was a gipsy look about the tenth customer, which seemed to stamp him as one of the gentle Romany. Even keen eyed Hagar was deceived.

"Are you of our people?" she asked, abruptly, after looking at him for a moment or so.

"I do not understand," replied the man, in very good English, but with a foreign accent. "What people you speak of?"

"The Romany—the gipsy tribes."

"No, lady; I no of dem. I know what they are—oh, yes, they in my own country as in dis."

"Where is your country?" demanded Hagar, vexed at her mistake.

"Iran; what you call Persia," replied the customer. "My name, lady, is Alee; I come from Ispahan dese two year. Oh, yes; a long time I do stop in dis town."

"A Persian!" said Hagar, looking at his swarthy face and deli-cate features. "I don't think I ever saw a Persian before. You are very like one of the Romany; not at all like a Gentile."

"Lady, I no Gentile, I no Christian; I am follower ob de Prophet. May his name be blessed! But dis not what I do come to speak," he added, with some impatience. "You give money on ring, eh!"

"Let me see the ring first," said Hagar, diplomatically.

Alee, as he called himself, slipped the ring in question off one of his slender brown fingers, and handed it to her in silence. It was a band of dead gold, rather broad, and set in it was an oval turquoise of azure hue, marked with Arabic letters in gold. The ring had the look of a talisman or amulet, as the queer hieroglyphics on the stone seemed the words of some charm, stamped thereon to avert evil. Hagar examined the ring carefully, as she had never seen one like it before.

"It is a queer stone," she said, after looking through a magnifying glass at the turquoise. "What do you want on it?"

"One pound?" replied Alee, promptly; "just for two—tree days. Eh, what! you give me dat?"

"Oh, yes; I think the ring is worth five times as much. Here is the money; I'll make out the ticket in your name of Alee. How do you spell it?"

The Persian took the ticket from Hagar, and in very fair English letters wrote down his name and address. Then with a bow he turned to leave the shop; but before he reached the door she called him back.

"I say. Alee, what do these gold marks on this stone mean?"

"Dey Arabic letters, lady. Dey a spell against de Jinns. 'In de name ob Allah de All-Merciful.' Dat what dem letters say."

"They say a good deal with a word or two," muttered Hagar. "Arabic must be something like shorthand. When do you want back the ring?" she asked, aloud.

"In two—tree days," replied the Persian. "Say dis week. Yes. Good night, lady; you keep dat ring all right. Yes. So."

Alee took himself out of the shop with another bow, and Hagar, after a further examination of the queer ring with its talismanic inscription, put it away on a tray with other jewels. She wondered very much if it had a story attached to it; and, having read the "Arabian Nights" of late, she compared it in her own mind to the ring of Aladdin. It looked like a jewel with a history, did that inscribed turquoise.

In the afternoon of the next day another Persian arrived. Hagar recognized him as such from his resemblance to Alee; indeed, but for the difference in expression the two men might have passed for twins. Alee had a soft look in his eyes, a melancholy twist to his mouth; while this countryman of his had a hawk-like and danger-ous fierceness stamped on his lean face. He was dressed similarly to Alee, but wore a yellow turban instead of a purple one, and gave his name to Hagar as Mohommed; also, he took out of his pocket the pawn-ticket, which he handed to the girl.

"Alee, my countryman, he send dis," said he, in broken but very fair English; "he want de ring which he leave here."

"Why doesn't he come for it himself?" asked Hagar, suspi-ciously.

"Alee ill; him bery bad; he ask me to get de ring. But if you no gib me—why, I tell Alee; he come himself den."

"Oh, there is no necessity for him to do so," replied Hagar, get-ting the ring. "You would not have the ticket with you if everything was not square. Here is Alee's property. One pound and interest. Thank you, Mr. Mohommed. By the way, you are a friend of Alee?"

"Yis; I come to dis place when he come," replied Mohommed, passively, "him very great frien' of me. Two year we in dis land."

"Both of you speak English very well."

"Tank you, yes; we learn our Inglees in Persia for long time; and when we here we spike always—always. Goot-tay; I do take dis to Alee."

"I say," called out Hagar, "has that ring a story?"

"What, dis? I no know. Him charm against de Jinn; but dat's all. Goot-day; I go queek to Alee. Goot-day."

He went away with the ring on his finger, leaving Hagar disap-pointed that the strange jewel with its golden letters had not some wild tale attached to it. However, the ring was gone, and she never expected to hear anything more of it, or of the two Persians. A week passed, and no Alee made his appearance; so Hagar concluded that everything was right, and that he had really sent Mohommed to redeem the ring. On the eighth day of its redemption she was undeceived, for Alee himself made his appearance in the shop. Hagar was surprised to see him.

The poor man looked ill, and his brown face was terribly lean and worn in its looks. An expression of anxiety lurked in his soft black eyes, and he could hardly command his voice as he asked her to give him the ring. The request was so unexpected that Hagar could only stare at him in silence. It was a moment or so before she could find words.

"The ring!" she said, in tones of astonishment. "Why, you have it! Did not your friend Mohommed give it—"

"Mohommed!" cried Alee, clenching his hands; and the next moment he had fallen insensible on the outer floor of the shop. The single mention of the name Mohommed in connection with the ring had stricken the poor Persian to the heart. His entrance, his behavior, his fainting—all three were unexpected and inexplicable.

Recovering from her first surprise, Hagar ran to the assistance of the fallen man. He was soon revived by the application of cold water, and when he could rise Hagar, like the Good Samaritan she was, conducted him into the back parlor and made him lie down on the sofa. But more than ordinary weakness was the matter with the man; he was suffering from want of food, and told Hagar faintly that he had eaten nothing for two days. At once the girl set victuals before him, and warmed some soup to nourish him. Alee ate sparingly but well; and although he refused to touch wine, as a follower of the Prophet, he soon became stronger and more cheerful. His gratitude to Hagar knew no bounds.

"You are as charitable as Fatima, the daughter ob our Lord Mohommed," said he, gratefully, "and your good deed, it will be talked ob by de angel Gabriel on de Las' Day."

"How is it you are so poor?" asked Hagar, restive under this praise.

"Ah, lady, dat is one big long story."

"Connected with the ring?"

"Yes, yes; dat ring would haf mate me reech," replied the Persian, with a sigh; "but now dat weeked one vill git my moneys. Aha!" said Alee, furiously, "dat Mohommed is de son ob a burnt fazzer!"

"He is a scoundrel certainly! How did he get the pawn-ticket?"

"He took it away when I ill."

"Why did he want the ring?"

Alee reflected for a moment, and then he evidently made up his mind what course to pursue. "I weel tell you, lady," he said, looking with thankful eyes at Hagar. "You haf been good to me. I weel tell you de story ob my life—ob de ring."

"I knew that ring had some story connected with it," said Hagar, complacently. "Go on, Alee; I am all attention."

The Persian obeyed forthwith; but, as his English was imperfect at times, it will be as well to set forth the story in the vernacular. Being still weak, it took Alee some time to tell the whole tale; but Hagar heard him patiently to the end. His narrative was not without interest.

"I was born in Ispahan," said the Persian, in his grave voice, "and I am a Mirza—what you call here a prince—in my own country. My father was an officer of the Shah's household, and very wealthy. When he died I, as his only son, inherited his wealth. I was young, rich, and not at all bad-looking, so I expected to lead a pleasant life. The Shah, who had protected my father, continued the sun of his favor to me; and I accompanied him to the Court at Teheran, where I speedily became high in his favor. But alas!" added Alee, in the flowery language of his country, "soon did I cover the face of pleasure with the veil of mourning, and ride the horse of folly into the country of sorrow." He paused, and then added, with a sigh: "Her name was Ayesha."

"Ah!" said Hagar, the cynic. "I was waiting to hear the name of the woman. She ruined you, I suppose?"

"She and another," sighed Alee, stroking his beard. "I melted like wax in the flame of her beauty, and my heart turned to water at the glance of her eyes. She was Georgian, and fairer than the chief wife of Sulieman bin Daoud. But alas! alas! what saith Sa'adi; 'Wed a charmer and wed sorrow!'"

"Well," said Hagar, rather patiently, "I know all about her looks. Go on with the story."

"On my head be it!" said Alee. "I purchased this Georgian in Ispahan, and made her my third wife; but so lovely and clever she was, that I speedily raised her to the rank of the first. I adored her beauty, and marveled at her wit. She sang like a bulbul, and danced like a Peri."

"She seems to have been a wonder, Alee! Go on."

"There was a man called Achmet, who hated me very much," continued Alee, his eyes lighting up fiercely at the mention of the name. "He saw that I was rich, and favored by the King of Kings, so he set his wits to work to ruin me. Having heard of my beautiful wife Ayesha, he told the Shah of her loveliness, which was that of a houri in Paradise. Fired by the description, my Sovereign visited at my house, and I received him with due splendor. He saw all my treasures—among others, my wife."

"I thought you Turks never presented your wives to strangers?"

"We are Persians, not Turks," corrected Alee, quietly, "and the Shah is no stranger in the houses of his subjects. Also, he has the right to pass the forbidden door to the Abode of Felicity."

"What is the Abode of Felicity?"

"The harem, lady. But to tell you the story of my ruin.

"The Shah saw my beautiful Ayesha, and her burning glances were as arrows of delight in his heart. He returned to his palace with a desire to possess my treasure. Achmet, who had right of access to the person of the Shah, strengthened this desire, and declared that I was unhappy with Ayesha."

"And were you?"

Alee sighed. "After the coming of the King of Kings I was," he confessed. "My wife wished to enter the royal harem, and warm herself in the glory of the royal sun. She was silent and melancholy, or cross and fierce. I did what I could to console her, but she refused to listen to me, treated me as dirt beneath her feet, and sometimes she even smote me on the mouth with her pearl-embroidered slipper. Tales of our constant quarrels were carried to the Shah by the perfidious Achmet who declared that I ill-treated my beautiful Georgian. At last Achmet told the King that I had wished I were rid of the woman, if only for the meanest jewel worn by his august self."

"Did you say that?"

"In a fit of rage one day I said something like it," said Alee, darkly; "but I never intended my foolish speech to be taken seriously. However these idle words were reported to the Shah, and he sent for me. 'Alee,' said he, 'it has been said that thou deemest the meanest thing worn by us of more value than your wife Ayesha. If that be so, take this ring, which we give thee freely, and surrender thy lightly-valued wife to dwell in the shadow of our throne. Thou hast my leave to go.' Lady, I bowed myself to the ground, I took the ring you know of, and I went."

"Did you not say that you wished to keep Ayesha?"

"No; the word of the Shah is law. Had I expressed such a wish I should have lost my head; as it was, I lost my wife. Returning home, I made known the Shah's desire, and urged her to fly with me beyond his power. Desirous of entering the royal serail, however, she refused, and so I carried her off by force. I drugged her one night, placed her on a camel, and set out for the nearest seaport disguised as a merchant."

"Was your flight successful?"

"Alas, no," replied Alee, in melancholy tones. "Achmet was on the watch, and had me followed. My wife was taken from me by force, but only too willingly on her own part. For daring to disobey the royal command I suffered the bastinado on the soles of my feet until I fainted away."

"Poor Alee!"

"Mad with anger, I let the wrath of the heart overpower the judgment of the mind, and rashly joined in a conspiracy to overthrow the King of Kings. Again my evil genius Achmet thwarted and discovered me. I was forced to fly from Persia to save my life; and all my wealth was forfeited to the royal treasury. A goodly portion of it, however, was given to Achmet for his having found out the conspiracy. After many adventures, which I need not relate here, I came to this land, where I have lived in poverty and misery for two years. My wife is a queen in the serail of the Shah; my enemy is the ruler of a province; and I, lady, am the exile you see. All that I carried out of the Shah's kingdom was the ring which he gave me in exchange for my beautiful Ayesha."

He paused, and Hagar waited for him to continue the story. Finding that he still kept silent, she addressed him impatiently: "Is that all?"

"Yes—except that since I have been here it has been told to me that both Achmet and Ayesha wish to get me back to Persia, that they may kill me. The Georgian never forgave me for carrying her away, and only my death will glut her vengeance. As for Achmet, he is never free from dread while I live, and wishes me to die also. If they can manage it, those two will have me carried back to Persia, and there have me slain."

"They can't take you out of London against your will."

Alee shook his head. "Who knows!" said he. "There is the case of the Chinaman who was lured into the Embassy to be sent back to China. If the Government of England had not interfered he would have been a dead man by this time. I keep always away from the Persian Embassy."

"You are wise to do so," replied Hagar, who remembered the case. "But about the ring. Why did you pawn it, and why did Mohommed steal it by means of the pawn-ticket?"

"There was a friend of mine in Persia," explained Alee, "who saved for me out of my property seized by the Shah a box of jewels. Knowing that I was starving in this land, he sent the jewels to me in charge of a servant. I received a letter from him, in which he stated that the servant had been instructed to give up the jewels to me when I produced the ring. I foolishly told Mohommed about this, and one night he tried to thieve the ring from me, thinking that he would show it to my friend's servant and get my jewels. In fear lest he should obtain it, I pawned it with you for safety, until the servant should arrive."

"Is the servant here now?"

"He arrived last week," replied Alee, mournfully, "and he is now waiting for me at Southampton. But, alas! I speak foolishly. When I fell ill after pawning the ring, Mohommed stole the ticket, and, as you know, he obtained the ring. I have no doubt that by this time he has shown it to the servant of my friend, and is possessed of the jewels. Mohommed the accursed is rich, and I remain poor. Now, lady, you know why a darkness came over my spirit, and why I fell as one bereft of life. Surely, I am the sport of Fortune, and the most unlucky of men! I am he of whom the poet spoke when he said:

'Strive not, contend not; thy future is woe;
Accept of thy sorrows, for Fortune's thy foe.'"

The poor man recited this couplet in faltering tones, and burst into tears, rocking himself to and fro in an agony of grief. Hagar was sorry for this unfortunate person, who had been so unlucky as to lose wife, and wealth, and country. She gave him the only comfort that was in her power.

"Here are twenty shillings," said she, placing some silver in his hand. "Perhaps Mohommed has not yet gone to Southampton; or it may be that the servant with your jewels has not yet arrived. Go down to Hampshire, and see if you can recover your ring."

Alee thanked her with great emotion, and shortly afterwards left the shop, promising to tell her of the issue of this adventure. Hagar saw him go away with the fullest belief in his honesty of purpose, and perfect trust in the truth of his story; but later on, when alone, she began to wonder if she had not been gulled by two sharpers. The whole story told by Alee was so like an adventure of the "Arabian Nights" that Hagar became more than a trifle doubtful of its truth. As the days went by, and Alee did not return as he had promised, she fancied that her belief was a true one.

"Those two Persians have played a comedy of which I have been the dupe," she said to herself; "it has all been done to get money. And yet I am not sure; the pair would not take all that trouble for a miserable twenty shillings. After all, Alee's story may be true; and he may be at Southampton trying to recover his ring and jewels."

In this conjecture she was perfectly right, for all the days of his absence Alee had been at Southampton vainly looking for Mohommed the thief. His twenty shillings had soon been expanded; but luckily he had met with an Englishman whom he had known in Persia. This gentleman, an Oriental scholar and a liberal-minded man, had recognized Alee, dirty and miserable, as he haunted the Southampton quays looking for the servant of his friend and the recreant Mohommed. Carthew—for that was the Englishman's name—was profoundly shocked to find one whom he had known wealthy in such misery. He took Alee to his hotel, supplied him with food and clothes, and requested to know how the Persian had fallen so low. Alee told this Samaritan the same story as he had told Hagar; but, versed in the craft and topsy-turvydom of the East, Carthew was not so surprised or sceptical as the gipsy girl had been. He was sorry for poor Alee, who had been for so long the butt of Fortune, and determined to befriend him.

"I suppose there is no chance of your regaining the Shah's favor?" he asked the unfortunate man in his own tongue.

"Alas! no. What is, is. I conspired against the King of Kings; I was betrayed by Achmet; so there is no way in which I can approach again the Asylum of the Universe."

"Humph! looks like it," growled Carthew, stroking his white beard. "And Achmet, that son of a burnt father, is high in favor?"

"Yes; he is the governor of a province, and as he is friendly with Ayesha, who is now the favorite of the Shah, he is above all fortune. It is strange," added Alee, reflectively, "that those so rich and high-placed should wish to get me back to my death."

"They know they have wronged you, my friend, and so they hate you. But you are safe in England. Even the Shah cannot seize you here."

Alee reminded Carthew, as he had done Hagar, of the Chinese kidnapping case which had created so great a stir in England. Carthew laughed. "Why, don't you see that the case is your very safeguard?" said he. "If the Persian Embassy seized you, they would have to release you. Remember, now that I have met you, you are not friendless. You stay by me, Alee, and you will be safe from the vengeance of your wife and Achmet."

"But I do not wish to live on your charity."

"You needn't," said the Oriental scholar, bluntly. "As you know, I am translating the Epic of Kings which Ferdusi wrote. You must assist me, and I'll engage you as my secretary. In a few months you'll be on your feet again, and no doubt I shall be able to find you some regular employment. As for that scoundrel Mohommed who stole the ring, I'll set the police after him. By the way, I suppose he dare not go back to Persia again!"

"No; he was a conspirator also," replied Alee. "We fled together from the wrath of the Shah. He was nearly captured and beheaded in mistake for me, as we are so like one another; but he managed to escape, and joined me in England. Still, he is safer here than I, as he has no powerful enemies who desire his return to Persia."

"It's a case of Dilly duck, come and be killed," said Carthew, with a grim laugh. "Well, we must hunt up the scoundrel, and find your jewels if possible. Who was the friend who sent them to you?"

"Feshnavat, of Shiraz. He was a friend of my father's, and is, as you know, a great merchant."

"Yes, I know him," said Carthew, nodding; "a fine old man. I have no doubt he recovered your jewels, and sent them here all right. The pity is that he made their delivery depend upon the showing of the Shah's ring. Though, to be sure, he never anticipated that a villain would rob you of it. Truly, Alee, you are the most unlucky of men!"

"Not since I met with you, O comforter of the poor!" replied Alee, gratefully "You have been charitable and good, even as the woman who helped me in the great city. But to both reward shall come. What says the poet:

'Give freely to the poor your gold;
What's spent will come back forty-fold.'"

"Ah, Alee," said Carthew, with a half-sigh, "your couplet and gratitude are but bringing the posey of the East into the prose of the West. You are in London, my friend—in ordinary, commonplace London; and not with Sa'adi in the gardens of Shiraz."

Carthew was as good as his word, and employed Alee to aid him in translating the Epic of Kings. With the first money which he earned the Persian visited Hagar—to repay her, and to tell her all that had befallen him since he had left her shop. Hagar was pleased to see him, and gratified at the refunding of the money; for such action quite restored her faith in Alee, which she had been beginning to lose. She asked after Mohommed; but concerning that rascal the Persian was unable to give any news.

"He haf took my ring and jewels," sighed Alee, mournfully, "and in some lan' far away he live on my moneys. But the justice of Allah, who sees the black beetle in the black rock, will smite him. He will fall in his splendor and evil-doing, as the people of Od went down to the dust. It is written."

In the meantime Carthew, who had a genuine liking for Alee, made all inquiries about the absent Mohommed and the missing ring. For many weeks he learnt nothing; but finally chance set him on the track of the thief, and in the end he learnt all. He discovered what had become of Mohommed and of the ring; and the discovery astonished him not a little. It was an Attaché of the Persian Embassy who revealed the truth; and Carthew judged it best that the lips of this same man should relate the story to Alee.

"My friend," said he one day to the Persian "do you know a countryman of yours called Mirza Baba?"

"I have heard of him," replied Alee, slowly, "but he has not seen my face, nor have I beheld him. Why do you ask?"

"Because he knows what has become of your ring."

"And of Mohommed? Oh, my friend, tell me of these things!" cried the Persian.

"Nay, Alee; it is better that the truth should come from the lips of Mirza Baba himself. I will ask him here to tell you."

"But he may learn who I am!" muttered Alee, in dismay.

"I think not, as he has never seen your face," replied Carthew, smiling, "besides—" He broke off with a nod. "Well, you'll hear the story as he tells it; but call all your self-command and Oriental impassiveness to your aid. You'll need courage."

"Let it be as you say," rejoined Alee, folding his hands. "To-day and to-morrow are in the hands of the All-Wise."

True to his promise, Carthew next day received Mirza Baba in his house, and introduced him to Alee, who gave his countryman a feigned name. The Persian of the Embassy, who was a very great man indeed, paid little attention to Alee, whom he regarded simply as the secretary of Carthew, and as one quite beneath his notice. This neglect suited Alee, who sat meekly on one side, and listened to his own story, and to the story of Mohommed and the missing ring. Mirza Baba, in response to the request of Carthew, told it over pipes and coffee, and greatly astonished Alee in the telling.

"You know," said the Mirza, addressing himself particularly to Carthew, and quite ignoring his own countryman," that this dog of an Alee, on whose head be curses! had the folly to conspire against the peace of the Shah—on whom be blessings! He escaped from the Land of the Sun, and came to this island of thine. Hither he was traced, and to assert the majesty of the Asylum of the Universe it was resolved that this son of a burnt father should be brought back to Persia for punishment. The Banou Ayesha, who is the Pearl of the East, was bent upon seeing the head of this traitor, to whom aforetime she had been wife, ere the King of Kings had deigned to cast his eyes upon her. Also Achmet, the most zealous of governors, who had discovered the conspiracy of the evil-minded Alee, wished to punish him. Orders were sent to our Embassy that Alee should be taken, even in the streets of London, and sent back in chains to the Court of Teheran; but this, it was difficult to do."

"H'm! I think so!" replied Carthew, drily. "The Chinese Embassy tried on that game with Sun Yat, and had to give him up. The English Government do not recognize the Embassies as so many neutral territories in London."

"It is true; I know it," answered Baba, coolly. "Well, as there was no chance of capturing Alee in that way, it was resolved to employ stratagem. A letter, purporting to be written by Feshnavat, of Shiraz, was sent to this traitor, in which it was set forth that a box of jewels, saved from the wreck of his property, was being sent to England, and that it would be given up at Southampton to the bearer of the Shah's ring. You know of the ring, my friend?" added the Mirza.

"Yes; the ring given by the Shah to Alee in exchange for his wife. Go on."

"That is so. The dog surrendered his spouse, who is now the Pearl of Persia, for the meanest ring worn by the Shah. It was known that he bore it to this land, so it was arranged by the Pearl and Achmet that such ring should be the means to lure this traitor to his death. Well, my friend," continued Baba, with a chuckle, "the plot contrived by the wit of Banou Ayesha was successful. Alee went to Southampton, and finding the supposed servant of Feshnavat, produced the ring, and demanded the jewels. This was at night, so at once the traitor was seized, and placed on board the waiting vessel to be taken to Persia."

"That was very clever," said Carthew, stealing a glance at Alee, who was painfully white. "And what happened then?"

"Lies and misfortune," replied Baba Mirza. "This Alee, when he learnt the truth, swore that he was not the man we sought, but one Mohommed, and that he had stolen the ring to get the jewels. Of course, no one believed this story, which, without doubt, was a mere trick to save his life. He was carefully watched, and was told that on arriving in Persia he would be beheaded at once. In fear of this death, the wretch escaped one night from the cabin in which he was confined, and threw himself into the sea. He left behind him the ring; and this, seeing that the man was dead, was taken to Persia, in proof that Alee had been seized. The ring is now worn by the Pearl of Persia; but never has she ceased regretting that Alee escaped her vengeance."

After telling this story, which was listened to, with outward composure but inward fear by Alee, the Mirza took his leave. When alone with the Persian, Carthew turned to address him.

"Well, Alee," said he, kindly, "you see Fortune has not forsaken you yet! She has saved you, and punished Mohommed for his theft."

"What is, is," said Alee, with Oriental impassiveness; "but in truth it is wondrous that I escaped the snare. Now I can live in peace; for, thinking me dead, neither Ayesha nor Achmet will seek me again. I have lost the ring, it is true; but I have gained my life. Now I shall take another name, and dwell for the span of my days in England."

"It is a queer ending to the story," said Carthew, reflectively.

"The tale is as strange as any of the 'Thousand and One Nights,'" replied Alee. "It should be written in letters of gold. It is of such that the poet writes:

"Go forward on thy path, tho' darkness hides it;
Thy destiny is sure, for Allah guides it."

12

The Passing of Hagar

IT WAS NOW two years since Hagar had presented herself to the astonished eyes of Jacob Dix, and one year since the death of the old miser had left her in sole charge of the pawnshop. During all these months she had striven hard to do her duty, for the sake of the man who had taken pity on her poverty. She had toiled early and late; she had neglected no opportunity to make bargains; and she had lived penuriously the meanwhile. All moneys accruing from the business she had paid into the bank; and all accounts of receipts and payments she had placed in the hands of Vark, the lawyer. At any time that Goliath chose to arrive, she was ready to hand over the pawn-shop and property to him, after which it was her intention to leave.

As yet she had no idea in her head what was to become of her when the arrival of the lost heir reduced her to the position of a pauper. It had, indeed, occurred to her that it would be best to return to her tribe again, and take up the old gipsy life. On account of Goliath she had exiled herself from the Romany tents: so when he came into his inheritance she would be free to return thereto. As a wealthy man, Jimmy Dix, *alias* Goliath, would not care to spend his life in roaming the country with vagrants; and thus she would be relieved of his presence. Hagar was getting very tired of the shop and the weary life of Carby's Crescent; and often the nostalgia of the roads came upon her. Several times of late she had wished that Goliath would claim his heritage, and relieve her of the irksome task which she had taken on her own shoulders, out of gratitude to Jacob Dix. But as yet the absent heir had not made his appearance.

Hagar knew very well that Eustace Lorn was looking for him. Pursuant to the promise he had given her, and expecting the reward of her hand on his return, Lorn had been these many months on the trail of the missing man. All over England and Scotland had he tramped, inquiring of every gipsy, every vagrant, every town scamp, the whereabouts of Goliath; but all in vain, for Goliath seemed to have vanished completely. Indeed, Eustace began to fear that he was not in the United Kingdom, else he would certainly have heard of him, or the man would have seen in the newspapers the advertisement inquiring for his whereabouts. From time to time Eustace wrote to Hagar of his ill success, and received replies wherein she expressed her detestation of the shop, and bidding him continue his search; whereupon, encouraged to fresh exertions, Eustace would resume his wanderings. His adventures while thus engaged were many and various; and in the end his efforts were crowned with success.

One day, while Hagar was seated rather disconsolately in the back parlor, the side-door, which had been used by Dix for such of his friends as wished to dispose of stolen goods—a form of business which Hagar had abandoned—was opened boldly, and a tall man strode into the room. Hagar rose indignantly to repel the intruder, who had no right to enter by that way, when suddenly she saw his countenance, and fell back a step.

"Goliath!" she said with a pale face.

The tall man—he was almost a giant in point of height and size—nodded and smiled. He had closely-cropped red hair, and a rather brutal cast of countenance, by no means prepossessing. Again familiarily nodding to Hagar, who recoiled from him in aversion, he seated himself in a large armchair by the fire, which had formerly been used by dead Jacob Dix.

"My father's chair," said he, with a grin. "I have come to take possession of it, my dear."

"I am very glad to hear it," replied Hagar, recovering the use of her tongue. "Certainly it was about time, Mr. Dix."

"Don't call me Mister, or Dix, my dear! To you I shall always be Goliath—your Goliath."

"Indeed you shan't!" retorted Hagar, in a spirited manner. "I hate you now just as much as I did when you forced me to leave my people."

"That is uncommon cruel of you, seeing as you have been wearing my shoes all this time!"

"I have been wearing your father's shoes, you mean, and for your benefit solely. I did so simply because your father was good enough to take me in, after you had exiled me from the Romany."

"Oh, I know all about that, Cousin Hagar. We're cousins, ain't we?"

"Yes; and we are likely to continue cousins. But I'm tired of this sparring, Goliath. Where have you been all this time? and how did you learn that your father was dead?"

"Where I've been I'll tell you later," replied Goliath, rendered surly by the attitude of Hagar, "and as to how I knowed the old 'un was gone—why, a cove called Lorn told me just after I got out."

"Got out!" cried Hagar, noting the queer wording of the phrase; "so you have been in prison, Goliath!"

"You're a sharp one, you are!" grinned the red-haired man. "Yes, I've been in quod though I didn't intend to tell you so yet. I was Number Forty-three till a week ago, and they ticketed me for horse-coping. I got two years, and was took just arter you gave me the slip in New Forest; so now you know how I didn't see your noospaper notice about the old 'un kicking the bucket."

"You might speak of your father with more respect!" said Hagar, in a disdainful tone; "but what can one expect from a convict?"

"Come, none of that, cousin, or I'll twist your neck."

"You dare to lay a finger on me, and I'll kill you!" retorted Hagar, fiercely.

"Yah! You're as much a spitfire as ever!"

"More so—to you!" replied the girl. "I hate you now as I did when I left my tribe. Now you have come back, I'll go."

"And who is to look after the shop?"

"That is your business. My task here is ended. To-morrow I'll show you all the accounts—"

"Won't you share the property with me?" asked Goliath, in a wheedling tone.

"No, I shan't! To-morrow you must come with me and see Vark, to—"

"Vark!" echoed Goliath, starting to his feet; "is it that old villain who is to hand me over my tin?"

"Yes; your father employed him, so I thought—"

"Don't think! there ain't no time for thinking! Job! I'd better get my money afore the head of old Vark is stove in!"

"What do you mean?" asked Hagar, bewildered by his tone.

"Mean!" echoed Goliath, pausing at the door. "Well, I was in quod, as I told ye; there I came across Bill Smith—"

"The mandarin customer?"

"Yes; we managed to talk—how it don't matter to you; but I guess, when Bill Smith's out of quod, that Vark is bound for Kingdom-come! And Bill Smith *is* out!"

"What!" shrieked Hagar, alive at once to the danger which threatened the lawyer. "Out! Escaped?"

"That's the case. He got away last week, and they ain't got him yet. I'd best go and tell Vark to load his pistols. I don't want the old villain choked until I get my property square. You come too, cousin."

"Not just now. To-morrow."

"To-morrow won't do for me!" growled Goliath. "You come to-day, quick!"

"Oh," said Hagar, very disdainfully, "it is no use your taking that tone with me, Goliath. I must get ready my accounts to-night; and tomorrow, if you come here, I'll take them with you to Vark. When everything is set out to your satisfaction, you can enter into your property at once."

"Then you won't come now?"

"No; I have given you my answer."

"You'd best give me a pound or two," said Goliath, crossly. "I'm cleaned out, and I need money to get a bed for the night. You are as obstinate as ever, I see; but if you won't come, you won't. But I'll go and see Vark myself, and tell him about Bill Smith."

After which speech Goliath, with money in his pocket, went off to see the lawyer, cursing Hagar freely for her obstinacy. The man entirely forgot how she had devoted herself these many months to looking after his property; all he thought of was, that he loved her now, as much as he had done in the old days, and that she was still set on having nothing to do with him. Had she been an ordinary girl, he might have broken her spirit; but it was useless to attempt bullying with Hagar. She could give as good as she get; and this great, hulking Goliath could only admire and desire this spirited gipsy girl who disdained him and his money.

"Well," said Hagar to herself as she saw the last of him, "I have had one unexpected visitor; so by all the laws of coincidence I should have another to-day. I never knew one strange event happen without another following on its heels."

Hagar did not think precisely in so bookish a fashion, but the gist of her ideas was as above; and this proved correct before nightfall, at which time the unexpected second event duly occurred. This was none other than the arrival of Eustace Lorn, who entered the shop with a smile on his lips and a love light in his eyes. The girl knew his step—by some intuition of love, no doubt—and rushed to meet him with outstretched hands. These Eustace clasped ardently in his own; but as yet—so dignified was the attitude of Hagar—he did not venture to kiss her. His speech was warmer than his actions.

"Hagar! my dear Hagar!" he cried, in rapture, "at last I have come back. Are you not glad to see me?"

"I am delighted!" replied Hagar, beaming with pleasure—"more delighted than I was to see Goliath."

"Ah! he has returned, then? I found him at last, you see; and I recognized him from your description."

"He did not tell me of your meeting, Eustace."

"Oh, it was in this way," replied Lorn, as they entered the parlor together. "I had searched for him everywhere, as you know, but could not find him. Where he has been all these months I cannot say, as at our interview he refused to tell me."

"Perhaps he had a good reason for his silence," said Hagar, noting the fact that Goliath had kept quiet concerning his prison experiences.

"I dare say," laughed Lorn. "He looks a scamp. Well, I was down near Weybridge, resting by the roadside, when I saw a tall red-haired man passing. Remembering your description of Jimmy Dix, I felt sure that it was him; and I called out the name 'Goliath.' To my surprise, instead of stopping, he took to his heels."

"Ah, he had a good reason for that also."

"Not an honest one, I am afraid. Well; I ran after him, and in spite of his long legs I managed to catch him up. Then he showed fight; but when I explained who I was, and who you were, and how his father had died and left a fortune, Goliath grew quiet and friendly. He fraternized with me, accepted the loan of a few shillings—which was all I could spare—and took himself off to London. You have seen him?"

"Yes; and to-morrow I make up my accounts and give him over his property. Then I shall be free—free! Oh!" cried Hagar, stretching her arms, "how delicious it will be to be free once more—to leave this weary London, and see the sky and stars, sunrise and sunset—to hear the birds, and breathe the fresh air of the moors! I am going back to my tribe, you know."

"I don't know," said Eustace, taking her hand; "but I do know that I love you, and I have an idea that you love me. In this case, I think that instead of going back to your tribe you should come to your husband."

"My husband—you!" cried Hagar, with a charming blush.

"If you love me," said Eustace, and then was quiet.

"You leave the burden of proposing on me," cried Hagar, again. "Well, my dear, I will not hide from you that I do love you. Hush! let me go on. I have seen but little of you, yet what I have seen I have loved, every inch of it. I can read faces and estimate character better than most, and I know that you are a true, good, honorable man, who will make me, a poor gipsy, a better husband than I dared to expect. Yes, Eustace, I love you. If you care I will marry you—"

"Care! Marry me!" said Lorn, in rapture. "Why, my angel—"

"One moment," interrupted Hagar more seriously. "You know that I have no money, Eustace. Jacob Dix did not leave me a penny. I refuse to take anything from Goliath, who wants to marry me; and to-morrow I leave this shop as poor as when I came into it two years ago. Now, you are poor also; so two paupers are foolish to marry."

"But I am not poor!" cried Eustace, smiling—"that is, I am not rich, but I have sufficient for you and me to lead the life we love."

"But the life I love is the gipsy life," objected Hagar.

"I also am Romany by instinct," said Eustace joyously. "Have I not led the life of a vagabond these many months while looking for Goliath? See here, my dearest girl; when I left you I sold the Florentine Dante to a collector of books for a goodly sum. With the money I sought a caravan, and stocked it with books suitable for the country folk. All this time, my dear, I have been traveling with my caravan from town to town, earning my living by selling books; and I find it, really and truly, a very profitable concern. I ask you to be my wife—to share my caravan and gipsy life; so if you—"

"Eustace!" cried Hagar, joyfully, and threw her arms round his neck. That was all; the situation adjusted itself between them without further words. When the pair stepped out into Carby's Crescent to see the caravan—it was round the corner—they were already betrothed. For once in this world the course of true love was running smoothly. To marry Eustace; to live in a caravan; to wander about the country in true Bohemian fashion—Hagar could conceive of no sweeter existence. At last she was rewarded for her toils in the pawn-shop.

"This is our future home, Hagar," said Eustace, and pointed to the caravan.

It was a very spick and span vehicle, painted a light canary color, picked out with pale blue; and on either side was inscribed—also in azure—the legend, "E. Lorn, Bookseller." A sleek gray horse in brown harness was between the shafts; and the windows of the caravan were barred with brass rods and curtained with the whitest of curtains. Hagar fell in love with this delightful Noah's ark—as Eustace playfully called it—and clapped her hands. As it was about six o'clock and twilight, the street was almost emptied of people, so Hagar could indulge in her raptures to her heart's content.

"O Eustace, Eustace! 'Tis beautiful! 'tis perfect!" she cried. "If it is as neat within as without, I shall love it dearly!"

"You'll make me jealous of the caravan," said Eustace, rather uneasily. "But don't look inside, Hagar."

"Why not?" said she, with a wondering look.

"Oh, because, because—" he began, in confusion, and then stopped. Hagar looked at the door of the caravan, and Eustace turned his eyes in the same direction. It opened slowly, and a face— a brutal white face—looked out. The man to whom this visage—it was covered with a hairy growth of some days—belonged peered out at Eustace; then his gaze wandered to Hagar. As the light fell on his sullen looks, she gave a cry; the man on his side uttered an oath, and the next moment, dashing open the door, he had leaped out, and brushing past the pair, was racing down the street which led from Carby's Crescent into the larger thoroughfare.

Eustace looked surprised at this sudden flight, and turned an inquiring look on Hagar, who was pale as sculptured stone.

"Why are you so pale?" he said, taking her hand; "and why did my friend run away at the sight of you?"

"Your friend?" said Hagar, faintly.

"Yes; for the time being at all events. He is only a poor tramp I found near Esher the other day. He was lying in a ditch half-dead for want of food, so I took him into my caravan, and looked after him till he got better. He asked me to take him up to London; and I was about to tell you about him when he ran away."

"Why did you not wish me to look into the caravan?"

"Well," said Eustace, "this tramp seemed rather nervous; I'm afraid a hard life has told on the poor soul. A strange face always made him afraid, and I thought that if you looked in suddenly, he might be alarmed. As it is—"

"As it is, he was alarmed when he did see me," burst out Hagar. "He well might be, as I know him!"

"You know him—that tramp?"

"Tramp! He is a convict—Bill Smith—the one I wrote to you about."

"What! that blackguard who was engaged in the mandarin swindle!" cried Eustace, taken aback—"who stole those diamonds! I thought he was in prison!"

"So he was; but he escaped last week. The police are looking for him."

"Who told you this, Hagar?"

"Goliath. He was in prison also, for horse-stealing; but he has just been let out—a few days ago. Bill Smith—Larky Bill as they call him—broke out, and he wants to kill Vark, the lawyer."

"Then I have unconsciously helped him to escape justice," said Lorn, in vexed tones. "I really thought he was a tramp; had I known who he was I would not have helped him. He is a brute!"

"He'll be a murderer soon!" cried Hagar, feverishly. "For heaven's sake, Eustace, repair your error by going to Scotland Yard and telling them that the man is in London! You may be able to prevent a crime."

"I'll go," said Eustace, getting on to the driving seat of the caravan. "I'll see about this tonight, and return to talk to you to-morrow. One moment"—he leaped down again—"a kiss, my dear."

"Eustace! there are people about!"

"Well, they didn't stop Bill Smith running away, so they won't object to a kiss between an engaged couple. Good-by, dearest, for the last time. To-morrow we meet to part no more."

It was in considerable agitation that Hagar returned to her pawn-shop. The coming of Goliath, the arrival of Eustace, the unexpected escape of Bill Smith—all these events crowded so rapidly into her life—in the space of an hour, as one might say—that she felt unnerved and alarmed. She did not know what the next day might bring forth, and was particularly careful in locking up the house on this night, lest the escaped convict should take it into his head to enter therein as a burglar. The next twelve hours were anything but pleasant to Hagar.

With the daylight came more assurance; also Vark and Goliath. The lean lawyer was much agitated at the news of the escape, and feared—as he well might—that his miserable life was not safe from so bitter an enemy as Larky Bill. However, his fear did not prevent him from attending to business; and the whole of that morning Hagar was busy explaining accounts and payments and receipts to Vark and Goliath. The lawyer tried hard to find fault with the administration of Hagar; to pick holes in her statements; but, thanks to the rigid honesty of the girl, and the careful manner in which she had conducted her business, Vark, to his great disgust, was unable to harm her in any way. Everything was arranged fairly, and Goliath expressed himself quite satisfied with the statement of his property. Then he made a speech.

"It seems that I have thirty thousand quid," said he, exultingly; "also a pop-shop, which I'll give the kick to. With the rhino I can set up as a gent—"

"That you can never be!" retorted Hagar, scornfully.

"Not unless you look arter me. See here, you jade, when I was poor you said naught to me; now I am rich you—"

"I say the same, Goliath. When you were an honest man I refused you; now you are a felon I—"

"Was a felon," corrected Goliath. "I'm out of quod now."

"Well, I won't marry you. I hate you!" cried Hagar, stamping her foot; "and indeed, if you must know, I'm going to marry Eustace Lorn."

"What! that puppy!" cried Goliath, in a rage.

"That man—which you aren't! I'll live in a caravan and sell books."

Here Goliath broke out into imprecations, and was hardly restrained from violence, so enraged was he. He swore that for her years of service he would not give Hagar a penny; she would leave the pawn-shop as poor as when she entered it.

"I intend to," said Hagar, coolly. "I shan't even take the mourning I wore for your father. My red dress is good enough for the caravan of Eustace; and to-morrow I'll put it on, and leave the pawn-shop forever."

This was all that Goliath could get out of her. He offered to settle the money on her, to go in a caravan round the country if she wished it; but all to no purpose. Hagar had surrendered her stewardship in such wise that not even Vark, who hated her, could find a flaw in the accounts. These things being settled, she declared that she was going away with Eustace, after one more night in the pawn-shop. First the altar and the marriage service; then the caravan and the country; and from this program Hagar never swerved.

That same evening Eustace came to see Hagar, and told her that he had given notice at Scotland Yard of Smith's escape, and that the police were now looking for him. While they were talking over this, Vark, pale and scared-looking, made his appearance. He told the engaged pair a piece of news which astonished them not a little.

"I went to the police about Smith," said he, rubbing his lean hands together, "and I found out that not only one convict escaped, but two."

"Two!" cried Hagar; "and the second?"

"Is Goliath—your friend Jimmy Dix. He got three years, not two; and he broke prison with Larky Bill."

"What a fool to come here!" cried Eustace, recovering from his surprise.

"On the contrary, I think he was very wise," said Hagar; "only I knew him as Goliath, and under that name he was arrested and sentenced. As James Dix, the heir of Jacob, the owner of thirty thousand pounds, no one would suspect him of being an escaped convict. But how did he get rid of his prison clothes?"

"The police told me," grinned Vark. "The two broke into a house and stole suits to fit 'em. Bill Smith was wounded by a steel trap, so hid in the ditch where Mr. Lorn found him. Goliath came up here boldly to get his money. If I hadn't heard his description at Scotland Yard I should never have suspected him."

"Did you tell them he was here?" asked Lorn, sharply.

"No; but I'll do so unless he gives me half his money—fifteen thousand pounds. If he does, I'll smuggle him over to America. If he doesn't—"

"Well," said Hagar, "if he doesn't, you Judas?"

"I'll give him up to the police."

"You beast!" cried the girl, furiously, "you low reptile! You make capital out of everything. Goliath has conferred nothing on you but benefits; why, he warned you about Smith, and so gave himself into your hands; yet you would betray him!"

"I thought you hated the man!" quavered Vark, astonished at this outburst.

"So I do; but I think you might let him enjoy his money in peace. If he has been in jail, he hasn't deserved it half so much as you."

"I want half his money," said the lawyer, sullenly.

"What good will it do?" asked Lorn. "Bill Smith may kill you."

"I'm not afraid of him!" snapped Vark, turning pale nevertheless. "I have Bolker to stay with me at night, and I've got my pistols. Besides, the police are after Bill, so he won't come here."

"Yes, he will," said Hagar, throwing open the door; "he'll gladly give his own neck to twist yours. Get out of this place, Judas! You poison the air!"

Vark whimpered and protested, but Hagar drove him out and locked the door on him. When in the street, he turned round and shook his fist at the house wherein dwelt the woman he now hated as much as he had loved. She had escaped his toils, she had run clear of the traps he had laid for her; and now, having discharged her trust towards the dead, she was going out into the wide world with the man she loved; poor indeed as regards worldly wealth, but rich in the possession of Lorn's honest heart. No wonder Vark was wrathful.

The house in which Vark lived, was down by the river, and near that ruinous wharf whither Bill Smith on a certain memorable occasion had dragged Bolker. It was a gloomy old ramshackle mansion, which had seen better days in the early part of the century, but now it was given over to the lawyer, his deaf old house-keeper, and the rats. On the present occasion Bolker was also staying there, by desire of Vark. The wretched solicitor, who had sold so many thieves, and who was now terribly afraid of one, insisted that the lad should stay by him, in case of need. But Nemesis was not to be tricked in that way.

Passing through the gloomy streets on his way to this den, Vark, who had grown a trifle hard of hearing, did not hear the stealthy footfalls of one who stole after him; nor did he see a shadow gliding close at his heels. It was a windy night, and the moon was veiled on occasions by a rack of flying clouds. The lawyer walked slowly on, until he ascended the flight of worn steps which led to his hall door. As he did so, a black cloud swept before the moon, and lingered there so long that Vark could not find the keyhole. When he did so, the door blew open with a crash, and Vark measured his length on the stone pavement of the hall. Bill Smith saw his opportunity of entering the house unnoticed, and flew swiftly up the steps, and past the prostrate man, who was so confused by his fall that he did not know of the man flitting by. At this moment Bill could have killed Vark easily; but he judged that the hall, with the open door, was too public; moreover, he wished to get into the room where the lawyer kept his safe. Vark once dead, and Bill intended to open the safe with his keys, and then escape well laden with plunder. But of all these dark plans against his life and moneys Vark was ignorant.

As he gathered himself up and closed the door, his housekeeper came down the stairs with a candle. Grumbling at her for being late, Vark made her precede him into a little room at the back, looking on to the river. Larky Bill took off his boots, grasped the knife he was carrying, and went after the old man and woman. When he looked through a crack of the door into the room, he started back and swore under his breath, for therein were Bolker and Goliath. Bill began to think he would not be able to kill Vark after all.

He hid in a dark corner as the housekeeper repassed him on the way up the stairs, and then returned to his vantage point near the door of the room, where he could both hear and see. What ensued made him more resolved than ever to kill Vark. Such an ungrateful bloodsucker, thought Bill, did not deserve to live.

"I am glad to see you here," said Vark to Goliath, who rose at his entry. "You got my note asking you?"

"Yes, or I shouldn't be cooling my heels in this hole of yours?" growled Goliath, savagely. "What do you want?"

"Fifteen thousand pounds," said Vark, tersely.

"Half the money left by the old 'un! And why?"

"Because I know you bolted from jail," replied Vark, coolly, "and that the police are looking for you."

"Do you intend to give me up?" asked Goliath, grinding his teeth.

Vark rubbed his hands. "Why not?" he snarled. "I gave up Bill Smith and got the reward; but I'd rather have half your money than put you in jail again."

"I've a mind to kill you."

"Oh, I'm not frightened," said Vark, with an ugly look. "Bolker sits here, and Bolker has pistols. You can't kill me."

"No; I'll leave Bill Smith to do that," said Goliath, coolly.

"Bah! I'm not afraid of that ruffian!"

Before Goliath could reply there was a roar like an angry beast's, the door was burst violently open, and Bill Smith, knife in hand, hurled himself into the room. Vark yelled shrilly like a rabbit caught in a trap, and the next moment was dashed to the ground by the infuriated convict. Bolker ran out of the room crying for the police, and flew through the passage, out of the hall door, and into the windy night. His shrieks roused the neighborhood.

In a flash Goliath saw a chance of gaining a pardon by saving Vark from being murdered. He threw himself on Bill, who was striking blindly with his knife at the struggling lawyer, and strove to wrench him off.

"Let be, curse you!" shrieked the convict. "He sold me; he said he'd sell you! If I swing for it, I'll kill him!"

"No, d—n you, no!"

Goliath plucked the wretch off the prostrate man like a limpet off a rock; and then commenced a furious struggle between the pair. Vark, wounded and covered with blood, had fainted away. The next moment, while Smith and Goliath were swaying together in a fierce embrace, the room was filled with policemen, brought hither by the shrieking Bolker. Seeing them enter, Bill, wrenching himself free of Goliath, snatched up a revolver that Bolker had left on the table when he fled, and fired two shots at the prostrate body of his enemy.

"Yah! Brute! Curse you! Die!"

Then he returned to the window which overlooked the river, and keeping the police at bay with the pistol, he wrenched it open. Goliath sprang forward to seize him, but Bill, with a howl of rage, dashed the revolver in his face.

"Curse you for rounding on a pal!"

The next moment he had swung himself out of the window, and those in the room heard the splash of his heavy body as it struck the waters of the Thames.

Two months after the foregoing event, a caravan, painted yellow and drawn by a gray horse, was rolling along one of the green lanes leading to Walton-on-Thames. It was the beginning of spring, and the buds were already running along the leafless branches of the trees, while the sharpness of the air was tempered by a balmy breath foretelling the advent of the warm months of the year. Beside the caravan strode a tall dark man arrayed in a rough suit of homespun, and near him walked a woman with an imperial carriage and lordly gait. She wore a dress of dark red, much stained and worn; but her eye was full of fire, and her cheek healthy. The pair were of humble condition, but looked contented and happy. As the horse plodded onward in the bursts of sunlight, the two talked.

"So Vark died, after all, Hagar," said the man, gravely.

"As you know," she replied, "the two pistol shots killed him; and Bill Smith was drowned in the river as he attempted to escape. He gave up his life to compass his revenge."

"I am glad Goliath was pardoned."

"Oh, as to that," said Hagar, indifferently, "I am neither glad nor sorry. I think myself that he only strove to save Vark in order to gain pardon."

"Well, he got what he wanted," said Eustace, reflectively.

"He wouldn't if the public hadn't taken the matter up," retorted Hagar: "but they made him out a hero. Nonsense! As if Goliath was the man to forgive Vark, who intended to sell him. Well, he is free now, and rich. I dare say he'll lose all his money in dissipation. He had much better have held on to the pawn-shop, instead of giving it up to Bolker."

"Bolker is very young to have a business."

"Don't you believe it," replied Hagar, drily. "Bolker is young in years, but old in wickedness. He bought the pawn-shop business with the reward he got from Lord Deacey for recovering the diamonds. Bolker will grind down the poor of Carby's Crescent, and develop into a second Jacob Dix."

"You are glad to be away from the pawn-shop?"

"I should think so!" she replied, with a loving glance at Eustace. "I am glad to leave dirty Lambeth for the green fields of the country.

I am a gipsy, and not used to the yoke of commerce. Also, my dear, I am glad to be with you always."

"Are you indeed, Mrs. Lorn?" said her husband, laughing.

"Yes, Mrs. Lorn," repeated Hagar, very sedately, "I am Mrs. Lorn now, and Hagar of the Pawn-shop, with all her adventures, is a phantom of the past."

Eustace kissed her, and then chirruped the horse onward. They passed down the lane, across the dancing shadows, and went away hopefully into the green country towards the gipsy life. Hagar of the Pawn-shop had come to her own at last.

The Adventures of a
Lady Pearl-Broker

Beatrice Heron-Maxwell

I

"WHAT I WANT is this," said Mr. Leighton, the prince of pearl merchants, throwing himself back in his chair, and looking severely at
me over the top of his glasses:

"I want a lady, a young lady, who is good-looking, smart, and
free of encumbrances, who has a nice manner, and a sweet voice,
is accustomed to society and yet knows how to hold her own, and
who, besides all these, has plenty of pluck."

I meditated for a moment.

"I have no encumbrances, Mr. Leighton," I said. "I am a widow,
as you know, and have few relations, and I am quite sure that I
have any amount of courage—but as to the rest of the qualities you
are in search of, I—"

"The rest are all right," he interrupted. "I don't require you to
tell me that, Mrs. Delamere; I can see it for myself. But"—he leant
toward me and tapped my chair with his glasses—"I think it only
right to tell you that there is a good deal of risk, which I share with
you, and a chance of danger which you must venture by yourself.
Are you prepared to do it?"

I reflected again.

"The risk would be both yours and mine?" I questioned. "In
what way?"

"In the way of monetary loss," he answered; "it would be possible for you to lose more than you could ever repay, and I should
have to bear the brunt of it, because it would be my property. You

couldn't guarantee it, and all I can do is to be assured—as I am—of your trustworthiness. The risk remains."

"And the danger," I concluded, "is entirely mine. Very well, Mr. Leighton, I consent."

"Not so fast," he said; "you must wait till you know what it is. In the first place you would get, as I have already told you, a good income from it, partly in salary, partly in commission, and the work would not be arduous. It would mean two or three hours a day three or four times a week; sometimes less, sometimes more. It would entail your living in town, in a house or rooms of your own, and keeping your own carriage. Now for the work itself. Have you heard of lady pearl-brokers?"

I replied that I had not.

"Well," he said, "it has been tried in Paris, and with great success. There is a certain number of ladies of good position who undertake to be mediums between pearl merchants and their clients. I do not mean to say that you have to solicit orders from your personal friends—not at all. You may occasionally treat with private people, who wish to lay out a large sum in gems; but, as a rule, your business would be with the heads of large jewellers firms, and as they are generally of the upper class, it is easier to approach them if you can do so on equal terms. The qualifications I have mentioned are all desirable in order to facilitate good business. And in addition, we find that ladies have an instinct for appraising the value of jewels. We in the trade of course learn how to distinguish between good and bad, but ladies seem to become experts without any training at all. They can almost detect a flaw with their eyes shut. But the risk is that you would have to carry about with you sometimes fifteen or twenty thousand pounds' worth of jewels."

He looked to see if I showed any sign of alarm, but I was gazing at him quite quietly, and he went on:

"Your only plan is to observe absolute secrecy as to your occupation; to choose your servants and house carefully; to drive in your own carriage with a coachman you can depend on, and, under all circumstances, to keep your head."

"And the jewels," I added. "I am ready to begin work as soon as you like, Mr. Leighton. I can arrange about my carriage in a day or two; and with regard to a house, I should greatly prefer, in any case at first, to stay on at the Howarth Hotel, where I am at present. I have been going in a little for journalism, as you know. I shall give out that I have some literary employment which necessitates my staying in town. I am really safer in many ways at an hotel, especially as I shall always carry the pearls about with me, in a safe place which I shall contrive in my dress. Let me try it at all events."

"Very well," he said; "I will let you manage things in your own way. Only remember that you must always be looking out for an attack. If it once gets known—and London thieves learn these things in the most marvellous way—that a woman is in possession of jewellery to any extent, she is marked at once, and sooner or later they have a try for it."

"It is worth some risk to have an assured income," I said, smiling. "Money is so easy to lose, Mr. Leighton; so hard to gain. And poor widows are looked upon in society so often as adventuresses. People seem to think it a disgrace that one's husband should not leave one enough to live on. Well! I will return in a week from to-day, and ask for instructions, and my first instalment of jewels."

"Think it well over," said Mr. Leighton, as, he shook hands; "put yourself in a pearl-broker's place—imagine yourself carrying about a small fortune with you, and think how you would act in the event of anything untoward happening to you."

I thought it a very good plan, and decided to adopt his suggestion, although I knew that nothing would now deter me from undertaking the work. As he showed me into the square courtyard that led to his office, I involuntarily glanced round in all directions to see if there were any suspicious-looking person about, or if my presence there were attracting any notice. The buildings all round the court looked mostly like counting-houses, or wholesale warehouses. There was very little sign of life; a clerk diligently adding up ledgers behind a very dingy window, two or three boys dodging each other round the posts that stood at intervals across the entrance to the square; a flower-woman, with a dilapidated basket, sitting in the gutter trying to rock an unruly baby to sleep. I went slowly down the steps.

Supposing that I was holding the jewels in my muff, instead of the very meagre purse it contained, would it be safe to cross the court and make my way to the thoroughfare beyond?

Quite safe, I decided mentally; and as I did so I glanced up at the house opposite. High up on the fifth story was an open window, and hanging out of it a little way, as though held there, was an Oriental-looking curtain.

Some movement in the curtain attracted my eye, and I looked still more closely. Half hidden by its folds, which he was clutching with one hand so as to shield him from observation, was a man with a strange, wild face, and matted black hair. He had a dark skin, and a Hindoo cast of feature, and he might have been anything from a fakir to a cloth merchant. I had seen such faces amongst the native workers, or the jugglers, at exhibitions; it was a familiar type; yet something in his fixed regard vaguely troubled me. We looked steadfastly at one another for a moment, then he dropped the curtain so that it concealed him. I walked away down the court with the absolute certainty in my mind that, as soon as my back was turned, he peeped out again after me.

I resolutely put him out of my thoughts; it would not do, I told myself, to be nervous because people looked at me, when I was soon going to undertake so great a responsibility. I must learn to be equable, and while noticing everything, not to give undue weight to trifles.

I took a cab and drove back to the Howarth Hotel, where, as I had often stayed from time to time before I was a widow and afterwards, I felt quite at home.

For the next few days I occupied myself entirely in preparations for my new undertaking, keeping always in my mind the thought of possible danger. But my nerves remained quite steady, and by the end of the week I was more determined than ever to go through it, and to make it a success. I had bought a neat little brougham, and a charming horse, and arranged to keep them in a private stable which was to let close by; and I had found a coachman who seemed the one of all others to be desired. Steady, sober, unmarried, with the very highest references, and carrying such a good character written across his honest face, I felt I was absolutely safe in his hands. He was to live over the stable, and intended, as he put it, to keep himself to himself; and I was very glad to hear it.

I had contrived secret pockets in various unexpected places in my dress, those I was especially pleased with being some small oblong ones in the lower part of my sleeves, on the inner side of the wrists under the cuffs. It would be impossible for me to lose anything out of them, and quite impossible for anyone to cut out the pockets while I had my senses about me. With regard to keeping the jewels at night, I bought a small safe, but, for fear of attracting attention, I did not have it fastened to the wall of my room or leave it out in evidence; instead, I placed it inside my trunk, which served as a settee in a corner of my bedroom, and was always covered with a rug; and screwed it right through the bottom of my trunk to the floor.

Then I enclosed the key in a brooch, the back of which opened with a secret spring. The receptacle had been originally intended for a portrait or a lock of hair, and the spring was concealed under one of the letters of my name, "Mollie," written in small brilliants across the front of the brooch. I had been in the habit of wearing it every day, and there would be nothing unusual therefore in my doing so. It fastened with a safety pin, and a small chain attached to it went round my neck.

It was a proud though an anxious moment for me when, at the end of my next interview with Mr. Leighton, I emerged from the office with pearls to the value of £11,000 concealed about me.

There were amongst them some specially fine ones, which he had first suggested should wait until I had had a little practice in my profession, but at my earnest entreaty he yielded them to me at last. I have always hated having things made easy for me—there is then no satisfaction in accomplishing them.

I glanced up at the window where I had seen my Oriental friend; it was closed, and there was no sign of anyone within.

But as I passed through the posts at the end of the court, a curious figure, half English and half Eastern-looking, turned out of the street, and was apparently going to pass me.

A pair of black eyes flashed into mine, and the man turned quickly and retraced his steps into the crowded street, where I lost sight of him in a moment.

This was the second time I had met his glance. I wondered what the third would bring me. I felt a sort of superstition about it. Those eyes had a knack of haunting one. They had pursued me before, both in my waking and sleeping dreams, after I had seen them the first time. I felt sure I was destined to be brought into contact with their owner in the future, and thought of him more than once.

But the business that occupied me during the next fortnight or three weeks helped to banish the remembrance of him from my mind, and an occurrence that happened at the end of that time drove him completely from it for a period. I was beginning to get accustomed to all the ins and outs of my new trade, and to find an exhilaration in the variety of experiences that it brought me; and the proverbial good luck that always waits on beginners had also not failed to attend my first efforts.

Mr. Leighton was so pleased with me that he doubled my commission on a transaction I carried through with a well-known jeweller who was noted for being difficult of approach. He said that I had shown great skill and tact, and made an opening for future business, and insisted on my profiting by it as well as himself.

I had almost ceased to be nervous about my valuable charge, and on the day that preceded the occurrence I speak of, I felt particularly cheerful and confident.

Mr. Leighton had intrusted to me a more valuable cargo than usual; there were some black pearls of great price amongst the white ones, and also a pink one of rare beauty that had already gained a name for itself. I had made up my mind to surprise him when next I demanded an interview, by telling him that I had placed them all—I had one or two clients in my mind's eye, and amongst them an Australian millionaire, whose latest fad, I had been told, was the collection of quaint or unique gems.

The pink pearl should be his; I had fully decided on that.

One small incident occurred on the morning of that day, but I did not attach any importance to it. I passed a man twice—once in the Strand, once in Regent Street; and noticing that he looked attentively at me, wondered why his face seemed familiar, and where I could have seen him before.

Later I remembered that I had passed him on the hotel staircase one day in the early part of the week, and concluded that this was the reason for his apparent recognition of me, and mine of him. He had a pale, fair, determined face, with a very unpleasant expression; that was all that I remarked about him.

I was rather tired when I went to bed that night, and I felt almost inclined to leave the pearls, just as they were, in the hiding places of my dress until the morning. But it was my rule to look at them, count them, and so make sure of their safety, every night, and I would not let myself break through it. I found them as I expected, all there, safe and sound.

Some sudden caprice made me stop when I was about to open my trunk and put them inside the safe, and I changed my mind, and placed them instead in a writing-case, the key of which I placed under the pillow with my trunk key, as well as the brooch containing my safe key.

I looked to my window to see that the fastening was right, fixed on to it, as usual, a small patent immoveable hasp, locked my door, and placed a wedge against it, looked into my wardrobe and under my bed, lit my night-light, and five minutes afterwards I was deeply and soundly asleep.

I dreamt that I was wandering at the bottom of the sea, and that all around me lay wondrous gems of every hue and shape; strange creatures floated near me with jewelled eyes; long seaweeds, fringed with pearls and diamonds, clear and bright as drops of water, brushed against my face, and twined themselves in my hair—it was a very Paradise of pearls. I thought I gathered some of all kinds until my hands and arms were laden, and soaring upwards with them through the clear water, reached the top of the ocean, and felt the fresh wind blowing on my face.

And then quite suddenly I realised that I was wide-awake, that the room was in total darkness, and that a cold air was coming from the direction of the window.

I strained my eyes towards the vague outline of the curtain, I strained my ears to catch the faintest sound, and in the silence, a hand came stealing gently, stealthily, amongst the folds of the sheet round my neck, feeling for my face, and an almost imperceptible rustle told me that someone was kneeling beside me.

My heart seemed to stop beating for one second, and then, with an awful surging rush of sickening terror, throbbed to suffocation; the pulses in my throat and head beat like iron sledge-hammers; I was too paralysed to scream or move, and like lightning the thought flashed through my brain of how absolutely helpless I was, through my own agency. The door was not only locked, but wedged—even if I made myself heard, they would have to force an entrance. I might pay the penalty of my life for the sake of saving the pearls.

As the stealthy fingers reached my lips, and drew aside the sheet, a deadly faintness seized me; I was almost unconscious, when, with a new thrill of horror, I recognised the strong, sharp smell of chloroform, and knew that something cold and wet was lying across my face.

The shock recalled me to new life and courage. I have never been rendered insensible by chloroform; I am strangely unsusceptible to it, as I knew from more than one experience of it.

For a minute or two there was a loud singing in my ears, a feeling of alternately diminishing and swelling, with a sensation of floating in air; then the effect had passed off, and I was absolutely myself. My eyes, accustomed to the darkness, could discern over the edge of the handkerchief a shadow that was bending over my trunk; the keys had evidently been removed from my pillow; the tray had been lifted out; the thief was now opening the safe. With a sigh of relief, I remembered that the jewels were not there; every moment's delay was precious to me. He would, of course, find the key of the writing-desk—unless he had missed taking it from under my pillow—and would try that next.

Against the dark space of the open window I could see the silhouette of a man's form, leaning on the ledge outside, apparently resting on a ladder. The other man raised himself from the trunk, looked towards the bed and approaching me, drew something from his pocket. I remembered with a shudder that I had heard if you wanted to bring people round who were under the influence of a drug, a sharp cut with a knife was efficacious.

He was close to me—he had removed the handkerchief; his fingers were at my throat lightly pressing it; his other hand was raised. I could bear it no longer—something in my brain seemed to snap. I opened my lips to scream, when shrill and clear from the room above me rang out an awful cry in a woman's voice, "Murder—Help!" The man made one bound to the window, and gaining the sill, stood there hesitating, and as shriek after shriek echoed through the hotel, and a sound of hurrying steps and voices arose, he dropped his feet over the ledge, and disappeared.

I sprang out of bed, and staggered to the door, but my limbs failed me. I could see the brightness of the electric light shining through the chinks; I could hear the shrieks upstairs dying away to hysterical sobs and laughter; I could distinguish that the voices and steps were coming towards my room, and that someone was repeating my number, 13, over and over again.

I felt that I should die there in the darkness, with that dreadful open window, in which I fancied I could still see the outline of a man's form close to me. They were knocking, they were calling to me to open the door.

With a supreme effort I pushed the wedge aside, dragged myself up to my knees, and turned the key, and as a flood of light and an excited crowd of people burst in, I fell back senseless.

For many days I was too weak and ill to think much of that terrible night, but gradually it recalled itself to me, and they told me how I was saved.

The lady who occupied the room above mine was in the habit—for which I invoke fervent blessings on her head—of sleeping with her window wide open, and mercifully had, on this particular night, forgotten to open it. She therefore arose at about two o'clock in the morning, and threw it up, putting out her head at the same time to see if it was raining. Perceiving to her horror the crouching figure of a man on the sill beneath, she proceeded to shriek until assistance came.

The thieves, of whom no trace has ever been found, had laid their plans well; they must have concealed themselves during the day on the roof, and had fastened a rope ladder to one of the chimneys; then descending, had neatly cut out a pane from my window, removed my patent hasp, and opened it.

I did not wish, of course, for my future safety, to betray my occupation to the public and I assured the hotel manager and the police that I possessed only a few valuable jewels, and that I thought the thieves might have mistaken my room for that of someone else. I had little doubt in my own mind that the man I had met on the hotel stairs and in the Strand had been shadowing me, and had discovered that I was worth robbing.

Mr. Leighton was so upset when he heard of my adventure, that he wished me to resign my post at once.

But I pleaded so hard to be allowed to continue, that eventually I won him over; as a concession to his fears for me, I gave up the hotel, and took a flat in Victoria Street.

"No thieves can get at me here without my knowing it," I said; "I shall be quite safe now."

But I spoke a little too soon.

2

"WELL, MRS. DELAMERE," said Mr. Leighton, as I entered his office one day, "are you still determined to go on with your work; or has your courage failed you now that you know the dangers of pearl-broking?"

"I have plenty of courage still," was my answer, "and it would take more than one alarm to make me give up my profession now that I have seriously adopted it. I have sold the black pearls for the price you wished. They have gone over to the Continent to-day with a foreign dealer, to be set in a pendant for a royal marriage. I have the pink pearl yet to place, but I am reserving that for a special mission. Will you let me have some white ones suitable for making a necklace? I fancy I might do something with them."

Mr. Leighton went to his safe, and unlocked it.

"I have not only the pearls here, but also the order for them—if they suit," he said.

He handed me a letter, of which at first I could make no sense, and watched me with an amused smile while I puzzled over it. Suddenly the solution of the puzzle came to me.

The letter was written backwards after the fashion of Hindustani and Persian epistles, and began with what I had at first taken for the signature.

It was couched in flowery and figurative language, difficult to understand, but I succeeded in making out that it was a request for some pearls, well matched and pure in colour, to be sent on approval for the writer to see before purchasing. He required them, it stated, for a Ranee of great wealth, who was willing to pay a high price for the desire of her fancy. It concluded by naming an hour when he would be ready to receive Mr. Leighton's emissary.

The address was printed very legibly after the name: 14, Saint Athelstane's Court. I lifted my head in surprise.

"Why," I said, "that is close to here, Mr. Leighton!"

"Just opposite," he answered. "I suppose that is how my Oriental friend came to think of me. It seems singular, though. These natives generally deal with each other. I don't altogether like it. Perhaps it would be better to let it slide."

He could not have said anything more certain to resolve my own doubts and indecision.

"Certainly not," I said. "I will take the pearls, and go to see Ali Mahomed Khan to-morrow."

Mr. Leighton would not give them to me at first.

"You must not be foolhardy, Mrs. Delamere," he said gravely. "I begin to feel a little worried about your adventurous spirit. If any serious harm comes to you, I shall never forgive myself. Give up this particular quest to please me."

But, partly from some impulse for which I could not account, and yet could not resist, and partly from a sort of resentful pique that had taken possession of me since my narrow escape at the hotel, I was not to be shaken from my resolve.

I carried off the pearls to my flat, and, placing them in the safe which was let into the wall of the passage, slept the sleep of the just and the unconcerned.

I felt fully prepared the next morning for Ali Mahomed Khan, and I did not doubt that it was he, or some person belonging to him, who had made me the object of scrutiny on the day of any first visit to Mr. Leighton's office. I recalled the swarthy face that had looked down on me from the opposite house, and again the chance meeting at the entrance posts.

His interest in me was accounted for; he was, no doubt, contemplating dealings with Mr. Leighton. I drove to the corner of St. Athelstane's Court early in the afternoon, and sent the carriage away, in order to avoid attracting attention, then quietly made my way to No. 14, and knocked at the door. It was opened immediately, and in the dim passage beyond I saw an *ayah*, who silently invited me to enter.

"Is Ali Mahomed Khan at home?" I said.

She nodded. "Waiting for you," she answered in English. As I stepped in, the door closed behind me, and I noticed, though it did not make any special impression on me at the time, that there was no visible lock or fastening—no more apparent mode of effecting exit from the inside than there had been of entrance outside.

The *ayah* passed in front of me to the stairs, and led me up four long flights, our footsteps echoing dismally through the silence of the house.

At the top of the first flight, a window, so encrusted with dirt that the panes were opaque, was slightly open, and through the space I could set a narrow vista of deserted back yard.

The rooms had evidently been used in former times as warehouses, and through the doorless apertures we passed on the way up I saw rows of empty shelves and cases.

Everything spoke of disuse and oblivion, and I felt that I should breathe more freely if I were a few yards off in the open street again. Finally we stopped before a heavy dark curtain shrouding an archway, and my guide, drawing back the folds with one hand, directed me with the other to pass through an open door beyond.

It was a singular transition from the desolate uncarpeted staircase to a room covered with soft thick rugs, filled to repletion with every sort of Oriental furniture and bric-a-brac, the atmosphere heavy with mingled scents—of sandal-wood, kuskus, lacquer, and attar-of-roses.

For a moment, as I entered, it seemed to stifle me, and I felt a little dizzy.

There were two men in the room—one plainly dressed, small and lithe, with a keen, handsome face, who was writing at a table; the other, more elaborate in his attire, seated on some cushions, a tray with cups of coffee and dishes of sweetmeats at his side.

He looked steadfastly at me, and I recognised the strangely brilliant eyes whose glance, encountered twice before, had left such a vivid imprint on my mind.

He rose quietly and came to meet me.

"Mrs. Delamere, I think?" he said politely.

I bowed.

"This is my friend, Abdullah," he continued, indicating the man at the writing-table, then in a tone of authority, "give Mrs. Delamere a chair."

The man wheeled a low armchair forward, and I sat down.

I remember thinking as I did so, that I should be glad when our interview was over, and that, in the event of any difference of opinion arising between us as to terms, I should close the transaction at once and take my departure.

"You wished to look at some pearls," I said. "Mr. Leighton handed your letter to me and I—"

"Pardon me," he made a courteous gesture of interruption. "You will first take a little coffee?"

He handed one of the cups to me.

"Thank you, no," I answered; "I never take coffee."

"At least some of these," he said, lifting one of the little dishes.

"I would rather not, thank you," I answered again, and as he frowned a little, I added apologetically, "I am not fond of sweets."

The frown deepened, and he said slowly:

"We do not understand your Western ways. In our country, business is conducted with preliminary compliments, and to refuse a proffered hospitality is an affront. May I not persuade you to take one."

He was still holding the dish towards me, and I wavered. If I refused again, possibly he would take offence and decline to treat with me. It would be a pity to lose the chance of a sale that meant such a large profit to me, and that would greatly advance my prestige with Mr. Leighton.

The sweets looked very harmless; there were some small red and amber jujubes, dusted with sugar, that were probably made of Rahat Lakoum. I could at least take one of them, and then my Oriental friend would, I suppose, proceed to business.

We were all silent as I took the sweet and ate it, and in the stillness I heard the door, which was behind me, gently closed from the outside, and the faint sound of retreating foot-falls on the stairs. A sudden perception of danger came to me with so violent a shock that I involuntarily swallowed the remainder of the sweet-meat, though at that very instant I had noticed an unusual taste which came from a little nut in the centre of it.

I glanced towards the two men; they were both looking down on the ground, their faces devoid of expression, politely waiting my leisure. For a moment I was reassured, then again doubt assailed me. I looked round the room; was there any window through which I could call for assistance if anything untowards occurred?

Both windows were blocked up half way with heavy inlaid cabinets, above which only the upper panes were visible.

My heart began to beat a little fast; I felt that I must summon all my courage, and direct my attention to business with the hope of getting through it quickly and departing. All this flashed through my mind while I passed my handkerchief over my lips and cleared my throat to speak.

"If you will kindly tell me which stones you would like to see," were the words I essayed to utter, but with the first syllables my voice broke and died away.

I had no sense of pain, but a strange difficulty of articulation had suddenly taken possession of me: any throat felt cold and dead; my tongue lay lifeless in my mouth and refused to do its office. I realised, with an awful throb of terror, that my speech was paralysed, and for an instant the room swam round me, and I thought that I must faint.

But the very intensity of my alarm, and the uncertainty of what precise danger threatened me, steadied any nerves and kept me conscious.

Ali Mahomed raised his eyes, and said, in a quiet, measured way:

"Do not try to speak; it will not be possible to you for the next two hours. That sweet contained a small quantity of the active principle of coca—for the present your throat and tongue are paralysed.

"You are a brave woman, or you would have lost your senses when you found that you had lost your voice. But you have no need to be alarmed—I do not seek your life, nor do I desire to rob you. My motives are quite different. Do you wish to learn them, or will you do exactly as I tell you without seeking to inquire the reason?"

He read the answer in my eyes.

"Very well. I am quite willing to tell you. But first, if you will drink some of this"—he lifted a liqueur glass from the tray—"it will give you confidence; it is only an ordinary restorative."

I shook my, head. I would trust him no further. It might be drugged, and I must keep my senses clear, or all chance of escape would be over.

"I am a native of Kabalpur. Here I am no one; I pursue my business unremarked. In my own country I have much influence and renown, and when there is a difficult thing to be done men come to me. Abdullah there is in my power, and bound to me by many ties; therefore, he does as I bid him, and, with his assistance and that of Guzra Bai downstairs, I defy even your London police." All the while he was speaking I was striving to keep my attention concentrated on his words, and not to allow it to dwell on my own terrible sensations.

The feeling of powerlessness that had come to me with my loss of voice was intense—the shock had left me weak and unstrung, and I felt as if I must burst into tears; but my determination to keep calm, and avail myself of the first opportunity for release that might come, was so strong that it upheld me, and kept me outwardly quiet.

"I have been watching you closely for some time past, Mrs. Delamere," the smooth voice went on, "and I know your history well. You have few relations; none near enough to busy themselves in inquiry after you at once if you should disappear suddenly. By the time they realise that you are not to be found you will be safe in Kabalpur, or well on your way there. The servants at your flat would, of course, give the alarm if you did not return to-night, but you will explain your absence satisfactorily in a note to them which you will write here, and which Abdullah will send presently. With regard to your occupation, of which I have ascertained all the details, and which has provided me with the means of obtaining this interview without difficulty, your employer, Mr. Leighton, will not expect to hear from you for a day or two. It rests with you to decide what you will write to him. Since you sell the jewels for a commission, it can no longer matter to you whether they are sold or not; you will not be in a position to receive the profit. If you have them all with you here, the matter is easy. You will write a note resigning your post, and returning the jewels. If on the contrary you have some in the safe at your flat, it will be best to say that you have sold them, and to enclose the necessary amount. I can arrange for a cheque from my agents here. You understand that my motive is not robbery."

He paused for a moment. I endeavoured to say something in reply; useless—I was still absolutely dumb. I looked round the room again. Was there no possible outlet through which help might come?

His glance followed mine, and for the first time he smiled.

"If it were possible for you to escape and you did so, Mrs. Delamere," he said, "I should have no fear of you. For your own sake you would never reveal the danger you had run. It would double the risks, already rather great ones, of your profession. It would encourage everyone to take advantage of you; in fact, Mr. Leighton himself would refuse to let you incur them any more. But escape is impossible. Put the thoughts of it aside. You know, or you may not know, that some years ago, in an attack of the hill tribes on a cantonment, a young and beautiful English woman was believed to have perished in the flames of a burning bungalow. This was, however, a mistake. She was captured while insensible by some of my countrymen, and was carried to the Rajah's palace. She has remained there as his wife ever since, and, though her son cannot inherit the throne, he is the Rajah's favourite child. The Rajah is very much attached to her, and since she pines for her own country and her own people, to which he cannot permit her ever to return, he has thought that it might add to her happiness if she had a companion of her own race. He has commissioned me to arrange this for him. The lady is to be of good birth, young and handsome, clever and high-spirited—a dull companion would be useless. She must be one who would not be quickly missed or sought after, as all traces of her must be obliterated, and the transaction must never become known. You fulfil all the requirements, and my intentions are to disguise you as a native woman, passing you off as Guzra Bai's sister, and to return to Kabalpur with you at once. It will be necessary to keep you to a certain extent under the influence of drugs, which, for the time, will deprive you of memory and the desire to escape. They will not injure you nor give you pain, and when you arrive at your destination you will regain your usual state. You will be treated always with the greatest kindness, and there is no reason why your life should not be a happy one.

"Now will you write the letter to your servants?"

I nodded assent. I saw that my only chance was to appear submissive, and to gain time—above all, to put off the moment when they would give me the drug of which he spoke.

Abdullah placed the table and writing materials before me and I took up the pen to write.

At that moment there was a subdued knock, and he went hastily to the door and held a whispered colloquy with the *ayah*, whose voice I recognised.

Ali Mahomed listened attentively, and then said something in his own language, which sounded like an interrogation.

Abdullah's reply evidently was unpleasant to him, and they argued for some moments. Finally, Abdullah gained his point, and left the room with the ayah. I heard their descending steps with a new sinking at my heart. Was I, then, to be left absolutely alone with this awful man?

He came slowly towards me; then, struck by some new idea, passed out on to the landing, and called softly down to the others. Guzra Bai's voice answered him from the bottom of the house.

Now was my chance my only chance! I rose for an instant my brain went round; I trembled so that my limbs failed me then, desperately, I pulled myself together. It was for life and liberty, I thought. I crept towards the curtain. Ali Mahomed was evidently bending over the stairs, still speaking. I drew the curtain aside his back was towards me. Now! In a flash I was past him and down the first flight. As I turned the corner he was so close behind me that his fingers caught the lace of my cloak. The force of my descent tore it away, and I reached the next landing with almost one bound. He was calling Guzra Bai. I could hear her beginning to ascend. I was at the end of the third flight, she was midway up the second, and he with hands outstretched within a few feet of me at the back. The staircase window was half open now, and a long yard extended below it, with a high wall all round and a door at the end.

I jumped from the last step straight on to the sill and dropped. I was conscious of no sensation at all as I did so. The peril was too imminent and deadly for me to realise that I was taking a leap of about sixteen feet, and the force with which I reached the ground almost stunned me, and sent a thrill of pain all through me. But instinctively I picked myself up, and ran straight on to the door, and, stumbling, fell against it. The latch, old and worn, gave way with my weight—the door opened afterwards—I staggered through—thank God! I was in a narrow alley leading to a street.

I reached the top of it, and as I did so saw Abdullah coming towards me, and within a few paces of me.

With a strangled scream I turned and fled in the opposite direction, the few passers-by stopping and staring at me as I ran. I think if they had tried to stop me, I should have been done for. My strength was almost spent, and a mist was gathering before my eyes. A hansom loitering across the top of the street stopped; I signalled to the man, pointed up the turning he had just quitted and jumped in. As he whipped the horse, and we backed and turned, I saw Abdullah halt a few yards off, and then retreat.

I had dropped my card-case at some time during my flight, but I had a letter in my pocket, and pushing up the trap door I handed the envelope to the cabman.

Then I burst into tears, and I can only remember dimly, as in a dream, arriving at royal Mansions, Victoria Street, and hurrying up to my flat, where the maids, shocked and distressed at my condition, vainly sought for some time an explanation of it.

When I at last regained my voice, and told them that some cocaine, taken by mistake, had deprived me of it temporarily, they concluded that I had been to a dentist, and that my sufferings at his hands accounted for my state of nervous exhaustion.

As Ali Mahomed had wisely said, I did not care to make public my terrible experience with him, since it would have seriously damaged my chances in my profession; and when, after a fortnight's rest, I went to see Mr. Leighton, I merely said that my Oriental interview had been unsuccessful, and that the price offered for the jewels was inadequate.

But I mentally resolved to be more wary in my business appointments in the future.

3

"So your Oriental venture proved a failure, Mrs. Delamere?" said Mr. Leighton, interrogatively, when I called at his office. "There are disappointments even in pearl-broking, are there not?"

"Blessed are they who expect not, for they shall not be disappointed," I answered flippantly.

He was looking at me keenly, and I was anxious to avoid all questions on the subject of my interview with Ali Mahomed Khan. I could scarcely think of it yet without shuddering. I believe Mr. Leighton saw that the reference was a distasteful one, for he changed the subject, and showed me some pearls that had lately come in, explaining their demerits, which to an outsider would have been inappreciable, and finally arranging that I should see the head of a large wholesale jeweller's firm and do some business with him.

Then we said good-bye, and I left the office, with his parting injunction ringing in my ears. "I do not think," he said, "there can be any great risk attached to these next projects of yours, but I confess to having an uneasy feeling about you sometimes, and I hope you will under no circumstances be venturesome. Be discreet—I ask it as a personal favour, Mrs. Delamere—and be distrustful of everyone."

It was a lovely day; after driving part of the way home, I felt inclined for a walk, and, getting out, sent the carriage away.

I had the jewels with me, certainly, but they were in their usual hiding places—and unless some accident happened to me, quite safe. They were, too, though fairly valuable, not so precious as some of my former parcels had been. The best was the large pink pearl, for which I had refused many offers—I meant to get a high price for it. I had just dismissed all anxiety from my mind, and was revelling in a vision of fair millinery at the Maison Nouvelle, when a child's clear voice, speaking in French, made me look round. A brougham was drawn up opposite the shop, and leaning out of the window was a little girl with a most charming face, framed in a picturesque tangle of dark curls surmounted by a pink silk bonnet.

I have a weakness for pretty children in pretty bonnets, and I was interested at once.

"*Tiens, maman,*" said the eager voice, "*regards cette jolie poupée là bas. Je veux bien la voir, laisse moi descendre.*"

A woman with a sweet foreign face, who was just passing by me into the shop, stopped and looked back, shaking her finger.

"*Tu ne peux pas descendre, Cléo, attends, je reviendrai à tantôt.*" And she went on into the shop.

The little face clouded over; Mdlle. Cléo looked wrathful; apparently she was accustomed to have her own way and at once.

I watched her with an amused smile as she opened the carriage door and jumped out; I supposed she was going to run after her mother and remonstrate. But instead she ran round at the back of the brougham, and was half across the road towards the attractive doll-shop, when there was a sharp tinkle from a bicyclist and a shout from an omnibus driver, both of whom were bearing down upon her from opposite directions. I had involuntarily moved to follow her from the first, and as this happened and the child hesitated in bewilderment, I ran forward.

Her momentary pause was fatal. The omnibus and the bicycle continued their progress, and, with a little cry of terror, she was darting right under the horses' heads, when I in hot pursuit caught her arm and pulled her back. Simultaneously the front wheel of the bicycle caught my dress and whirled me off my feet, dashing me violently to the ground. My head struck the curb and I was stunned.

When I came to myself the usual crowd was surrounding me, and a policeman, in whose arms I was supported, said kindly:

"That's right, miss; now, if you can hold up, there's a chemist over the way; he'll soon put you right."

I staggered to my feet, feeling sick and dizzy, and realized that a handkerchief was bound over my forehead, and that the latter was cut and bleeding.

I was only too glad to take refuge in the chemist's shop, where the cut on my head, a very slight one really, was properly bathed and plastered, and whence, after the attentions of the crowd had been gently but firmly repulsed from the doorway by my policeman, I emerged feeling almost myself again.

As I did so, a brougham drew up close to me and a lady got out. I recognised her as the mother of the child, and she hurrying up to me, held out both her hands and caught mine in them.

"How can I thank you," she exclaimed in broken English, "for your goodness, your nobleness in saving Cléo. You will let me drive you home. Oh! but you must; you are not fit to go alone. I am so ashamed to think I have not been with you, but I was so occupied with Cléo at first, and when I found she was unharmed we looked for you, and you were gone."

"She is quite safe?" I asked. "Not hurt at all?"

"Not hurt at all," was the answer, "only frightened, the naughty little one. Do come and see for yourself." She drew me to the carriage, and, as I felt rather weak and trembling, I yielded to her persuasions and got in.

The little girl was still sobbing, and as one or two witnesses of the scene loitered round the carriage, she clung to her mother, imploring to be taken away from the men who stared.

"Drive on," said the lady, and for a few moments she occupied herself in quieting the child; then she turned to me.

"I do so hope you are feeling better," she said. "I do not know how to express my gratitude—will you tell me your name?—I feel that I owe my child's life to you."

"It was nothing," I said, "I was watching your little girl at the moment and happened to see her danger—that was all. Anyone else would have done the same. If you will kindly drive me home I should be very grateful to you. My head aches a little, but I shall be all right as soon as I get home and lie down."

She pulled the check-string. "Where shall I tell him to drive?" she said.

And even as she said it, her face faded away from me, and I sank back fainting.

I remembered nothing more, until I awakened to find myself lying on a sofa in a room that was strange to me, and it was some time before I could collect my thoughts sufficiently to recall what had happened before I was brought there.

At last it all came back to me, and, sitting up on the couch, I looked round for someone to question. But I was quite alone.

My hat, jacket, and bodice had been taken off, and were lying on a chair close by; on another chair were salts, a bottle of sal volatile, some brandy in a wine-glass, and eau-de-Cologne.

The room was a boudoir, exquisitely furnished, and hung with rose silk draperies, festooned here and there to display panelled mirrors. A book on one of the tables attracted my attention; I took it up and looked at the fly leaf. "*Amélie Berthe de Mérgas*" was written in thin foreign writing, and above in bolder characters: "*A la Comptesse, hommages.*"

So! my invisible hostess, doubtless the mother of Cléo, was a countess, or was at all events called so. And this was an offering from some admirer.

But where was she, and why was I left alone?

It seemed a little odd. I recalled at the moment Mr. Leighton's injunctions. Be discreet and distrustful.

Heavens! I hoped my jewels were safe.

At the thought my energy returned. I dressed hastily, and examined my hidden pockets for the stones. They were all there except one—the pink pearl was missing!

I looked for a bell to ring, but could see none—then I went to the door. I would find someone if possible, I thought—at all events I would not waste another moment there. The door was locked— and on the outside. All my lurking uneasiness took shape when I found that I was a prisoner, and I seemed to suddenly understand that something strange was going to happen to me; that what had occurred already was a sort of preliminary which seemed to be leading up to some approaching climax.

There was a window, but when I looked out I found that a descent from it would be impossible—it was too high up, and beneath was a court-yard with a high wall all round it.

I do not know what made me go straight to one of the mirrors, when I turned in despair from the window, and, pulling aside the rose-silk curtain, press my fingers on a knob that was concealed under it.

It was a veritable intuition. The knob slid into a groove, and, the mirror receding, showed me a passage with a glass door at the end of it.

I walked along it, and looked through. There were curtains hanging at the other side, but they were parted, and between them I could see a large oblong table, round which sat nine men, one at the head and four on each side.

The one at the top of the table was leaning his head on his hands, and I could not see his face.

The others were talking together.

For a minute or two their words were indistinguishable then, as my ear grew accustomed to their voices, I found I could hear what they were saying.

"It is the rule of the society," said one man, with a dark, dangerous-looking face; "do we make rules to break them?"

"There are exceptions to all rules," broke in another, whose face and voice were both much more pleasant than the first speaker's. I moved to get a clearer view of him. He looked little more than a lad; a handsome, well-bred face that seemed familiar to me.

"In this case," he continued, "the intrusion has been an involuntary one. It is impossible that there could be any plot connected with it. The whole affair happened by chance. The lady was absolutely unconscious, and has not yet regained her senses. Is it not so, Countess?"

The changed inflection of his voice in the last sentence betrayed a sentimental interest in the person he addressed.

To my surprise, the reply was in the Countess's own voice. She was there, then; I could not see her, as my limited range of vision only permitted a clear view of those in the direct line of the door.

"She has not yet recovered; I have left her in my room, and the door is locked. None of the household know she is there. It would be easy to remove her before she comes to herself, and I would greatly prefer it to the other alternatives. Remember, gentlemen, she has just saved my child's life."

"Of course, if sentiment is allowed to weigh with the society—" began the dark man, with a sneer.

But he was interrupted by a murmur of disapproval from several of the others, and a unanimous demand for a speech from the president.

The man sitting alone at the end of the table, of whom I could only just catch an oblique glimpse, slowly raised his head from his hands, and looked round at his colleagues.

I caught my breath, and almost betrayed my presence by an audible cry.

The sight of his face made the whole thing, and the danger of it, clear to me at once.

I had fallen literally into a "den of thieves."

The president was the man who had tried to chloroform and rob me at the hotel.

He looked pale and harassed, and spoke in a tired tone.

"Let us review the matter," he said, "and put it to the vote. My wife arrives home to-day with a strange lady, in a state of insensibility. She tells us that the lady rescued our child when on the point of being run over. The countess offered in gratitude to drive her to her own house, but the lady fainted before giving her address. There was, therefore, no choice but to bring her here. If my wife drives her at once to a doctor's house it will no doubt be easy for him to restore her, and she can then go home. Even if she should recover before starting, or during the time that she is carried downstairs and placed in the carriage, I do not see that there could possibly be any danger to the society. If you insist on the observance of the rule, we shall have to wait until she is conscious, and to have her brought before us here; when, after being informed of our exist-ence, which seems to me wholly unnecessary, she will be given her choice of two courses, either to become one of us, or to forfeit her life. The latter alternative is one we have never had to contem-plate yet, and seems to me to involve us in a far more serious dan-ger. However, I put it to the vote."

There was a dead silence for a few moments. I do not know how to describe my own sensations during this interval; I felt as if the whole occurrence must be a dream, or as if it were happening to someone else, and I was merely a spectator. I did not attempt to make any plan! I simply waited for their decision.

The silence was broken by the Countess, who said hurriedly:

"Gentlemen, I hope you will consider me in this matter. Some of you have children of your own. Imagine your feelings if you were obliged to repay the saviour of your child's life by forcing on her the choice you speak of. I cannot believe that you will place me in such a position. There is honour I have been told even among—"

But she was interrupted fiercely by the dark man.

"Do you wish to insult us, madam?" he cried, springing to his feet.

"Silence," said the fair boy, also standing up, "I will complete the Countess's sentence, and you can direct your questions to me. There is honour even among thieves."

As he spoke, I suddenly remembered him; he was the son of an old friend of mine, a man who was proud of a good old name, un-tarnished and well-known. I had heard of this boy's gambling proclivities, but nothing worse of him. We had met sometimes in society—I had even danced with him. I wondered idly whether I should ever have the chance of meeting him in society again. It did not seem like it—nevertheless it was to be so.

"Your votes, gentlemen," said the president.

As he spoke, a slight sound behind me made me turn; and I saw Cléo standing in the aperture left by the open panel in the boudoir.

If she spoke I was lost! I hurried to her, putting my finger to her lips, and gently pushing her inside the room, was about to close the panel, when the door was quickly unlocked, and the Countess entered.

She saw at a glance what had happened, and turned as white as death.

"You have been listening?" she said breathlessly. "You know? Then what am I to do?"

She told me quickly that the majority of the votes were against me in one respect; that is to say, if I were still unconscious I was to go free—if otherwise I was to appear before the council.

"I must return to them in a few minutes," she said, "and I will not give you up to them. What can I do?"

She wrung her hands in distress, but Cléo pulled at her arm and whispered something.

"Yes, that might do," the Countess said, "that must do. See! the child will confess that she unlocked the door and came in to you during my absence—and that you asked her to show you the way out as you were anxious to get home. When you find yourself in the road, turn quickly to the right and walk across the heath to some red houses, where they will direct you to a station close by. I will tell my husband you have taken the other road. Promise me never to betray us—remember, though you have done much for me, I have done much for you, and that it would mean ruin to me and mine."

"I promise," I said, and she put her arms round my neck and kissed me.

Then, guided by the child, I made my way quietly down a back staircase, and through a side door into the road, and afraid even to look back, I hurried away across the heath as she had directed me.

When I reached the row of red brick villas that fringed the common, I asked which was my nearest station, and found, to my great relief, that I was close to one on the District Railway, and that I should be at home in half-an-hour. I have never told, and I shall never tell to anyone, the name of that station, nor any detail that could lead to the recognition of that house where, for a time, my life hung in the balance. My promise is sacred to me for the sake of "the Countess" and little Cléo, who had both won my heart.

My grief at the loss of the pink pearl was very great, but it did not last long; for before I had time to communicate it to Mr.

Leighton I received a registered letter by post, and found to my joy it contained the pearl.

A small type-written paper inside held these words:

"My husband recognised you when he carried you into the house, and I am therefore able to trace your name and address. He wishes me to restore this to you, and to assure you that you are perfectly safe from any kind of danger at his hands in future. None of the others know who you are, and he will never tell them. Cléo happens to be the only thing in the world he cares about, and his gratitude therefore equals mine. We are your friends henceforth, and we trust to your honour that you will be ours."

So my third adventure ended very quietly after all, and I began to hope that it would be my last, for my taste for unusual experiences was greatly modified since I began pearl-broking.

I had fancied till then that in London one must be absolutely safe, but there are many hidden tragedies there, submergences that make no ripple on the surface; and although my experience of a very dangerous society was personally a unique one, I believe that this superior Association of Gentlemen Burglars is not by any means the only one, nor the most unscrupulous, that lives and thrives in and near our law-ridden city.

4

I GAVE MYSELF a holiday for a few days after my involuntary exploration of the Society of Gentlemen Thieves, and then I turned my attention steadily to work again, and accomplished a great deal of business to my own and Mr. Leighton's satisfaction. It had taken me about three weeks to finish a commission entrusted to me by the head of a Bond Street firm for a necklace of pearls, three rows in graduated sizes, and I was much pleased when after matching those in the last row, over which I had had a somewhat unusual difficulty, I took them to Bond Street, and handed them to the senior partner.

"These will do nicely," he said, "our customer is very particular, and will criticise every pearl separately. But these are perfect."

I was rising to go, when an assistant came in with a small ring-case, and asked for some directions as to its being sent off. The senior partner opened the case, and showed me the ring, asking me if I did not think it very nice.

"It is splendid," I said. "It makes me feel quite covetous."

The five diamonds, as large as could possibly be worn in a ring, were beautifully set and of a most dazzling lustre.

"A wedding present?" I said interrogatively, as I handed it back.

"A betrothal ring," he answered, "sent for in a hurry. It is the lady's birthday to-night, and, as the engagement is to be announced at a dinner party, she wished to have her ring. It had to be made smaller for her."

"I wonder if it can be Miss Somers-Brand," I said, "it is her birthday to-day, and they are giving a large dinner to which I am going. If so I hope it is to Sir Charles Merivale."

The senior partner smiled.

"Sir Charles is an old customer of ours, and his father and grandfather were before him," he said. "His bride will not need to envy anyone's jewels. We are doing up the family rubies now."

I felt sure, though my question had received an indirect reply, that my surmise was correct. Sir Charles' devotion to Miss Somers-Brand from the first moment of their meeting at her coming-out ball had been apparent to everyone. But though she was very pretty and charming she was undowered, and people had wondered whether such a very desirable party, both as to rank, and riches, as Sir Charles Merivale would select her from the many eligible young ladies amongst whom he might have chosen.

I saw that I was right in my guess as soon as I arrived at the Brands' house that night. Amidst a group of men on the hearthrug, Mr. Somers-Brand and Sir Charles Merivale stood conversing together with marked cordiality, the latter beaming with the assured and triumphant happiness of a newly-engaged man.

Nellie Brand, all pink chiffon and blushes, came forward to shake hands with me, and when I laughingly lifted her left hand and looked at the ring sparkling in all its pristine beauty on the third finger, she blushed still more, and nodded an affirmative to my unspoken question.

There were a great many people present—it was a party of twenty-four—and I was the last to arrive, so that I had not time to notice all the other guests, and almost immediately after my entrance we paired off and went downstairs.

I was taken in by the son of the house, and as he and I were friends of long standing, and had not met for some time, we were occupied at first in giving a mutual account of ourselves, and getting as it were "up to date " with each other.

Now and then the voice of a man seated on the same side of the table as myself, and hidden from me by the intervening couples, broke in and arrested my attention. It was a familiar voice certainly, but besides that it gave me an odd feeling of anxiety.

Where had I heard it last? It was associated with some uncomfortable experience I felt sure; but when and how?

I glanced in the direction of it once or twice, but I could not catch the man's face.

At last it worried me so that I said to Tom Brand:

"Tell me who is sitting on our side of the table? There's a voice I recognise, and I cannot fit the person to it."

He mentioned the names of the four couples, and I stopped him at the last.

"Of course," I said, in a sort of surprise, "Gerard Beverley! Why, dear me, he is a—"

I broke off suddenly, realising the betrayal of which I was on the verge.

Tom smiled at my apparently unnecessary excitement and confusion.

"He is a son of old Admiral Beverley," he said, "and he is a confounded young fool; throws all his money away on betting, and gets into no end of scrapes; but I don't know anything worse of him than that. Why do you look so horrified about him? You knew him when he was a lad down in Hampshire, didn't you?"

"Yes," I answered, "I knew them all quite well; I loved Mrs. Beverley; she was such a sweet, gracious old lady, and so devoted to her boys. What a grief Gerard must be to her."

Tom laughed again.

"Oh, he is only a scrapegrace; he'll get over it some of these days, I expect. You seem very down on him, Mrs. Delamere, which is not like you—you are generally so charitable. Has he been so unlucky as to offend you?"

"No," I said, "quite the contrary. But I happen to know something about him which I would greatly prefer not to know. I would not say even so much as that to you, but it just occurs to me that perhaps you could look after him a little. You know his people better even than I do. Could you manage to convey to them that he wants a very great deal of looking after, much more than they think;

and that the kindest thing they could do to him, would be to pay all his debts—for I am sure he must have many—and send him out to some definite work abroad. Will you try to do this?"

"I certainly will if you are as much in earnest as you seem to be," he replied; "you shall tell me just what you want me to do presently when we can have a quiet talk together."

At this moment there was a little stir, and a buzz of louder conversation.

We had reached the dessert stage, and an old friend of the family had insisted on proposing a toast—"the engaged couple."

We all looked and spoke our compliments to them, and Sir Charles Merivale said a word or two of thanks for himself and Nellie, and then someone asked to see her ring, and she took it off and handed it round for general inspection.

It passed Tom and me, and I handed it on to my next door neighbour; then our attention was attracted by an exciting story of an Indian loot, told by an old general who had taken part in it, and whose recollections were aroused by the brilliance of Nellie's diamond ring.

The whole party listened to the story—a stirring one and well-told—and it was not till the general had concluded, and the comments were subsiding that Nellie said with a laugh: "Please may I have my ring back now? My finger is catching cold."

There was a little murmur of reply, and then she said in a decisive voice:

"But I have not got it, indeed; it has never come back to me."

Several people began looking about, moving the plates and wine-glasses; one or two sitting near Nellie stopped and looked on the floor; finally, Mr. Brand rang the bell for the butler, and Nellie, getting up, shook her dress, thinking it might have fallen into the folds.

But the ring was not forthcoming!

It came upon me with a sort of shock that I knew with absolute certainty where the ring was, and yet that it was impossible for me to reveal my knowledge, because such a revelation would have made me a traitor, though indirectly, towards someone who claimed my loyalty, and would—though in justice to myself, I must say this was a secondary consideration to me—have been very dangerous to me.

A complete search was made all over the room for the ring; each one saying in turn that it had been passed on to the next person at the table.

When, after an interval of ten minutes it was still invisible, a sort of hush fell over the whole party, and the extreme unpleasantness of the situation dawned on most of them.

I say most of them, because I knew that there were two people whose feelings were totally different to those of the others, and one of those two was myself.

"I don't know what to do," said Mr. Somers-Brand at last; "it is a most extraordinary thing, and seems like magic. The ring seems to have disappeared from the face of the earth."

He looked appealingly round at his guests; it was really a most awkward predicament. Mrs. Brand seemed inclined to make a move to the drawing room.

I felt desperate; I seemed such a traitor either way.

A thought occurred to me; I spoke a few words rapidly to Tom.

Fortunately I knew him well enough to feel assured that he would not misconstrue my agitation.

He interposed at once between his mother and the door.

"Don't go, mother," he said, "stay and help us to solve this problem. Who else was in the room besides you?" he continued, turning to the butler.

"Only William, sir," that decorous official replied, with the imperturbable demeanour which is so admirable in butlers.

"Ring for William," said Tom.

As soon as William, the footman, had made a sheepish appearance, Tom proceeded to address the whole company.

"With my father's permission," he said, "I will make a suggestion, and I hope that you will all approve of it, and that you will appreciate the motives I have in making it. It is this. That the door should be locked and the key held by my father; that we should all resume our places at table; and that the lights should then be turned off. That after a minute or two they should be turned on again. I should like to say that I have a theory about the disappearance of the ring which I am anxious to prove. If this way is unsuccessful I shall suggest another. But I fully believe that when the lights are turned on the ring will be visible.

"I apologize to you all for asking you to do this, but I feel certain that you would all prefer that the ring should now be found, if possible. Do you agree to my suggestion?"

Apparently everyone did, and it was carried out in every detail.

When the electric lights flashed up again we were all dazzled for an instant, after our temporary eclipse, and looked vaguely at each other as though we expected to see the ring suspended in mid air or lurking in some unusual place like a conjuring trick.

Then Nellie Brand gave a little glad cry, and, stooping forward, picked the ring out from the folds of yellow ribbon that meandered about amongst the flowers in the centre of the table.

"Ah!" said Tom, with an accent of relief, "a practical joke as I thought, and very cleverly played! Now, mother, we will consent to part with you."

He telegraphed to me a look of grateful acknowledgment as I passed out of the room; I saw him turn and go towards Gerard Beverley.

I had no need to be assured by the ghastly look on the boy's face that he was a thief, for from the moment that Tom told me to whom the voice, so oddly familiar to me, belonged, I had identified him with the Countess's impetuous champion in the Gentlemen Burglars' Club, on the memorable occasion when I was the unwilling witness of one of their meetings, and when the question of my escape with life and honour hung and trembled in the balance.

Scarcely any other subject was spoken of either in the drawing-room, or, as I heard from Tom afterwards, in the dining-room that evening.

Many were the surmises as to the perpetrator of the joke, or the theft, that had made such a sensation, but neither Tom nor I betrayed our knowledge.

When we managed to have a few quiet words together just before I left, I explained to him the suggestion I had made, and which he had adopted by saying that I had heard of it being done, and with the same successful result on a very similar occasion.

But I did not acknowledge to him, either then or later, that I knew Gerard Beverley to be a thief, for I felt that to do so might lead eventually to the discovery of the club, and that I should then have broken faith with my kind little "Countess."

Nevertheless, I cannot doubt that Tom guessed the real state of affairs for himself; he told me that he saw Gerard home that night, and took the opportunity of having a serious talk with him.

The wretched young fellow completely broke down, confessed he was in worse trouble than anyone imagined, and, only after immense persuasion, consented to make a clean breast of it to his father.

Poor old Admiral Beverley collected all his son's debts, settled them up, got him a berth as overseer in one of the new South African settlements, and told Tom, the last time they met, that Gerard was writing more hopefully and reasonably than he had ever done before, and that they hoped to make a decent fellow of him yet.

The ruffled complacency of the dinner guests of that evening was restored when they heard that both the butler and footman had given indignant warning to the Somers-Brands the very next day.

"You may be quite sure," said Sir Charles Merivale to me subsequently, "that the butler and footman were in league, and it was one of there who took it. They got frightened when Tom suggested his experiment, and were afraid of a search coming next; so they decided to put it back. It was a clever idea of Tom's—saved any disturbance, and restored to Nellie her ring without any more fuss!"

I smiled demurely. For the "clever idea" was a happy inspiration that I have often congratulated myself upon since then.

5

In spite of the fact that there were frequently in my safe jewels sufficiently valuable to make it well worth the while of a professional burglar to invade my flat, I had never experienced the least nervousness on the subject.

A flat always seems so safe and self-contained! When you close your front door you seem to shut yourself up in your castle and pull up a metaphorical drawbridge between yourself and the world, and there is an added sense of security in the knowledge that though enclosed in your own domain you are not really isolated, and there are human beings within call at your desire.

My safe, a small unostentatious one, was set into the wall of my bedroom, and the door of it draped with a little frivolous hanging curtain of art muslin tied up with knots of ribbon, which imparted to it the guileless appearance of a medicine cupboard. I flattered myself that to the casual eye there would seem to be nothing more valuable behind those delicate folds than sal-volatile, and that no one would imagine a small fortune often lay concealed there.

I had only two maid-servants—sisters. Comely, honest country girls, for whom I had sent to the Hampshire village, where I had spent my youth, and whom I knew to be thoroughly trustworthy. Having cautioned them in a general way not to pick up chance acquaintances, nor to gossip too much with their neighbours, I felt a tranquil assurance of safety.

But I confess to having now and then an uneasy feeling that it was time for me to have another adventure of some sort, a vague presentiment of something unpleasant in store for me; and I was especially careful in all my business appointments and meetings.

My employer, Mr. Leighton, had just received a fresh consignment of pearls, amongst which were some very fine ones, and arrangements had been made for me to interview several important dealers.

I brought the pearls home one afternoon and put them into my safe.

Usually I locked the door of my room while I was transferring the jewels from their hiding-places in my dress, but on this occasion by chance I forgot to do so, and just at the moment that they lay on my dressing table, while I was unlocking the safe, Kate, my parlour-maid, opened the door abruptly without knocking.

"I beg your pardon, ma'am," she said, "I thought you were still out; I was going to shut your window."

"It's all right, Kate," I answered carelessly, unwilling to betray the vexation I really felt, and moving between her and the pearls.

But she had seen them already, and lifting up her hands in surprise, she said: "Oh what lovely pearls, ma'am, and what a lot of them."

"Yes; they are pretty," I said, "but they don't belong to me. I am taking care of them for someone else. I hope they will not get lost during the few days they are in my charge."

I consoled myself after she had left the room by the reflection that she was not likely to speak to anyone about them, and would probably forget the subject all the sooner because I had not made it of special importance, and as she was absolutely honest herself, there was nothing else to fear.

Two days had passed of the three that were to elapse before the interview at which I hoped to arrange the sale of the pearls.

On the evening of the third day I was engaged to dine out with some great friends, and as I was to meet an artist whose latest success in portraits was adorning the walls of the New Gallery, I decided that I ought to go and see it that afternoon.

I had spent a pleasant hour at the Gallery, and was moving away, when some American acquaintances pounced on me and carried me off to tea with them at the Cecil; so that it was late in the afternoon when I got back. And I found that I had only just left myself time to dress.

I was startled to hear a loud sob from Kate as she opened the door to me, and to see that she was in floods of tears.

"Oh, ma'am," she said, "we are so glad you have come back; we didn't know what to do. Mother is dying, and Mary and me feel we must go to her."

She handed me a telegram containing the words: "Mother had accident, cannot live through the night, both come at once."

"This is dreadful," I said, "I am so sorry. You must go, of course."

"But how can we leave you alone?" she answered.

"Oh, I must manage somehow," I said, "I could not think of keeping either of you in such a case."

They were naturally both eager to be off, and there was barely time for them to catch their train, so that I was too much occupied in giving them the money and directions for their journey, and dispatching them in a hansom, to think of anything else until after they had gone.

Then a disagreeable recollection of the pearls, and the thought that I should be quite alone in the flat that night, flashed across my mind.

But there was no possibility of getting any one in so late in the day, even if I had been able to go and hunt somebody up, and I was due at the Anstruthers' dinner in three-quarters of an hour.

There was nothing for it but to dress and go, taking the latchkey with me, and reassuring myself with the thought that no one could possibly know I was suddenly bereft of both my servants, and that my wisest plan was not to mention it at all. As I passed through the hall on my way out, I saw the ill-fated telegram lying crumpled up on the floor, and picking it up mechanically, smoothed it out and carried it with me. Although I told myself, as I drove towards Eaton Square, that there was nothing to worry about, and that in the morning it would be possible, if the maids did not return, to find someone to take their place, I still felt an indefinite sense of uneasiness. If only I had returned home earlier that afternoon I should have had time to arrange something.

I glanced at the telegram to see when it had arrived, and noticed, without at first taking it into my mind, that it had been sent off from Paddington at four o'clock.

I read it over more than once with a sort of puzzled feeling of something being wrong, without knowing where or why.

It seemed quite simple: the mother had met with an accident, and the brother had telegraphed for his sisters to come to her.

But why Paddington, when they lived in Hampshire? I suddenly asked myself. Why Paddington?

How was it that the telegram, instead of being sent off from their own village, had started from Paddington?

I was still seeking a solution to this problem when I reached the Anstruthers, and was obliged to dismiss the whole matter from my mind.

The artist, a Mr. Charles Seton, turned out to be a very charming man, who spoke little of art, but talked well on all subjects, and in the interest roused by his conversation I quite forgot the incident of the telegram, and enjoyed myself very much.

He had brought with him, at the special invitation of the hostess, a splendid dog, the original of one of his own paintings. It was a Russian boarhound, massive and ferocious-looking, but as gentle as a kitten under his control, and he laughingly introduced it to all, making it present a huge paw to each of us in turn.

"Serge is not accustomed to dinner parties," he said, "but he is too well-bred to be shy. Give your paw to Mrs. Delamere, Serge."

The dog did as he was told in a dignified manner, and then lay gently down beside me, and put his head on my lap.

"Serge has adopted you as one of his personal friends," Mr. Seton said; "that is a sign of his especial approval and protection."

Mrs. Anstruther declared that she was jealous, and when we went down to dinner, and Serge leisurely followed me and disposed himself under the table at my feet, she tried to lure him away from me with bribes, but unsuccessfully.

After dinner he followed us up to the drawing-room, passing his master with superb indifference, and stalking solemnly after me, much to everyone's amusement.

"I wish I could take you home with me," I said. "I should feel so nice and safe with such a companion."

And then I told Mrs. Anstruther about the unavoidable exodus of my maids, and my enforced loneliness that night.

"My dear," she said, "I wouldn't be you for the whole world. I should not sleep a wink. Why don't you borrow Serge to take care of you? I am sure his master would lend him."

I laughingly repudiated the idea of being nervous, and negatived the suggestion, but in her impetuous good-nature she continued to insist upon it, and finally, when the gentlemen joined us, she told Mr. Seton that she had arranged for Serge to spend a day or two with his new friend. I became rather embarrassed at last, and declared that I should be more afraid of Serge himself than of anything else, but this quite offended his master, and I was obliged to retract it.

"I assure you, Mrs. Delamere," he said, "I have only to say to Serge, 'This lady is in your charge; on guard,' and your safety is guaranteed. He would neither harm you himself nor allow anyone else to do so."

Finally the dog himself settled it by walking out of the room after me and following me down-stairs.

"Very well," I said, "You shall come. I will send you back to-morrow."

I felt a sort of relief that after all I should not be absolutely alone in my flat that night—my nerves had not been quite so strong since my first two adventures—and a dog is very much better than nothing in the way of a companion.

He seemed perfectly contented with the arrangement, and waited quietly when we reached the door of my flat while I opened it with my latch-key, exactly as though he had been accustomed to do so always.

We entered together, and I closed the door and turned into the little room I called my boudoir, out of which on one side led my bedroom, having another door into the passage, further on.

Serge pricked his ears, and looked fixedly at the door between the two rooms, which was slightly ajar, and involuntarily I laid my hand on his collar, and stood still waiting for something—I did not know what. There was dead silence for a moment, then a chink as of some metal, a stealthy movement, and, the door opening towards us, showed a man cautiously peering; through the aperture. He had a coarse, clumsy face, with a smile of triumph on it, and in his hand he held a small packet, rolled up in a torn newspaper. I knew my pearls were there.

I held the dog more firmly. The room was in semi-darkness, and I was between him and the man, who, therefore, did not notice him.

Before I had time to speak the man pointed a Derringer at me.

"Scream, and I fire," he said. "I don't want to hurt yer, but I've got to get away. I didn't reckon on you coming home so soon."

I released the dog.

"Fetch him, Serge," I said.

The dog's onslaught was so rapid, that if the man had been one step away from the half-opened door, he couldn't have saved himself.

As it was, he dropped the package in his terror, and it fell just where it prevented the door from shutting.

Serge seized it with his great teeth, and whirled it away, and the man pulled the door to and locked it. The dog tore and bit furiously at the barrier thus interposed between them, and I dropped trembling into a chair. What was I to do next?

The man's voice, changed from its first brutal defiance, came now in subdued accents of entreaty.

"If you call the dog off, I'll come out and go away quietly," he said. "You needn't be hard on me; I haven't took nothing."

"You are safe from the dog where you are," I replied, "and, since you are armed, it would be impossible for me to let you out. Besides, how do I know that you would take nothing with you?"

"You can count the stones," he said, "they're all in that package."

I picked it up and proceeded to do so. Yes, they were all there, thank goodness.

But what was I to do about the man?

If I raised an alarm I should be obliged to give him in charge, and to state that he had broken open my safe. This would lead, perhaps, to a revelation about the pearls, and in accounting for their presence in the safe my occupation would become known.

This was exactly what I wished to avoid. At the same time, if I called the dog away the man might open the door and fire straight at me.

I was afraid as it was that he might fire through the door and succeed in wounding poor Serge. I thought it best to assume more decision than I really felt.

"I am going to summon help from down-stairs," I said, "and I shall leave the dog on guard. If you attempt to come out he will tear you to pieces."

"For God's sake, let me off!" he said; "it's my first job. I've never tried it on before, and I never will again, s'help me. It was your girls talking about the wonderful lot of pearls you'd got, that put me on to it. I thought I'd step in while you was all out and make off with them."

"You sent the telegram then?" I said.

"Oh, yes," he answered; "they didn't mean no harm, but they got talking to me about their mother and all that, and it seemed as if the whole job was really for me. You see they thought I was a labouring man come up from their part of the country to look for work. They never said a word about the dog, though."

"I suppose, but for the dog, you would have shot me?" I said.

He did not answer, and we remained silent for several minutes.

Serge was lying close to the door, with his head on his paws, and his eyes fixed on the chink of light that came from under it.

Presently he gave a low growl, and, getting up, sniffed all along the chink, and then stopped listening. I wondered what the man was trying to do, and whether he would still manage to outwit me in getting away.

I wished that, after all, I had given the alarm at once.

In spite of Serge's presence I began to feel frightened. Suddenly, with a snarl of rage and a terrific bound, he sprang past me through the door leading to the hall; there was a crash, a strangled oath, and then a horrible sound, the sound of an animal and a human being in deadly conflict.

I rushed out. The man was lying on the floor with his head and shoulders jammed into an angle of the wall; one arm wedged underneath him by the weight of the dog, who was straining every effort to reach his throat with its huge jaws, while he vainly strove with his hand wound into its collar to choke it off.

His face was covered with blood, and purple with the agony of his effort.

I thought he would be killed, torn to pieces before my eyes.

"Serge," I cried, "Serge, come away; down, good dog, down."

I seized his collar, and pulled him back. He never attempted to bite me, but continued snarling and showing his teeth at his enemy.

I was only just in time. The wretched man was quite spent, and lay still with closed eyes.

I picked up the Derringer which had fallen in the struggle; it was unloaded, a rusty, useless thing. I suppose he had hoped to frighten me with it, and indeed he would have succeeded but for Serge.

I felt dizzy and faint myself with the sight of that ghastly struggle.

The man had got out of the bedroom by the door leading into the passage, and stealing round, had hoped to get through the hall door before the dog caught him.

I fetched him some brandy and water, and a wet sponge for his face, and the dog watched him all the time, not letting him stir a yard.

Then I ordered Serge to keep still, and, leading the man to the door myself, put him out.

He began muttering some thanks and protestations, but I cut him short.

"You had better get away as quickly and quietly as you can," I said. "If the porter catches you at the door, he will be sure to ask for your business, and make it unpleasant for you."

He slouched away down the staircase, dazed and crestfallen, and presently the sound of the hall-door closing quietly, assured me that he had managed to escape unseen.

When I sent Serge back to his master the next day, I felt basely ungrateful in not mentioning the good service he had done for me; but I thought it best to tell no one on account of the risk it would add to my business if it became generally known.

Since then, I am glad to say, circumstances have enabled me to tell the whole story of that night, and to thank Mr. Seton more fully for the loan, which was such a fortunate one for me, of his dog.

He insisted on making me a present of Serge, which he said was the most fitting reward for the dog's gallantry, and I feel that as long as Serge lives I shall never need to fear a burglary again.

My maids, on finding out that they had been hoaxed, for what reason they never knew, were anxious to return to me at once, but I thought it safer to get two new ones. Honesty is a very good quality as far as it goes, but a little discretion is a necessary adjunct to most virtues, I fancy, and, but for the lucky chance of Serge's advent, I should have suffered an irreparable loss, in consequence of their careless loquacity.

6

I was beginning to get over the phase of nervous inaction which resulted from my unpleasant interview with the burglar, and to feel that I was once more mentally and physically ready for work, when Mr. Leighton wrote for me to come to the office, and told me that he was anxious to send a consignment of pearls on approval to a large firm in Bristol, and that, if I liked to undertake the business, he would be pleased to place it in my hands. He did not apprehend any danger, since it was not even remotely probable that anyone would know either of my journey or its object; and he should like me to he his emissary, because these would be his first dealings with the firm, and to establish a friendly footing between them was very desirable from a business point of view.

I gladly undertook the commission, and made preparations for my journey without any misgivings.

I had never been to Bristol, though I had often received invitations to pay it a visit from relations of my mother who lived there, and I decided that, now fate had brought me the opportunity, I would take full advantage of it, and, my business once finished, and the pearls safely transferred from my keeping, would roam about for a time and give myself a holiday.

I was in such high spirits all the day before that fixed for my departure, that some friends who were calling on me rallied me on my cheerfulness, and one of them, as she said good-bye, laughingly asked me if I had just had a fortune left me.

"I have never seen you so gay, Mrs. Delamere," she said, "what is the reason of it? Do tell me."

"There is no special reason," I answered; "I am going out of town to-morrow, and am rather looking forward to it. I don't know that I have any other cause for rejoicing."

She looked at me attentively. She was a Scotch girl, a Miss Burnley, and very superstitious. "Then you are 'fey,'" she said, "that's what it is, and something is going to happen to you."

"What sort of something?" I asked; "and why do you think so?"

"I know it," she said; "when a person is unreasonably happy and excited, the Scotch call them 'fey,' and say it means coming danger. Have you had any unusual experience lately—during the last twenty-four hours, say?"

I pretended to reflect. She was quite in earnest, and I am not superstitious.

"The only one I can remember is that a man stared at me very rudely yesterday," I said at last, "and wrote something down in a book about me; at least it seemed to me as if he did so."

She looked quite startled.

"If you see that man again," she entreated, "avoid him! No matter how difficult it may be, go away from him. He is your evil genius."

"Good gracious!" I said, "how alarming. Do you know, I believe he was only a surveyor taking measurements."

"Never mind," she replied, as she went away, "don't let him come near you if you can help it. He means danger."

I was a great deal too busy to think of her warning again, and too intent on so disposing of the pearls in various much-concealed pockets in my attire that they should be safe. I carried a handbag with me—one of the ordinary dressing-cases of travel—but I never placed anything very valuable in it, reserving it for small accessories of comfort.

I had sent it to Mappin's for a little necessary repair, and had fetched it away during my drive that day, on the occasion when the trifling incident of which I spoke to Miss Burnley had occurred.

The man, a respectable-looking loafer, had sauntered past my carriage twice, and had stared in rather a marked manner; finally, after jotting down something in a note-book, had lounged away.

I was going by the morning train to Bristol, which meant an early start, and I had intended to be in good time, and to choose my carriage carefully, but various small obstacles cropped up, and made me so late that I only reached the platform at the moment of the train's departure.

The guard hurried me on, and opening the door of a first-class carriage, signed impatiently for me to enter.

I saw that it was empty, and gave a hesitating glance to the window of the next carriage.

A man and a woman were sitting opposite to each other; the woman was facing me, and even in my momentary glimpse I saw that she was young, fair, well-dressed; the man had his back towards me, and I caught only his profile.

But that was enough. It recalled, with a flash of memory that included Miss Burnley's warning, "he means danger," the face of the man who had stared at me.

Instinctively I turned and entered the empty carriage.

I had intended to find a compartment with three or four fellow-travellers; the train was an express, and went right through to Bristol; therefore, if I started well there was nothing to fear.

But after all, to be alone was safer than travelling with only one other person.

I wondered idly whether the resemblance between the man in the carriage beyond, and the impertinent loafer, was a real one or only fancied, concluded that in any case it could not matter, and gave myself over wholly to the charms of a new novel.

We were nearing the end of our journey, and had just entered the Box Tunnel, when I was startled back from romance to reality by a short, sharp scream, apparently strangled in the very middle of its utterance, coming from the next carriage, followed by a thud against the partition behind me.

I sprang to my feet and listened intently; the beating of my heart quickened with sudden unrealised terror.

No sound for an instant, then another cry, a low sobbing one, ending in a horrible choking gasp.

I flew to the alarm and pressed it, while all sorts of vague thoughts rushed through my brain. What was happening to the woman next door?—for it was a woman's voice. Was she being murdered? Was the man a thief—an escaped lunatic? Miss Burnley's warning, "he means danger," ran like a dark thread in and out of my brain.

We were nearly through the tunnel; the train, which had slackened speed half way before I sounded the alarm, was now slowing down. Glimpses of daylight came from the opening ahead of us.

I leant out of my window, debating whether I should open the door and step along to the next or not, and as the thought occurred to me I saw the guard swiftly emerge from his van and come towards me.

Then the door of the next carriage opened, and a white, furtive face looked for an instant into mine, while the man swung himself down, and fled through the tunnel into the darkness which we had just left.

I tried to scream, but my voice would not sound right.

The guard, however, saw the man descend and run, and, springing down, followed him, shouting out to the guard at the other end.

By this time every window was alive with eager curious faces, and voices clamouring to know the reason of our sudden stop. I stepped out on the footboard, and into the next carriage.

Horror! a woman was lying on the floor, her distorted purple face bruised and bleeding, her eyes staring upwards in mute and desperate appeal.

The lace ruffle round her neck, at which one of her hands were clutching convulsively, had been twisted and strained with such force, that it looked like a narrow ragged string on either side of which the flesh rose in two dark ridges.

I thought she was dead, but I threw myself down on my knees, and cutting the edge of the ruffle with my pocket-knife, was able to get a finger under it, and to untwist it.

By this time one of the guards was with me, and we lifted the poor thing on to the seat, and supporting her head, I gently wiped the swollen lips, round which a foam had gathered, and stooping, held my ear against her heart.

It seemed to me that a slow, heavy beat was faintly perceptible, and when the next moment someone came with a flask of brandy, I forced the discoloured lips and clenched teeth apart, and poured some down her throat.

There was a quiver of the eyelids, they closed, a tremor ran through her whole frame, and a sobbing sigh came, as she swallowed the brandy.

"I am a doctor; will you allow me?" said a man entering.

We made way for him gladly, and, during the half-hour that passed before we ran into Bristol Station, he and I, under his directions, gradually restored the sufferer to consciousness.

"You are alighting here?" he said interrogatively, as we began to stop.

"Yes," I said.

"I should advise your taking her at once to the nearest friend's house," he continued in a low voice, "or a hotel; she should be kept perfectly quiet. She is your sister, I suppose."

I gave an astonished negative.

"She is no relation; I do not even know her."

He looked mystified.

"But," he said, "I thought, of course, she was with you and she is so like you."

I looked at the face, the poor disfigured face it certainly, except for the accidental alteration of it, might have been very like mine.

She was, too, evidently about the same height, and was dressed in black with touches of white as I was.

I began to tell him hurriedly the circumstances of the case, and then the train stopped, and we were surrounded at once by officials, with the stationmaster at their head.

I related exactly what had happened, and my story of the man who descended from the train and escaped through the tunnel was corroborated by the guard.

The man who had succeeded in escaping, he said, must have dived between the carriages to the other side of the train and got out of the tunnel on the further side; the train had to proceed, and they had wasted several minutes as it was trying to catch him.

The poor woman was, after the attack, far too weak and ill to answer any questions; she glanced about as if in search of something, and on the guard producing a handbag which he found in the tunnel, and which must have been dropped by her assailant in his flight, she made a feeble sign of direction for us to open it.

We found a card-case inside, which revealed her name and address, and she was carried to a fly, and driven to Grove Villa, Clifton, accompanied by a detective, the doctor, and myself.

It appeared that she was the wife of a lawyer, Westall by name, and that she had been paying a visit to her own people in town and was on her way home.

Her husband, for whom we sent at once to his office, was absolutely at a loss to account for the murderous attack on his wife, and could only suggest that the man must have been mad.

For three days Mrs. Westall was so ill that it was hopeless to attempt to find out anything from her; and, indeed, the doctors were afraid that she would succumb to the nervous shock; but she pulled through, to my great joy. For not only was I deeply interested in her recovery from ordinary feelings of compassion and kindliness, but I had a vague indescribable feeling of participation in this mysterious crime as though I were in some way, unknown to myself, involved in its guilt.

The face of the man in the tunnel haunted me. It was most certainly the same as that of the loafer who had stared at me.

I felt sure that in some inexplicable fashion I was mixed up with his attempt on Mrs. Westall's life.

At last she rallied sufficiently for the doctors to sanction a legal interview with her, the result of which I learnt as soon as possible.

It appeared that when she first got into the train at Paddington, there was another lady in it, but that a minute or two before starting a man passed up and down in front of the carriage, and apparently stared rudely at this lady, who, on his preparing to enter, murmured an expression of annoyance, and got out, changing to another carriage higher up.

Mrs. Westall, a little startled, thought of following; but seeing that the man appeared harmless, and at once engrossed himself in a newspaper, decided not to. He was perfectly nice on the way down; spoke to her once or twice with reference to the window, and other trivialities, and she felt no alarm at all.

On entering the Box Tunnel, however, he suddenly got up, and was about to lift down her bag, which was in the rack above her, when she stopped him.

"Excuse me, that is mine," she said.

"It's going to be mine, now," he said. "I know what you have got in it, well enough, and you will have to do without this little lot of pearls."

He pushed her aside and made for the door. But knowing that all her money, her ticket, and a few jewels were in the bag, she would not take its loss so calmly.

She grappled with him, and succeeded in wresting the bag from his grasp and throwing it behind her.

He tried to reach it, but failing to do so, threw her down, and told her he would "do" for her, and have the bag all the same.

She struggled desperately for a moment, and then he got his hand into the ruffle at her neck, and twisted it until she lost consciousness.

She remembered nothing more till her restoration.

"Either he was a madman," she said, in her deposition, "or he must have taken me for someone else."

Alas! poor thing; I saw only too plainly that she had been mistaken for someone else, and in my horror at this confirmation of my undefined dread, I nearly betrayed myself.

But I felt that it would be unwise and a mistake, both for my own sake and my employer's, that this should be known publicly, and as soon as I had finished my commission at Bristol, sold the pearls, and ascertained that Mrs. Westall's recovery though slow was sure, I hurried back to town and told Mr. Leighton the whole story.

He commended my discretion.

Since the man had escaped, and was still in ignorance as to his own mistake, there was no object to be gained in our explaining it to the public.

From my description of him, Mr. Leighton felt quite sure that he was a discharged employé of his, who had doubtless been lurking about the office, had guessed my business there, and, possibly, overheard my arrangements with Mr. Leighton.

He had recognised me when I was waiting at Mappin's for my bag, had concluded that I intended to convey the pearls in it, and, jotting down a few notes as to my dress and general appearance, had laid his plan to rob me on the way down.

Mrs. Westall's unfortunate—for her—chance resemblance to me in all these details, and choice of the same train, coupled with my own very late arrival at Paddington, had misled him, and had ended in her being my involuntary substitute.

"He must certainly have thought I was someone else," she said constantly, "because he spoke more than once of 'the pearls.' 'I'll have those pearls,' were the last words I heard him say, 'if I swing for it'—or else he was quite mad."

But both Mr. Leighton and I feel convinced that there was method in his madness, and that I was saved marvellously from a struggle, which might possibly in my case have ended fatally.

Indeed it must have done so in hers, had I not sounded the alarm, and so interrupted the murderer, and saved her life.

I am most inexpressibly thankful that it turned out so; for I could never have forgiven myself otherwise.

It is one thing to risk one's own life, when one's living depends on it, but quite another thing to involve others, however accidentally, in danger.

Mr. Leighton was inclined, for my own safety, to give me my dismissal; but I persuaded him at last to reconsider it, and promised to be very careful, and to have no more adventures if possible.

7

It was many weeks after my narrow escape on the journey to Bristol before Mr. Leighton would hear of my undertaking any large or difficult commission for him.

"You are too confident, Mrs. Delamere," he said gravely, when I urged him to give me some work worth doing, "too reckless. Certainly you manage to escape scathless from danger in the most wonderful manner, but you know in all cases of risk it is only a question of time. Sooner or later I am afraid something bad will happen to you, and then how should I forgive myself?"

"Nonsense, Mr. Leighton," I said, "you are over-cautious and over-sensitive. You are giving me, at my earnest desire, the opportunity to earn a comfortable living in a congenial way. If you take it from me, then I must become a governess, or a companion, or a typist, or something equally arduous, and for an income that will only just clothe me. Surely you have nothing to blame yourself for, whatever happens."

"Well," he answered, "a woman, and especially a wilful one, generally manages to get her own way. Since you insist, Mrs. Delamere"—he handed me a letter that had been lying on his desk.

It was a very ordinary letter, and worded in a terse business-like manner that did not suggest any possible romance. The writer said that, having heard of Mr. Leighton's reputation as a pearl merchant, and being anxious to match exactly two pearl earrings, he would be obliged if some trustworthy and intelligent person could be sent to see him, and to take his order. He named a day and hour.

The letter was signed, Arnold Gervoise, and addressed from St. Bernard's Mansions, some new flats in Mayfair.

I folded the note up and put it in my card-case; then rose, and holding out my hand to Mr. Leighton, said: "Good-bye. I will be at St. Bernard's Mansions punctually at ten on Thursday."

Mr. Leighton smiled.

"No hesitations?" he said; "no suspicions, Mrs. Delamere? How do you know this is not a fresh plot against you personally?"

"I am convinced it is not," I answered; "and, anyhow, I'm going, Mr. Leighton." And I left the office before he could raise any fresh objections.

Thursday came, and at ten o'clock I found myself in a charming room, half dressing-room, half boudoir, awaiting the pleasure of Mr. Arnold Gervoise.

Presently the door opened, and a wheel-chair, propelled by its owner, appeared.

He piloted himself in skilfully, shut the door, and then came quite close to me, saying apologetically:

"I am extremely sorry to have kept you waiting; I had no idea Mr. Leighton's representative was a lady, but in any case it was unavoidable. I hope you will excuse me."

"Certainly," I said; "it does not matter at all; I am not in any hurry. Mr. Leighton entrusted this business to me because I have done a good deal of work for him before."

He looked at me with increased scrutiny and, while feigning to glance in another direction, I returned his criticising glances in a mirror that reflected him.

He was young and handsome, though with a weary, worried look about him that told of some mental strain in addition to his physical incapacity.

"I am a wretched cripple, as you see," he broke out impatiently, "and therefore dependent on others for the management of my affairs to a great extent; but I wish to keep this matter entirely between ourselves. I trust that I may count on you not to mention it to any of my household?"

I bowed.

"I shall certainly not do so," I said.

He looked at me questioningly for an instant, and then wheeled himself to the door and disappeared.

When he came back he had a small velvet case in his hand.

"I want you to take the exact design of these," he said, showing me a pair of magnificent earrings. "You can make a drawing of them if you like, only you must be very quick. And I want you to bring me a pair that will match these exactly in three days."

I obeyed his first directions in silence. When I had finished a rapid sketch, I observed:

"These will be very expensive, and I cannot promise them faithfully in three days, though we will do our best. The black pearls will be the difficulty."

The earrings were two splendid diamonds set in a circle of large white pearls, and each depending from a single black pearl.

The setting was peculiar and old-fashioned. He seized the case from me, and hurried once more out of the room.

When he returned he seemed more tranquil and relieved.

"I am greatly obliged to you," he said, "and I shall be still more so if you can accomplish the copies successfully within the three days."

I assured him that Mr. Leighton would do his best, and took my leave, not without some wondering questions in my mind as to the meaning of all that had happened.

I had reached the public staircase, and was waiting for the lift, when it ascended, and a very beautiful woman alighting from it gave me a glance of curiosity, and passed on to the flat I had just left. She was exquisitely dressed, tall and graceful, and, before the lift descended with me, I had time to see that, on the opening of the front door, she walked straight in without inquiry. She was, I felt sure, the wife of the man who had given me the order for the pearls.

I fulfilled Mr. Gervoise's commission by dint of much perseverance and trouble, and managed to get the earrings completed within half-an-hour of the time he had appointed for my arrival at the flat with them.

I hoped that this slight difference of time would not matter, and when I was shown into the same room as before, I expected that Mr. Gervoise would make his appearance at once, and that the whole affair would be speedily settled.

But one quarter of an hour passed, and another, and yet another, and still I was sitting alone with no sign, either visible or otherwise, from Mr. Gervoise.

I began to feel very uncomfortable.

Had he not laid such stress on my secrecy, I should have rung the bell and sent a message to him; as it was I did not know what to do. But my patience was very nearly exhausted, and I decided at last that I would stay only five minutes longer, and would then quietly take my departure, and wait for further instructions through Mr. Leighton.

The time had almost expired when the door suddenly opened, and there swept into the room the same woman I had seen in the lift.

I was struck anew with her extraordinary beauty, and with a strange, startled expression in one of the loveliest pairs of eyes that I have ever seen.

She stopped dead on seeing me, and Mr. Gervoise, who was wheeling himself rapidly after her, stopped also, and made me a signal that seemed to be of entreaty.

"What do you want?" she said quickly and imperiously; "are you waiting to see me? I was not told that anyone was here."

I had already risen, and I answered quietly, though I felt I was in a awkward dilemma: "Perhaps there is some mistake. I fancied that this was the flat to which I was sent for on business, but—"

I concluded by answering Mr. Gervoise's look of appeal with one commanding him to speak.

"Of course," he said, "it is someone for our predecessor again, Vera. We have only just taken this flat," he continued, to me, "perhaps it was Mr. Thurston you wanted." This time his look was one of the most agonised entreaty.

I bowed, and walked towards the door.

"I am sorry," I said, "that there has been a mistake. I did not know that Mr. Thurston had let his flat to you."

And, having reached the passage, I fled to the door and let myself out without further delay, mentally resolving never to enter it again.

I had no desire to be mixed up in Mr. Gervoise's mysteries, and I felt that I had been very unfairly treated, and was well out of an uncomfortable situation.

But the next day came a letter, addressed to Mr. Leighton, to be handed to me, in which Mr. Gervoise apologised for having given me a fruitless errand, and said that he would fully explain everything if I would call at six o'clock on the following afternoon, and that he must beg that I would not transfer the matter to other hands, but would come myself.

I confess that my curiosity to learn the secret of all this mystery greatly helped his persuasions, and I found myself quite unable to resist going, in spite of my former resolves.

At six o'clock therefore I found myself again in the little room, and in the presence of Mr. Arnold Gervoise.

"Look here, Mrs. Delamere," he said, "I am going to make a clean breast of it to you. You must think it all very queer and suspicious, and I am anxious to avoid suspicion. If you will consent to keep my confidence, I should prefer to confide in you. I am sure I can trust you."

I told him that I thought it would be best for him not to confide any secret he might have to a total stranger like myself, and that if he would kindly settle for the pearls I could take my leave, and the matter would be ended.

But he was, as I could see, an impressionable and excitable person, and this did not suit him.

"Here is the cheque," he said, handing me an envelope. "But I must ask you to listen to me, and to hear my explanation of what cannot but seem to you my unusual conduct.

"It is like this. I have a wife to whom I am passionately devoted. She was penniless, and she married me for a home, not for love. I am determined to win her in time, though, and I will let nothing stand in the way of it. A few months ago I had an accident out hunting, and was disabled for a time; I shall get over it presently. Some friends of mine lent me their country house to rest in and get convalescent.

"My wife went there with me. Our hostess has some fine jewels, and one evening she showed them to my wife, and told her the value of a particular pair of earrings. Soon after, she and her husband went away to Monte Carlo, leaving us in their house, which they offered for our use while they were away. One night"—he bent forward, and his voice sank to a whisper with repressed agitation— "I saw my wife get up, and go out of our room. I watched for her return, and when she came back she had these earrings in her hand. She put them into a secret compartment of her dressing-case and locked them up. The next day I asked her if she knew where our hostess kept her jewels, and whether she had taken them abroad with her. My wife told me that she knew where they were kept usually that, in fact, she had been told the word which would open the lock of the American safety-lock, to open which you must set the correct password, but she added that she had forgotten the word and also that she believed our hostess had taken all her jewels with her. Then I knew that she was a thief; that my wife, the woman whom I worshipped, had stolen the earrings deliberately. I tried every plan to lead her to confess, but she wouldn't.

"Finally, hearing that our hostess was on her way home, I came up here and determined to match the earrings; to place the new ones in the secret drawer of my wife's dressing-case, and to get the original ones conveyed in some way to their rightful owner. As you have helped me in the first part of my scheme, will you help me with the second? Will you try to think of a plan to get the jewels back without rousing their owner's suspicions against my wife?"

Amazing as this story was, there was no doubt about its truth, and that Mr. Gervoise was thoroughly in earnest in his resolution to hide his wife's crime, and yet to atone for it.

"Give me the earrings now," he said, "and I will put them in the dressing-case, and hand the others to you, if meanwhile you have thought of any way to return them. My wife is out, and this may be our only opportunity."

He took the case, looked at the earrings, and admired the ex-
actness of every tiny detail to the pattern ones, and was wheeling
himself towards the door when it was flung open, and Mrs. Gervoise
came in, carrying a small silver lamp.

"Oh, you are here, Arnold," she exclaimed, "and in the dusk
too. What are you—" she caught sight of me and stood still, the
lamp in one hand and the other resting on her husband's shoulder.

"Who is this lady?" she said. "Was she not here the night before last?"

He did not answer, and she stamped her foot with annoyance.

I felt exceedingly annoyed myself, but there was no escape.

Then she saw the case in his hand.

"What is that?" she demanded. "I insist on seeing."

She snatched it from him, and gave a cry of astonishment or
alarm—I could not quite tell which.

"What is the meaning of this?" she said. "Mrs. Hamilton's earrings' here! What are you doing with them? Good Heavens, Arnold,
you are not—" she faltered—and then burst out again—"how did
you get them?—speak—tell me at once, or I shall think you are a
thief."

He caught her hand.

"You know I am not," he said; "I want to replace those that have
been stolen."

"Stolen!" she echoed. "Are you mad, Arnold? If they are stolen,
you must have taken them yourself."

They had both of them forgotten me completely, so absorbed
were they in their own impetuous feelings.

"Oh, Vera, Vera," he said, "why won't you acknowledge that you
stole them? I would forgive you, darling—I have forgiven you already—if you would only—" He caught her hand, but she wrenched
it free. Her eyes were blazing with anger, and she could hardly
speak for rage and agitation.

"How dare you say that to me?" she stammered; "to accuse me—"
she choked with passion. He clasped her hand again, and was going to speak, when, freeing herself with a violent gesture, she

dropped the lamp which she had been holding, and in an instant, with the crash of splintering glass, a liquid stream of fire began to spread itself like lightning over the carpet.

I had involuntarily sprung forward as she dropped it, and the swift flame caught the edge of my dress, which, being of light material, blazed up at once.

In my panic I was going to lose my head and rush from the room, but Mrs. Gervoise caught me, threw me down and rolled me in an Indian rug, extinguishing the flames.

Meanwhile the servants, in answer to her screams, had come and managed to put out the fire.

Then I fainted, and when I came to myself I was in bed in the Gervoises' spare room, and my scorched ankles had been bound up with some soothing ointment.

For some days I was too ill to be moved, and both the Gervoises were kindness itself to me, though I could see that they were not on friendly terms with each other.

At last, when I had been carried to the sofa in the boudoir, Mr. Gervoise offered to read to me, and as soon as we were alone told me all that had been happening.

"My wife is furious with me," he said. "She declares I stole the earrings myself, and invented the whole story in order to get power over her. She insisted on sending the original ones back anonymously to their owner, and she will not speak to me on the subject again. I can see she hates me. What am I to do?"

"It is very singular," I mused. "A theory has occurred to me, Mr. Gervoise. I wonder if you would be willing to make an experiment."

"Anything you like," he answered, "provided she forgives me."

It was a very simple little plot, and before I left them we carried it out, and I proved that my surmise was a correct one.

Mrs. Gervoise was, unknown to her husband and even to herself, a somnambulist, and was in the habit, if anything had interested or excited her brain, of walking in her sleep, and doing things of which she had no remembrance afterwards.

She had slept in the room with me the first two nights after the fire, because I was feverish from the shock and the pain of my burns; and it was her walking about and talking in her sleep that gave me the possible solution to her husband's mysterious story about the earrings. She was quite unaware that she had gone to her friend's jewel-case, made use of her knowledge of the pass-word, and, taking out the earrings, had hidden them away. When the truth came out, she was touched with her husband's goodness to her, in spite of his knowledge of her theft, and I think she learnt to care for him more as a result of this experience than she ever would have done otherwise.

At all events, when I parted from them, they were the best of friends, and she had graciously accepted the gift of the second pair of earrings from Mr. Gervoise. I was lame for some time afterwards, but otherwise there was no ill result from what might have been a serious, if not fatal, accident to all three of us.

8

"ARE YOU SURE that you have recovered from your last unlucky experience?" said Mr. Leighton doubtfully to me, when I presented myself at his office and asked for some work.

"Quite sure," I answered; "and, indeed, though it is not pleasant to be scorched, I cannot call my last adventure an unlucky one, since it has been the means of bringing happiness to two people, and setting right a very grave mistake. I have been idle some time now, Mr. Leighton, and you must really let me return to business. Is there any special thing on hand that I can assist you in?"

"Well," he said, "I have been asked to supply some curious specimens of pearls to an old gentleman who is interested in them. I fancy he is a man of many hobbies, and that his latest is the acquisition of quaint, unset gems. He does not insist on their beauty or great value, provided that they are uncommon."

"And have you found any for him?" I asked.

"Here are one or two he might possibly fancy," replied Mr. Leighton, unlocking a drawer and handing me a case.

The pearls inside, seven in number, were, I could see at once, not very good, but were all of singular shapes; one exactly resembling a tortoise, another a beetle, and a third a human heart. This last was set as a pin, and was transfixed by a diamond dagger, tipped with rubies.

"I could send these by post," said Mr. Leighton, "but, if you like to take them to him on approval, it is possible you may arrange some further dealings with him. He lives a little way out of town, just beyond Brentham, and I hear is a bachelor, well off, and leading the life of a recluse, always engrossed in some new fad. Here are the name and address," he said, handing me a card, on which I read:

MR. PHILIP MAGNUS,
The Gables, nr. Brentham.

"I think I may as well go," I said, "if you have nothing else for me to do just now. It may lead to something further."

"Yes," he assented, "only I do trust, Mrs. Delamere, that the something further may not be any new and startling adventure for you. Pray, be careful, and if Mr. Philip Magnus does not seem a desirable client from a personal point of view, have nothing to do with him, and bring the pearls back."

I promised to be very cautious, and, having arranged an appointment by letter with Mr. Magnus, I found my way to The Gables, taking the train to Brentham, and driving from the station in a fly.

The house was a mile or two out, and stood quite by itself in a large garden at the end of a straggling bit of common.

"You can wait for me," I said to the cabman, as we drew up at the outside gate, beyond which only a footpath was discernible, winding away through close shrubs.

"Sorry I can't do that, my lady," was the reply, "I'm engaged to meet a party coming down by the next train. I could come back for you in an hour or two."

I told him with vexation that that would not do at all, and that he ought to have mentioned his engagement before we started. The only thing now was for him to send me another fly as soon as he reached the station; this he promised to do, and drove off.

It was with a certain amount of reluctance that I wended my way up the path, and arriving at the house, which was quite hidden from the road by trees, rang a very rusty, unused-looking bell that hung at the side of the door.

The sound of my departing fly wheels had already died away, and I seemed suddenly cut off from the outer world, and felt a sympathetic resemblance to Mariana of the Moated Grange stealing over me.

The door had glass panels, but they were so encrusted with dirt as to be opaque, and gave me an impression of discomfort and isolation that was not encouraging.

"I am on the right side of the door now," I reflected. "I wonder if I had better remain there, and give up the attempt to penetrate into Mr. Philip Magnus' privacy."

But I allowed myself one moment's hesitation, and in that moment I was lost, for the door opened, and a middle-aged woman of stern demeanour, but immaculate tidiness, stood surveying me.

"What may you be pleased to want?" she asked frigidly.

Evidently I did not find favour in her sight. "I have an appointment with Mr. Magnus," I said; "can I see him?"

"I think there's some mistake," she replied, "Mr. Magnus never receives visitors. He is expecting someone now on business."

"Yes, that is quite right," I said, "I have come on business," adding, as she still barred the doorway, "from Mr. Leighton."

"Oh," she said, reluctantly moving aside, "then I suppose you must come in. I understood it was a gentleman Mr. Magnus expected."

She looked curiously at me, as though questions were hovering on her lips, but I declined further parley, and, stepping in gave her my card. She went away with it and during the moments that followed I was struck anew by the loneliness and silence of the place.

Returning, she signed to me to follow her up-stairs, which I was proceeding to do when she stopped half-way, and said suddenly: "Mr. Magnus is rather a strange gentleman. It's years since he has seen any woman to speak to except me. I'm used to his ways, but a stranger might not understand them. He means no harm, only he's queer."

"Oh, I dare say it will be all right," I said with a cheerfulness that I confess was assumed.

She still eyed me doubtfully.

"He had a trouble some years ago, to do with a lady," she said; "he lost someone he was fond of. As long as you don't remind him of her it won't matter though."

"I shall certainly not do so," I remarked. "But if you think Mr. Magnus is likely to be upset at seeing me, perhaps I had better not go up."

"I'm afraid it would disappoint him now," she said. "He's been looking forward to having some new toys for his collection. Only I thought I would warn you that he's queer."

And with this reassuring speech she led the way to a room on the first floor, and announced me.

As I passed her in the doorway she pointed to another room opposite, and said in a low voice:

"I shall be in there."

Then I found myself confronting Mr. Philip Magnus.

He was a benevolent, rather nice-looking elderly man, clad in a flowered dressing gown, that trailed on the ground, with a skull-cap on his head; and he was sitting in pleased contemplation of a table laden with cases of all shapes and sizes, some open, some shut, all containing apparently the treasures he had been collecting. The walls were hung with odds-and-ends of every conceivable description and nationality, and the tables and cabinets and even the chairs were covered with bric-à-brac, some portions carefully assorted and labelled; others mingled together anyhow as though their owner's interest had suddenly failed.

The chair in which Mr. Magnus sat was in an angle of the wall, and he seemed to be almost blocked in by the huge table in front of him. I noticed that on the wall close to him hung the pulley of a lock; one of those old-fashioned locks which consist of a brass bolt suspended from a cord, and a socket fastened on to the door of the room. The suspending cord ran round the edge of the ceiling to Mr. Magnus' favourite corner, and then dropped within reach of his hand; so that he could lock or unlock the door of the room without moving.

He rose and bowed, looking at me in a stealthy way from under his eyelids that I did not much appreciate; then edged himself out of the recess and came towards me.

I handed to him the case of pearls with a few brief words of explanation.

I noticed that in taking them from me his hands shook perceptibly, and he gave me another quick stealthy glance.

He walked, without replying, to the table, and opening the case, began talking to himself.

"So like," I could hear him muttering, "so very like. But why does she come with the pearls? Does she want to gain forgiveness through the pearls?"

I felt a little uneasy, and wondered whether the housekeeper was within reach of the sound of my voice.

He was still standing with his back to me, and I could see that he was holding the heart-shaped pearl and examining it intently.

I told him in the most matter-of-fact tone I could assume that I did not recommend the pin as a jewel, merely as a curio; but that, if he preferred to have valuable pearls for his collection, Mr. Leighton would be pleased to procure them.

He listened attentively, and said, without turning round.

"What is the history of this one?"

"I don't know;" I answered. "Possibly it may have one, but it has not been told to me."

He looked at all the other pearls in turn, then went back to the heart, and again he began murmuring to himself.

"A heart," he said; "mine—pierced with a dagger—a dagger tipped with blood. Treachery was the dagger she used—black treachery. I swore I would kill her for it."

Then he wheeled round suddenly.

"What have you come back for?" he said more loudly.

I rose to my feet, and looked him straight in the face.

"I don't understand you, Mr. Magnus," I said. "I think you are mistaking me for someone else."

"No," he said, "there is no mistake this time. I was sure you would come back some day, and I knew you as soon as you came in."

He took a step towards me, and though I was still not greatly alarmed, believing that he was a harmless lunatic who wanted humouring and controlling, I thought it might be wise to retreat.

I therefore backed away from him towards the door, but with a movement as rapid as it was unexpected, he turned, ran round the table into the corner, and released the pulley.

Instantly the lock fell into the socket on the door, and I was a prisoner.

Even if I could have reached the door I was powerless to get out, for the lock was high up on the top panel beyond my reach. But yet I did not feel at all overcome with fright. The housekeeper was within call; surely no great harm could happen to me.

Nevertheless, the face that was now looking at me was very different from the one I had seen on entering. Then it had worn a bland smile and was almost childlike in its expression; now it looked mad, and there was a cunning leer in eye and mouth that foreboded evil.

"I must ask you to unlock the door, Mr. Magnus. I have other appointments to keep. I can come back another day when you have decided about the jewels," I said very quietly and distinctly.

He began feeling about with one hand amongst the cases on the table, in a strange, covert manner, while with the other he pointed towards me.

"No, you don't go," he said, "you will stay here now, with me—always with me. It was foolish of you to come back—I warned you not to—you stabbed my heart with a dagger; you killed me with poisoned words and false kisses, and then you laughed. Yes, you laughed when my heart was bleeding; you didn't care—and you went away on his arm, and I vowed if I ever saw you again I would kill you—I'm going to kill you now; I'm going to pierce your heart, as you pierced mine, and laugh as you laughed at me."

He had found what he was searching for on the table; a long, narrow case, and when he pressed the spring I saw that inside lay a stiletto.

And I realised all at once, with a flash of sickening terror, that whatever he had been up to the moment I came, he was a raving madman now, and that I was alone in the room with him, with a locked door between me and any possible help.

He had taken the stiletto from its case, and was beginning to creep round the edge of the table towards me.

I dared not lose another moment.

With a loud call for help, I darted to the other side of the table, and made a dash for the pulley.

But, quick as lightning, he pushed the table towards me, jamming me securely between it and the wall, with my outstretched hand just a foot away from the cord on which my salvation depended.

And then he laughed, and I turned a little dizzy, for a madman's laugh at such close quarters is not good to hear, or to see. The woman was battering now at the door, calling incoherently to him to open it, and to me to tell her what was the matter. He paid no attention to her cries. I do not think he heard them. He leant forward over the table, the length of which just prevented his reaching me, and struck towards me with the stiletto, laughing all the time. I summoned all my strength to push the table away, and release myself sufficiently to reach the pulley.

Useless! What was my power compared to a maniac's? He held me there, securely pinioned.

"Get someone to break the door open," I shouted to the woman outside, and I heard her run along the passage, screaming wildly. Then a new thought seemed to flash into his mind.

"I must be quick," he said, and he pulled a chair towards him, and began to wedge it between the table and the wall behind him.

I felt desperate. The woman had ceased calling, and must have run out into the garden, for there was no sound at all in the house; in another second Mr. Magnus would come to my side of the table, and it would be a struggle at close quarters, with long odds on his side, since he was armed and free.

I gave one piercing scream for help; the next instant Mr. Magnus had sprung towards me, and I was struggling for my life.

To me it seemed an eternity; but in reality it cannot have lasted a moment, for just as my frenzied grasp of his wrist relaxed, there was a crash of broken glass, and with a bound a man had leapt from the window-sill across the room, and seizing the madman from behind, dragged him off me.

I don't know what happened during the next quarter of an hour, for though I was not unconscious, I was too shaken to realize what was going on; but at the end of that time I found that Mr. Magnus, dissolved in imbecile tears, was lying, bound and helpless, in an arm-chair, with a huge, stalwart man standing over him, while the housekeeper was hovering round me, sobbing out distraught apologies.

"I knew he was queer," she reiterated, "but I never thought he would break out like that. You must have reminded him somehow of the lady that jilted him, and that always did upset him. Dear, dear, another minute, and he would have killed you!"

"What are you going to do with him now?" I asked. "It is most unsafe—he is quite mad."

"Oh, my husband will look after him right enough," she answered, indicating the stalwart man. "He would never have left the house at all, if he had known a lady was coming. But we will send for the doctor, the one that knows Mr. Magnus, and if he must be put away, why he must be. Only it means the loss of home and wages to us."

The sound of approaching wheels told me that my cab had come, and so thankful was I at my newly-regained safety that I am afraid I did not trouble my head with any further considerations as to the advisability of Mr. Magnus being at large. I simply gathered up my small amount of remaining strength and fled from The Gables, shaking the dust thereof from my feet, and thinking how very unpleasant it would have been if the housekeeper's husband had come just too late, and Mr. Magnus had succeeded in plunging his stiletto into my heart.

To Mr. Leighton I merely said that, as Mr. Magnus did not seem quite right in his head, I had not pursued negotiations with him, and that I thought the best plan would be to write about the pearls. This he accordingly did, and receiving a cheque by return of post, the matter dropped.

But I have often thought of my narrow escape, and wondered whether Mr. Philip Magnus, of The Gables, near Brentham, will yet succeed in avenging his wrongs, and also whether in such a risky profession as pearl-broking the game was always worth the candle.

At all events, I resolved that I would have no more private interviews with unknown customers, and that in future discretion should take the place of valour with me.

9

THERE IS NO DOUBT that a profession entailing continued anxiety about other people's property is rather a strain on one's faculties, and although some weeks had passed since my last alarm, I felt that a rest would do me no harm, and that I should work all the better if I put aside pearl-broking altogether for a few days.

So I accepted the invitation of some old friends, the Brockhursts, to Hampshire, and gaily bade adieu to my employer, Mr. Leighton, telling him not to expect me until he saw me.

I returned to his keeping all the pearls that remained unsold of those confided to me, retaining only one, the pink pearl, which was so perfect as to be almost priceless.

I had been unsuccessful in one or two attempts to sell it to jewellers at the price I demanded, but I still hoped to effect the sale of it privately to some collector of rare jewels, and I therefore took it everywhere with me in a safe and secret pocket in my dress.

When I arrived at Hurst Dene I was warmly welcomed by the Brockhurst family—father, mother, and children and Mrs. Brockhurst led me to my room, and prepared to have a long talk with me.

"I am free, for a wonder," she said, "and I want to hear all your news and tell you all about everybody here, and then we shall start fair."

"I suppose you have a tremendous party, as usual?" I said. "You are never happy, Fannie, unless you are entertaining about two dozen people. What have you done with them all?"

"My dear," she said, "I have sent all of them to the flower show. George and I felt as if we must have a little peace; so I said I must be in to receive you, and he conducted them all there, and then sneaked away home. Now I'll tell you all about them."

It was even a larger house party than I had anticipated.

To begin with, there was the newest millionaire, an Australian, young, good-looking, pleasant, with more money than he knew how to spend, and a generous, liberal way of spending as much as he could on all his friends.

There were three young couples, the usual riding, bicycling, tennis-playing pairs that one finds in country houses, three unattached young men, and a rich cousin, old and cranky, who had come uninvited in order to look after his only daughter and heiress, whom he was always suspecting of a latent tendency to make a mésalliance.

Their name was Fenton, and I had met the daughter, Adela, in town more than once, and liked her very much.

Lastly, there was the millionaire's secretary, a Mr. Blount, who went everywhere with him, and had more influence over him, people said, than anyone else in the world. They were, in fact, almost like two brothers, though two more opposite men could not be imagined, Mr. Anderson being tall, fair, débonnair, and social, and favoured exceptionally by fortune in every way, while Mr. Blount was rather short, dark, saturnine, and, barring his lately acquired salary, penniless.

At the moment that I was introduced to them I felt a presentiment that Mr. Blount and I would have some unpleasant experience together.

Outwardly we got on very well from the first, and indeed he very soon singled me out for attention, but I felt sure that he did not like me really any better than I liked him, and that his apparent admiration, a little too obtrusive sometimes, was assumed for the sake of frustrating the friendship which Mr. Anderson began to establish with me.

"Mollie," said Fannie Brockhurst to me, seriously, at the end of the first week, "I wish you would not encourage Mr. Blount. He

is not half good enough for you, and besides—" she broke off, hesitating.

"Besides what?" I said, "I don't like Mr. Blount at all, and I
find it difficult to be always civil to him."

"Oh, that's all right," she rejoined brightening, "then I may
speak openly to you. The fact is, dear, I have seen him playing the
same game before; he may be in earnest this time, but on every
occasion when Mr. Anderson has shown preference for any
woman's society, Mr. Blount has paid her marked attention, and
with the same result. Mr. Anderson, who has a charming nature,
has thought it unfair to put himself in rivalry with his secretary,
feeling that his own wealth might place Mr. Blount at a disadvan-
tage, and has, therefore, withdrawn.

"Mr. Blount has then pretended that his suit is rejected, and
has withdrawn also, his only motive being to prevent Mr. Anderson's marriage, which would not suit his plans at all."

I quite agreed with Mrs. Brockhurst's opinion, but it was difficult, if not impossible, for me to shake off Mr. Blount, so persistent was he in his efforts to monopolise me.

Mr. Anderson's great friendship for him made it still less easy,
for he often spoke to me in glowing terms of "Dick," as he called
him, and would have resented any slight offered to his secretary.

A singular chance, namely, the accidental mixing up of two tele-
grams, one intended for me being placed in Mr. Blount's envelope,
and vice versâ, revealed to me that this apparently prosperous
young man was in serious money difficulties, and was in want of a
large sum in cash within a very short time. He made a plausible
explanation to me of what the message meant, when the mistake
was discovered, and I accepted it as though the whole matter was
a joke, and of no consequence to either of us, but I had caught a
look on his face when I handed him the telegram and asked for my
own, that told me he was exceedingly wroth and troubled.

It was only a day or two after this that another slight mischance
occurred, which also seemed trivial enough at the time. This was the
breaking of a string of pearls that Adela Fenton wore always round
her neck. They were strung in a single row, with a diamond clasp,

and there was a history attached to them, which Adela had laughingly related one night when someone had admired the necklace.

"Father gave it to me on my last birthday," she said, "and he
was told that it belonged formerly to a famous singer who prized it
greatly. It was a royal gift to her, on the occasion of her first brilliant success, and she had never unclasped it from her neck since
the night when a King's hand placed it there. She was taken ill some
years afterwards with a malignant fever, and at her death the necklace, which had remained round her neck all the time, was found
to be quite discoloured. The stones looked like dull grey pebbles.
Her heirs removed it, and sold it to a jeweller, who had it carried
down by divers to the bottom of the sea and fastened there to a
rock. After thirty years it was brought up again, when the pearls
had recovered all their former whiteness and lustre."

I was interested in this legend, and asked to look at the necklace.

"I seldom take it off," said Adela, "only now and then to break
the spell in case I should share the actress's fate. Here it is, Mrs.
Delamere."

I looked at it with attention the pearls were remarkably good
ones, and I noticed that it had lately been re-strung. It was handed
round for inspection, and I fancied that two people looked at it
with special interest, Mr. Blount and a young barrister called Harry
Duncan, who was thought to be in love with Adela, and was in consequence severely snubbed by her father.

At the moment when the necklace broke, Adela had just finished a game of tennis, and we were all standing in a group dis-
cussing the play, and making up a new set.

She gave a cry of dismay, and the next instant the pearls fell in
a shower around her.

We all stopped to pick them up, and Mr. Blount dived under a
rose-bush for some, and came out with several in the palm of his
hand. She collected and counted them all gradually, and, putting
them into a small box, carried them up to her room.

When we went upstairs to bed that evening she linked her arm
affectionately in mine, and asked me to come and brush my hair in
her room.

I was longer than usual in undressing, as it happened, and when at last, brush in hand and clad in a dressing-gown, I ran along the passage to her bedroom, it was nearly twelve o'clock, and the lights in the upper part of the house had been put out.

As I passed a corner of the passage, the rustle of a dress and a subdued whisper caught my ear.

In the flickering light thrown by my candle I could only distinguish the back of a man moving quickly away, but the other person who was coming towards me, and who had not seen my light quickly enough to evade me, I saw quite plainly before she turned aside into a room and shut the door. She was one of the housemaids, a rather pretty, untidy girl whom I had seen, without noticing her much, once or twice.

I wondered who her fellow whisperer was, and what she was doing, and thought it was probably nothing very interesting.

The only point to which my mind recurred was that the man who was hurrying away seemed familiar to me. It was, I felt sure, not one of the men-servants, but one of the gentlemen staying in the house.

"How late you are," said Adela; "now come and sit here, and I'll brush your hair for you. I always admire your hair, Mrs. Delamere, because it's so wavy and such a glorious colour, and what a heap of it you have."

I guessed from her manner that she had something to confide in me, and I drew her on gently until at last it all came out. She and Henry Duncan were in love with one another, and were secretly engaged, but the affair was hopeless, as her father had said he would never permit her to marry anyone who was not in receipt of a minimum income of £1,000 a year.

Harry had £150 a year allowance from his people and his profession, a briefless one at present. What was to be done?

She had been putting away some of her jewellery while she talked and as she took out a tray containing the broken string of pearls I asked leave to look at them.

I examined the clasp, and I saw that the string close to it must have been partly cut through before the final threads gave way.

Then I looked at the pearls. I had a sort of detective feeling on me, and felt a sudden impulse to do these things.

Adela was silent, waiting for my advice about her engagement.

"When did you last take this necklace off before it broke," I asked.

She blushed vividly, to my surprise.

"Why do you ask?" she stammered.

"Because," I said, handing them back to her, "your pearls have been changed since that night when you told us their history. Some are the same and others very good imitations, that is all."

The colour fled as suddenly from her cheeks as it had come into them.

"How do you know, Mrs. Delamere?" she gasped. "Oh, it can't be true! What makes you think so?"

"I don't think so," I said; "I know it. I have studied pearls, and I can detect imitations at once. I can tell you something more about your necklace, if you wish to; but I don't want to distress you, Adela. Only it is safer, perhaps, for you to know it."

"Tell me," she said hurriedly.

I could not account for her agitation; it was, I felt sure, caused by some feeling outside the natural grief at the loss of her stones.

"The string has been partly cut," I said, "see, here by the clasp. Your necklace was bound to break before long."

She clasped her hands together and burst into tears.

"Oh, what shall I do?" she said. "No one must ever know it. Mrs. Delamere, promise me you will keep my secret."

I promised not to tell anyone against her wish, and gradually soothed her, and finally she gave me the whole of her confidence.

The only occasion on which the necklace had been taken off was on an evening, two days before it broke, when Henry Duncan had unclasped it from her neck, and, forgetting to put it back, had kept it in his pocket for some hours, till an opportunity came for returning it.

"I know he is very hard up," she sobbed, "but I am quite certain he would not change my pearls; only supposing it should come out that he had them in his possession that day, how awful it would be. I would not risk it for the world."

I quite sympathised with her feeling about it, and at the same time I felt a most absolute conviction that Henry Duncan had not taken the pearls, and that someone else in the house had done so, and had made a deliberate plan beforehand.

When at last I left her, consoled by my promise that no one should know without her permission, my mind was full of vague surmises, and I lay awake all the rest of the night trying to solve the problem.

And just before morning the possible solution flashed into my head with the sudden certainty of an inspiration, and I decided at once what I would do in order to discover the thief and take the weight off poor Adela's heart. Accordingly, I engaged Mr. Anderson in conversation, and leading him skilfully to the subject of his hobbies, I found that he was interested in the acquisition of curios, and especially of rare jewels.

This was exactly what I hoped for, and I followed it up by telling him that I had been entrusted with the sale of a pink pearl whose price was almost prohibitive, and that I would show it to him if he liked.

I took it to the library so that he might examine it quietly, and away from the other guests, and here we were joined by Mr. Blount, who never failed to interrupt any conversation between us as quickly as possible.

Mr. Anderson did not hesitate at all about the price for the pearl, large as it was, and arranged for the immediate purchase of it. When this was completed, and I handed the pearl to him, he said he should like to show me some other stones and jewels of various kinds which he had bought from time to time.

He asked Mr. Blount to fetch the case containing them, and when it arrived, he detached a small gold key from his watch chain, saying: "Just open it, Dick, old man; I want to show some of my pretty things to Mrs. Delamere, and we will put the pearl in here, too."

Then turning to me, he added: "I never part with that key; it's always on my chain, and under my pillow at night in company with my revolver. I have a dislike to keeping things in banks or safes; I like to have my things about me, ready to hand when I take a fancy to look at them."

I pretended to be absorbed in the contents of the case, and deliberately asked Mr. Anderson to let me take an amulet he was showing me to the light, knowing that he would consent, and would follow me to the window.

Then I watched Mr. Blount, and saw him adroitly withdraw the key, hold it in his hands for a moment with his back to us, and then slip it into the lock again.

That was all I wanted.

There was nothing else to be done now, but to wait for Mr. Blount's next move.

It was not long in coming.

The next day he said he must go to town for a few hours, on important business.

I waited till he was well on his way, and then I sought out Mr. Anderson.

I told him in confidence, having wrung an unwilling consent from Adela, the whole story of her necklace; and then I said to him:

"Mr. Anderson, I am quite sure that I have traced the thief, but it is the very last man whom you would suspect, and before I tell you his name, I want you, if you don't mind, to get your jewel case, and see if your pink pearl is safely there."

He was amazed, and even the liking I knew he felt for me was scarcely proof against his evident annoyance.

"I will do as you wish," he replied, "but I am at a loss to understand what you can possibly mean."

He fetched the box and opened it, lifting up each of the trays in turn.

The pearl was not there!

"Now," I said, "I am going to ask you one more favour. Will you say nothing about this occurrence to anyone? Will you wait quietly till to-morrow, and will you then open your jewel-case when you are alone? If the pearl is there will you bring it to me?"

He hesitated for some moments, then he acquiesced.

Mr. Blount returned from town that evening, and devoted himself to me more persistently than ever.

I detected a new motive in this.

He had felt mistrustful and suspicious of me ever since the sale of the pink pearl; he did not understand how it came about that I was in a position to sell jewels of this value, and no doubt it had occurred to him that possibly I understood pearls, and that danger lay in that direction.

He had urged Mr. Anderson to leave Hurst Dene, telling him that some business in town required his personal attention, and it was settled they should depart in two days' time, and I knew that the reason was to divide me and the pink pearl as much as possible.

The next day Mr. Anderson sent a message asking me to come and speak to him in the library.

I guessed his reason, but I was a little nonplussed when I found Mr. Blount awaiting me there too, though the look on his face told me something had happened.

"Mrs. Delamere," said Mr. Anderson, "I can see you are surprised to find Mr. Blount here. But I like doing everything as much on the surface as possible, and I have had an affection for this man that was almost brotherly; therefore I wish to let him down easily. Here is the pearl; I found it replaced in the box this morning, and I asked him"—he carefully avoided saying "Dick,"—"if he knew anything about its temporary disappearance. He then confessed to me that he had felt doubtful as to its real value, and had taken it to show an expert who had pronounced it all right. It was exceedingly kind of him to act in my interest in this matter, no doubt; but I am not sure I appreciate the kindness. In fact, I have just owned up to him that there is a mystery in which you and I are interested, that we should be glad of his help to clear up. Do you give me leave to tell him more?"

"Let me see the pearl, please," I said quietly.

After scrutinizing it I handed it back. "This is not the pearl," I said, "though it is an excellent imitation of it. I have something more to tell you, Mr. Anderson, which I have learnt since we last spoke of this. The under-housemaid here has just confessed to me that she partially cut the string of Miss Fenton's necklace at the instigation of a gentleman staying here—who asked her to do it in order to help him to win a bet he had made that the necklace would break—she declines to tell the name of the gentleman, and she only confessed it at all because she was offered a higher bribe than he gave her, and was assured that the fact of the string having been cut by her was already known. If pressure were put upon her, no doubt she would give the name, but I have left that for you to decide."

I forebore to look at Mr. Blount, but his voice told me what his sensations were.

"I congratulate Mrs. Delamere on her cleverness," he said, "and if I had known that a lady detective was disguised as a guest of this house, I should have laid my plans better. What are you going to do with me?" he concluded, defiantly, turning to Mr. Anderson.

"You have played your last card badly," Mr. Anderson answered. "If you had not ventured to insult this lady you would have done better for yourself. As it is, I don't intend to prosecute you. You must hand over to me as much of the price you got for the pearl as remains in your possession, and you must sign a confession. I shall, of course, buy back my pearl, and Miss Fenton's also. And you can go to the—" he stopped.

"I won't say what I was going to at this moment," he continued. "Kindly sit where you are, and don't attempt to leave the room. I wish to speak privately to Mrs. Delamere."

He led me to the window-seat, and spoke a few words to me, and then I left them together. They departed for town the next day, and a few days afterwards, when I returned to my flat, taking Adela Fenton with me for a visit, Mr. Anderson called, and we had a long talk together. And the result of it all is, that Adela Fenton has her pearls back again, and is engaged, with her father's consent, to Harry Duncan, who is Mr. Anderson's new private secretary at a salary of £850 a year.

And the pink pearl has again changed hands, for it belongs now to me, and was given to me, as one of my wedding presents on the happy day when I became Mrs. Anderson, and gave up the profession of pearl-broking once and for all.

Coachwhip Publications

CoachwhipBooks.com

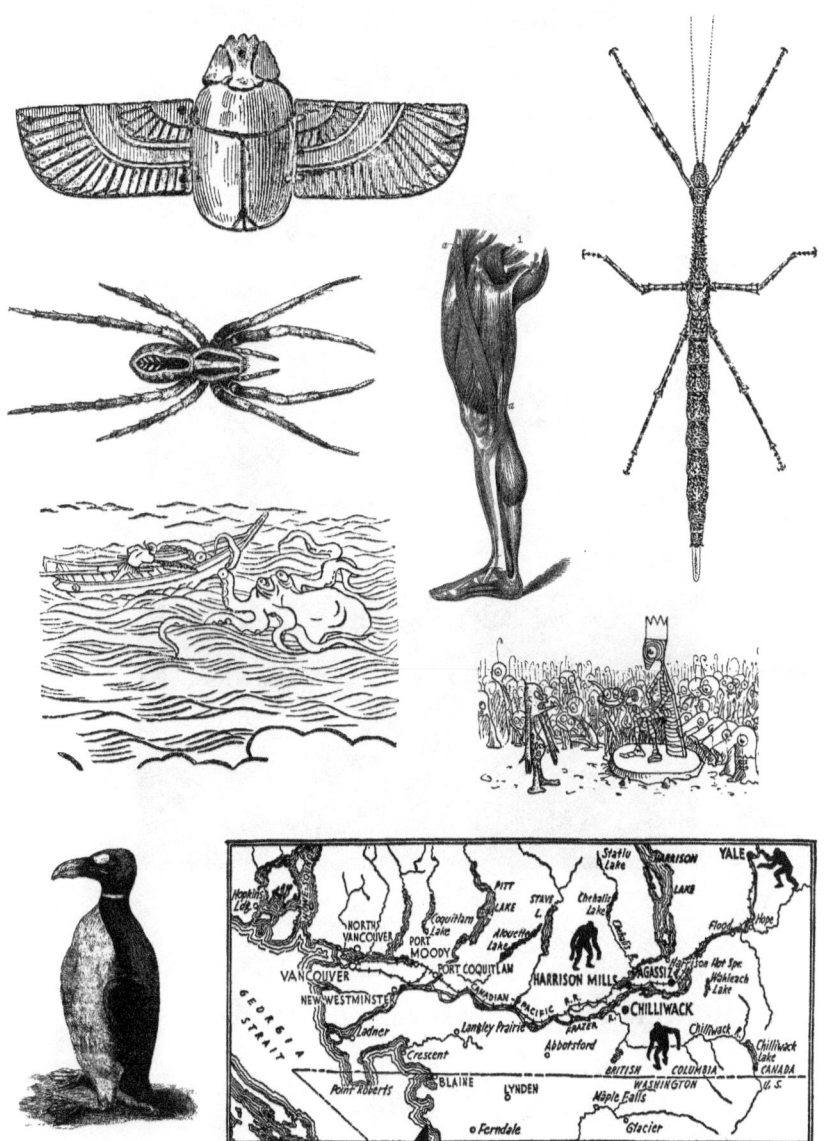

THE CHRONICLES OF ADDINGTON PEACE /
LUTHER TRANT, PSYCHOLOGICAL DETECTIVE

ISBN 1-61646-097-0

DETECTIVES 2

AVERAGE JONES
SAMUEL HOPKINS ADAMS

DR. FURNIVALL, PHYSICIAN-DETECTIVE
GEORGE F. BUTLER

AVERAGE JONES/
DR. FURNIVALL, PHYSICIAN-DETECTIVE

ISBN 1-61646-098-9

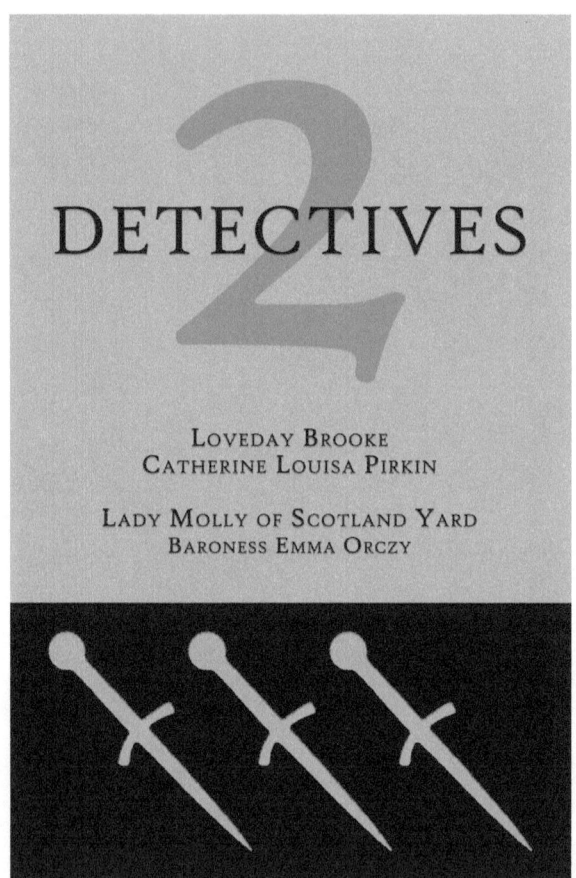

DETECTIVES 2

LOVEDAY BROOKE
CATHERINE LOUISA PIRKIN

LADY MOLLY OF SCOTLAND YARD
BARONESS EMMA ORCZY

LOVEDAY BROOKE /
LADY MOLLY OF SCOTLAND YARD

ISBN 1-61646-112-8

DETECTIVES 4

MISS MADELYN MACK
HUGH C. WEIR

VIOLET STRANGE
ANNA KATHARINE GREEN

MISS VAN SNOOP
CLARENCE ROOK

FLORENCE CUSACK
MEADE & EUSTACE

MISS MADELYN MACK / VIOLET STRANGE /
MISS VAN SNOOP / FLORENCE CUSACK

ISBN 1-61646-156-X

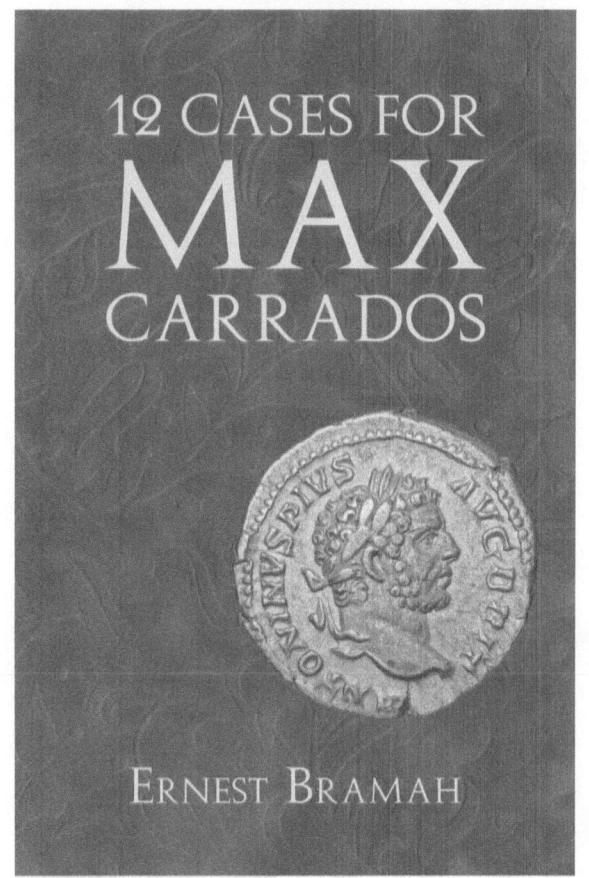